MASTER OF ILLUSION

A CELINE SKYE PSYCHIC MYSTERY

NUPUR TUSTIN

Foiled Plots Press

Master of Illusion
A Celine Skye Psychic Mystery
Foiled Plots Press

Typesetting services by bookow.com

Acknowledgments

A contemporary mystery needs as much research as a historical! For insights on art heists and the Gardner theft, I am grateful to Stephen Kurkjian, Edward Dolnick, and Matthew Hart. The Gardner Museum's Anthony Amore was good enough to respond to emails.

Photographer Luther Gerlach provided insights on camera obscuras and a blueprint to construct one. (I left the actual construction to my ever-devoted husband, Matt.)

On matters Paso Robles, I'm indebted to Karen Christiansen of the Paso Robles City Library and Scott Brennan, Publisher, *Paso Robles Daily News*. (I made up the bit about tickets being sold at the Paso Robles Intermodal Station.) Iris Nolasco of California FarmLink and Suzie Roget of ASFMRA provided key facts about land prices.

On wine-related matters, Elise Keeling of J. Lohr Vineyards & Wines was ever helpful. Thanks to the San Antonio Winery in Los Angeles for the most informative wine tour I've been on.

The staff at Adelaida Vineyards and Sculpterra in Paso Robles allowed me to pepper them with questions as I tasted their excellent wines. (I am still savoring the Viogniers!)

SinC Members Lisa Preston, Heidi Hunter, Thonie Hevron willingly answered questions on police procedure, money laundering, and police dispatch. Donnell Bell pointed me in the right direction.

For forensic matters, I am thankful to Elaine Pagliaro of the Henry C. Lee Institute. LAPD detective Adam Richardson and his Writer's Detective group stepped up to the plate every time I had a question; as did Patrick O'Donnell's Cops & Writers group. Thank you for your service!

Finally, thank you Re, Gun, and Hun for letting Mom work on her novel. And Matt, thanks for that lovely trip to Paso Robles. I'd love to do it again.

Greater Boston, March 2019

FBI, Boston Field Office. It was 3 a.m. when the tip was called in on the FBI hotline.

"Hello." The bleary-eyed intern manning the line lifted the receiver with one hand, crisply mouthing the greeting as she reached across her desk for a Styrofoam cup of coffee with the other.

The line crackled, then a hoarse voice she had to strain her ears to hear came hesitantly over the wires.

"Is the FBI still interested in recovering the Gardner art?"

The intern's ears perked up. "Yes sir, we are."

She straightened up, her coffee forgotten.

The FBI had considered the Gardner Museum heist, the boldest art heist in the twentieth century, all but solved when Robert Gentile, a small-time crook, had been arrested last year. But Gentile would soon be released.

And agents were no closer to recovering the art. So the FBI phone lines remained open, ready to follow up on any viable leads.

The voice at the other end of the line cleared its throat.

"This information is for Special Agent Blake Markham."

"Yes sir." The intern drew a Post-It pad toward herself, licked the tip of her pencil, and jotted down the name.

Special Agent Blake Markham was the youngest member of the FBI's Art Crime Team—a team spread through the country, its efforts coordinated by the law enforcement organization's Art Theft Program.

Markham's name was in an article on the Art Crime Team. Buried in the FBI website's pages, true, but easily discovered by anyone tenacious enough to look for the information, as this caller must have been.

It was unusual for a tipster to ask for an agent by name. Even more so for anyone to identify the particular unit their information should go to. Most people would have asked for the Special Agent-in-Charge, a fact obligingly provided on the upper right-hand corner of each field office's home page.

This might actually be good.

"And your information, sir," the intern prompted, pencil at the ready.

"The Vermeer," the caller whispered into the line.

"The Vermeer," the intern repeated. She wrote the name down.

The caller cleared his throat again. "I have information about Vermeer's painting, *The Concert*." He sounded tentative. "It was stolen from the Gardner."

"You've seen it somewhere?" the intern gently probed. A leading question might get the facts out of the man more readily than the usual even-handed approach the FBI favored: *Have you seen the painting?*

The caller went silent. Had she spooked him?

"I know where it is," he eventually said. "Make sure Special Agent Markham gets the news," he said a little more firmly. "I'll deal only with him."

The intern nodded, realizing a fraction of a second too late that the movement was invisible to her caller. "Yes sir."

She wanted to ask where he'd seen the painting, but sensing she could very easily lose him, she asked instead for a number at which Special Agent Blake Markham could get in touch with him.

All calls to the FBI hotline can be traced with some degree of accuracy.

Within minutes of the call ending, the intern had discovered that the call had originated from San Luis Obispo County, California.

❧

Boston, 8 a.m. The caller from San Luis Obispo County wasn't the only person interested in getting in touch with Special Agent Blake Markham. But Grayson Pike, a long-time Boston resident—middle-aged and washed-up now, with a beer belly—knew better than to call the hotline.

This tip was hot, and Grayson wanted to make sure Special Agent Markham himself received it. He peered at his cell phone and tapped out the number listed on the Boston FBI's home page. When the well-modulated automated voice prompted him to, he keyed in Markham's extension.

Markham wasn't in. Grayson hadn't expected him to be. Fortunately, neither was his personal assistant. That was good. Grayson wasn't interested in chitchat or answering bureaucratic questions.

He simply wanted the one hundred thousand dollars the Gardner Museum was offering for a certain ten-inch-tall bronze eagle that had once graced the top of a flagpole that Napoleon Bonaparte's First Regiment of Imperial Guard had used to proudly hoist their flag.

A stilted, female voice instructed him to "leave a message for Special Agent Blake Markham after the beep."

He waited for the promised beep.

"I have word on the Gardner's eagle finial," Grayson said. "Better than that—I know where it is. I've seen it. I can arrange to have it back. Possibly the rest of the Gardner works as well. Call me when you get this, and—"

No, he wasn't going to mention the other long-time Boston residents who might be interested in the news.

"Just make it quick, Markham. You'll make news. Trust me."

As instructed, he pressed the pound key to finish recording his message, hung up, and smiled. He was quite sure Markham would bite. The young agent was eager to make his mark on the art crime scene; hungry for the kind of headlines this lead—properly followed through—promised to make.

A hundred grand. He could almost feel the notes rustling in his palms. *One hundred thousand dollars. Yeah, baby!*

❧

Chelsea, 9 a.m. The pizzeria was empty when Special Agent Blake Markham swung open its glass door and sauntered in. It took him no more than a second to pass under the arched entrance of the brownstone-and-brick building and step onto the polished tile floor.

Here he paused, hand on the door handle, surveying the neat rows of double-sided wooden benches—each facing a small rectangular table—that lined the pizzeria floor and turned around the corner of the L-shaped interior.

No customers. And no Grayson Pike.

That fact didn't bother Special Agent Markham. After all, it was Grayson who had gotten in touch with him. And he'd seemed more than eager to share his "hot tip." The washed-up former art student wasn't going to skip the meeting.

Markham checked his watch. It was precisely nine o'clock. He'd returned Grayson's call a half-hour ago and after some haggling they'd arranged to meet here. For Markham, it was a seven-minute walk from the FBI's office on 201 Maple Street.

But for Grayson, it would be a twenty-five-minute commute from the low-rent rathole he called home in downtown Boston to Chelsea where the Boston field office and this pizzeria were located. Twenty-five minutes, if he was lucky.

Special Agent Markham released his hold upon the pizzeria door and strolled around the corner. The bearded, middle-aged man behind the counter glanced curiously up at him.

"Welcome to Buccieri's." A cautious half-smile accompanied the greeting, as though the man didn't quite know whether Markham was here to interrogate him or to place an order. It was the sort of tentative greeting the agent was accustomed to.

He'd never be good at undercover work. There was something about the wide set of his shoulders, the muted pinstriped suits he habitually wore to work, and what a one-time girlfriend had referred to as his "swagger" that marked him as an FBI man.

Markham smiled, an intentionally wide smile designed to put the man—*Pete*, according to the brass nametag pinned on the left strap of his red apron—at ease.

"I'm here to meet a friend," he said, resisting the urge to extend his arm over the counter. He doubted a friendly handshake would do anything to convince Pete that, at this time, he was just a customer.

He eyed the tray of calzones behind the counter. It was too early to eat, but he figured he'd place an order in any case. He could always brown-bag it for his lunch.

"I'll have the meatball Parmesan," he said, pointing to the crescent-shaped turnover. "And for my friend"—he glanced over the day's specials listed on the laminated card on top of the counter—"the roast beef sub."

He watched as Pete grabbed a paper plate and thrust a pair of tongs inside the glass case for his calzone. He waited until the calzone had dropped onto the plate before saying: "Can you set the sub aside and keep it hot until my friend arrives?"

Markham took his plate, paid for the food—his and Grayson's—with cash, and then selected a table along the white-tiled side wall. It was discreetly located, shielded from any curious passersby who might choose to peer in through the windows on either side of him.

But he had only to tilt his head back to get a quick glimpse of whatever was going on outside.

Just the way he liked it. The way he'd always liked it. To be able to observe undetected.

You could never be too careful. Although he had to admit, as he sat down, there was very little chance of running into any of his FBI colleagues here.

It was too early in the day for one thing; and for another, almost everyone in the Boston field office favored Floramo's, also on Everett Street, but only a minute's walk from the FBI office rather than the seven minutes it had taken him to walk to Buccieri's.

That was just one of the reasons he'd decided to meet Grayson at the pizzeria. The second was that unlike Floramo's, the pizzeria didn't boast a bar. If it did, he'd have no chance of keeping Grayson sober and on point.

The third hadn't really been in his hands. Floramo's didn't open until eleven in the morning.

That Buccieri's was cash-only worked in its favor as well. Markham didn't want anyone to know about this meeting until he was ready to talk about it.

Other than Grayson's message on his office line, there was no evidence of any kind of connection between the two men—on this matter at least. He himself had taken care to return Grayson's call from an unregistered cell phone he kept for such purposes. Calls on his personal cell phone and on his FBI-issued device could be detected and monitored.

He took a bite of his calzone. It was excellent—the meatballs moist and tender, the Parmesan delicately nutty, and the sauce nicely flavored.

He glanced at his watch again. Where was Grayson?

If this tip was good—it certainly sounded good . . .

Markham put down his calzone and wiped a paper towel across his mouth.

Ordinarily, he would have ignored Grayson's message. When it came to the Gardner case, there was nothing more to be learned from the man who had been one of the two guards on duty on the day the heist took place: March 18, 1990.

The other night watchman had been Richard Abath.

Grayson had not been on duty the night before when George Reissfelder and Lenny DiMuzio, the two men who'd robbed the museum, had done a dry run of their plan. But Abath had.

And on both nights, it was Abath who had flouted security protocol to let Reissfelder and DiMuzio—dressed as cops—into the museum.

Although Grayson had been quickly dismissed as a suspect in the case, law enforcement officials at the time had been convinced he knew more than he was letting on. And Blake Markham suspected they were right.

Since then Grayson had kept in touch, first with the FBI office and then with the Art Crime Team, calling in tips now and again. Most of these had panned out, but Markham's colleagues had always felt that these were tidbits fed to Grayson by someone with skin in the game.

Someone who wanted to keep tabs on the Art Crime Team and was using Grayson to do it.

Someone likely connected to the Gardner Museum heist since that was the biggest unsolved case the team was up against.

Markham took another bite of his calzone. Had Grayson really seen the eagle finial? Or was someone simply trying to find out what the FBI had uncovered since Bobby Gentile's arrest last February?

Chapter One

The chair, diagonally across from where she stood vigorously polishing the horseshoe-shaped counter, had been empty the last time Celine Skye glanced up.

Now, barely seconds later, her green eyes found themselves staring at the Lady.

Celine had always thought of her that way—compelled, she had no idea why, to be deferential. The Lady herself would have stood for nothing less.

Not that Celine could've explained just how she knew that.

It was a few hours to closing time at the Delft Coffee & Wine Bar. Most of the bar's patrons had left. Only a handful of customers lingered within its vast, softly lit interior, buried in the sumptuous leather armchairs scattered about the wood floor, drinks—wine at this hour, not coffee—in hand.

And among them, perched upright upon the uncompromisingly hard seat of a plain spindle-backed wooden chair sat the Lady.

Dressed as always in a low-necked black gown, tailor-made to encase her figure. Her smile muted, her pose graceful. Exuding an aura of wealth and confidence so unmistakable, a child could've picked up on it.

Although even as a child, Celine had never mistaken her for a flesh-and-blood person.

Unable to withdraw her gaze, Celine stared, fingers clutched around the bottle of lemon-scented furniture polish her employer, Dirck Thins, insisted she use. Her heart muscles contracted painfully. A sure sign.

Someone was going to die. Yet again.

Who? Celine asked.

The Lady sat still, unresponsive—like a painted figure. In all the time Celine had known her, she had never spoken a word. She remained silent now.

But the coils of tension in Celine's chest constricted painfully.

She closed her eyes, lips clenching against the slowly intensifying pain. It had been seven years since she'd last seen the Lady. Seven blissfully ordinary years, free from visions of murder Celine could do nothing to prevent.

It's time, Celine.

She heard Sister Mary Catherine's voice in her head. It was the nun—in life, a student counselor at the private Catholic school Celine had attended in Los Angeles—who had insisted Celine's visions had a purpose.

"You can't prevent an unjust death, Celine," she had said. "But you *can* fight for justice. Let the memory of what you couldn't do for your parents spur you on."

Sister Mary Catherine had passed on. But death hadn't prevented her from staying close to Celine.

It's time, the nun said again. *Are you ready, Celine?*

Ready for what?

Celine opened her eyes. The Lady sat—immovable, unrelenting, her blue eyes fixed on Celine's face.

Ordinarily, she lingered close to the person Death had fingered—her proximity a sure sign of what was to come. This time she sat apart, simply staring at Celine

Is it my turn? Celine silently asked.

The question went unanswered. Instead, the Lady's gaze bore relentlessly into Celine's brow—penetrating her skull with the intensity of a bullet.

It is my turn now, isn't it?

The pain in Celine's chest sharpened; a fine mist of furniture polish spurted out as her fingers jammed down on the nozzle.

"Hey!" A customer's wine-sodden voice protested.

"Sorry," Celine mumbled, noticing the middle-aged man seated at the bend of the horseshoe-shaped counter. He looked like an aging, drunken Liam Neeson.

A Liam Neeson gone to seed, she thought, apologizing to him again.

She pushed the rag in her right hand into the grain of the countertop's wood surface, determined not to be unsettled by the news she'd just received. What good would it do to let it rattle her?

At least she had advance warning of what was to come. What would it be —a knife or a bullet—that would snuff the life out of her?

Her hand trembled. She held herself still—unwilling to admit she was shaken.

She'd learned a long time ago that you couldn't change the future.

You might see what was to come—in a hazy, obscure fashion. But you could never change it. There was no point trying.

Not that Celine hadn't tried; all those years ago when the Lady had issued her first warning. Her parents had smiled, shaken their heads, and dismissed her vague fears.

That was when Celine had realized humans have no real agency. If they did, her parents would still be alive. Not mangled in a car crash.

She'd only been twelve when she'd woken up to that fact.

She thought she heard Sister Mary Catherine's voice again, but she drowned it out.

No. Don't tell me how I can fight for justice from beyond the grave!

"Wassa matter? You seen a ghost?" The same wine-sodden voice broke into her thoughts.

Celine stopped scrubbing and looked up, his words as provocative as a red flag to a bull.

"No, actually, I haven't."

Forgetting he was a customer, she glared at him. Why were people so ready to assume she saw ghosts?

The man raised his hand unsteadily, palm facing out.

"No need ter bite my head off," he slurred out the words. His wrist sagged, palm dropping drunkenly down.

❧

"Everything all right?" Dirck's quiet voice sounded behind her. His hand rested lightly on her shoulder.

"Y-yes." Celine swung her head back, the movement causing her waist-length, red-gold hair to flutter about her face.

The Lady, she saw at once, had vanished. *Thank heaven for that!*

She forced herself to smile. "I'm just a bit tired and on edge."

Dirck nodded, his eyes sliding over to the cause of the problem who sat alone at the bar counter, noisily slurping down the last of his wine. The customer slapped his glass down and tapped the rim.

Dirck glanced back at Celine.

"I can finish up here," he offered, making Celine feel guilty about the white lie she'd told. He looked tired himself—his cheeks shrunken and gray; a web of tight wrinkles at the corners of his eyes.

"No, it's okay. I'm not that beat." She reached for the man's wine glass and poured him some more of their finest Syrah—a Mechelen Vineyard product priced at about eighty-five dollars a bottle.

Personally, she thought the wine was wasted on the guy. He looked more like a beer-drinker.

Dirck nodded again and resumed his position behind the cash register. A couple of customers came up to settle their bills and headed out.

"Say, wha's t' word with those paintings?" the man said as she set the glass down in front of him. He pulled a few bills from his wallet and pushed them over to her.

Celine turned toward the paintings that covered the wall behind the counter.

"They're mostly by local artists. Those are for sale." She pointed to the obligatory seascapes for the Paso Robles tourist crowd.

"The others were painted by Dirck Thins, the owner of the bar, and his friend John Mechelen, the guy whose winery produced your Syrah." She twisted around and smiled. "*They* aren't for sale. They have sentimental value. They document Dirck and John's early days on the Paso Robles wine scene."

The man managed an energetic nod as he took a large gulp of his wine. He peered over the counter, his eyes narrowing as if to appraise the value of the Delft's art. It seemed like a pose to Celine. He didn't look any more like an art connoisseur than he did a wine aficionado.

But he'd taken her mind off the Lady and her own imminent death. There was something to be said about that.

"That a Rem-bran'?" the man asked. "A self-pawtrait?"

"That's actually John Mechelen," Celine said. "Dirck painted that. They thought it would be fun to dress up like Rembrandt." There was another just like it in Dirck's office. That one was a portrait of Dirck painted by John Mechelen.

An odd thing to do, now that she thought about it. And the man, inebriated though he was, seemed to think so as well. He stared at her.

Celine shrugged. "I guess it was an homage to their Dutch ancestry . . . I don't know."

"Dirck Thins?" the man asked. He jerked his chin at the owner of the Delft. "That t' guy?"

"Yes."

"Dutch, you say?"

"Well, his grandparents or great-grandparents were, I guess. He's from Boston."

"B-aw-ston?"

The man smiled, a broad, beaming smile as wide and smarmy as the Cheshire cat's grin.

"I'm from B-aw-ston. On vacation, would ya believe it?" He stretched his hand out. "Greg," he introduced himself.

That drew a sharp glance and a flicker of a smile from Dirck. Although in all the years Celine had known him, she'd never seen her employer go out of his way to reach out to patrons from back East.

And God knew, the Delft received several from the area—tourists anxious to sample the best the wine capital of the country had to offer, but more prone to eventually settle for the familiar lattes and café mochas the bar kept on hand.

Few of the Bostonians who came into the bar would have identified Dirck as a fellow Bostonian. The heavy nasal twang that marked Greg's speech had all but faded from Dirck's. His years on the west coast had taken their hold on him.

When the last customer had paid up and departed, Dirck drifted over to where *B-aw-ston* Greg sat, his elbows propped on the counter, fingers entwined around a half-empty glass of wine. His sunken blue eyes were fixed on the portrait of John Mechelen dressed as Rembrandt.

Celine twisted around to look at it. She had never seen anyone quite so taken with it. It was a nice enough piece of work, but nothing special. In her estimation, at any rate. Not that she knew anything about it. It was years since she'd stayed current with the art world.

"Reminds me of someone," Greg said, gesturing toward the painting with his chin. "Damned if I can remember who."

"Oh, yeah?" Dirck stood motionless against the counter, fingers gripping the edge.

Greg nodded. "It'll"—his voice barely pronounced the "t"—"come to me." He lifted his right forefinger and scratched his chin. A few minutes later, he lifted it again and gave his chin a few more strokes.

"You r'ember tha' big museum heist?" He raised his head and turned it slowly toward Dirck. "T' papers were all over it. St. Patrick's Day, 1990. Lotsa paintings stolen."

"We'd already left Boston by then," Dirck said. He stood stiff and awkward. Celine had never seen her employer act so embarrassed. Not that there was anything to be embarrassed about. Few people would have taken the trouble to keep up with news from a place they'd left.

On the other hand, Dirck had always prided himself on his knowledge of the art world. It was the reason why the Delft offered wall space to local artists. Her boss had always had a good eye for what was likely to sell.

But there was no shame in not knowing every last detail about an art heist, no matter how big. Even back East, the story of the Gardner heist had all but faded from public memory. It had merited no more than a single mention in her art history class. In the context of a lost Vermeer and a few stolen Rembrandts.

The theft had reared its head again during an unfortunate incident at the Montague Museum. It had cost Celine her job. But for that, it might have completely escaped her memory.

"Paso Robles is a small town," Celine explained for Greg's benefit. "It's unlikely any of that big-city news made it out here. Or that it would have been relevant to anyone in the wine business."

Dirck and John Mechelen had been trying to break into the business at the time. Celine doubted they'd had time to consider anything other than the weather and its effect on the grapes and any news that might affect the price of the wines they'd ultimately be selling.

"Well, issa strange thing," Greg's voice slurred. "But that pi'ture of your friend there." He pointed to it again. "You wouldn' believe it, but it looks the spitting image of Earl Bramer."

"Earl Bramer?" Dirck's voice barely rose, his curiosity so mild, it was clear the name meant nothing to him.

"Was that the man responsible for the heist?" Celine poured the last of the Syrah into Greg's glass. The bottle was almost empty; and Greg was so drunk, an ounce or two more could hardly make a difference.

Greg took a large gulp of his wine.

"Tha's wha' the feds think. Not tha' the heist was solved. Never will be, if you ask me."

"Why not?" Dirck asked, staring at the man.

Greg wiped his mouth. "Word is, Earl an' a frien' were charged with transpaw'ing the loot. A few days after the Gah'ner was broken into, Earl and his friend Duarte died. Biggest cah crash you ever saw. Cah went up in flames as did the aht."

"That's terrible!" Celine said. "But how could the police be so sure the works were in the car?" Any canvas in the car would have been reduced to ashes.

"They mus've been." Greg shrugged. "They stopped looking for them." He took another gulp of his wine. "*Unofficially*. Officially, they're still on the case."

"Seems a pity to give up so easily on finding them." Celine frowned as she moved over to the bar sink stacked with wine glasses and coffee cups. Although, from what she'd seen, it seemed par for the course.

Close a case as quickly as possible, that was the motto of most detectives charged with solving a crime. She'd only met one who was different.

"Why bother looking for the art if it was all burned to a crisp?" Dirck quietly said, still watching Greg closely.

"To know what really happened, of course." Celine wondered why he'd even needed to ask.

To this day, she didn't know how her parents had died. Not officially.

Unofficially, she knew exactly what had happened.

The police had been long on theories—her parents may have been driving under the influence; driving too fast—short on any facts that could confirm what she knew. Len and Viv Skye had been murdered.

"Those works of art may still be intact," she said with more conviction than was warranted given her complete lack of knowledge of the case. "Perhaps they flew out of the car during the crash. Maybe those men faked their deaths . . ."

"Now that's a theory." Greg looked at her with interest. "Faked their deaths, eh? No one's thawht of that. Wonder why?" His head swiveled toward Dirck. He slurped down the last of his wine and slapped his glass down on the counter.

"Nice painting," he said, pointing toward Mechelen's portrait. "Nicely done." He extended his arm across the counter. "Wouldn't min' seein' more of your stuff."

"Sure," Dirck said to Celine's surprise. He'd never before shown any interest in showing his art to anyone or in trying to sell it. "Any time."

He reached across to grip Greg's palm.

Chapter Two

"Go on home, Celine," Dirck said after Greg finally left the bar. "I know you're tired. I can finish up here."

On any other night, Celine would have appreciated the offer. But tonight, after what she'd learned, she hated to be alone.

"No, it's all right," she started to say.

"You can go home now, Celine." Dirck's smile was tight. His face weary. He held himself against the countertop as taut as a guitar string. "I have things to do."

Then why send me home? she wanted to ask. *If I clean up, it frees you up to do whatever else it is you need to do.*

But she sensed she'd get nothing meaningful in response to that out of her boss. Ever since his friend John Mechelen had passed six months ago, Dirck had seemed depressed, weary, a decade older than his fifty-four years.

She gripped the countertop, reluctant to leave. "Are you really going to sell that man your paintings?" she asked instead.

"Do you think I shouldn't?" he countered. He looked down at her, his smile more relaxed, the nervous tension easing out of his body.

Celine's cheeks flamed. The paintings weren't hers. Nothing in the bar was.

"It's part of our history," she said. The words felt strange. She hadn't realized until now how closely she identified herself with the Delft and the Mechelen vineyard. "I just didn't think you and John would want to let that go. And now with John gone . . ."

"I don't think John would mind, Celine." Dirck clasped his hands together, fingers closely intertwined. "I really don't."

Celine nodded, accepting the explanation without comment, and turned her attention to the wine glasses that stood drying on a black tea towel.

But Dirck stopped her. "No, Celine. I mean it. Go home. I can handle things here."

Celine bit her lip. Out of the corner of her eye, she could see the Lady was back. She didn't want to leave. Not just yet, anyway. Not without saying goodbye.

From the time she'd fled the art world and Dirck Thins and John Mechelen had taken her in, Dirck had become the closest thing to a father she'd had since losing her parents.

"Is there anything I can do for you?" she asked. "One last thing before I go?"

Dirck's face brightened. "Actually, yes, there is. Thanks for reminding me. There are several bags of empty wine bottles that need to be driven back to the Mechelen."

"Of course."

For the longest time, Dirck and John had been sterilizing and reusing wine bottles from the Delft. And for a couple of years now, customers had started bringing their own empty bottles back to the bar as well for a small discount against their next wine purchase.

"I'll help you load the bags into your trunk," Dirck said, heading toward the wooden wall that faced the countertop.

He pressed a button concealed in the wood paneling. The wall slid aside, revealing a spacious, parlor-like interior.

"And there's one other thing here I need you to take charge of as well."

❧

It was a few minutes past eleven o'clock in Chelsea, Massachusetts when the ringing of the phone jolted Special Agent Blake Markham out of the light doze into which he'd fallen in front of his computer.

Instantly alert, he sat up. The screen on his laptop was grayed out, but a touch of the start button brought it awake. A secure website with a map of a small town in San Luis Obispo County, California and a large yellow circle marked Grayson Pike showed up on the screen.

Pike had made contact with the target hours ago, and Blake had been monitoring him from the time he returned to his apartment. The agent stared at the screen, his eyes dry and blurry.

A gray button flashed insistently on the sidebar letting the agent know Pike was initiating a call from the tracking device he'd worn since he'd left the Boston FBI office a week ago.

They'd decided to start monitoring Pike even before he'd departed for his mission. And now he was checking in with them, as instructed.

High time, the agent thought, although he wished Pike had used his cell phone instead of the two-way call system on his tracker. This wasn't an emergency. *Now where in the hell was his phone?*

He could hear it still ringing, the sound coming from somewhere around the narrow perimeter formed by the couch and two easy chairs in his living room. His eyes darted around, homing in on the coffee table with his black jacket thrown over it.

Bingo!

Blake reached under his jacket, pulled out the phone, and flipped it open.

"You have it?" he asked tersely.

The only reason the FBI had agreed to fund Grayson Pike's excursion out west was that there was a chance—a very small chance, true, but a very real one nevertheless—of recovering some of the works stolen from the Gardner Museum nearly three decades ago.

The turd better have something for him or there'd be hell to pay. Although, as Blake had pointed out to his supervisor, how in the hell could you ignore a tip like that? Not one tip, but two, pointing to the same geographical location?

That was no coincidence.

The only question was: could an aging, washed-up, half-drunk former art student-turned-informal informant pull it off?

"What, no 'ello, no hi? Is tha' any way to greeta frien'?"

Blake clenched his lips. Pike was drunk.

"Do you have it?" he repeated.

"No—hey, hey, slow down. Look, I said I'd ge'it fer yer. I will."

"Have you even seen it?" Blake asked.

"No, but, hey wait. I 'ave infer-may-shun. Yer gotta lissen to this. I's good!"

"I'm listening." Sending Pike out had been a big mistake. He should've checked the tip out himself. Thing is, a week back, it had all seemed so farfetched. Despite the two tips he'd received—one from the hotline, the other from Pike himself.

But following up on them had even then seemed like the right thing to do. A way of letting the Gardner Museum officials know the FBI was still on it, investigating leads even if they were most likely a waste of time.

And, boy, had the Director of the Museum been pleased when he'd called her. A chance to finally recover some of the art; to know what had really happened all those decades ago. She'd sounded as excited as a girl going to her first prom.

"Lissen, you'll never guess who I saw?"

"Get on with it, Pike!"

"Simon Duarte, Blake. Simon Duarte is alive."

Blake tensed. Shortly after the theft, two museum employees—Simon Duarte and Earl Bramer—had been discovered dead in a fatal car crash, their bodies almost completely charred in the fire that had followed the crash.

The fire had been hot enough to singe a large swath of wild grass at the bottom of the cliff where the black sedan registered to Duarte had been found. But the medical examiner had still been able to return a positive ID on the dead bodies.

That the dead men were both museum employees and art students hadn't escaped the notice of Blake's predecessors. And when word filtered through —brought in by Pike himself, according to Blake's files, via a notoriously shady fence the team had been tracking at the time—that the Gardner art had been consumed in the fire as well, no one had questioned the fact.

But when William L. Worth, the fence, had been brought in for questioning on an unrelated illegal weapons charge, he'd promptly denied being the source of that information much less having any knowledge of it.

There the matter might have rested had not an undercover agent said he'd heard Worth make the same claim. Bramer and Duarte had died attempting to double-cross the mob, and the art they'd stolen had died with them.

Yet less than ten years later, Worth claimed to know where one of the Rembrandts was and had even taken a Boston Herald reporter to a warehouse to show him the painting. That had left agents completely flummoxed.

Because although the paint chips Worth provided had not matched the Rembrandt, they had been consistent with pigments used in Johannes Vermeer's *Concert*.

Had all the art with the exception of the Vermeer been destroyed? That had been the working theory the FBI had operated on.

But if Duarte and Bramer had survived the flames that engulfed their car, could the stolen art have survived as well?

"You saw Duarte and Bramer?"

"Not Bramer," Pike clarified. "Gather 'e died some mon's back."

"You speak with him? Duarte, I mean. You talked to him?"

"Sure did."

"Did he say he has the art?"

"Not in so many words. But c'mon, he must 'ave. I see 'im in a bar called the Delft owned by a man called Dirck Thins. The co'nci'ence, man!"

Vermeer had lived and worked in Delft, at the time a city in the United Province. But it was only when Pike said, "Thins, get it?" that Blake recalled the other connection to the Dutch master.

When he'd joined the art team and been assigned to the Gardner theft, Blake had read several books on the artist. He'd learned less than he needed to about Vermeer, but far more than he ever wanted to about the Dutch artist's mother-in-law, Maria Thins.

"Okay. You flap your lips to anyone else about this?"

"'Course not." Pike sounded indignant. "Just spoke 'bout some art wi' some young girl. Anyway, I think Simon got th' message. Ah'm headed back ter t'is place later to see th' works. See ya!"

The call ended before Blake could ask any more questions. He reclined in his easy chair. Calling Pike back and badgering him with questions would just be a waste of time. While he didn't share his informant's confidence, the lead so far sounded promising.

He reached for his jacket again and pulled out his work phone. Time to check in with his supervisor with an update on Operation Project Recovery.

Chapter Three

"Well, that's everything." Dirck hoisted one last hefty bag into Celine's trunk. He glanced over his shoulder, giving her a half-smile as he pulled the rear hatch down. It closed with a firm, business-like click.

"You'd better get going now," he continued. "It's late."

It was in fact no later than usual. If anything it was earlier than she'd been leaving since John Mechelen had passed and the Mechelen Estate had come into Dirck's hands. But Celine just nodded, and after a moment's hesitation reached out to hug her boss.

"See you tomorrow?" Her voice was hesitant, the Lady's presence at the back door of the Delft reminding Celine that it was no sure thing that they would.

"Of course. Same time, same place." Dirck withdrew from her embrace. "Now get going or you'll miss Bob."—That was Bob Massie, the handyman-slash-guard who manned the guard room at the Winery. He was on duty until ten. It was barely eight now, and the Mechelen was only six miles out of downtown Paso Robles.

But Celine didn't bother pointing that out either. It was clear Dirck wanted her gone—and soon. It was puzzling and somewhat hurtful, but Celine wasn't about to make a fuss. She opened the driver's-side door and maneuvered herself in behind the wheel.

Dirck gave her a smile and her arm a couple of quick taps— like a parent sending a needy child off to school. "Off you go."

It was a few minutes past eight o'clock when Celine pulled out of the parking lot behind the Delft into the alley. Just before she made her turn onto Pine, she glanced up into her rearview mirror, wanting to give her boss one last wave. But he'd already returned to the bar.

The dull ache in Celine's chest and the knot of pain in her stomach intensified. She wouldn't be seeing him again—not like this, anyway, one living person interacting with another—and she knew that. She gripped the wheel harder. It felt cold beneath her hands and she shivered.

It had been a warm day with temperatures in the seventies, but now her car thermometer claimed a chilly sixty-five. To someone like *B-aw-ston* Greg, that might've seemed pleasant. A fine spring evening. And shortly after she'd returned to California, Celine herself would've agreed.

But after seven years back in the Golden State, she'd gotten accustomed to eighty-degree days. And anything below seventy heralded either the coming of winter or its last gasp.

Celine rolled up her front windows, turned up the heat—just a slight turn of the knob to get some warm air going—and shivered again. She was on 13th Street now, headed east.

❧

She cruised toward Paso Robles Street, wanting to take in every storefront, every street corner, as she left downtown. She'd made the same journey, from the winery to the bar and back again nearly every day for the past seven years. That routine hadn't looked like it was going to change any time soon—until today.

Aren't you being a bit maudlin, my dear? Sister Mary Catherine's sensible voice suddenly boomed out in the stillness of the car. Celine smiled, oddly reassured. In life, the nun might have been willing to coddle Celine's sensibilities. But in death, Sister Mary Catherine had shown no such inclination.

Everyone died. But death wasn't the end of life. Celine was in a better position than most to realize that.

It had been disconcerting at first to hear a disembodied voice, and one with such strong opinions at that. But Celine was used to it now.

I can't manifest both voice and form, the nun had explained when Celine had asked her about it some years ago. *It takes more energy than I have to do both. Besides, my voice is more useful to you than my face.*

True enough, Celine now thought, pushing down on the gas pedal when she saw the light at Riverside Avenue up ahead turn green. But the Lady's presence that evening had been so persistent, the signs so clear, it was clear to her that death was coming.

And she didn't like it.

An untimely death, Sister Mary Catherine said, *but not—*

"Oh my God!" Celine jammed her foot down on the brake. She'd been about to go through the intersection at Riverside Avenue when the figure passed in front of her car. It turned toward her as she squeaked to a halt a half-inch past the white line that marked the intersection.

The Lady. Oh God, it was just the Lady.

Celine closed her eyes in relief, heart pounding, clammy hands clinging to the steering wheel.

What were you thinking, Celine? Sister Mary Catherine's voice was so loud, it was nearly a bellow. *You'll get yourself killed, driving like that.*

"I *am* going to die," Celine replied.

Not tonight, you're not. Not unless you keep driving like a madwoman.

"What else was I to do? You saw her. I know you did."

Celine opened her eyes. But the Lady was gone.

"Make her stop doing that. Please." Her hands gripped the wheel. "I can't handle it. Not now. Not while I'm driving."

Still breathing heavily, she eased off the brake.

❧

Traffic had been fairly light, and now as she left downtown, passing by Paso Robles Street and heading toward South River Road, it thinned out even further.

Confident Sister Mary Catherine would keep any disturbing visions at bay, Celine hit the gas a little harder.

In a little over ten minutes she was on Linne Road, following the street as it wound left toward the gates of the Mechelen Estate at 5125. The winery and its grounds went back to the mid-nineties when John Mechelen had bought and cultivated the lands, planting his first Cabernet Sauvignon.

Since then the vineyards had expanded to include Zinfandel, Merlot, Cabernet Franc, Mouvedre, Viognier, and Syrah.

Now the ninety-five-acre plot belonged to Dirck, passing into his hands when John had died, childless and single, last October. The strain of running a huge estate and a wine bar must've gotten to Dirck because since John's death, Celine had noticed her boss slowly going to pieces.

He'd been staying ever later at the bar, but his focus was on running the vineyards he'd inherited. That had forced Celine to pick up some of the slack at the Delft, help that Dirck had welcomed until just a couple of weeks back.

Then he started insisting she leave shortly after the bar closed. At the time she figured he felt bad about allowing the burden of the business to fall mostly on her shoulders.

But tonight, Dirck had positively shooed her out of the bar.

Why, Celine wondered.

And why was Dirck even considering the idea of parting with the art he and John had labored over? That was their history—*a visual history*, he and John had called it.

Celine had even put up images of it on the *About Us* page on their joint website. Along with short, catchy captions, the art had provided a more vivid, colorful narrative than the usual "Our Story" most other estates included on their sites.

He does need to put his affairs in order, Sister Mary Catherine reminded her quietly.

"So he does," Celine agreed. Dirck, like John, had remained single and childless, happy to enter into more or less casual, no-strings-attached relationships with women who weren't looking for commitment either.

But now the thought of who was to inherit the vineyards John had cultivated and the bar Dirck had built up probably consumed him as well. Was Dirck planning to sell the business? Before a sudden heart attack took him as abruptly as it had his friend?

The thought felt like death to Celine. The bar was all she'd known since-

She shook her head, trying to rid her eyes of the film of tears that was beginning to blur her vision.

Dirck could sell the vineyard, she thought, driving through the gates of 5125 Linne Road. She could live with that.

But she'd built a life around the Delft. What would she do if that were taken from her? Was that the death the Lady's presence portended? A metaphoric death—the death of a life and a career?

Celine couldn't bear the thought of that happening. Not again. It had been devastating enough when it had happened seven years ago.

Chapter Four

Bob Massie had left one leaf of the Mechelen's wrought iron gate open for Celine. He was waiting for her by the guard room as she rolled in, and flagged her to a stop.

"Dirck called," he said, opening the passenger-side door of her Honda Pilot and hopping in. He settled into the wide leather seat and fastened his seat belt. "He wants them bottles stored in the barn by the guard's cottage."

"The barn?" Celine repeated. But the empty bottles weren't in cardboard wine carriers. There'd been no time to pack them into the special boxes with corrugated inserts they used to transport, ship, and store bottles, regardless of whether they were full or not.

And the barn didn't have any crate wine racks either.

"Did he tell you to get some of those crate racks from the bottling room?" she wanted to know.

"Nope. Why? Do we need any?"

"Yes, unless you want the bottles rolling around in hefty bags." Celine shifted her gear into *Drive* and followed the packed dirt driveway as it wound past a gentle slope dotted with oaks.

Bob sighed. "Guess I'll have to get some, then."

"I'm sorry. I'd have packed them myself if I'd known that we'd collected enough for the bottling plant to clean. But the new girl—the intern—had already put them in hefty bags, and . . ." And Dirck had wanted her out of the bar.

She glanced over at Bob. "I can get the bags out of the trunk while you go get us fixed up," she offered.

He nodded. "I'll need your car, though. It'll take forever if I have to walk them racks over one rack at a time."

"Sure." She knew he could've stacked the crates on one of the many aluminum hand trucks scattered about the estate. But Bob, stocky, with thinning hair and a beer belly, usually preferred to take the easy way.

He probably wouldn't even help her unload the trunk. But Celine didn't really mind that. Not this evening. Not with the one hefty bag, among all the others, that Dirck had entrusted her with.

"You're the only person I can trust with this, Celine," he'd said. "Find a secure place for it somewhere on the estate. Far from prying eyes."

And grouchy Bob Massie's eyes tended to be more curious and prying than most.

The driveway twisted around, opening out onto a beautifully laid ornamental garden.

Outdoor lighting cast a fairytale light over the circles of rich green boxwood that enclosed trees and flowering plants. It illuminated the stone porch and glass-and-wood doors of the Mechelen Estate Tasting Room behind the garden.

And it threw a faint glow over the estate's guest cottages with Spanish-tiled roofs that stood on the left.

Only one of them was let out now. To a Ms. Hood, Celine recalled. A silver-haired woman with a wide mouth, a ready smile, and shrewd blue eyes. The few times they'd met, she'd reminded Celine of Sister Mary Catherine, the nun who'd become her guardian angel.

The barn, a rustic structure constructed out of rough-hewn gray-black stone, was on the right. The driveway ran along past it to the main production facility and bottling plant at the back.

Celine stopped the Pilot directly in front of the barn but left her key in the ignition and the engine running.

"I'll unload the trunk and then you can get going," she told Bob as she popped the rear hatch and jumped out. To her dismay, he cut the engine and lumbered out of the SUV as well.

"No need to do it all by yourself. I can help. I'm no spring chicken, but I'm not past my prime either."

"No, no, of course not," Celine said hastily. She stood by the truck, wondering how to stall him.

He had just hoisted the first hefty bag from the trunk, the bottles clinking loudly as he swung the bag over his shoulder when an image flashed into Celine's mind—a white cotton blanket with colorful patches and a red border spread out on a cold stone floor.

She didn't need to hear Sister Mary Catherine's voice whisper, *The Christmas blanket, Celine*, to know what she needed to do.

"Bob, wait. Let's throw down a blanket on the floor. The Christmas blanket is still in there. In the plastic box on the bottom shelf, remember?" She'd asked Bob to put both box and blanket up in the rafters in January. It was March now, and he still hadn't done it.

"Throw down a blanket?" Bob seemed puzzled. "The Christmas blanket? You want it on the floor?"

"To provide some cushioning for the wine bottles," she explained. "So they don't crack or shatter when we set the bags on the floor." Under Bob's less-than-gentle handling, that situation wasn't entirely unlikely.

And even if it hadn't been for the box Dirck had put in her care, she'd have needed to take every precaution possible to ensure the wine bottles remained intact and ready for use.

"You sure you want the Christmas blanket, though? Thought you wanted me to put it into storage."

"I did. But since you haven't, there's no reason not to use it, is there?" She knew she was beginning to sound a bit testy, but she couldn't help it. Bob, with all his questions, was trying her patience. Why couldn't he, just for once, get on with it?

"Oh-ka-ay." Bob swung the bag around, about to plonk it down heavily on the ground when Celine intercepted it.

"Here, let me hold onto that."

She set the bag gently down as Bob retreated into the barn. She could hear him shuffling around inside, probably trying to locate the blanket even though it was right in front of his eyes.

She worked quickly, unloading as many bags as she could, but four or five still remained when Bob emerged again.

It was just her luck that the bag he sought to lift out was the one with the cardboard carton in it.

"Hey! This one has a wine carrier." He fumbled with the zip tie, trying to loosen it and peer inside.

"That one's mine." Celine grabbed the bag out of his arms. "Needs to go into storage." She clutched it close to her body.

"O-ka-ay."

"Sorry, I didn't mean to snatch. It's just . . ." she hesitated, casting around for an explanation.

Your parents, Sister Mary Catherine prompted.

"It's some stuff that belonged to my parents . . ." Celine grasped the lifeline eagerly.

It wasn't exactly a lie. From what Dirck had told her, whatever was in the box had greater sentimental than actual monetary value.

Bob nodded. He knew about her parents. Almost everyone did by now. He lowered his head and returned to his work.

In about fifteen more minutes all the hefty bags were piled up on the thick cotton quilt that was usually spread around the Mechelen Christmas tree stand to hold the presents that John and Dirck gave the employees of both the bar and the winery.

"I'll get the racks, then," Bob said, plodding toward the driver's side of her Pilot. He yanked the door open, pushed her car seat back, and eased himself in.

Chapter Five

The Pilot disappeared from view and Celine returned to the barn to consider the problem of where to store the object Dirck had given her. She glanced at the barn door. The hefty bag stood just inside it, the outlines of the cardboard box it contained visible through its creases.

She'd gotten the impression it contained some type of gewgaw—the kind of showy bronze ornament that someone's Great-aunt Mildred might have proudly displayed above her mantelpiece about a hundred years ago.

It was most likely old enough to be considered an antique now, but that probably didn't make it any less god-awful.

Had the black hefty bag not been secured with a zip tie and were Bob not likely to return any moment, Celine might've sneaked a peek just to see how ugly the thing was.

"It's no Cellini or Riccio." Dirck's smile had been wry as he recalled the sixteenth-century Italian sculptors whose bronze figures he and John had drooled over in a Christie's catalog online.

Celine still couldn't understand why Dirck wouldn't let her store it in her cottage. It would've been the best place for it. But Dirck had been adamant.

"I'm not sure how safe that would be," he'd said, his voice so firm she'd realized there was no arguing with him. "At this point, it's worth more than a few pesos."

He'd dragged the bag out of a closet that Celine had never even known existed. It was in a room concealed behind the Delft's wall panels. No one would've suspected the existence of a room there, much less a secret closet.

Controlled by what looked like a thermostat.

"It *is* a thermostat," Dirck had informed her. "But it's also programmed to open and close the closet." He'd shown her the code to punch in to open the closet and the one you punched in to lock it.

"Both codes are changed every week," he'd told her. "From now on that's going to be your job."

Celine had known about the room. She and Dirck frequently sat there after the bar closed to go over accounts and inventory and to plan events. But in all the time she'd worked at the Delft, she'd never guessed about the closet.

The loud tick-tock of the wall clock caught her attention. Bob would be back any minute now.

But where on the estate could she find a hiding place as safe from detection as that closet?

Put on your thinking cap, Celine, Sister Mary Catherine urged her. *The solution is staring you in the face.*

"You mean, right here? In this barn?"

Where else?

It was as good a place as any, Celine figured. She surveyed the clutter of tools and odds-and-ends that jostled for space on the stone floor and the shelves that lined the walls.

The barn must have been what Dirck had in mind as well.

Why else had he called Bob out of the blue, insisting that the empty wine bottles be stored here? Dirck must've figured Bob would have to go to the bottling room to get wine racks, giving Celine several precious minutes alone to find a good hiding place inside it.

Celine whirled around, scrutinizing every inch of the place. There didn't seem to be anything in here quite as impregnable as the Delft's secret closet.

The barn had originally been used for horses. The stalls had long been dismantled and the stone flooring extended to what had once been packed dirt covered with rubber mats. But a large square of hardwood floor remained in what had once been the tack room. An old green wheelbarrow was parked here, surrounded by gardening tools.

Dirck and John's gardening tools.

Celine's gaze kept returning to it.

If all she was looking for was a temporary place to store whatever it was and keep it out of sight, did it really matter if it wasn't all that secure?

"John and I were taking care of this for a woman we both knew." Dirck had stared down at the bag in his arms. "She meant a great deal to us once. Still does."

He looked up at Celine.

"I just don't think I can hold on to it any longer. It needs to go back. But until it does, we have to keep it safe."

❧

Celine stared at the wheelbarrow. It contained a few bags of potting soil and a trowel or two.

A hoe, a rake, and a spade, all three of which looked like they went back to their owners' Boston days, stood propped up against the barrow.

In the early days, Dirck and John had enjoyed working together on the Mechelen gardens. Afterward, when a team of gardeners had taken over the main grounds, their efforts had been restricted to the small plot that fronted the twin cottage they shared on the estate.

But on the day he'd had his heart attack, John had been alone in his garden, using his spade to turn over a dry patch of soil.

Under the wheelbarrow, Celine, Sister Mary Catherine suggested. *No one will think to look under it.*

"But you don't have to move it to see under it," Celine pointed out.

Just move the barrow.

Celine sighed. It was true most people might think a hefty bag stored under a barrow contained nothing more than gardening tools. But who was to say, someone wouldn't open it?

On the other hand, of course, no one but Dirck and John had ever used those tools. The team of gardeners the Mechelen employed had their own gardening shed. And Bob Massie had never touched a gardening tool in his life.

Maybe it was the perfect place. Hiding in plain sight. *Safe from prying eyes,* just like Dirck wanted.

She propped the hoe, the rake, and the spade against the wall, and pushed the barrow out. Its wheels creaked as it reluctantly yielded to her efforts and moved. A layer of potting soil and dust coated the floor where the barrow had stood.

Celine was using one of the trowels to brush it aside when she noticed one of the floorboards was loose. Curious, she lifted it up.

Then a couple more.

Underneath the loose floorboards, housed between two floor joists was a large, coffin-shaped steel container with a lid.

A heavy-duty steel ring was installed in the middle of the lid. Celine grabbed hold of it and pulled the lid open.

The container was empty.

She peered inside. The space was perfect for the hefty bag with Dirck's cardboard box.

And Sister Mary Catherine was right! No one would think to look for anything under an old wheelbarrow.

Celine got off her knees and ran back toward the barn door. She needed to get this taken care of before *Curious* Bob returned.

Make sure the floorboards are flush with each other when you're done. Sister Mary Catherine reminded her.

Celine carefully hoisted the bag into the steel container. Breathing heavily from the effort, she closed the lid and started putting the floorboards back.

And push the dirt and potting soil back over the area before you wheel the barrow back.

❧

She had just finished when the low hum of the Pilot's engine reached her ears. Bob was back. She stood up, dusted the knees of her denim jeans, and sprinted toward the barn door.

Bob cut off the engine.

"Took me a bit of time. But I found what we needed."

He plodded toward the back of the car and popped open the rear hatch. Wine crates stacked the cargo area.

"Got as many as I could."

"I see that."

"Take a couple in and start filling 'em up. I'll bring in the rest."

Back in the barn, Celine swiftly opened up hefty bags and began transferring empty wine bottles into the racks Bob had brought back. Bob lumbered in, bringing in a couple of racks at a time as she worked.

"Don't forget that stuff of yours that needs to go into storage," he reminded her.

Trust Bob to remember something as trivial as that.

"You'd better get it back in your car."

She glanced up. He was standing, crate in hand, looking at her.

"I will. When I'm done here."

She'd known he'd remember and she was prepared.

While she unloaded the bottles, she'd been collecting the empty bags and piling them into one large hefty bag. Now, as Bob set his crates down and trudged out the barn door, she reached over to zip-tie it.

Then she carried it out to her car, dumping it on the rear passenger seat.

The barn floor was still sufficiently strewn with hefty bags for Bob not to notice that she'd gotten rid of some.

Twenty minutes later, she was back in the Pilot, circling past the barn to a small cottage behind a thick row of lush green boxwood.

She was finally home.

Chapter Six

Celine dug into the slim navy blue purse that rested almost constantly against her right hip—its long slender strap descended from her left shoulder and across her body—and fished out her cottage keys.

As she slid the main key into the lock of the blue cottage door, an inexplicable feeling hit her. She twisted her head up and around.

Her gaze circled over the clear night sky studded with tiny pinpricks of starlight; the hedges—black in the darkness—that shielded her cottage from view; and the pebbled path between two neat pockets of grass that led to her door.

It felt like the end of something.

The sensation was so strong, her fingers reached for her phone, ready to text Dirck. Celine wanted to let him know where she'd kept the cardboard box. That it was safe.

Mainly she wanted to hear that he was all right.

But Dirck had told her not to contact him at all that night. "I know you can handle this. You don't have to report back to me. In fact, I'd rather you didn't."

The end is nigh. It is coming, she thought.

But the end of what exactly, she had no idea. It was just a feeling she couldn't shake off

She stepped into the cottage and flicked a switch by the door. The light that came on illuminated a large open area—a kitchen and dining space to her left and a cozy living room on the right. She pulled her purse strap over her neck and set the purse and her keys on top of the granite-topped island that separated the kitchen from the dining area.

Very little in the cottage belonged to Celine. It had been given to her fully furnished when she'd gratefully accepted Dirck's offer to join the Delft Coffee & Wine Bar as its Marketing Manager.

That had been seven years ago. She'd agreed to have a small sum deducted from her bi-weekly paychecks as rent, but after the first few months, Dirck had stopped taking the amount out of her salary.

"Consider it a perk of the job," he'd said when she asked him about it. "Well-deserved, too. You do far more than the job calls for."

That was true. How many marketing managers tended bars and helped harvest grapes? But getting involved in the business—at John Mechelen's suggestion—had helped her understand its unique challenges and devise ways to address them.

Still, the perk had never sat right with her. It had always felt more like a favor. How could living rent-free be a justified benefit when she was doing no more than it took to do the job well?

Not that she wasn't grateful to Dirck.

She just wasn't convinced she deserved the benefit. And she hated being beholden to anyone.

Celine grabbed an apple from the fruit bowl on the island and flung herself on the living room couch. The apple, at least, was hers. She'd paid for it— and the rest of the fruit in the bowl and all the food in the small kitchen refrigerator. The clothes in the bedroom closet were hers as well.

If she ever had to leave, these were the only things she'd be able to take with her. Everything else would stay right here.

And that was all right with Celine. Ever since her parents had died, she'd felt like a traveler through life. There was no point collecting very much or getting attached to your possessions.

Not when you weren't destined to have a permanent home anytime soon. Not when you had to be ready to move at a moment's notice. Wanderers traveled light.

But in the seven years that Celine had been in Paso Robles, she had never felt she would have to move on.

Not even when John Mechelen had unexpectedly died last October.

Her cottage on the Mechelen Estate had felt like as much like a permanent home as a cottage that you didn't own could feel.

She took a bite out of her Gala apple. Its crisp juiciness filled her mouth.

Why was she so sure it would all come to an end soon?

The first inkling of unease had come, Celine realized, when Dirck had agreed to show *B-aw-ston* Greg his art.

"Showing someone your art doesn't necessarily mean you're ready to sell it," she said to herself as she took another bite of her apple.

And selling the art didn't mean anything either, did it?

But her objections were as persuasive as some smarmy politician's promise to waive all debt and make everything free. Dirck was getting ready to leave —

Celine stopped short. The thought, popping into her head out of the blue, had left her stunned. Was Dirck really preparing to leave—the bar, the winery, everything he and John had built together?

She took another bite of her apple and chewed slowly. What had happened to make her believe that?

Her mind rewound the day's events.

And stopped at the moment her employer of seven years had revealed that the bar she'd worked in contained a secret closet.

It had taken Dirck seven years to reveal its existence to her. *Seven years.*

Why had Dirck taken so long to confide in her?

Chapter Seven

Dirck had always said he trusted her. That she was like the daughter he'd never had. After all, Celine had been born the very year that he and John Mechelen had arrived in Paso Robles—with nothing but their paintings, their gardening tools, and a desire to start a new life.

Had John known about the secret space? Celine was sure he must have. Especially if he and Dirck had taken joint responsibility for the gewgaw concealed inside it.

And Dirck in turn probably knew about the steel container fitted between the floor joists under the barn floor. It had been perfect for the cardboard box she'd just stored there.

So perfect she wondered if the container had been custom-built.

The width of it, about fifteen inches across, was a precise match for the dimensions of the cardboard box. Too precise for it to be a coincidence, Celine thought.

And Dirck hadn't mentioned that either.

She clamped her lips together and gripped her apple in both hands.

If Dirck doubted her, could she blame him? He'd taken her in, given her a job, a home. That was as much as she could expect. Especially after the way she'd lost her position at the Montague Museum back East.

She'd been innocent of the charges, but could you blame someone for having their suspicions? And being cautious?

He didn't want to burden you, Celine. Sister Mary Catherine sounded exasperated. *Is that so very hard to understand?*

"Burden me with what? The knowledge that we have a secret space that until now held a somewhat valuable item that he and John have been keeping for a friend? And what about the steel container in the barn?"

He knew you'd find it.

"What if I hadn't?"

They both knew she was being contrary. She'd had the nun to guide her. In hindsight, there'd been no question that the container would be found.

And Dirck knew that, Celine. I made sure of it. He obviously had no idea where his certainty came from. But even the densest human being is open to spiritual suggestion.

There was no arguing with that. You didn't have to be psychic to receive insights in the form of a dream or a sudden inspiration. Nor did the nun have to remind Celine that while John was alive, their secrets hadn't been Dirck's alone to share.

The thought calmed her down.

❧

She sank deeper into the couch, reclining her head against the armrest.

"But why tell me about all this now?" she wondered. She took a few more bites of her apple and chewed thoughtfully.

Had Dirck intended to share the information with her all along, simply waiting for the right moment? Or had circumstances compelled him to make the revelation?

There'd been such an air of finality in the way he had shown her how to change the codes that opened and closed the closet. Dirck had acted like a stage IV cancer patient revealing details of bank accounts and ATM pin codes to a surviving relative.

Like a person who knew he wouldn't be around for much longer.

And now, all of a sudden, the task was hers?

Celine took a bite of her apple. It was almost gone, and her teeth met core and seed. She spat the stuff out onto a paper napkin, tossed the napkin and the remnants of the apple into the trash can by the countertop, and got up to get herself a drink of water.

Taking a sip of the ice-cold water, she returned to the couch. For as long as she'd known him, Dirck had a heart condition. Just like John. But unlike John, Dirck was always careful to take his medication and comply with his physician's recommendations.

He'd seemed exhausted these past few weeks, but Celine couldn't believe his condition had worsened. She hadn't noticed any change in his prescriptions—in the medications themselves or the dosages—when she'd refilled them at the Apothecary, a few doors down from the Delft.

She twirled the glass in her hands.

No, she didn't think Dirck had originally intended to say anything about the secret closet and its codes. Telling her about the cardboard box, showing her the closet, had all seemed to come as an afterthought—when she'd asked if there was anything she could do before he chased her out of the bar that night.

And he'd been in quite the hurry to get her out of that bar.

Her mind, like a river following its course, turned to the curio Dirck had been storing for his friend. Why had he been so eager to remove it from the Delft's premises?

It needed to be in a secure place. But what could be more secure than a closet whose existence no one but Dirck knew about?

Unless its location had been compromised. Did someone else know about the closet? Or, more likely, that the item was at the Delft?

Was that why Dirck was insisting it be returned? Because it was no longer safe for him to store it for his friend?

No wonder he'd been so adamantly opposed to her storing it in her cottage, either.

"He's in some kind of danger," she muttered to herself. "And I would be, too, if I had the thing anywhere near me."

She sat on the edge of the couch, certain her instincts were on the mark, but unsure what to do about it.

The danger was likely imminent if Dirck was unwilling to wait until the morning for Celine to either hand-deliver or mail the item back to his friend.

Does brooding about the matter really help? Sister Mary Catherine's voice startled her.

"Yes, it does," Celine said firmly. "I'm trying to figure out what's going on."

You'll know soon enough. There'll be time enough to figure things out then. But until then, I'd get some sleep if I were you.

Celine frowned. "What will I know soon enough?" she wanted to ask, but she knew she'd get nothing more out of her guardian angel.

Besides, there were things that even Sister Mary Catherine, despite the vantage point death gave her, didn't know.

And most likely the item, whatever it was, was safe in the barn. Celine doubted that any person—even someone covertly watching them on a regular basis—would suspect it had been smuggled out of the Delft.

Transporting empty wine bottles to the Mechelen was a routine chore for anyone who worked at the bar.

She finished her water and headed to the bedroom.

Chapter Eight

"Celine!" Dirck's voice was urgent. She heard it a second time, a little louder "Celine!"

Where was he? In the darkness, Dirck's voice seemed to come from all around her. Celine searched the blackness, her desperation growing.

When she finally turned around, her heart nearly stopped.

A dark sedan, torched by flames, sat right in front of her. She felt its searing heat now, scorching her skin.

Dirck? She tried to say his name, but its single syllable remained trapped within her vocal cords.

Then she saw his form emerge, dazed, from the burning car. A surge of relief flowed through her. *He's alive.* A hand reached out to help him.

The Lady?

Celine wasn't sure.

Then relief gave way to despair. They were at the bottom of a ravine. She could dimly see its high walls reaching up beyond her. Her head arched back as she followed the rugged outline of rock toward an ashy gray sky.

There'd be no getting out of here. The flames would eat them alive.

"Celine!"

Dirck was closer to her now. She saw the red, splotchy burn marks that dotted his face.

He stretched his hand out to her, palm upturned.

"The pills, Celine."

He staggered forward, clutching his chest.

"The pills."

❧

Oh my God, she'd forgotten the pills.

Celine's eyes opened. She bolted upright, her heart pounding, and reached for the large tote perched on a woven cane armchair by her bed.

Inside the bag, her hand felt its soft silk lining, then her fingers closed around a plastic bottle.

Dirck's prescription. She'd picked it up yesterday and forgotten to give it to him.

She glanced at the clock. It was 2 a.m., hours past the time he was supposed to take it. She'd have to wake him up.

She swung her legs down to the floor.

Not in his cottage, Celine. Sister Mary Catherine's voice startled her. *He's not there.*

"Not in his cottage?" She thought the question rather than uttering it out loud.

No, Celine.

"Then, where?" she demanded, her voice nearly shrill from agitation.

❧

Special Agent Blake Markham's eyes opened to a gray dawn in Massachusetts. His mouth felt dry and chalky. He passed his tongue over his lips, grimacing in distaste at his own stale breath.

What time was it? His eye passed over the coffee table with his laptop, its screen still up, sitting on it; the flat-screen television in its recess on the back wall; and settled on the pine display clock in a smaller recess above it.

Jesus F'in' Christ! He'd missed Pike's call. The last vestiges of sleep dissipated.

He couldn't believe he'd slept through the raucous ringtone he'd set on the unregistered phone he was using to communicate with Grayson Pike. Goddammit, where was the damn phone?

In the gray light that filtered through the blinds, Blake's fingers fumbled around on the seat of his easy chair and then around the laptop. He found the device at last behind his laptop. Impatiently, he flipped it open.

The plain blue screen showed him the date and time. Blake swore. Pike was supposed to have called three hours ago. He hit *Menu* and then selected *Call Log* from the list of options. The most recent call listed was the one he'd received from Pike shortly after 11 p.m.

Nothing since then. *Nada.*

That was troubling. Had Pike failed to retrieve the art? Or had he . . . ?

Blake leaned forward and hit the power button on his laptop.

Three hours ago, Pike's tracker had been where it was supposed to be. At the wine bar where he'd arranged to meet with Duarte.

The screen came to life, showing the secure website he was using to track Pike's movements.

Blake peered at the screen. The green circle showing Pike's location was outside the wine bar now, not within it. And it wasn't blinking. There were only two explanations for that, one of which could be ruled out immediately. The battery on the tracker was near full charge.

The only other explanation for an unblinking green circle, according to the product manual, was that the subject was motionless.

The agent considered. Pike had been drunk when he'd last called. Had he downed a few more beers and passed out near the bar?

With the art? Or without?

Either option was distasteful. He ought to have known Pike would mess the whole operation up. What had he been thinking?

You weren't thinking, Markham, that's the problem. Over twenty years later, and he could still hear the rants of his fuming scoutmaster. What a disastrous camp trip that had been.

But Blake was damned if he was going to let the situation get out of hand this time. He was an FBI agent, not a kid. And he had resources.

Clenching his lips together, he hit *Contacts* on his phone and scrolled down to the number on Pike's tracker.

No answer.

He glanced at his laptop. The flashing gray button on the sidebar indicated the call had gone through. Why wasn't Pike picking up?

Chapter Nine

The wheels of the Pilot squealed as Celine reversed out of the gravel parking area in front of her cottage and onto the driveway. She glanced at the clock as she shifted the gear into Drive.

2:20 a.m.

What was Dirck still doing at the Delft?

The gate out of the estate was unlocked, one leaf still open. It was confirmation of what Sister Mary Catherine—and her own fleeting search of the estate grounds—had already told her. Dirck hadn't returned.

The Pilot drove out and swung left in a single smooth curve. *2:21 a.m.* She'd be there in ten minutes. She punched the gas. The streets would be empty at this hour.

Downtown Paso Robles was eerily quiet. She turned onto Pine Street and then into the alley. Dirck's van was still parked in its spot, the only vehicle in the parking lot. Celine pulled in beside it and stopped the engine.

Her skin prickled—tiny pinpricks of unease on the back of her neck and down her arms. Something wasn't right.

She surveyed her surroundings. The back door to the bar was firmly closed. The buildings overlooking the alley behind her showed no signs of life.

It was quiet.

So quiet, Celine would have expected Dirck to hear her pulling into the parking lot. If he was still awake—and well. But she'd seen him clutching his heart only minutes ago in her dream.

She grabbed her leather tote with his prescription, jumped out of the car, and pushed against the back door.

It remained closed. She looked at it, puzzled. Was it stuck?

She thrust her body against it, hard. It didn't yield an inch.

She pushed again, harder this time. Nothing.

The door was locked.

Dirck had locked the back door to the bar. Why?

Celine's skin prickled again. Clutching her tote, she walked out of the parking lot, into the alley, and turned left.

A narrow walkway separated the café next door from the Delft. It was the quickest way to the front door on 13th Street. She walked carefully, alert for any suspicious sounds or activity.

She'd just emerged onto 13th Street when she stumbled, the sensation of a hard, round object penetrating the leather soles of her shoes.

Celine stepped back and looked down. It looked like a watch of some kind. Probably a customer's. She bent down, picked it up, and dropped it into her purse. It could go into the Lost-and-Found basket once she'd made sure everything was all right with Dirck.

Her head pivoted left, then her eyes widened and her form went rigid. The Delft's front door was ajar. A dim light filtered through the crack.

That didn't make sense. Why would Dirck lock the back door only to keep the front door ajar? The bar was air-conditioned. Neither door was ever kept open. And when either of them remained in the bar after hours, only the front door was ever locked.

Was Dirck expecting someone? Was someone already in there with him?

Celine's arms tingled. Her feet felt icy. She took her phone out of her tote and, pulling the bag over her front like a shield, advanced cautiously forward.

❧

For the past fifteen minutes, Special Agent Blake Markham had been pacing the floor of his small living room in Chelsea. He flipped his work phone nervously from one hand to the other, debating the wisdom of calling his supervisor.

But there was no way to spin the current situation without admitting Operation Project Recovery had gone south. At best, Pike was lying in a drunken stupor in a Central Coast city alley.

At worst, he'd taken off his tracker and fled with the finial and whatever else he'd been able to recover from Duarte. This wasn't a scenario Blake was willing to consider. His stomach tightened as it entered his mind yet again.

He gave his laptop a fleeting glance as he passed by it on his way to the living room window. The green dot indicating Pike's location showed no signs of life.

Blake stopped at the window and peered through the slats in the blind. Was there any reason for Pike to dishonor his agreement with the FBI?

If he made away with the eagle finial, Pike would be foregoing the hundred-thousand-dollar reward the Gardner Museum was awarding for its recovery. Moreover, he'd be turning himself into a felon. He'd be charged with theft and possession of stolen property. And worse.

The black market value of the finial, once it was discovered to be a stolen item, would be no more than seven to ten percent of its true value. Even if Pike managed to sell it as just another Napoleon finial—there was more than one of those floating around—Blake doubted he'd get very much more than the reward money the Gardner was offering.

No, there was no logical reason for Pike to welsh on his agreement.

Blake turned pensively from the window. He was about to resume pacing toward the back wall when Pike's green dot blinked to life. Stunned, he moved closer to his laptop.

Sure enough, Pike was moving. Away from the alley and . . . Then Pike hovered by the street. He'd better not be going back to the bar.

The green dot pulsated. *Get on with it, man!*

Blake stared at his laptop screen. Pike seemed rooted to his spot.

Then, seconds later, he began moving again—back toward the bar instead of away from it.

But at least the shitstain was moving. Blake's call, made fifteen minutes ago, must have jogged the bozo into action.

Blake tossed his phone from his left hand to his right. He'd give Pike another fifteen minutes. That would be time enough for the slimeball to get everything he needed and get out of the area.

If he hadn't called back by then, Blake would check in.

Chapter Ten

"Dirck," Celine called softly.

Icy barbs of fear suddenly stung her skin, and she leaned back, out of sight, against the wall. It's just a door, she told herself. Nothing more sinister than an open door.

Dirck must have wanted to let in some fresh air; he was often short of breath.

But the fear persisted, accompanied by the strong sense that she was about to encounter something menacing.

Still holding herself against the rough, stucco surface, she tilted her head cautiously out to peer into the interior of the Delft.

"Dirck," she called again. "Are you there?"

She stepped forward.

Dirck was obviously not in the main area of the bar open to the public. As far as Celine could tell there were no lights switched on here.

The soft glow that illuminated the floor and spilled out onto the front step was coming from a powerful light switched on somewhere beyond.

Celine clutched her bag and edged herself into the crack left by the open front door and entered the bar.

"Dirck!" she called a little louder. The kitchen door on the left was closed and deep in the shadows. But the wall panel on the right that led into the concealed room had been slid open.

She glanced over her shoulder at the open front door. A curious odor filled her nostrils—burnt, smoky. Someone other than Dirck was here—or had been until quite recently. She was sure of it.

Celine took several deep sniffs of the air around her. Along with the cool night breeze curling around the doorway, she detected the acrid smell of burning cigarettes. It was dissipating thanks to the gusts of fresh air blowing in, but the heavy odor of cigarette smoke still lingered.

Dirck didn't smoke. Whom had he brought in here?

Celine turned to look at the wall panel. The concealed room was a space so private, she'd been the only employee Dirck and John had trusted to go in there. No one else even knew of its existence.

She walked toward it.

"Dirck, it's Celine. I forgot your pills. I—"

❧

At first she thought Dirck was asleep. On the carpet in the middle of the room that he'd always kept hidden. His legs spread in a misshapen heap on the left, his head and neck twisted to the right. His arms resting loosely on the carpet, hands bunched into fists.

Then she noticed the Lady sitting at his feet. The Lady looked up at Celine, her features sorrowful. The smell of cigarette smoke was even stronger here.

Celine's gaze shifted to Dirck. Circular burn marks dotted his face just as they had in her dream. Dirck's features were contorted into a painful grimace. A slender gash scored the skin around his neck, branded into his sunburned flesh like a thin red band.

From where Celine stood, she could make out blood glistening on jagged bits of skin.

Who had done this to Dirck? A shrill, sharp, long-drawn cry assailed her ears.

Screaming won't bring him back, Celine. Sister Mary Catherine's voice startled her. *Call 9-1-1.*

❧

"Ma'am!" The 911 dispatcher's voice cut into Celine's narrative and the visions flooding her mind. "Ma'am, I need you to stay calm."

It was an unfamiliar voice, cold and dispassionate. Celine had expected to hear Peggy, the police dispatcher who answered the Paso Robles Police Department's non-emergency phone line during the day.

Or someone like her—warm and vibrant and full of sympathy.

I am calm, Celine wanted to say. About as calm as could be expected under the circumstances. She'd turned her back on the scene, but there was no escaping the image of Dirck's body lying tortured and helpless on the floor.

Or the other images invading her mind. Stubby fingers relentlessly holding a glowing cigarette against Dirck's weathered cheeks. The beefy fists tightening a thin wire behind his neck.

They were all seared into her memory.

Peggy, the police dispatcher, would have realized that. "Don't you worry, honey. I'll send someone over right away."

But the woman who'd responded to her 911 call sounded like an automaton. Celine had barely managed to mouth the words, "I need help," when the woman had asked her to confirm her location. Was she calling from Paso Robles?

"From within the city limits?" the woman had asked. "And the address?"

Celine had tried to explain about Dirck's weak heart, the unusual burn marks on his face, the gash in his neck. And the dispatcher had asked her if Dirck smoked!

Was he having a heart attack now? Was he conscious? Was he breathing?

"Ma'am, I can't help you unless you answer my questions."

Celine inhaled deeply and tried again. "There's no fire here," she said answering one of the first questions the dispatcher had asked. "Just a strong odor of cigarette smoke. Dirck, my boss, didn't smoke. Even if he did, he wouldn't have pressed the end of his cigarette into his skin.

"He isn't conscious, and . . ." And she'd assumed he was dead. She stole a look at him over her shoulder. "I don't think he's breathing, but I . . ."

"Ma'am, can you see your boss? Is he in your line of sight?"

"Yes. He's in the room behind me. I'm at the door."

"Ma'am, I need you to focus on your boss's abdomen, the upper part of his abdomen. Can you do that for me, please?"

Celine swiveled around, cell phone pressed to her ear.

"Okay."

"Focus on the point just below the ribcage. Do you see the diaphragm moving? You should be able to detect a rise-and-fall movement. Lay your hand at that point, if necessary."

"I don't see anything," Celine reported. *He's dead*, she wanted to shout. *Please just send someone, he's dead.* She bent over his lifeless body and placed her palm on his ribcage. "I don't feel anything."

"I need you to do one more thing for me, ma'am. Turn up your boss's wrist. Place the tips of your fingers at the base of the thumb. Can you feel a pulse?"

Celine knelt beside Dirck's body and gingerly lifted his wrist. It was limp and flabby. Not cold, but the warmth of life had long departed.

"There's no pulse."

"Thank you for your cooperation, ma'am. An officer from your city will be with you shortly. Please stay where you are until he arrives."

"When will he be here?"

"As soon as he can, ma'am."

"But he's dead." Murdered, most likely.

"Yes, ma'am. He doesn't need Emergency Medical Services."—So that was it! Dirck was dead, so there was no need for anyone to rush to his—or her —aid. "There's nothing more we can do."

"But Dirck didn't do this to himself."

The visions returned. Two separate sets of hands, one jabbing the end of a glowing cigarette onto Dirck's cheeks; the other straining to tauten a wire around his neck.

"I understand, ma'am. Is the person, or persons, who did this to him there?"

"No, of course not." Just their hands torturing Dirck.

Why wouldn't the images leave her? Why couldn't she see their faces?

"Are you in fear for your life, ma'am?"

"No!"

"Then, I need you to be patient, ma'am. Someone will be with you shortly."

Chapter Eleven

Celine dropped her phone into her purse and lurched unsteadily to her feet. For the first time since she'd walked in, she noticed the state of the room.

The chairs had been roughly shoved against the wall. She saw a burly arm sweeping them out of the way. A thick-soled, black leather shoe had kicked the coffee table back, making the burgundy contents of the wine glasses splosh out.

An image of Dirck cowering in the background flashed into her mind, then her gaze honed in on the wine glasses. Why were there two glasses? A slender rivulet of alarm trickled slowly through her being.

Had Dirck been expecting two men or was the wine for someone else? Someone other than the two men here?

An image of the open door swirled into her brain.

Then the impressions receded. Celine walked toward the coffee table, hand outstretched toward the wine glasses. Her fingers brushed against the rim, when she remembered the courses on criminal justice she'd taken at Durham College years ago.

Never touch anything at a crime scene, the instructor had said. *It's all evidence.*

Hastily, she withdrew her hand. The ornaments lining the mantelpiece above the faux fireplace had been cast off the marble ledge onto the floor. She could see a beefy fist reach toward the painting that hung above it, and she heard Dirck's wild, mocking laughter.

An intense, inexplicable sensation of loathing engulfed her.

"You'll find nothing here, my friend," Dirck rasped out. She saw the tortured smirk on his face and clenched her fists in suppressed anger. "It's hiding in plain sight, but not here. Not—"

Celine had barely time to wonder at the emotions surging through her when an incessant buzzing rocked her out of the vision. Her cell phone. Where was it?

She dug into her purse, but by the time she pulled it out, it had ceased its vibrating. She stared down at it, puzzled. The screen, instead of showing her a missed call, was dark. She hit the power button and tapped in her code to access her phone log.

Nothing. It was as though the call hadn't happened. But she could have sworn she'd felt it vibrating in her purse.

Still puzzled, she slipped the phone back into her purse. It was an older phone, true—a hand-me-down from Dirck when he'd acquired the newer iPhone 8. But it had been relatively unused when Celine had first received it. It seemed unlikely that either the battery or the phone itself should now need to be replaced.

A few seconds later, she felt its urgent vibration again. She pulled it out of her purse, but the vibration had stopped and the screen was still dark. Was someone trying to reach out to her?

"Is that you, Sister Mary Catherine?" Celine whispered, looking into the dark bar beyond. But even as she asked the question, Celine knew the nun wouldn't resort to manipulating electronic devices to communicate with her. There was no need to. Celine could hear her as clearly as she heard the living.

"Dirck?"

Dirck is gone, my dear.

"Did you know this was going to happen? Did you know?" Celine's voice was shrill. "Did the Lady know?"

Yes, dear. We did try to tell you. You didn't seem to want to understand.

"But why?"

His time was up, my dear. Dirck knew that. He knew what he was setting in motion. He knew you'd be able to carry on for him.

❧

Her phone clutched in her hand, Celine wandered out into the bar.

Carry on? How was she expected to do that? She had no real experience running a vineyard, winery, and wine bar. The wine bar, she might be able to manage. But the vineyard and the winery? No way.

Besides, what authority did she have in the matter? Even if Dirck had left a will, there'd been no one to leave the business to.

Unless he'd made some arrangements with one of the other wineries in the region. Celine fervently hoped he had. She would stay on as Marketing Manager, of course. Do whatever she was called upon to do. But someone else needed to be at the helm.

The bar was still unlit, but the illumination from the concealed chamber where Dirck's body lay had lightened the darkness into an obscure gray. Oddly enough, nothing was in disarray here. The barstools were still pushed in under the counter. The chairs and tables still neatly arranged.

But something was projecting out from the bar counter. What was it?

Celine flicked on the light switch.

Dear God!

Almost every painting on the wall was face-down upon the countertop. She moved closer.

Using a bar napkin, she carefully lifted the corners of the one closest to her. It was one of the many paintings the Delft displayed on consignment. A seascape, charming enough, but nothing out of the ordinary.

The next two were similar—one a painting of elephant seals sunning themselves along a line of gray boulders; the second an image of a harvest festival with women in colorful skirts and bandanas stomping grapes in a large oak barrel. Again, nothing special. A five-hundred-dollar painting in acrylic.

Undamaged, fortunately, although Celine couldn't understand why they'd been taken down and left on the countertop. She stepped around the horse-shoe-shaped counter, inspecting each painting as she came to it.

Then her gaze fell on the last one, and she froze, eyes dilated, breath trapped, mid-passage down her throat. She could hardly believe what she was seeing. A jagged slash separated most of the left edge of the canvas from its stretcher. Loose threads spurted out all along the ragged fringe.

Why had they done this? Why ravage a work of art in this brutal manner?

Her hand reached up to stifle the shocked cry that threatened to burst out of her. Calmer now, she propped one edge up, bent her head down low, and peered at the canvas. The purple-blue waters of Morro Bay at sunrise swirling away from a massive outcrop of rock came into view.

Dear God! Celine lowered the painting back down. The damage would have been bad enough had the work been one of Dirck's or John's. But this was a painting the Delft had accepted on consignment.

It wasn't the thought of the compensation that would have to be paid to the artist that bothered Celine. The Delft's actual liability for any damage sustained was nominal—about ten percent of the sale price. But there was an unspoken understanding that any work the Delft accepted would be treated with the utmost care.

It would not be vandalized. It would not be slashed or ripped. Nothing like this had ever happened before.

What had Dirck's attackers been looking for? And among the Delft's art consignment at that?

Then came a chilling realization.

The ruffians who'd done this—the man with the red, beefy hands and the guy with the short, stubby fingers—had been interrupted in their work.

In the early morning silence, they'd detected the soft purr of her engine as she pulled into the parking lot. They'd heard her banging on the back door and calling out to Dirck.

And they'd left minutes before she entered the bar. That was the reason for her seemingly irrational fear when she'd seen the open front door. She had sensed the raw energy of their presence as she approached the bar.

She knew then that they'd left not because they were afraid of being discovered. They hadn't wanted to get their hands dirty killing another person. It wasn't worth their while.

Celine's head swiveled toward the front door. It was still ajar.

She crept toward it and peered out. The streets were empty. When would the patrol car be here?

She twisted the leather strap of her purse. What if Dirck's attackers returned? They hadn't found what they wanted; they would be back. That much was clear.

She untwisted the strap and twisted it again.

They were unlikely to be back tonight. She knew that. Yet, somehow, that didn't make her feel any better.

She turned resolutely in. Tomorrow—tomorrow, she'd send all the art back. It was a breach of the consignment agreement, but each work would be safer with its owner than here at the Delft.

She stared at the clock. Only five minutes had elapsed since she'd made her 911 call. During the day, it could take as long as fifteen minutes for an officer to come by. And that was with four patrol cars in the area. But at night, according to Peggy, the Paso Robles Police Department dispatcher, there might be no more than one—perhaps two.

Celine took a deep breath. She was tempted to call 911 again, but the woman who'd taken her call had been so brusque, Celine knew there was no point.

If only she could call someone to wait with her. She didn't want to be alone.

Chapter Twelve

Call Julia, Celine. Sister Mary Catherine's voice filled her head. *Call Julia.*

Julia? Julia Hood, the woman renting the guest cottage on the Mechelen Estate? Celine wondered if she had misheard the nun.

She can help you, the nun urged.

"But she'll be asleep," Celine protested, although the idea was more appealing than she cared to admit. An image of the short, sturdy Julia Hood with her silver hair pulled back into a ponytail, a web of wrinkles at the corner of her shrewd, compassionate blue eyes floated into Celine's mind.

Julia—capable, resilient Julia—would know what to do. And, as inexplicable as the thought seemed, Celine had the strong impression that Julia was no stranger to scenes such as the one in the Delft where a man had been left brutally murdered. A call such as this one would leave Julia unfazed.

Julia would ask no questions. She would simply come.

But even if that were true—and Celine had no way of knowing one way or other whether it was—Julia was on vacation and it was—

Celine glanced at the clock. It was nearly 3 a.m. No time to be calling a woman she barely knew—a guest, no less.

An image of Julia sitting up in her bed and checking her phone swam into her consciousness.

She's awake, Celine, Sister Mary Catherine said, *and she's waiting for your call.*

Special Agent Blake Markham was beginning to lose it. The urge to fling his phone hard against the wall was damn near irresistible.

But he balled his fingers into his palm and resisted the impulse. He'd called Grayson Pike twice in the last half-hour since he'd detected his tracker moving.

But the turd had ignored his calls.

According to the tracker, Grayson was still in Paso Robles. Still at the bar known as the Delft.

Blake had tried Pike's cell phone. After a single ring, the call had gone to voicemail. A sure sign Pike had either blocked his calls or that his cell phone was turned off. Goddamn the man!

The agent flung himself into his easy chair and powered up his laptop. What time was it in California? About 3 a.m.? Something like that, he figured. So what in the hell was Pike still doing at the Delft?

He hit the Google Chrome icon on the taskbar at the lower left corner of the screen, and when the Google tab opened, typed in *Delft Bar, Paso Robles* into the search engine. He ignored the listings that came up, focusing instead on the map and photos on the right. The bar's hours were posted underneath them.

The latest the bar stayed open was 7:30 p.m. That was every Wednesday and Friday. Last night had been a Wednesday; there was no indication the bar had remained open any later than usual. How had Pike arranged to meet Simon at the Delft, then? How was it possible, he was still there?

Blake navigated away from Google and back to the LSS web site that was keeping track of Pike's movements.

Yep, Pike was still at the Delft. The green dot vibrated, indicating that the person wearing the tracker was moving about, but otherwise it remained more or less in the same spot it had been minutes ago when Blake had made his calls.

He thought back to Pike's call last night. Pike had informed Blake he'd be returning to the Delft—a business owned by a man called Dirck Thins—to meet Simon and to look at the paintings.

Blake scratched his chin. The tip that the FBI hotline had received a little over a week ago had also originated from the Delft. (It had taken the threat of a court order to elicit that information from the provider.)

But did that mean Simon was an employee of the Delft? Clearly, a trusted employee with access to the premises after hours. It was the only way Pike could arrange to meet with him in the middle of the night.

And who had called in the tip about the Vermeer? Simon? Somehow that seemed unlikely. Why would he call the FBI after all these years? For nearly three decades everyone connected to the Gardner heist had been convinced that Simon Duarte and Earl Bramer were dead.

Did Simon really think he could cut a deal with the feds, get some of the reward money for one of the two most valuable works of art stolen from the Gardner Museum?

Not likely.

But if not Simon, then who? Simon's employer, Dirck Thins? Or someone else at the Delft?

Grayson Pike had been charged with making contact with the tipster, a man who'd insisted on being called "Rembrandt." But Grayson had met Simon Duarte instead.

And Simon had agreed to show him the stolen art?

Why?

That Duarte and Pike were planning to pull something off was clear. But what exactly?

Blake navigated back to Google. The Delft opened every morning at 11 a.m. That was 2 p.m., Eastern Time. He'd call Dirck Thins at exactly that hour.

Chances were Dirck wouldn't know Simon Duarte by that name. Simon may have kept his first name, but it was unlikely he'd retained his last.

Even so, a description of Simon—and Grayson—might help to put Operation Project Recovery back on track.

Chapter Thirteen

It was 3:05 a.m. when Amtrak Thruway Coach 4768 pulled up at the Paso Robles Intermodal Station. The man seated on a black metal bench within the vestibule, formed by the station's gable roof and its green walls, waited until the coach eased alongside the curb directly in front of the entrance.

When the bus came to a stop and the two passengers ahead of him had finished boarding, he emerged from his shelter, took a cautious look around him, and got onto the bus.

Finally, he thought, *finally*, barely acknowledging the conductor's greeting. After what he'd seen, the sooner he could escape from El Paso de Robles —Pass of the Oaks—the better.

Eventually, they'd track him down. He was under no illusions about that. But he was about to bring the trail to an end. And if all went well, the General's men would be going around in circles following the crumbs he intended to leave for them.

He took a seat at the rear of the bus and settled down for the forty-minute drive out of the city. His muscles still ached from the distances he'd walked. From 13th Street to his motel room on Spring Street, where he'd changed into a fresh set of clothes. A dark jacket, denim jeans, and a clean white shirt.

He'd stuffed the wine-stained tee shirt and jeans he'd been wearing earlier into his duffel bag and had left it in plain sight on the chair facing the bed. Let them think he was still in the city. By the time they realized he'd departed, he'd be long gone.

Not wanting any trouble at the motel, he'd taken the time to check himself out. He'd waited until the clerk on duty left his desk before slipping his room key and a pile of hundred-dollar notes under a clipboard. He didn't want to leave any unpaid bills in his wake. Didn't want to be hounded.

Still, it would take some time for the motel to realize he'd checked out. And as for the bozos after him—they'd never think to make inquiries at the desk.

He caught sight of his reflection in the window and smiled. That eased the expression of tension in his face, but his blue eyes remained narrow and wary. His hair was disheveled, one brown lock falling across his forehead. He brushed it back as best he could.

His toilette case with his comb was back at the motel. No problem. He'd buy himself another. He passed his tongue over his teeth. He'd been tempted to brush his teeth, but leaving behind a wet toothbrush would have given the game away. He didn't want anyone thinking he'd returned to his room.

He peered at his reflection. Good! There was already a prickly, brown-gray growth of stubble on his upper lip and chin. A few more days of shunning a razor and shaving cream, and he'd have a full-on beard and mustache. No disguise necessary. He'd slip back home and merge seamlessly with the crowds.

He looked away, stretched his legs out, and winced. Boy, he couldn't remember the last time he'd had to walk that fast. It had taken him all of seven minutes to get to his motel. From there to the newsstand on 13th Street had been another seven or eight minutes. Then he'd hightailed it back to Spring Street and the Paso Robles Intermodal Station for the first ticket out of town.

He put his head against the backrest, closed his eyes, and made a mental note of the items he'd purchase with the prepaid card he'd bought for himself at the newsstand. His smile broadened.

That would be the first crumb.

The purchases were necessary. But paying for them with a prepaid Visa card was not.

❧

"You poor girl," Julia said when she arrived. She drew Celine into her arms and held her tightly. "What you must be going through."

She released Celine and gazed at the front door of the Delft. Unable to stand being inside a minute longer than she had to, Celine had emerged from the front door and stood waiting in the chilly night air on 13th Street.

"I had a bad feeling," Julia confessed. "Couldn't sleep. When you've been on the job as long as I have, you sometimes . . . you get this feeling in your gut. You just know that something bad will go down." She shrugged. "Nothing you can do about it but wait."

"I know the feeling," Celine said softly, thinking back to her visions earlier that evening. A thought popped into her brain and before she could analyze it the words were out of her mouth: "You're from the FBI—a federal agent, right?"

Julia's head swiveled sharply up to meet her gaze. Then she smiled. "That obvious, is it?" Her smile broadened. "No, don't answer. I'm sure it is. I've been an agent for thirty years. It rubs off on you."

Celine nodded, processing the older woman's response. Julia had been waiting for her call—had she told Celine that? Or had it been Sister Mary Catherine? Celine couldn't remember, but it left her more perplexed than ever.

"So, you're a federal agent, and you're here because . . . because you thought Dirck might be killed?" She frowned. "You knew?"

Julia shook her head vigorously. "No. No, I had no idea . . . I'm retired, Celine. I'm here on vacation. But . . ." She shook her head. "We can talk about all that later. First, tell me what we have here."

She strode into the bar, Celine at her heels. But once inside, the former federal agent slowed down, walking around the perimeter of the bar, apparently absorbed in her surroundings. The tilt of her head, cocked back toward Celine, was the only indication that Julia was paying any attention to the younger woman's account.

Unlike the 911 dispatcher, Julia heard her out with barely an interruption or two.

Her lips clenched when she saw Dirck's body. "Yes, I see," she said when Celine pointed out the burn marks on his cheek and the angry red gash around his neck. "Tortured and garroted," she murmured to herself, but Celine caught the words, nevertheless.

"I'd like to return the paintings," Celine began as they returned to the main area of the bar, but Julia shook her head.

"No, I'm afraid you can't do that. That's evidence." She paused and looked over her shoulder at Celine. "All of it is evidence."

"Fingerprints?" Celine ventured. Could they get DNA from the picture frames and canvases—from sweat, perhaps? Celine didn't know.

Julia came to a halt at one end of the horseshoe-shaped bar counter. "More than fingerprints. We need to know why Dirck's attackers were interested in these works."

Celine sighed. "I don't know what they thought they'd find. Those are inexpensive works—charming and picturesque in their own right, but not worth much."

"Ostensibly worthless," Julia said. She turned to look at Celine. "We don't know what's beneath the surface of any of these works."

"What could there be but gesso or some type of primer?" Celine wanted to know.

"Oh, my dear, you'd be surprised."

Julia walked around the counter and stared at the painting that had been slashed.

"About fifteen years ago, we nabbed a forger on the East Coast. His name won't mean anything to you, so I won't bother mentioning it. But he was a well-known crook, and we'd been after him for some time. He'd developed an almost foolproof method to hand over stolen works of art to the shady collectors who'd commissioned their thefts.

"Know what he did?"

Celine shook her head, although Julia, absorbed in the painting, couldn't have seen the gesture. She was about to speak up when Julia went on.

"The wily son-of-a-gun covered each stolen piece with this sort of"—Julia waved a disparaging hand over the paintings on the bar counter—"touristy stuff. Then he'd have the owner of a local bar display the works on consignment. I'm sure you can guess the rest. Collector walks in, takes a fancy to some piece or the other, and hands over a few thousand for a painting worth millions. No one's any the wiser."

"That's not something Dirck would've done," Celine said, instantly protective of her employer's reputation. She felt tears welling up and angrily brushed them aside. "He wasn't like that."

Julia regarded her. "I'm not saying he knew what was going on, but"—she turned back to gaze at the paintings—"you have to admit, something was. Going on, I mean."

A moment's silence followed, then Julia pointed to the painting that had been slashed. "Who is this by, do you know?"

Celine walked over to where she stood and gazed down at the painted waters of Morro Bay. "It's by Simon—"

"Simon?" Julia broke in, her brow furrowing. "Simon who?"

"Simon Underwood," Celine said. "He's a local painter. Originally from —"

"Boston?"

"Yes, how did you—?"

But Julia ignored the question.

"So the rumors are true. Simon is alive."

Chapter Fourteen

A hard rap on the door startled them both. "You reported a dead body, ma'am?"

Celine whirled around. An officer stood by the door, one hand on his belt, the other, encased in a cream-colored latex glove, lightly touching the door. He looked from Celine to Julia, his eyebrows raised, his eyes wide.

Through the door, Celine could make out the black quarter panel of a Paso Robles Police Department patrol car. Intent upon examining the Delft's art, neither she nor Julia had heard it ease up to the curb.

"Yes," she said, gathering her swirling thoughts together. A quick glance at the clock told her it had been twenty minutes since she'd made her 911 call.

The officer must have noticed, for he shifted uneasily on his feet. "It's been a busy night, ma'am, and there are only two cars out on patrol. And when the dispatcher called in a dead body . . ." He shrugged.

"You knew it wasn't going anyplace anytime soon," Julia offered. "Is that about right?"

A sheepish expression had begun to descend upon the officer's features, but, struck by a sudden thought, it quickly dissipated. He frowned. His gaze shifted toward Celine.

"Dispatch said you were alone, ma'am."

"I was when I made the call," Celine confirmed. "But I didn't want to wait alone, so I called Ms. Hood."

"In the middle of the night?" The question was quietly uttered, the officer's voice barely rising, but his gray eyes were cold and steely.

"I'm a federal agent, Officer," Julia said, showing the officer her badge. "I'm used to being called out at all hours of the night. And Celine was aware of that."

It was a small lie, and Celine was grateful for it. It stalled any further questions on the matter. It would have been hard to explain why she'd thought of calling Julia or been so sure her call would not go unanswered in the middle of the night.

The officer seemed to accept the explanation.

"Has anything been touched or handled? Detectives will want to know." He walked toward the bar counter, his eyes on the paintings. He stopped a few inches from them and looked up. "Where is the body?"

"In there." Julia pointed. "As you can imagine, Officer, this isn't my first rodeo, so, no, I didn't touch anything. Did you, Celine?"

Celine shook her head. "My fingers may have brushed against the wine glasses in there. And the dispatcher had me check whether Dirck was breathing."

"What about doors, windows, light switches?"

"The back door was locked. That was unusual. I banged against it and tried to twist the knob open. But the front door was ajar. I may have pushed it open a little wider to let myself in. The main area of the bar was in darkness. I turned on the light switch later when I noticed those"—she indicated the paintings behind her—"but the light was still on where Dirck is."

While she'd been speaking the officer had walked around the bar, and then poked his head into what Celine had always considered Dirck's sanctum— the room, concealed behind a wall panel, where his body lay.

"There was a strong smell of cigarette smoke when I first came in. That's what alerted me to the fact that there may have been intruders."

The officer turned around. His gaze circled around in search of elusive smoke tendrils as he took a cautious sniff.

"It's dissipated now," Julia added. "But you'll find splotches of gray cigarette ash on the rug." Celine turned to her in surprise as Julia continued to speak; she herself hadn't spotted any traces of cigarette ash, but some had to have dropped on the floor near Dirck. The former federal agent's eyes were clearly still sharp enough to detect such minute quantities. "And then there are the burn marks on the victim's face. Clearly done with the butt-end of a cigarette."

The officer nodded. "I'll have the Coroner's Unit come out," he said. "The Sheriff's detectives roll with them, and they'll take your statement. In the meantime, I'll need you to wait outside the bar."

"No problem." Julia propelled Celine toward the door. At the door, she turned and gestured toward the paintings on the bar counter.

"Let them know, Officer, that the man, or men, who attacked the victim was after the art he sold on consignment. This is probably not just a case of gang or mob violence. There's more to it than meets the eye."

❧

Celine looked over her shoulder as she and Julia passed through the Delft's front door and stepped out onto the sidewalk. The cold air hit her hard, making her shiver, and she buried her hands deep inside the pockets of her sweatshirt.

What had Dirck's attackers been expecting to find concealed in the art the Delft sold on consignment? And who were they? The sporadic impressions she'd received inside had failed to reveal their faces.

It's your point of view, Celine. Sister Mary Catherine's voice made itself heard above Celine's thoughts. *It limits what you can see.*

Celine frowned, not understanding what the nun was trying to say. Did Sister Mary Catherine think Celine was letting her biases get in the way of her intuition? But that simply wasn't true.

She heard Julia's voice speaking, but didn't catch the words over the din in her own head.

"I'm sorry, my mind was elsewhere. What did you want to know?"

Julia tipped her head in the direction of the door. "Has anyone expressed more than a casual interest in those works of art recently?"

"No, our patrons—" Celine was beginning to say when a memory surfaced. "*B-aw-ston Greg,*" she said with a gasp.

"Who?"

"I've never seen him before. A tourist, I imagine. He didn't seem the type to appreciate either wine or art. But he asked several questions about those works." She paused. "The only thing is he seemed more interested in Dirck's works than the ones we have for sale."

She turned to face Julia. "He even asked to see some of Dirck's art. And Dirck agreed, surprisingly enough."

In her mind's eye, she saw the two Merlot-filled wine glasses in Dirck's sanctum. Had Dirck arranged to meet Greg later that evening? Was that why he'd hustled her out of the bar? And had that fatal decision led to his death?

They'd have to find Greg, but how?

"Does the interior of the bar have security cameras?" Julia's brisk voice broke into Celine's musings.

Celine's head jerked up. "Yes, yes, as a matter of fact we do. You think that'll help?"

For the first time, she felt a twinge of hope. And Julia's response was especially reassuring.

"It gives us a face and an image to work with." A determined expression settled on Julia's features.

Greg would have to disguise himself if he wanted to stay hidden. But with law enforcement officials sending out images of him, he'd be found in no time at all.

"It's a start. A very good start, really," she assured Celine.

The former federal agent hugged herself tight and stomped her feet, clad in sensible black shoes, on the gray sidewalk.

"I could do with some coffee. Wish I'd thought to bring some in a flask with me. But when you called, all I could think of was getting here as quickly as I could."

Celine looked wistfully out over 13th Street. Vic's Café, right across the street, didn't open until 7 a.m. It was the earliest any of the cafés in the vicinity of the Delft opened. She could almost taste the hot, strong, aromatic espresso she'd order when Vic's finally did open.

"If Dirck remembered to turn the pot on," she said, "there'll be coffee ready to brew right here in the bar. But it won't start until 10:30 in the morning, a half-hour before we open."

"Damn!" Julia cursed under her breath.

She rubbed her hands together. "Any other impressions of the scene of the crime?" she asked.

Celine stared. This wasn't her first crime scene, but no law enforcement official, retired or otherwise, had ever expressed any curiosity about *her* opinions of a crime.

Julia stared back. "You do get impressions, don't you? Keith Elliot—"

"Detective Keith Elliot?" Celine asked. "Of the Durham Police Department?"

He'd helped solve the murders of her college friends, Sonia and Nicole. That had been many years ago, but Celine would never forget the man who'd recognized her psychic visions for what they were.

There'd been the Montague Museum case, a few years after that. But despite her visions and Elliot's efforts, it had gone nowhere. At the time, he'd mentioned having an FBI contact. *Julia*? If he'd provided a name, she couldn't remember it.

"*Lieutenant* Elliot," Julia said. "But yeah same guy. Retired now."

"*He* sent you here?" Detective Elliot had been gifted with second sight as well, although his visions weren't as strong as Celine's.

"Thought you might be in trouble. He wanted me to make contact with you, keep an eye on you. I didn't say anything earlier because . . . Well, I didn't want to spook you. And quite frankly, I was skeptical."

She looked back at the bar with a sigh. "Not anymore, though."

An impression filled Celine's mind, and she decided to confirm it. "That's not the only reason you're here, is it, Julia?"

Julia looked at her, then slowly shook her head. "No, it's not. Keith thought I might find answers to a case I've devoted most of my career to. A nearly thirty-year-old case that's yet to be solved. The Gardner Museum heist."

That again! Celine let out the breath she hadn't even been aware she'd been holding.

The Gardner Museum theft had come into play in the unsolved case in Durham as well. The killer had gotten away then. She hadn't thought about it until earlier this evening when . . .

"Greg brought that up as well. The Gardner Museum heist. But what does that have to do with Dirck and our art?

"I don't know, kiddo. I just don't."

Chapter Fifteen

It was when Grayson's tracker began moving toward the Paso Robles Police Station that Special Agent Blake Markham began to worry. At first he'd thought Grayson was finally heading back to his motel.

The tracker had moved west on 13th Street and then turned left onto Spring Street where Grayson had booked a motel. Blake knew that because he'd seen the tracker at the location of the inn. The FBI wasn't springing for a hotel. It had made Grayson's travel arrangements, but that's as far as it went.

As for the rest, Grayson had been issued money in the form of traveler's checks and told to fend for himself. Grayson had griped long and hard about being handed an obsolete form of currency; one that required going to a bank—during regular business hours—for ready cash.

But the FBI had figured that this way any money the washed-up former artist-turned-informant was given would be less likely to be gambled away or wasted on liquor. It was a form of control; a way of keeping an unreliable operative on a fairly tight leash.

All these thoughts had passed through Blake Markham's head as he stared, bleary-eyed, at his laptop screen. He was at work now; had been for hours. His eyes felt dry, but although he'd felt in his drawer for his prescription eye drops and had them in his hand, he hadn't torn his eyes away from the screen long enough to put the drops in.

The tracker was literally blazing down the streets. Grayson was obviously in a car. With whom? Simon Duarte? Grayson hadn't rented a car; the tracker hadn't been near a car-rental place since it had first shown up in Paso Robles, even though there were two near his motel.

Why get into a car now? Because Grayson had managed to get control of all thirteen pieces stolen? Blake's hopes surged. That would be quite something. Maybe that's why Grayson and Simon had been so long at the Delft. The art was probably all stashed in the bar—cleverly concealed, no doubt.

Blake had refrained from calling, either on the tracker or on Grayson's cell phone. If the guy was with Duarte, Blake's call would only compromise the operation. No doubt, Grayson would call him as soon as he got to his motel room. A team would be sent out to retrieve the art the second Grayson gave them the go-ahead.

But then, inexplicably, the tracker had turned left on 10th Street, and then right on Park Street and cruised straight into the local police station.

Goddammit! Grayson was in a car all right. But it was a police car. What exactly had gone down at the Delft?

Blake leaned back in his leather office chair; the chair swiveled to the right. He glanced at the clock on the wall and made some quick calculations in his head. Not time for the Delft to open yet, but if police had been called to the bar, there might be someone there to answer the phone.

He swiveled back to his desk and pulled his phone toward him. He could hear the phone ringing at the other end. It kept on for some minutes. He hung up and tried again. And again.

Even if there were crime scene technicians there—the only reason not to answer a ringing phone—they'd get so tired of the incessant, ear-piercing *trr-rrring*, someone on the team would pick up the receiver just to make it stop.

"Hello."

"Yes, I'd like to speak with the owner, Dirck Thins, please?"

"Who wants to know?"

"A customer." Blake hesitated. "From out of state."

"I'm sorry to inform you Dirck Thins is dead, sir. Murdered, from the looks of it."

Murdered?

Before Blake could ask any more questions, the voice at the other end had advised him to call the Mechelen Winery to place his order, given him a phone number, and hung up.

Murdered? Dirck Thins had been murdered. By whom? Grayson Pike?

But a few discreet inquiries had yielded no further information. The owner of the Delft had been discovered tortured and garroted; somehow that didn't sound like Grayson.

The Sheriff's Office was handling the case. But no one by the name of Greg—Grayson's code name for the operation—had been arrested by either the Paso Robles Police Department or the Sheriff's men.

A chilling realization struck Blake Markham. Grayson Pike had ditched his tracker—must've ditched it sometime in the early hours of the morning. Just outside the bar, and someone had picked it up. Who? Not the police? Whoever had found and reported the body most likely.

The tracker was probably in the hands of detectives by now—a clue to the killer.

A clue to Grayson—code-named Greg—Pike.

The media would have a field day with this. Blake could just see the headlines: *FBI Informant Kills Prominent Businessman.* It was the last thing the Agency needed after the Russia collusion debacle. If word of Grayson the shitstain's involvement got out, it would be the final nail in the coffin of alleged FBI corruption.

Jesus F—in' Christ.

He could lose his job over this.

Blake banged his fist on the desk. *Dammit!* He needed to find Grayson. Today.

So the bastard had ditched his tracker? Had he ditched his phone, too? Would the motel Grayson had booked himself into know anything?

Blake's gray eyes were blazing as he mentally composed the instructions he'd give his personal assistant. He didn't need a state-of-the-art LSS3i tracker to find Grayson. He could find that piece-of-shit lowlife without all that high-end gadgetry.

"I will hunt you down, bastard!" he snarled.

❧

"What exactly did your employer know, Ms. Skye?"

Detective Rick Mailand folded his arms one over the other on the desk and eyed Celine as though he suspected her of withholding information.

They were in the Paso Robles Police Station interview room, but Detective Mailand, a man with a deeply tanned face and craggy features, was one of the Sheriff's detectives. He'd accompanied the Coroner's Unit when they'd finally arrived shortly after five o'clock to process the crime scene—and had stayed.

He'd caught the case—and Celine suspected that, given the circumstances, he meant to keep it.

But the question he'd put to her still hung, unanswered, in the air.

"About what?" she responded finally. She was stalling. The words *Gardner Museum Heist* had fluttered across her mind in golden letters. She deliberately wiped them off her mental screen as she pushed the stirrer into the Styrofoam cup of coffee Detective Mailand had handed her.

Clumps of powdered creamer floated in the tawny-brown liquid and grains of a packet of sweetener flecked the surface. No amount of stirring would dissolve either. Celine sighed. She'd been yearning for an aromatic cup of espresso. Instead, here she was with a cup of what looked like muddy brown water straight from the Salinas River.

Satisfied that her mind was completely blank, she looked up and gazed into his eyes—the color of mahogany rimmed with gray. Unusual eyes. Attractive eyes. And, at this point, deeply suspicious eyes.

"I don't know, Ms. Skye. I was hoping *you* could enlighten me. He must have had knowledge about something to be tortured and killed the way he was. You were a trusted employee, were you not?"

Celine nodded.

"Did he ever mention anything that seems relevant now in the light of what's happened? There were cigarette burns on your employer's face. He was garroted. That seems to indicate a personal motive for the murder, Ms. Skye. Rather than that Mr. Thins was just a random victim of a break-and-enter."

"I was a trusted employee, Detective, but I wasn't Dirck's confidante." She paused. "I think he *was* meeting someone. He hustled me out of the bar and when I returned I noticed the glasses of wine in the sanctum." She was repeating the information she'd already given him. "He may have been expecting two people. There were *two* glasses of wine."

Celine was quite sure now that Dirck had been expecting to see only Greg. The other glass of wine would've been for himself. But she had no other way of conveying her impression that there'd been two men attacking Dirck not one.

"You'll have to figure out a way of telling the police that," Julia had advised her, "without letting them know about your visions." Perhaps it was just as well, Celine thought, that she didn't have any identifying features to share about Dirck's attackers. There'd have been no explaining how she'd managed to get hold of that information.

Detective Mailand nodded, pushed his notebook out from under his hand, and peered at the penciled squiggle marks on its lined pages.

"And you think one of those two people was the patron called Greg?"

"It seems to be the only explanation that fits, Detective," she replied. "Greg was interested in the art hanging on our walls, very interested in seeing Dirck's art and in the fact that he was from Boston as well."

Detective Mailand regarded her from under a pair of broad, well-marked eyebrows. "Mr. Thins was from Boston? Did he have any associates there? Any connections he was still in touch with?"

Celine shook her head and smiled for the first time that night. "Dirck and John left Boston in 1990, Detective. They haven't been back since and if they left any friends there, they've long been out of touch."

A memory stirred as she spoke. Surely there was someone Dirck still knew back in Boston. Not that there was any point mentioning the possibility to the detective—she glanced at him. He might have been handsome had it not been for the furrows etched on his forehead and the deep lines creased into his stubble-coated cheeks.

A sensation—possibly attraction; it had been years since she'd felt anything of the sort—arose within her. She thrust it aside and returned to the matter at hand.

No, she didn't know whom Dirck might still have known in Boston or even why the thought had occurred to her.

"In 1990, eh?" Detective Mailand cupped his chin, allowing his broad thumb to pass back and forth over the stubble dusting his chin.

Celine stared back. Had Julia mentioned the Gardner Museum theft to him? What clues to the robbery could Paso Robles hold?

"1990," Detective Mailand repeated. "Was it after or before the infamous museum heist?"

Julia had mentioned it, then. Or maybe the detective was just well-informed.

"I don't know, Detective." Celine's fingers closed around the edge of her seat, gripping hard. "What I do know is that neither he nor John Mechelen could have had anything to do with the Gardner. They both had too much respect for art to steal it."

The impressions she'd received within the Delft's sanctum crowded back into her mind. The attackers had been after some object or other; something that could be easily concealed behind the back of a painting.

Money?

Drugs?

Whatever it was, Dirck had known about it. *It's hiding in plain sight*, she heard his voice taunting his killers.

The only thing hiding in plain sight was the gewgaw she'd concealed for him. But that could hardly be concealed in the back of a work of art. Besides, he'd said it belonged to someone else and needed to be returned.

No, no. That wasn't it at all.

"Ms. Skye."

The detective's voice pulled her abruptly out of her reverie. She looked up, startled.

"Yes?"

He regarded her with resigned patience. "Was there any significance," he began, enunciating each word slowly, "to the paintings that were taken off the walls? Not all of them were, as you might recall."

She did recall, and it puzzled her. Greg had wanted to see Dirck's art, but all of his paintings and John's had been left hanging on the wall. The ones taken down had been—

"The ones we sell on consignment, Detective. Those were the pieces the men who did this were after."

The specific work they'd been after had been painted by Simon Underwood.

Simon. The name had struck a chord in Julia.

There'd been a Simon implicated in the Gardner theft, too, hadn't there? A Simon Duarte? A simple coincidence? Celine wasn't sure anymore.

Simon Underwood was from Boston as well. And Greg had mentioned that John's portrait in the guise of a turbaned Rembrandt bore a remarkable resemblance to Earl Bramer, Duarte's friend.

Was it possible her boss, Dirck Thins, had been harboring the men who'd been behind the notorious heist? What other information could he possibly have had? Surely not the art itself?

Her fingers tightened around the wooden seat, abrading against the head of a nail roughly pushed in. No, no, never that.

Chapter Sixteen

"We'll need a warrant to ping his phone, Blake." Ella Rawlins, a dark-haired, bespectacled, young woman encased in a stylish skirt suit that emphasized her figure, poked her head around the edge of her desktop screen and peered up at her boss.

Special Agent Blake Markham felt irritation, like bile, rising up within him as he stared down at his personal assistant. Ella may not have been questioning his orders, but it sure sounded like it to him.

It was a habit of hers—to tell him what *they* needed to carry out any of his commands. As though Blake didn't quite know the law and needed a constant reminder of the innumerable ways in which it circumscribed his power.

He saw Ella's gaze drop to his hands, expecting to see the piece of paper that, in her mind, would authorize their operation. The mildly anxious expression her face habitually wore deepened when she saw he was empty-handed.

"Don't we?"

"No, we don't," he snapped. "Exigent circumstances. Grayson Pike is MIA on an undercover operation. He could be in trouble."

Or wanted for murder.

Not that Ella needed to know that.

"Just do it, okay?" Without waiting for a response, he turned brusquely on his heels and re-entered his office, resisting the urge to slam the door.

This would go a lot faster without Ella questioning his every move. But he'd given her a solid reason to get on that ping. If she'd had any further objections, she wouldn't have hesitated to run in after him to voice them.

Now to call Grayson's motel. He walked over to his desk and picked up the phone, too tense to sit down.

"Checked out?" He repeated the information the clerk gave him. "When?"

"The night clerk didn't see." The voice sounded apologetic. "He was either using the restroom or doing his regular check of the grounds. We don't have security cameras covering the exterior."

The night clerk had returned to find Grayson's room keys and a wad of cash to cover his stay stashed under the hotel register. There'd been an extra couple of hundred that even the night clerk had realized couldn't have been part of an exceptionally generous tip.

Grayson must have left in a hurry. Had he deliberately avoided the night clerk? Or was the absence of a witness just a coincidence?

"Will your friend be wanting the additional amount sent back to him, sir?" the clerk inquired, the tone of his voice suggesting that he hoped the answer would be, *no.*

"No, that's quite all right. Keep it." Blake was about to hang up when a thought occurred to him. "You said there are no cameras outside the motel. Are there any inside?"

"Only in the lobby. The footage is grainy."

"Check it for me, will you?" He wanted to make sure Grayson had voluntarily checked himself out, although it was hard to imagine a burly, five-foot-ten guy being dragged out against his will.

But at this point, Blake wanted hard facts. Not assumptions. Receiving an assurance of a callback, he hung up, sat on the edge of his desk, and stroked his chin. He was trying to be objective. He didn't have very many facts to draw any conclusions, but he had to admit to himself it wasn't looking good.

Grayson had ditched his tracker and quietly checked out of his motel. Not something an innocent man was likely to do.

His worst fears were realized when Ella opened the door and poked her head in.

"Looks like Grayson's cell phone was switched off around about 2 a.m., Pacific."

And judging by its current location, the phone itself had been ditched in an alley off of Spring Street in Paso Robles. Grayson was officially on the run.

"Anything else you want me to do, Blake?"

"Call the airlines and see if anyone named Greg or Grayson left San Luis Obispo Airport last night." It was a long shot. He didn't actually think Grayson would have used either his real name or the ticket the FBI had purchased for him in his code name."

He barked out a few more instructions and then began planning his next move.

❧

The call from the motel on Spring Street in Paso Robles came sooner than Blake had expected. Despite the poor quality of the security camera footage, there was no doubt in the day clerk's mind. It was the occupant of Room 64 who'd checked out. The time stamp on the camera showed it was a few minutes past one.

"But the extra money your friend left behind won't cover the damage to the door, sir."

"What door?" Blake wanted to know.

"The door to Room 64. The cleaning staff found it smashed in. Maybe your friend tried to come back for his things, but—"

"What things?"

"The things he left behind. He had nothing in his hands when he checked out. He should've asked the night clerk for his key back instead of smashing the door in. We can't let that room out until the door's fixed. And we don't have a credit card on file."

Blake sighed. He was tempted to suggest that the repairs be charged to the FBI, but that would be a surefire way of drawing unwanted attention to the fact that his CI was AWOL. Not something he wanted to do.

"Fine. Put it on my account." He pulled his wallet out of his pocket, drew a credit card from it, and read out the number. He tried not to balk at the figure the clerk quoted. Five hundred dollars to fix a broken door at some two-bit motel! Seriously?

But something else the clerk had said stirred in his memory. "How can you be so sure it was my friend who returned? I thought you said no security cameras cover the exterior of the motel."

"Who else would be interested in a duffel bag stuffed with his clothes —mostly dirty—or a toothbrush he'd been using. Then there's the tube of toothpaste, razor, shaving cream, a bottle of cologne. The cleaning staff can confirm it's all his."

It took a minute for Blake to absorb the significance of this information. "You mean the items are still in his room? He didn't take them after all?"

There was silence on the other hand. Blake couldn't even hear the sound of the desk clerk's breathing. He figured the clerk had come to the same conclusion he had. Grayson hadn't returned to the motel room. Why would he, only to leave his belongings behind?

"Yes, but the damage," the clerk huffed.

"You can still charge it to me." But for five hundred dollars, he wanted more.

"Call me if someone comes looking for my friend in the next day or two." He paused a fraction of a second. "And if I were you, I'd wait on fixing that door."

He hung up and paced the floor. Either Grayson hadn't left Paso Robles, which meant he might still return. Or whoever was looking for him would, to see if Grayson had stuck around. Most likely, though, Grayson had split, leaving his belongings as a decoy for whoever was after him.

Blake massaged his forehead, pushing his fingers deep into his brow. If Grayson was a fugitive, who was he running from? The FBI? Simon Duarte? Or Dirck Thins' killer?

Blake reviewed the facts. Grayson had jettisoned his tracker—a custom-made FBI tracker that made his movements accessible to no one but the agents monitoring Operation Recovery—outside the Delft Bar.

What exactly had happened to make him do that? It didn't seem likely that he'd garroted Thins. Could he have made off with the art?

Unlikely. Not without a car. And the only time the tracker had been in a car had been on its ride to a police station.

Even if all Grayson had was the Vermeer, it was a bulky item, not easily carried while walking. Of course, it was possible Grayson had a pretty good idea where the Vermeer was.

But was that reason enough to run?

Blake considered the other option. What if Grayson had witnessed Dirck Thins' murder? But if so, why hadn't he called Blake immediately? Ditching the phone was understandable. Anyone could use it to track him. But getting rid of the tracker was not. Only the FBI could monitor him on that—

Unless—

Blake stopped pacing. The very thought made him sick.

Did Grayson suspect the FBI was behind Thins' murder? Did Grayson Pike fear he was next on the hit list? But why?

What could he have seen? What could have aroused his suspicions?

Special Agent Blake Markham strode toward his desk. Grayson had to be found.

Chapter Seventeen

Geoff Brandt pushed a metal shopping cart laden with items out of the Costco warehouse in San Luis Obispo and surveyed the parking lot. It was a warm day, the sun blazing down on the dark asphalt of the vast lot.

There'd been no more than a few cars when he'd walked in a half-hour ago, minutes after the store opened. Now they cruised past in a steady stream, deftly maneuvering in between the white lines that demarcated each parking space. He craned his head, peering over the rows of parked vehicles, trying to locate his Mrs. B.

Getting out of the parking lot wasn't going to be easy, but with his Brandt Plan, they'd save several precious minutes. Instead of wheeling the cart over to the car, he'd have her meet him in front of one of the spots closer to the exit. Then, he'd quickly unload his items into the trunk and get in the car.

The trick was to find either an empty parking spot or one with a car whose owners were still shopping inside. If all else failed, you blocked an elderly shopper, the kind that takes a half-hour to walk three shopping bags from the cart to the car. They were never in a hurry to go anywhere and were usually too polite to complain.

His head on a swivel, he caught sight of a brick-red Toyota Camry abruptly catapulting out of a parking spot. That impatient maneuver along with a glimpse of blonde hair falling past large shades was all he needed to pinpoint Mrs. B.

He gripped the cart handle and shoved. It lurched forward, wheels rattling, as Brandt guided it toward a lane that wound round to the exit. Cars swept past, impatiently searching for empty spots in a lot that was fast filling up now. He couldn't have Mrs. B pull up in front of an empty spot. No, they'd have to block a parked car.

Or better still, a shopper getting ready to leave. A slow-as-molasses seventy- or eighty-year-old. And there, as luck would have it, was one. She was loading the trunk of her ancient Volkswagen Bug. Brandt gave her a quick nod and smile as he rolled to a stop just inches past her.

He glanced over his shoulder. Mrs. B was making her way toward him. His smile widened, but he doubted she could see him.

He angled the cart slightly out toward the center and waited. In a few minutes, Mrs. B's tires squealed as she turned the corner into his lane, gaining speed. He pushed the cart out a little more, raised his arm in a cheery wave, and bared his teeth in a wide smile.

But Mrs. B seemed in no mood to stop. Brandt's grin faded.

"Hey, wait!" he called out, thrusting the cart out in front of her.

"Asshole!" she yelled, careening to the left to avoid the cart, which creaked to a stop just behind her car. She jerked her middle finger up at him and shot out the exit.

"Damn!" Brandt cursed. "What is it with that bitch?" He pulled the cart back toward himself. "Goddammit!" He banged his fist hard into the metal handle, about to express himself a little more strongly when he noticed the elderly owner of the Beetle gaping at him, eyes wide, jaw slack.

Brandt rubbed his bruised knuckles against his thigh and gave her an apologetic smile. "Sorry about that, ma'am." He gestured toward the street that Mrs. B was now streaking past. "That was my wife. And"—he shook his head ruefully—"my ride to the airport."

He patted his pockets, in search of his iPhone, but there was no such thing in his pockets. "Must've left it in the car." He sighed as he dropped his hands, deflated.

He wheeled the cart around.

"They're not going to take that stuff back, you know," the woman's voice quavered after him.

Brandt looked over his shoulder.

"You may be able to return the clothes. But not the food. They won't take that back. And you've got a lot of food in there."

Brandt glanced down at the cart. There was a lot of food.

Two rotisserie chickens, hot from the oven, a large round container of brownie bites and another with mini cinnamon buns, a party pack of chips, and several ready-to-eat containers of pulled pork and chicken marsala.

"I'm taking the clothes. Those are for me. But all this food"—he gestured toward it—"was for my wife. To keep her going for the few days I'll be out of town unable to cook for Her Highness. She can come get it if she wants it."

"You're going to leave it here?" The woman asked, her reedy warble rising in shrillness. "Right here, in the parking lot?"

"You want it?" Brandt responded, seeing her gaze lingering on the items. "I can't take this with me on the plane. And I'm sure as hell not going to walk it back home."

He reached into his pocket and pulled out a card. "Here, you can have this as well. It's a gift card. I was going to give it to my wife to make up for being away for her birthday, but after that stunt she just pulled I'd sooner flush it down the toilet."

"How are you going to get to the airport?" she asked, still staring, bedazzled, at the food in his cart.

"Don't know. My cell phone's in the car. I can't call a cab. And even if I do, my passport's in the car as well. So I'm—pardon my French—royally screwed."

The woman cocked her head. "Well, they do accept other kinds of ID, you know. My nephew tells me anything with a photograph will do. As for your other problem, I don't have a cell phone—never could figure out how to use one—but I might be able to help out."

❧

The moving tracker caught Blake's attention. The San Luis Obispo County Sheriff's Office might be handling Dirck Thins' murder, but surely even a department as tiny as the Paso Robles Police Department could afford to handle the investigation of the crime scene itself.

He'd have expected the tracker and any other evidence found at the Delft to be retained at the local police office. But, no, it was clearly moving out of the police department.

It wasn't proceeding in the direction of San Luis Obispo, though. The agent watched in amazement as it traveled down 13th Street out of downtown Paso Robles, over the Salinas River, and then onto South River Road.

So the tracker hadn't been handed over to the police. It was the first ray of hope Blake had experienced in an otherwise gloomy morning. Whoever had picked up the tracker had obviously not realized what it was or that it might be connected in any way with Thins' murder.

That was good. Very good. It gave him a little more time to track down Grayson before a certain malodorous substance hit the fan.

The sense of relief didn't last too long. A knock on the door and Ella Rawlins' disapproving face behind it brought Blake scudding back to reality.

Chapter Eighteen

"I'd like to meet Simon Underwood, Celine," Julia said as she waited on the paved walkway in front of Celine's cottage. After nearly two hours at the Paso Robles Police Station, they'd finally been allowed to go. Exhausted, they'd decided to return to the Mechelen. "The man who painted—what was it called again?"

"Purple Water." It was the painting that had been slashed. Celine glanced over her shoulder. She twisted the key in the lock, her hand on the door handle, and hesitated.

"You don't think Simon Underwood had anything to do with what happened, do you?"

"You'll have to go meet him, won't you?" Julia responded with a question of her own. "I could tag along with you."

Celine acknowledged both the question and Julia's suggestion with a nod. She did need to meet with Simon. She'd have to let him know his work had sustained some damage—nothing serious; it could be fixed. But it wasn't a conversation she was looking forward to having.

Having Julia accompany her might make it easier.

She'd have to break the news to the other artists as well that their works were now in the custody of the San Luis Obispo Sheriff's Office—silent witnesses to a murder. Her gaze drifted beyond Julia's short, squat figure, and she sighed.

The Spanish-tiled roofs on the estate's buildings, the crystalline blue sky with wisps of clouds scudding across the surface—it looked like it had been lifted straight out of a Francesco Guardi landscape—and the palm fronds waving in the breeze were such a stark contrast to the impressions of ruthless savagery she'd glimpsed at the Delft.

It was a day like any other in Paso Robles—with one stark difference. Dirck was gone. And she'd been left to drift in the wind—again. Dirck's lawyer would have to be informed, as would the estate's Italian winemaker, Andrea Giordano. She'd let Andrea convey the news to the estate's employees. She couldn't bear to do it herself.

Her gaze shifted to Julia's blue eyes, narrowed into a squint against the glare of the sun.

"You can come along, but I still don't understand why you want to meet Simon. He would never hurt Dirck. They've known each other for years."

"That may be so. But don't you want to know what it was about Simon's paintings that would lead someone to torture and kill Dirck just for the sake of possessing them?"

"But we don't know if it was Simon's work they were after. It was the first piece they began to examine when I interrupted them." Celine hesitated again, but the thoughts flooding into her mind were too strong to ignore. "For some reason, you're convinced Simon Underwood is Simon Duarte. Am I wrong?"

Julia's eyes widened. "You've heard of Simon Duarte?"

Celine nodded. "From Greg," she began to say when Julia touched her arm and gestured toward the door. "Let's talk about this inside."

❧

"There were three flights out of San Luis Obispo this morning," Ella announced.

"Just three?"

"I assumed you were only interested in flights to Boston. Weren't you?" The light from the window behind Blake hit Ella's round glasses, making them gleam. He couldn't see the expression in her eyes, but her lips, tightly pursed, left no room for doubt.

Ella Rawlins, his personal assistant, wasn't pleased with him.

She made it across the floor to his desk in three rapid strides and dropped a sheaf of papers on his desk.

"American Eagle flight AA 2588 at 6:15 a.m., United Airways flight UA 5660 at 6:18 a.m., and United Airways flight UA 5644 at 7:40 a.m. No one by the name of Grayson Pike or Greg Peters was on any of them."

Blake glanced down at the bundle of papers on his desk. "What are these?"

"Passenger manifests for the three flights. I've highlighted the names of the passengers who purchased tickets for same-day travel—"

"Thank you, but could you check the other early morning flights? Actually, could you check every early bird flight out of San Luis Obispo?" If

Grayson thought he was on a hit list, he'd get on the first available flight out of central California—with or without fake ID. That's what Blake would've done.

Ella sighed—a heavy, drawn-out sigh that even Blake in his current preoccupied mood couldn't miss. "I think that's going to be a waste of time, don't you? We really need to go about this in a strategic manner."

"I thought we were," was all Blake could think to say.

Ella shook her head, pulled out the chair on the other side of his desk, and thrust herself into it. "I'm afraid not. If we were thinking this through, we'd realize there's no way Grayson could be on any early bird flight out of San Luis Obispo County Regional Airport."

"Why not?" He leaned forward, genuinely puzzled by her certainty.

"He was in Paso Robles when he abandoned his tracker and cell phone, right?" Ella waited for Blake's slow nod before continuing. "This was at about two, three, in the morning. At that hour, how would he get from Paso Robles to San Luis Obispo County Regional Airport?"

Sensing it was a rhetorical question, Blake waited for her to tell him.

"If he decided to rent a car, the earliest he could do it would be at 8 a.m. And that means the earliest flight he could take would be at about 10 a.m. There is a flight to Boston a few minutes after ten and two more an hour later. I can check all flights out of the airport between the hours of ten and noon, if you like."

Blake tapped his forefinger against his chin. Ella had a point. But unlike her, Blake didn't think Grayson would hang around until sunup in a city where he felt unsafe. He'd be out of there sooner than that.

❧

"Greg told you that Simon Duarte and Earl Bramer were responsible for the Gardner Heist?" Julia pushed the filter basket in place and flicked the coffeemaker switch on.

The rush of freshly brewed coffee gurgling and hissing into the carafe filled the room. It was accompanied by the rich, coconut-flavored aroma of Don Francisco's Hawaiian Hazelnut medium-roast. Julia inhaled deeply and sighed, mouth broadening into a satisfied smile.

"Ice water won't cut it," she'd said minutes earlier when Celine—her own craving for coffee long gone—had offered her a glass. Julia had busied herself making coffee, listening intently all the while as Celine tried to recall the details Greg had shared at the Delft.

It all seemed to have happened eons ago, even though it was just yesterday that Greg had walked into the bar. Just yesterday that she'd heard the names Simon Duarte and Earl Bramer in connection with the Gardner Heist.

"Weren't they?" Celine asked as Julia approached the easy chair by the couch where she sat nursing a tall glass of ice water. "Greg said that's what the feds thought."

"Responsible for the heist, no." Julia sank into the chair. "No one thought that. Involved in it, sure. But no one outside the FBI and the few CIs we were using at the time would've even known we suspected that."

"So, Greg couldn't have known about that?" Celine tilted her glass, and stared as the water in it swirled around, ice cubes tinkling against the clear sides of the container. Greg hadn't seemed like a federal agent. Of course he might have been undercover, but somehow she doubted that.

Could he have been a CI—a confidential informant? But if so, why had he been in Paso Robles, at the Delft?

She looked up. "If it wasn't common knowledge, how did Greg know?"

Julia's eyes narrowed as she considered the question.

"It was an odd coincidence, I'll grant you that. The car crash and deaths of two young Gardner employees just five days after the museum itself was hit. For us not to suspect, and investigate, a connection between the two events would have been irresponsible."

A muted beep indicated the coffee was ready. Julia got up to pour herself a cup.

"But it would have been equally irresponsible," she said, stirring creamer and sweetener into her cup, "to publicly speculate about such a connection. The FBI tends to keep that kind of information close to its vest. We didn't even include the Boston Police, who'd initially responded to the Gardner theft, in our investigation—rightly or wrongly."

The swirling of Julia's spoon slowed and she looked up, eyes narrowed, shadowed by mists of the past, forehead furrowing in an effort to remember.

"I just don't think any of the information we released would've led a member of the general public to draw the conclusions we did."

She lowered her head to the rim of her mug, wincing as her lips came in contact with the hot brew. "Sure you don't want a cup?"

Celine smiled and shook her head, no.

"Did the media cover the crash?" she asked.

It might have been irresponsible for law enforcement to speculate, but newspapers and television media rarely played by such rules. It took only the slightest hint made by a journalist for the most tenuous possibilities to spread and be accepted as Gospel truth.

By the time the truth eventually came out, the lies would already have taken hold.

Julia smiled. "Sure, they covered it."

She dropped her spoon in the sink and returned to the easy chair. Hands securely wrapped around her mug, she perched herself on the edge of the seat.

"It wasn't front-page news. But there were articles in the *Boston Globe*, the *Boston Herald*, and several of the other papers in the region. But we're talking about a different time, Celine. Journalists merely reported the facts then. Conjectures were left to the public."

Celine nodded, sipping her water. But the only conjecture that would have made sense was that Duarte and Bramer, both Gardner Museum employees, had been killed because of what they knew about the heist.

Greg had said they'd been involved.

"Was there any truth to the stories that they'd made off with the art?" she asked. "Or that it had all burned in the car crash?"

"We had an informant who came in with that tip. He'd worked as a guard at the Gardner Museum. In fact, he'd been on duty the day before when his co-worker had flouted security procedure to let someone in after hours. He said he'd gotten the word from a shady local antiques dealer."

"But there was nothing to it?" Celine guessed.

"The antiques dealer categorically denied it. In fact, it was he who brought us one of the more credible leads in the case. Flakes of paint that could've been from one of the works stolen."

"Then the works do exist?" Celine leaned forward, a frisson of excitement pulsing through her nerves. She had no idea why the thought excited her. It just did.

"That's what we thought." Julia gazed into her coffee. "It was hard not to do so. But then when lead after viable lead fizzled out, I think we began to wonder if those works of art hadn't just burned along with Duarte and Bramer."

"But now you think Duarte may be alive?" Celine returned to the question that had initiated their discussion. Her gaze lingered on Julia's face until the former federal agent finally looked up.

"It was something I overheard at a bar shortly before I left Boston. After what Keith Elliot had told me, that I'd find the answers I'd been seeking here in Paso Robles, it seemed like a plausible lead. After all, if Simon Duarte hadn't died, perhaps the art had survived as well."

"Isn't it a stretch to think Simon Underwood is the man you're looking for?"

"Why? Because Simon Duarte wouldn't have been foolish enough to retain his first name? When you're on the run and the slightest slip can give you away, you keep the lies to a minimum. That was why I was always Julia when I went undercover. It's my real name. I didn't have to train myself to respond to a new name and—more importantly—train myself not to move a hair if someone addressed me by my real name.

"If Simon Duarte is alive, he wouldn't have lasted very long if he'd decided to change his first name."

"And you think Dirck knew?" Hot tears pricked Celine's eyes. Neither Julia nor Detective Mailand had met Dirck. They couldn't possibly know that accusing Dirck of having anything to do with a notorious art heist was as absurd as accusing Len Skye, her art historian father, of such a crime.

Julia's eyes, soft with compassion, rested on Celine's face. "You were very fond of him, weren't you? That says a lot about the man he must have been."

"Then why do you think—?"

"Because Detective Mailand is right. Dirck Thins was tortured and killed either because he knew something or his attackers thought he did. We need to find out what it was. And Simon Underwood might just be our best lead now?"

"And Greg?"

Julia sighed. "I think Greg was sent by the Boston mob, Celine. It's never been fully proven, but there's a solid case to be made for the mob's involvement in the heist. If there's any truth to the rumors about Duarte and Bramer, the only other people interested in finding them will be the mob."

Chapter Nineteen

"And the estate, *cara*? What will happen to it?" After the initial shock of hearing about Dirck's murder, winemaker Andrea Giordano's mind had turned to more practical matters.

Celine had decided to phone Andrea right after Julia left her cottage. She could nap later. But now she regretted calling him. She had no answers to the questions he was asking.

"Am I to also tell our workers that they will lose their jobs?"

"I don't know, Andrea." Celine brushed strands of her red hair back, holding them in place with her fingers. "I'm not sure about my job either." She sighed. "I'll have to call Dirck's lawyer." She'd been looking forward to a nap. Instead she'd be discussing legalities with Charles Durand, the Mechelen's lawyer. "I'll call him right away."

"And until then, *cara*, what do you want me to do?"

Celine wanted to say she didn't know, but with Dirck and John both gone, claiming ignorance wasn't a luxury she could afford. She considered her options. She wanted Mechelen's employees to hear about Dirck's death from a representative of the estate not from the newspapers.

The Delft would need to be closed for a few days. Wine tastings would go on as usual at the Mechelen Estate. And the work on the estate—cutting the previous years' canes to make way for new canes and shoots and pruning the early shoots that emerged, pulling away excess foliage while still leaving a sufficient quantity to protect the vines from the growing heat—could continue as well.

If Dirck had died intestate and the estate was taken over by the government, she imagined it would soon be up for sale again—to one of the winemakers in the region perhaps.

"*Bene*," Andrea replied when she'd communicated all of this to him. "But find out what you can, okay? We cannot afford to lose anyone at this crucial stage."

"I will," Celine promised. "And there's one more thing—there was a party booked for a wine tasting at the Delft at noon. Could you—?"

"Of course. I will have someone call and change the venue, if they are agreeable, to the Estate Tasting Room, yes?"

"That sounds perfect, Andrea. Thank you."

❧

"There's got to be twenty-four-hour shuttles to the airport," Blake said. "Check Greyhound. Check Amtrak. I'd be surprised if Grayson was anywhere near Paso Robles at eight in the morning."

He'd have suggested Ella check for reports of stolen vehicles as well, but Blake didn't think Grayson had the ability to hotwire a car.

He waited until Ella had left the room before shifting his attention back to the laptop screen. The tracker was now at the Mechelen Winery. That was the place the guy at Thins' bar had asked him to call, wasn't it?

So one of the employees had picked up Grayson's tracker. And discovered Dirck Thins' body. Blake wondered who it was. He reached for his jacket hanging on a hook behind his desk and pulled out his unregistered private cell phone.

A heavily Italian-accented voice answered his call. "Andrea Giordano. Mechelen Winery. What can I do for you?"

Pretending to be an out-of-state customer, Blake complained about the Delft Bar not answering his calls. "I was told to call first thing today to confirm my order."

There was a moment's hesitation, then the voice said, "The bar will remain closed for some time, unfortunately. Our owner suffered a sudden death."

"You're observing a period of mourning," Blake said, his voice vibrant with sympathy.

"You could say that." The voice sounded mildly amused. "But it is an enforced and indefinite period of mourning. The police are investigating Mr. Thins' death. I would suggest speaking with our marketing manager, Celine Skye, but it was she who found the body, *la poveretta!*"

"She needs time to grieve," Blake said. So it *was* an employee—her name sounded familiar; had he seen it on the website?—who had the tracker. She obviously had no idea what it was. Probably thought it was a watch that one of the bar's patrons had dropped.

"The owner's death must have hit Simon hard as well," he added on a hunch.

"Simon? You mean Simon Underwood? Yes, yes, I suppose it does. But Mr. Underwood can sell his paintings wherever he chooses. He only placed them on consignment at the Delft as a favor to Mr. Thins."

Ah! So there was a Simon. Had Grayson seen Underwood and realized it was Duarte?

Ordering a wine basket he neither needed nor wanted—maybe Ella could take it off his hands—Blake hung up.

❧

Celine braced herself against the wall and closed her eyes, putting off for a few minutes her next call to *Lance, Douglass & Durand.* Charles Durand had been with the law firm for almost as long as Dirck and John had been its clients. Andrea had put her through her an interrogation that would have put a CIA operative to shame. She wasn't looking forward to fielding the same questions from Durand.

What had Dirck been doing so late at the Delft? Why had she herself returned? How could she have forgotten his heart medication?

You didn't forget, Celine. It was her guardian angel's voice.

Her eyes were instantly wide open. "What?"

You didn't forget his medication, Celine. You tried to give him the bottle in the morning, don't you remember? Dirck put you off.

The memory surged back. How could she have forgotten? Dirck had pushed the bottle away. "I'll take it from you at closing," he'd said. But he never had.

"That doesn't make it any less my fault. Dirck was preoccupied. I should've reminded him."

Guilt is an indulgence, Celine. You have to carry on Dirck's mission now. Belle needs your help now.

Belle? Celine straightened up. Who was Belle?

Before she could voice the question, the shimmering image of the Lady appeared, a pleading expression on her face.

Seven years ago, you promised her your help. It's your time now, Sister Mary Catherine said.

"But what about Dirck?"

This is what Dirck would have wanted you to do, my dear. Belle's waited long enough. What belongs to her must be returned.

The last thing Celine remembered before she collapsed onto the floor was the Lady's outstretched arms. Was that the Lady's name . . . *Belle*? But who *was* she?

And how had Dirck known her?

Chapter Twenty

It was the one call Special Agent Blake Markham had been dreading. Penny Hoskins, Director of the Gardner Museum, wanted an update on Operation Project Recovery.

Not that Blake could fault Hoskins' eagerness; the Gardner had waited nearly thirty long years for a break like this. Still, this wasn't a call he was especially looking forward to fielding. Not now with the operation going pear-shaped.

He lifted the receiver reluctantly up to his ear, cursing Ella, his assistant, for putting the Museum Director through.

"Agent Markham!" Hoskins' fluty voice greeted him in a breathy trill. She was close to fifty and looked it, but her voice over the phone sounded as sweet and naïve as a young girl's. "I hope you have good news for me. Although any news would be welcome at this point."

Blake winced. Since he'd first informed her of the leads they had—he'd emphasized their tenuous nature—he hadn't bothered to keep in touch with her.

"Agent Markham? Are you there?"

"Yes." Blake held back a sigh. He had news—plenty of it. None of it good, that was the problem. Certainly nothing he wanted to share with this woman, who grasped so eagerly at every straw, disappointment was inevitable.

She reminded him of his mother. Like Roseanne Markham, Penny Hoskins was the sort of woman whose imagination soared at the slightest promise. Never doubting its fulfillment; never imagining that life might come in the way.

Until the very moment that her hopes were shattered. Then, the letdown would be brutal, felt as keenly as a dagger to the heart.

"Nothing . . ." Blake paused, unsure of the wisdom of using the word "good."

"Nothing concrete, I'm afraid," he said. He paused again, as though debating whether to reveal sensitive information. He hated stringing her along. But it had to be done. "Are you familiar with the name Simon Duarte?"

"He was a gardener at the museum at the time of the heist, wasn't he?"

"Yes."

"I thought he was dead. Isn't he?" Penny's voice rose a little, trembling with hope.

Blake expelled an intentionally audible breath. "It turns out he might not be. Our man in the field may have seen him. Nothing's been confirmed yet, you understand . . ."

"Yes, but if he isn't dead, we have a definite hope of recovering the art, don't we?"

"I'm cautiously optimistic." He was. He truly was.

Someone associated with the Bulger family—Whitey the notorious mobster, his brother William a state senator—had years ago let fall into Penny's disbelieving ears rumors of Duarte and Bramer's involvement in the heist.

The fact that both men had died in a burning car meant, the Bulger associate had hinted, that the stolen works were lost, too. There was no point looking for them.

The tip had convinced many agents that Whitey Bulger, on the run from the law at the time, was in some way connected to the heist. But Whitey had been arrested and had been killed in prison without ever bringing up the Gardner Museum or the thirteen works it had lost.

Penny Hoskins had veered predictably from disbelief to despair, but now Grayson's reports of having sighted Duarte might help to shore up Penny's flagging hopes long enough for her to leave Blake alone.

"This still needs to be checked out," he reminded her. "And nothing may come of it . . ." He let his voice trail off.

"Yes, of course. I understand. But listen, now that you mention it, I'm quite sure our employee files said Duarte had a sister. She was listed as his emergency contact—probably his only relative. From what I understand, they were quite close. If he was still alive—and on the lam, as you'd put it— I think he'd have kept in touch with her, don't you?"

This time Blake's sigh was genuine. "You want us to check it out?"

"Why not? She'd be just the person to lead us to him."

"I'll discuss it with my colleagues and we'll see what we can come up with." He was eager to get off the phone now before she had him committing to doing anything more than that.

Duarte could wait. The art could wait. He needed to find Grayson Pike first. That was priority number one.

Much to Blake's relief, Penny seemed satisfied with his assurance that the FBI would give her suggestion some thought. It was the sort of insincere promise Blake had never been comfortable making. But after years on the job, he had to admit the Communication specialist at Quantico had been right.

It got people off your back.

"Wouldn't you rather spend more time chasing down leads than arguing with outsiders who don't know how the job's done?" she'd asked when Blake, a recalcitrant young recruit at the Academy, had questioned her recommendation to substitute a conciliatory—and in his mind phony—"maybe" or "I'll think about it" for a blanket "no."

But as he returned to the sheaf of papers spread out on his desk, his relief was dampened by the memory of his father's words: *Never make promises you can't keep.*

I might just look into it, he said to himself as he studied the passenger manifests Ella had printed out for him. These weren't manifests for the early bird flights. Blake had agreed with Ella that there was no point scrutinizing those. Short of a miracle, there was no way Grayson could have made it to San Luis Obispo County Regional Airport in time to board any of those flights.

But the late morning flights were another matter altogether. And of the three that had made it out of San Luis Obispo that day, two seemed especially promising. The United Airlines flight at 11:50 a.m. and the Alaska Airlines flight at 11:10 a.m. had, between the two of them, a total of ten passengers who'd bought tickets for same-day travel.

But the two passengers who had paid for their tickets with cash were both women. That ruled out Grayson, unless—

He held the thought in his mind, scanning the names of the six men on the two flights. The UA flight via San Francisco had a Solomon Elder, Jake Liu, and a Gary Portland. Blake's gaze lingered on the last name.

The initials were the same as the real and code names of his target. Could Grayson Pike, Greg Peters, and Gary Portland be the same person?

Blake tapped his fingers against his desk as his gaze slid to the passenger manifest for the Alaska Airlines flight via Seattle. He passed over Rick Nolte. But his eye caught on Juan Perez. The name was to the Hispanic community what John Doe or John Smith was for your average white guy. A dead giveaway for an alias.

Was Grayson being cute, assuming a Spanish name? Not likely. He'd need fake ID to go with the name. And the decision to adopt a Hispanic name would draw far more attention than Grayson—too pale to be regarded as anything but Caucasian—would be willing to risk.

The last name on the Alaska Airlines flight was a Geoff Brandt. After his recent conversation with Penny Hoskins, the name reminded Blake of Rembrandt. Three of the famous artist's works had been included in the stash the thieves had nabbed from the Gardner. Some people had taken that as hard evidence that Rembrandt van Rijn was the primary target of the looting.

But the Gardner had lost a total of thirteen works. Why bother with Degas sketches and Chinese vases, if Rembrandt was the main target? Blake shook his head. In this case, theories were a dime a dozen. Everyone had one.

His eyes were drawn back to the passenger manifest for the United Airlines flight. Gary Portland was their most likely bet if Grayson had managed to get himself a prepaid credit card. His index finger hovered above the red buzzer on his intercom, preparing to issue instructions to Ella, when the door opened and his personal assistant barged into the room.

Her face was flushed; the ends of her blunt-cut bob, curving sharply up like the black edges of a crescent moon, flicked her cheeks. She braced herself against the open door for a moment, her lips parted in a triumphant smile.

Then, pulling herself away to let the door swing shut, she marched across the room.

"I've got something," she announced, unceremoniously dumping a pile of papers on Blake's desk.

❧

"Simon is dead," Celine heard herself say.

Afternoon light filtered in through the muslin curtains at the living room window. The couch on which she sat was upholstered in a faded, worn red fabric. A newspaper lay crumpled on the coffee table.

She saw the large Old English font of its title through the corner of her eye. But her gaze was focused on the woman standing distraught in the middle of the room, tears raining down upon the letter bunched up in her hands.

Celine wanted to draw her into her arms, wanted to tell her not to cry, but she remained seated, her hands folded in her lap.

"It'll be okay," she wanted to say.

"He'll be watching over you," she said instead, mouthing the words awkwardly. "Simon will look out for you."

"How can he, when he's gone?" The woman sobbed uncontrollably.

"Bella," Celine began. *Bella. Belle?*

⸨

When her eyelids jolted open, the stiffness in her neck was Celine's first conscious sensation. She was slumped on the wood floor, phone in her hand, back pressed hard against the white cabinet below the black quartz kitchen sink.

Her neck ached; her back was sore. She eased herself up, massaging the dull pain out of her neck.

Her eyes circled the room. It took a moment for recollection to set in. She was in her cottage. On the Mechelen Estate. In Paso Robles.

Not Boston.

Her eyes surveyed the room again, making sure of the fact. Then, bracing her hands against the floor, she pushed herself up.

The dream she'd had was so vivid, there was no questioning what it was. A psychic dream. For the half-hour or so that her physical body had been unconscious, her mind had occupied another time, another place.

Boston. She'd been in Boston. How did she know that? She closed her eyes.

The Old English letters of the newspaper's title came into focus.

The Boston Globe.

Had she been in Boston in the present time? She peered at the newspaper, but the date, in print too small to see, eluded her.

The woman's name had been Bella. *Or Belle?* The same person that Sister Mary Catherine had mentioned? The one who sought Celine's help?

Her eyes flew open. *And Simon was dead.* Which Simon? Simon Duarte? Or Simon Underwood?

Chapter Twenty-One

Recalling her promise to contact Dirck's lawyer, Celine glanced down at her iPhone. The battery indicator blinked red, prompting her to charge the phone—an unforeseen but fortuitous reason to put off her call.

She plugged her phone in, poured herself a cup of coffee, and sat down. She desperately needed to sort through her impressions.

Sister Mary Catherine's last words to her before Celine had collapsed had given rise to some unpleasant memories. Ten years ago cancer had claimed the nun's life—at the same time that a brutal serial killer had claimed the lives of Celine's college friends, Sonia and Nicole.

The killer had been apprehended and the girls had crossed over, but the incident—Celine's second encounter with murder—had been hard to bear. The memory of it—her inability to prevent her friends' murder—was as raw as that of her parents' untimely death.

Celine wrapped her arms around herself and rocked back and forth, trying to will away the intense pain that threatened to consume her.

Concentrate, she whispered to herself. *Concentrate.*

After she'd died, Sister Mary Catherine had shed light on the visions Celine received every time an untimely death occurred. The image of the Lady at such times portended more than death. They were a reminder of Celine's mission to fight for justice—the Lady herself standing in need of Celine's help.

She'll return when you're ready to help her, Sister Mary Catherine had said.

And now, according to the nun, the time to help the Lady had finally come.

But what did any of this have to do with Dirck? Had Dirck died trying to help the Lady? How had he even come in contact with her—the spirit of a dead woman?

Dirck didn't see the dead, my dear. Sister Mary Catherine's voice intruded upon her thoughts. *He was trying to right a wrong.*

❧

"Sonovabitch! He's in San Luis Obispo."

Blake rubbed his hands together, too elated to care that Ella, a woman and his personal assistant, was within earshot when he'd uttered the epithet. You never cussed in front of a woman or one of your underlings. But what the heck, it wasn't every day a guy had a break like this.

"I knew it!" He jabbed at the untidy heap of papers on his desk. "I knew we'd come up with something sooner rather than later."

Following paper trails wasn't exactly sexy work. Blake knew that. It was a slow, time-consuming process that required a patient, methodical mind. His colleagues, preferring to work the streets or go undercover, frequently teased him about his penchant for scrutinizing documents, calling him a pencil-pusher.

But right now Blake felt vindicated. Poring over paperwork was a solid way to develop leads. And it always paid off.

They now knew that at 3:15 a.m., Pacific, Grayson Pike had boarded an Amtrak motorcoach at the Paso Robles Intermodal Station.

"The station is a four-minute walk from his motel via 8th Street." Ella's nail, manicured and painted a bright red, traced the route from the Paso Spring Inn to the station on the printout that sat between them.

"He arrives at 3:55 a.m., walks to Santa Barbara and Church, and takes a second Amtrak bus at 6:21 a.m."

"To where? The airport?" Blake had pulled the printout toward himself as Ella spoke and now read her notation scrawled in the margin. "*To LOVR?*"

He looked up.

"Los Osos Valley Road," Ella explained. "It's a bus stop. There are several on that street. Grayson got off at the Laguna Village stop."

"Why?"

Ella shrugged. "It may have been the only one available to him."

Blake leaned back in his chair and frowned. "So 6:32 a.m., Pacific, at the Laguna Village bus stop in San Luis Obispo is the last we hear of Grayson. Where could he have gone from there?"

"If he'd had a car, he could have made it to the airport in eight minutes. There's a bus at 6:45 a.m. that could have gotten him to the airport by 7:40.

If the poor sap decided to walk it, it would have taken him an hour to get to the airport.

"Doable, considering he had nothing more than a shopping bag."

Blake considered this. If Grayson had to hoof it to the airport, he probably would. But it was unlikely that he had. No, the Grayson he knew—a lazy bugger if ever there was one—would've waited for a bus or conned someone into driving him to the airport.

"A shopping bag, that's all he was traveling with?" He raised his eyes. Ella, her head tilted to one side, was gazing earnestly at him.

"Yep, that was it." She nodded.

"And he didn't check in any baggage?"

Ella confirmed his hunch. That meant that Grayson didn't have the art with him.

Blake pondered the information they'd gathered so far. Grayson had left his belongings behind in his motel room. Deliberately, it would seem. He'd gotten rid of his cell phone. And now he was in San Luis Obispo. Presumably, he'd ditched his FBI code name as well; the Amtrak tickets had been booked in his own name, not the alias assigned to him.

He'd need some form of ID to fly out of the city. Fake ID since none of the flights they'd checked had any passengers by the name of Grayson Pike. He'd either gotten it and made it to the airport or he was still in San Luis Obispo, waiting for it. Or waiting to return to Paso Robles.

Either way, Grayson was going to need a couple of things to keep going: an unregistered phone and a credit card.

"Keep looking for a Grayson Pike flying out of San Luis Obispo," he told Ella. He pulled the passenger manifest for the late morning United Airlines flight out from under the printout they'd been studying.

"And I want to know more about Gary Portland. If Grayson managed to get some form of ID in time to catch the 11:50 flight, that could be the alias he's using. If it is, Portland will have paid for his ticket with a prepaid credit card."

Ella nodded and rose to her feet. "So you still think Grayson—"

"No, actually, I think he's probably still in San Luis Obispo. Find out what he purchased before he left Paso Robles. I'm betting it was a burner phone and some prepaid cards."

"But you still want me to keep checking flights out of SLO County Regional?" Ella didn't look too happy about the prospect. *Not an efficient strategy*, he could hear her thinking.

"I just want to cover our bases." If Grayson had his eye on the art, he'd probably make it back to Paso Robles. On the other hand, if he'd been sufficiently spooked by Dirck Thins' murder, he'd get out of California as fast as he could.

But, bottom line, the art was still in Paso Robles. Grayson hadn't taken it out of the city. Blake's pulse quickened as the thought occurred to him. Operation Project Recovery wasn't off the rails just yet.

"Check flights," Ella was muttering to herself as she pushed her chair in and turned to leave. "Keep checking flights."

"And this time, focus on passengers who used prepaid credit cards to purchase their tickets," Blake called after her.

Trying to right a wrong? Celine repeated the nun's words. If that was the case, Dirck must have had some information—or evidence—of a crime.

"And he died for his efforts," Celine whispered to herself. Whatever Dirck had known, whatever it was he was trying to do, it had caused his death. That much seemed clear.

He knew he'd die, Celine. Now it's up to you.

Up to her? Detective Mailand's question to her that morning—*What exactly did your employer know?*—replayed in Celine's mind. What had Dirck discovered?

The words *Gardner Museum Heist* flashed across her mind—just as they had that morning in the interview room of the Paso Robles Police Station. She'd been loath to consider the possibility then, but now Celine pondered it.

Hadn't Julia said that the clues to what had happened in Boston might lie in Paso Robles? Could Dirck have somehow stumbled across those same clues? She recalled all the late nights Dirck had spent at the Delft.

It had been shortly after John had died, and Celine had simply assumed it was because of the additional responsibility of taking over the Mechelen vineyard and winery.

Now she wondered if the real reason for the long hours Dirck had been putting in had less to do with the burdens of running two businesses and more to do with whatever it was her employer had unearthed.

Was the timing of his discovery significant? It appeared to have been soon after John's death. Did that mean there'd been something in John's papers . . . ?

No. No, that wasn't possible. That would mean John Mechelen had been involved in the heist.

He's a dead ringer for Earl Bramer.

B-aw-ston Greg's words rang in her ears. Had Greg—possibly connected with the mob—recognized the man the Boston mob knew as Earl Bramer? Was that why Greg had come to the Delft—a beer drinker at a wine bar; a mob-affiliated philistine pretending to be an art lover?

Dear God! And she'd left Dirck alone to deal with that? Celine buried her face in her hands. She ought to have stayed in the neighborhood. Tried to see what was going on.

She shook her head. Guilt is an indulgence, her guardian angel had said. And wallowing in it wasn't going to help her get to the bottom of the situation. Whatever evidence Dirck had discovered was "hiding in plain sight." That's what he'd said to his attackers.

That meant it was somewhere in the Delft. In the concealed closet he'd shown her, perhaps? She'd have to check it out.

Dirck hadn't confided in her, but could he have shared his discoveries with someone else? His lawyer, Charles Durand? Simon Underwood?

Simon is dead.

Celine sat straight up on the barstool. If Dirck had confided in Simon Underwood, he might well have put the artist in danger.

Celine glanced at the kitchen clock. She and Julia would need to get to Simon before the mob did. But first she'd make a quick call to Charles Durand.

⟡

"What happens to the business now is your decision, Celine," Durand informed her. The news of Dirck's murder hadn't come as a surprise to his lawyer.

Celine surmised Detective Mailand had already given Durand the news—why? To find out about whether Dirck's legal and financial affairs provided anyone with a motive to kill him?

It seemed unlikely given the scene of the crime. But Detective Mailand was likely just following protocol—making sure to have all his bases covered.

She forced herself to concentrate on the bombshell Durand had just hurled at her.

"But Charles, I have no standing—I'm not—"

"Dirck and John put their businesses in a trust, naming each other as beneficiary. When John died, Dirck listed you as his successor. He and John had thought long and hard about it. They wanted the business to continue and they felt it would flourish under you.

"There's some minor paperwork involved, but it shouldn't take too long. And I can take care of it all for you. You are now the legal owner of all of Dirck's assets. I'm surprised Dirck never mentioned it to you."

"No, he didn't. I guess he never got around to it." The evidence Dirck had uncovered about the Gardner Museum theft must have been horrifying; it had preoccupied his entire attention.

She hesitated, tapping her foot on the kitchen floor.

Now that she had Durand on the phone, she thought it unlikely that Dirck had confided in him. But the question had to be asked.

"Did Dirck mention anything else to you?"

"Anything else?" Durand sounded puzzled. "About the business, you mean?"

"No, not the business. But anything else he might have needed to take care of. Anything to do with Boston." She was rambling now. "Connections, relatives in Boston. Surely he had some?"

"No, neither one of them did. Is that what you're worried about—that someone might come out of the woodwork and lay claim to the business?"

Celine sighed. "If only that were the case. I'd be all too happy to have someone take the winery off my hands."

"You can always sell. Want me to look into it?"

"No. Not just yet, anyway. I don't think a decision to sell right this minute will make our winemaker too happy."

She turned the conversation to the matter of compensation for the artists who'd left their works on consignment at the Delft. Could a check be made out to each one of them? It could, Durand assured her. Was there anything else she needed help with? No?

"Well, all right, then. Call if you need anything. I work for you now, remember?"

Chapter Twenty-Two

Celine's fist was about to rain down upon Julia's cottage door for the third time when the door opened and the former federal agent appeared within the doorway—clad in a light peach bathrobe, eyes still narrowed into a sleepy squint, strands of gray hair falling out of her ponytail.

"I'm sorry, were you sleeping?" Celine slowly lowered her arm. She'd driven to Charles Durand's office, picked up the checks for Simon and the other artists, and then returned to the Mechelen Estate to pick up Julia.

Julia rubbed her eyes and blinked. "Yes. Weren't you? I thought you wanted to get some shut-eye."

"I did. But I think we need to go see Simon Underwood at once. He might be in danger."

"And you know this how?"

"I had a dream," Celine began.

Julia held up her hand. "Tell me about it later." She pulled the door back farther and stepped away from the doorway. "Come in while I get dressed. You can make us some coffee for the road."

Twenty minutes later they were on the 101 freeway driving to Morro Bay where Simon Underwood the painter lived in a two-story house overlooking the crown-shaped volcanic mound known as Morro Rock. The mound featured prominently in many of Simon's paintings, including the one that the Delft had been carrying.

"Morro Rock? Is that one of the Nine Sisters?" Julia asked, referring to the series of nine volcanic plugs that stretched from Morro Bay to San Luis Obispo. The wind whipped her gray ponytail to the front and held it against her cheek.

Celine nodded, her eyes on the road. "The smallest of them." They'd been formed twenty million years ago when magma had hardened within the vents of active volcanoes. Now they were a tourist feature. She stepped on the gas.

Flat, dry grassland interspersed with short, stubby trees spread out on one side of the freeway. On the other, a steep incline covered in yellow-green grass stretched above them. The road curved before them, virtually empty.

"*El Camino Real.*" Julia craned her neck out the window to read the words painted on the road.

"I imagine parts of the 101 follow the historic route. The Royal Highway or the King's Highway is what it translates to." Celine smiled. "A fancy name for a dirt road."

The 600-mile trail had in Spanish colonial times connected twenty-one Spanish missionaries, *presidios*, or fortresses, and *pueblos*, or settlements. She mentioned it to Julia, the rich history of Central California a more pleasant subject than the oppressive thought of Dirck's murder.

"All the way from San Diego to Sonoma," Julia said. "I know; I've read the entry in my guidebook, Celine. What I really want to talk about is your dream."

Celine sighed. She'd wanted to pretend if only for a few minutes that she was a tourist hitting the road instead of a victim in search of answers. She had already recounted the broad details of her dream to Julia. The interpretation, in her mind, couldn't have been clearer. Simon Underwood was in danger.

"Is there any way of knowing which Simon was meant?" Julia pressed on. "Whether you were in the past, the present, or the future?"

"I don't recall ever having informed anyone that a man by the name of Simon was dead. I think I'd remember something like that."

"If it was a psychic dream, you may not have been inhabiting your own body," Julia countered. "Many of the psychics I've worked with—"

Celine gave her a sharp glance. "You've *worked* with psychics?"

"Sure. The FBI has on occasion called in psychics. You have to be careful who you work with, but there's no reason not to draw upon a particular expertise, unconventional though it may be. We've had better luck with cold case homicides than with the Gardner heist, but I hope that's about to change."

"Meaning me?" Celine gave Julia another quick glance.

"Yes, you," Julia replied impatiently. "That's why I'm here."

Celine pursed her lips. The thought of being involved in this affair any more than she already was made her nervous. She was quite sure she wasn't cut out for it. Although, of course, if Dirck had uncovered anything about the theft, she'd do her best to follow through on what he'd initiated.

"As I was saying," Julia cut into her thoughts, "many of the psychics I've worked with find themselves tapping into either the victim's psyche or the criminal's. Based on the visions you've shared so far, it seems you tend to tap into the criminal's head. That's probably why you can't see the faces of Dirck's attackers."

"It's my perspective," Celine murmured, remembering her guardian angel's words. "It limits what I can see."

"Precisely. On the other hand, you have access to the criminals' thoughts and feelings. And that can furnish us with vital clues. Now in the case of this dream you had—"

"I was in my own body, Julia. And if I wasn't—if this was something that happened in the past—wouldn't that just confirm Simon Duarte's death—in 1990? Because Simon Underwood is still alive—I hope."

Julia was quiet. "I just don't think Duarte died in 1990. If he did, that would mean the art is gone, too. That . . ." She shook her head "I can't explain it, but that theory just doesn't sit right with me."

Celine's hold on the steering wheel tightened. Julia was right. The Gardner art had survived. She didn't know how she knew that, but she could feel it in her bones. She was about to confirm the former federal agent's impressions when the tinny sound of her cell phone playing the first few bars of Vivaldi's famous concerto—Summer—sounded.

❦

Celine pulled the phone out of her shoulder purse. "Hello?"

"Ms. Skye?" It was Detective Mailand. "Have I caught you at a bad time?"

"No, Detective. What can I do for you?" Out of the corner of her eye, she caught Julia staring at her. It couldn't have been more than three hours since they'd left the police station. They hadn't expected the detective to have any fresh leads on the case quite so soon.

"Were you aware that the security cameras outside the Delft and in the interior were disabled?"

"Disabled? What—no! That's impossible."

"It doesn't look like the cameras were tampered with. In fact, our best guess would be that either you or Mr. Thins turned them off and erased the day's footage. The only question is why."

"Those cameras are supposed to run 24-7, Detective. We never turned them off. If Dirck switched them off, he was forced to do it." Although another more unpalatable explanation had come to mind as well. If Dirck had a clandestine meeting planned, he may well have disabled the cameras.

"Are you saying all the footage from the entire day has been erased as well?" Celine barely heard his mutter of acknowledgment. "I don't see why . . ." Unless Dirck's attackers hadn't wanted Greg identified. Possibly because locating Greg would lead the police straight to them.

"Maybe." Detective Mailand's response to her theory when she suggested it to him was lukewarm at best. Could he really suspect her of disabling the cameras? Or erasing the footage? For the twenty odd minutes she'd been alone at the bar, it hadn't even occurred to her to check the security camera footage.

Celine suspected Mailand already knew she'd inherited both the Delft and the Mechelen—a sizeable inheritance for a woman as young as herself. She was barely twenty-nine. In his eyes, no doubt, that gave her a motive for killing Dirck. He didn't press the issue, however, merely requesting that she come in to work with a sketch artist. She agreed readily.

"The cameras were disabled and all the footage from yesterday erased," she explained to Julia after she'd disconnected. "Any hope we had of tracking Greg down through that footage is gone."

"Then we'll just have to rely on your memory, won't we?" Julia said. "But that's not what's bothering you, is it?"

Celine chewed on her lip. A sign flashed by. Exit 219 to Morro Road was a quarter of a mile away. If she didn't concentrate, she'd miss it.

"I'm pretty sure Dirck disabled the cameras. I think I understand his reasons for doing so. What I don't get is why he decided to erase all the footage." She turned right onto Morro Road. "I have a feeling that was his decision, not something he was forced to do."

She took her eyes off the road.

"Why would he have wanted to protect Greg, Julia?"

❧

The tracker was moving out of Paso Robles again. Blake watched its movement on his laptop for a few minutes. Celine Skye was clearly still unaware that she had an FBI tracker on her person.

He turned away after a while, giving up on his attempt to guess her destination. He'd know soon enough.

Simon Underwood's house and studio was on the left corner of South Street and Morro Avenue. Gusts of moist, salty air heavy with the spray and fishy odors of Morro Bay whipped into Celine's features and blew back her red-gold hair as she eased to a stop in front of 462 Morro Avenue.

"This it?"

Julia stared at the expansive structure with its façade of light-peach siding. A brick-covered section—set with a dark cedar tilt-up garage door and its own red-slate gable roof—protruded from the main building. A short, rust-red stamped cement walkway curved between mounds of green lawn from the sidewalk to the front stoop.

"Yes, this is it." Celine turned off the engine. Its soft purr was replaced by the noisy screeches and squalls of gulls flying overhead. She threw open her door and climbed down. She had wanted to satisfy herself that Simon was all right. But now that she was here, her urge to see the artist had dampened considerably.

She had nothing more concrete than her dream to point to that Simon was in danger. Would that be enough to persuade him the threat was immediate and serious? She hoped Simon was out, but that expectation dissolved when a young man carrying a large portfolio under his arm and an artist's bag in the other hand emerged from the front door.

He looked up at them and smiled. "Looking for Simon? He's up on the deck painting."

A winding flight of stairs on the side of the house led up to the deck. Followed by a huffing Julia—"I'm so out of shape!"—Celine climbed up. Simon, clad in a loose-fitting white shirt and faded blue jeans, had his head thrust into a wooden, pyramid-shaped frame covered on three sides with a dark blue curtain. A thick cylinder projected up like a telescope from an opening at the top.

"What is he doing?" Julia hissed in a stage-whisper. "I thought he was supposed to be painting."

"He is painting." Simon's muffled voice boomed out from within the pyramid before Celine could respond. "I'll be with you in a minute."

"It's a camera obscura," he explained, withdrawing his head from the device a few minutes later. He laid down a paintbrush tipped with black paint

onto a palette and rubbed his hands on the thick cotton apron he was wearing; it had once been white, but was now a pale gray-beige flecked with
splotches of black and minute traces of other colors.

"What brings you here, Celine?" Seeing the white envelope in her hands,
he smiled. "Don't tell me *Purple Water* has sold already?" He turned to Julia
and his smile widened.

Celine suppressed a sigh. So Simon hadn't heard the news yet.

"The Delft was broken into," she said, "and a number of our paintings were
. . . handled roughly. Yours, I'm afraid, was slashed."

She held the check out, but Simon didn't take it. "Why didn't you bring
it back? I'm sure I could've fixed it." He regarded her, his faded blue eyes
puzzled, a frown forming under the thatch of white hair that perched atop
his head.

"Celine didn't have much choice in the matter," Julia said, briskly drawing
the reins of conversation into her own hands. "You see, your painting along
with all the others that were . . . *roughly handled*"—she raised an eyebrow
as she echoed Celine's terminology—"are now in the custody of the police."

"Why?" Simon pulled his apron over his head and dropped it onto a deck
chair that stood near his easel and a table with his art supplies. His gaze
shifted from Julia's face to Celine's. "I don't understand. Did Dirck—?"

"Dirck is dead, Mr. Underwood. The men who manhandled your painting
also, we believe, killed your friend. He was your friend, wasn't he?"

"Yes, yes, he was." Simon stared at Celine. "Surely, that isn't in question."
It took a few moments for the substance of Julia's remarks to sink in. "Dirck
is dead?" he asked softly, a troubled expression on his face.

"I take it the police haven't called," Celine said.

Simon shook his head mutely. He stretched his arm out toward a bundle
of brushes on the table, fingers absently toying with the bristles.

"Is there any reason you can think of, Mr. Underwood, why someone interested in your painting would have wanted Dirck dead?"

"I . . . er . . . I just don't see the connection," Simon mumbled.

Celine's heart went out to him. *Poor Simon.* His plump pink cheeks looked
wrinkled and gray like a balloon that had popped and had all the air suddenly sucked out of it. An image of a long-haired man in a dark, slashed
waistcoat and baggy breeches, seated on a stool before an easel, floated into
her mind. Unsure of its significance, she cast it aside.

"Simon," she began tentatively. "Julia is a former FBI agent who worked on
the Gardner Museum theft." That caught Simon's attention. Celine thought

she saw his eyes widen, but a fraction of a second later wondered if she'd imagined the reaction.

Simon cleared his throat. "I see." He looked at Julia and attempted a smile. "I was in Boston at the time, but I swear I had nothing to do with it."

"No one thinks you do," Celine said quickly before Julia could say anything to contradict her. She had the feeling the former federal agent remained convinced that Simon held the key to the Gardner heist. "But we think Dirck may have uncovered some clues about what happened. And I expect he confided in you—"

"No, he didn't."

"But you were one of his closest friends."

"We went back a long way"—Simon turned to Julia—"all the way back to when we were students at Boston University." His eyes returned to Celine. "But if he uncovered any clues about the heist—and I seriously doubt he did —he didn't share his discoveries with me."

"You know that, Mr. Underwood." Julia gazed out at the deep blue waters of Morro Bay and the rock that rose high above the waves that surrounded it. "We know that. The question is"—she turned to face him—"does the mob?"

"The mob?" Any trace of pink that had remained in Simon's cheek was now gone.

"The Boston mob. They were behind the heist. I'm convinced they were responsible for Dirck's murder. And I strongly suspect they're after you."

Chapter Twenty-Three

"But I've never heard Dirck mention the Gardner Museum or Simon . . ." Simon Underwood frowned, trying to recall the names Julia had mentioned.

"Simon Duarte and Earl Bramer," Celine prompted.

The artist nodded. They were seated in a spacious living room beyond the deck. Simon had listened to Julia's theory regarding Dirck's murder with growing bewilderment.

"And I don't understand it, even if Dirck had found out anything about the heist, how exactly would the Boston mob have gotten word of it?"

Celine was quiet. She didn't doubt the details she'd seen or Julia's interpretation of them. But Simon was right. How had the mob gotten to know? From the way Julia's eyes had widened, Celine knew the former federal agent hadn't thought to ask the question either.

"There are only two things you can do with the kind of information we think Dirck discovered." Julia uttered the thought in a slow, pensive tone; her eyes were on the floorboards of the deck visible through the open door.

Celine knew exactly what Julia meant, and reacted immediately.

"Dirck wasn't the kind of person to blackmail anyone." The words burst out of her more forcefully than she'd intended. But the idea that Dirck Thins, a well-to-do business owner, would need—or want—to profit from his knowledge of a crime was preposterous.

"I said there were two possibilities," Julia interjected mildly.

"If Dirck did anything at all with what he knew, it was to call the authorities. His phone records will prove it."

"No offense, Ms. Hood," Simon cut in before Julia could respond, "but what if Dirck's only mistake *was* to call the FBI? The Boston FBI isn't exactly known for its integrity. I recall a *Boston Globe* article from 1988 insinuating —"

Julia shook her head vehemently. "That we were hand-in-glove with Whitey Bulger? Yes, that's true. Every organization has bad apples, and the FBI, unfortunately, is no different. But that's all in the past. And the Art Crime Team has never had any connections with the mob."

But Celine sensed the note of uncertainty underlying her words.

"The agents may not have any mob connections, but a CI might." Confidential informants, Celine remembered from the few criminal justice classes she'd taken in college, were frequently criminals themselves, trying to work off minor, or major, offenses by working with law enforcement.

But Julia was quick to dismiss the suggestion. "And why would an agent who'd been contacted with the kind of tip we're talking about need to get in touch with a CI?" she snapped. Her thick ponytail swung from side to side as she shook her head.

"And the fact remains"—Julia turned to Simon—"that the mob is involved. Or someone just as dangerous. But whoever it is, they're interested in your paintings. What would they find on the canvas under your works?"

Simon smiled. "I can show you," he offered, getting up, and gesturing toward the deck. "It's quite fascinating."

❧

Blake stared at the information Google had pulled up. Noticing the tracker had stopped moving, he'd taken down its current location and typed it into the search engine. 462 Morro Avenue was the street address for Simon Underwood's studio.

What business did Celine Skye, current owner of the Delft—Mailand had shared that interesting tidbit—have with Underwood? If she'd needed to inform him of Dirck Thins' death, wouldn't a phone call have sufficed?

Unless of course—Blake recalled the information he'd received from the Mechelen's Italian winemaker—the terms of Underwood's consignment arrangement with the Delft needed to be renegotiated.

Or simply restated.

He pulled up Underwood's website. Snippets of text—quotes from art reviewers—floated across the screen. Underwood had been praised as a *Master of Illusion*; in his treatment of light and shadow, *a veritable Vermeer*.

Blake's thumb flicked rhythmically across his chin. Underwood's consignment arrangement with the Delft had been undertaken, Blake recalled, as a favor to its owner. What did that mean? That Thins had known something about Underwood himself—or his art?

Was Underwood sufficiently skilled to disguise an old master, covering it in layers of new paint?

Or had Thins made some kind of discovery about his associate? And been killed for it?

Penny Hoskins' tip to check out Duarte's sister was making more and more sense.

❧

Fifteen minutes later, Simon withdrew a sheet of oil paper from his camera obscura and said, "This is what you'd find, Ms. Hood."

An image was blocked out in black acrylic on the oil sheet. Simon turned it over and carefully pressed it upon the prepared canvas that stood ready on the easel by the pyramid-shaped device. Rubbing his palm firmly over the sheet, he transferred the image.

Then he peeled the sheet off and turned to look at Julia. "That's what you'll see if you examine *Purple Waters* or anything else I've created."

A black-and-white image of gulls wheeling above the water was impressed upon the canvas. There was a curious quality about it, Celine noticed.

A startling contrast between light and shadow that would give the work a luminescent quality once Simon started working over it with colored pigments. Unlike an artist's preliminary sketch, the shapes here were defined by negative spaces and the shadows they cast.

"No lines," she murmured to herself, peering closely at the canvas.

Simon nodded but didn't say anything, watching Celine instead. She had the impression there was some connection he hoped she'd get. The image that had flashed into her mind earlier re-surfaced—a painter in a slashed jacket and balloon-shaped breeches seated before an easel. It took her a moment to recognize it.

Johannes Vermeer's enigmatic portrayal of the artist at work.

"Is that how Vermeer began his compositions?" She looked up at Simon. He was grinning, his cheeks flushed pink.

"Remember that from your art history classes, do you?"

Celine shook her head. "We discussed the effect—the fact that all you see is a black-and-white image of the subject—not how Vermeer achieved it. I remember reading about Lawrence Gowing's X-ray examination of *Girl With a Pearl Earring*."

She turned to Julia, who stood looking at them with a bemused expression on her face. "Vermeer's underdrawings have been a source of endless speculation for art historians. There are no preliminary sketches or guiding lines, just light and dark shapes, all put down without any hesitation.

"It's as though a step is missing and we don't know how Vermeer began his work. Even if he used a camera obscura to trace his subjects, you'd think there'd be some remnants of the lines he used for his tracings."

Julia stared at the canvas, her features expressionless, then scrutinized Simon's face. "So no art historian has figured this out. But you have? How?"

"It's a long story," Simon said with a smile.

"I'd like to hear it." Julia looked at Celine, who nodded. "Sure."

But she didn't understand Julia's interest. How could knowing Vermeer's techniques help?

Simon led the way back into the living room. As he stepped over the threshold, he glanced over his shoulder at Celine.

"You know, this is how Dirck and John and I met. All those years ago in Boston. We were brought together by our work on this puzzle and our mutual fascination with Vermeer."

Chapter Twenty-Four

"In the mid-eighties," Simon Underwood said as he walked around his living room, peering at the many prints that hung on the walls, "I was a graduate student in the art history program at Boston University."

He'd picked art history because he didn't think he'd qualify for the studio art program.

Celine stole a glance at Julia; the former fed seemed riveted by Simon's remarks. Dirck and John had rarely spoken of their Boston days. Now they were both gone, Celine found herself wanting to know more.

But she'd have been the first to admit, none of it seemed particularly relevant to either the Gardner case or Dirck's murder.

"There was enough focus on painting to satisfy me." Simon turned briefly to look at Celine and Julia, and then returned to the task of selecting prints to show his visitors. "I was fortunate enough to have an advisor who did more than speculate on the reasons why any particular artist had chosen his subject."

A failed artist himself, Professor Francis van Mieris had been fascinated by the techniques artists used to achieve their effects. He'd even encouraged his students to experiment with those techniques and methods in an attempt to replicate—and understand—the effects they produced.

Dirck must've enjoyed that, Celine thought with a smile.

"It was theory put into practice." Simon stopped before a panoramic view of what looked like Venice's *Bacino di San Marco*. Innumerable vessels crowded the dark, placid waters of the basin.

"Is that a photograph?" Julia whispered.

"No, it's a Canaletto," Celine whispered back. "An Italian view painter. I recognize it because my father specialized in *vedute* art." She didn't understand what Canaletto, an eighteenth-century painter, had to do with Vermeer, a seventeenth-century Dutch genre painter.

They watched Simon select three other prints: one a detailed image of a woman playing the clavichord—a genre painting, although Celine wasn't familiar with the artist; the other two recognizably Vermeer. He brought them over to the coffee table.

"These are all examples of realistic painting: Canaletto, Vermeer, and a near-contemporary of his, Gerrit Dou," Simon said. "Look at them closely. See any differences?"

A few minutes later, Julia shrugged. "I give up. What am I looking for?"

But Simon didn't respond, turning to Celine instead. "Well?" he pressed.

Celine struggled to put what she saw into words. "Canaletto's works look the same from a distance as up close—as though they were produced by a professional photographer. Gerrit Dou's work has the same quality in terms of its details, but the illusion is lost because of the staged, stiff posture of the woman. That poor woman must have had to sit like that for hours."

You could tell she was posing for a painting, not actually making music. Vermeer would have captured her in the moment—playing the clavichord, looking up for just a second to see who'd walked in the door. A snapshot of reality.

"The kind you can only achieve with a digital camera or an iPhone," Celine said. She'd always been intrigued by this aspect of Vermeer's art.

But she'd never realized Dirck and John had also found Vermeer just as fascinating. Her eyes roved over the print.

Then something else caught her eye.

She turned sharply toward Simon. "Up close, Vermeer doesn't always offer the level of detail you'd expect." Her voice reflected her surprise. "Nothing like what you see in the other two works."

"Exactly." Simon beamed. "And that was the question that preoccupied Frank van Mieris—after his wife, an artist, made precisely the same remarks." He sat down. "There's no question Vermeer made use of a camera obscura, right?" He paused to look at Julia.

The former federal agent bobbed her head. "Yes, you can tell from the discs of confusion in his paintings—those white highlights. And the difference in scale between foreground and background objects." She frowned, hesitating. "And the perspective," she said. "Philip Steadman."

Julia seemed to be reciting facts she hadn't considered deeply. But it was clearly enough for Simon that she accepted his premise.

"So Vermeer uses a camera obscura, yet his paintings are only an illusion of reality. Not a precise depiction of it. Frank wanted to know why. Vermeer wasn't the only Dutch artist to play with lenses. Gerrit Dou used them as well. Nor was Vermeer the only artist interested in realistic painting. But his works have more of a painterly quality than that of most other realistic painters."

"Painterly?" Julia asked.

"Not trying too hard to be photo-realistic," Simon explained. "Typically, you'll see dabs and splotches of paint that resolve themselves at a distance into what the artist wants them to represent."

Simon held a magnifying glass over the print of Vermeer's *Lady Standing at a Virginal.*

"Even Rembrandt, despite his freer approach, can depict pearls realistically. Take a look at the pearls in his portrait of Maria Trip. You can even see the white string connecting them."

He pressed a thick index finger against the pearls worn by Vermeer's *lady.* "But look at how Vermeer doesn't actually paint a string of pearls, he suggests the idea of them—a thin gray line dabbed into the woman's skin tone, and then globules of paint, overlapping as they round her neck."

Julia sat back. "And that means, what exactly?" she asked.

Simon put the magnifying glass down. "Well, Frank figured taking a look at Vermeer's underdrawings might reveal something of his method. Perhaps he wasn't capturing as much detail at the initial stage as you'd expect." He waved his hands. "Maybe the lines were fuzzy. I don't know what any of us thought we'd see."

Celine raised her eyes from her scrutiny of the fourth print, Vermeer's *Lacemaker.* Isolated from the rest of the subject, the spool of red and white threads looked like an untidy and entirely accidental splatter of paint. "So you looked at the underpainting and saw what Lawrence Gowing had seen."

"Yes, and for the life of us, we couldn't figure out how he'd done it. How had Vermeer captured an image without putting down any lines?"

Frank van Mieris had been the type of professor who'd brought his theories and research projects into the classroom. The graduate students in the art history program and the undergraduates taking a mandatory art history unit over at the College of Fine Art had both been treated to Frank's ideas and invited to participate in his quest for the truth.

"Dirck and John came up with the idea of a tracing. Vermeer could have traced the image he saw within his camera obscura onto a sheet of paper and then transferred it onto his canvas. The problem was no such papers had been found in Vermeer's possessions. Frank dismissed the suggestion."

But Simon had been convinced the young artists were onto something. In another course, he'd been introduced to the fifteenth-century Italian painter Cennino d'Andrea Cennini and his treatise on art.

"Oil paper," Simon said. "Cennini recommends it for making tracings. He even has instructions on how to make it. We knew enough about Dutch life to know that oil paper would have been readily available to Vermeer. His wife would've had it in her kitchen to wrap food."

"And did Vermeer have any oil paper sketches?" Julia asked.

"I thought no sketches were found in his inventory," Celine said.

"You're right, none were. And if he used oil paper, that would explain why. Oil paper has a very short shelf life. The oil degrades it. It was the only explanation that fit."

"And then what?" Celine asked.

Why hadn't Dirck and John ever mentioned any of this? It was cutting-edge research; they'd been part of it. And they'd never said a word about it.

But then again, Simon hadn't either.

He grinned now. "Then we tried it. We made our own Vermeer. It wasn't enough for Frank to just have a plausible theory. He needed to demonstrate that it worked.

"And he did it in his own spectacular fashion."

Blake scarfed down the last of his meatball sub, licked the greasy tomato sauce and cheese off his fingers, and turned back to the fresh pile of passenger manifests Ella had left on his desk. He'd decided to look at some of the other morning flights—those that didn't have Boston as their final destination.

He stifled a yawn, sleep deprivation finally catching up with him. Even for a man who enjoyed poring over papers, this was a mind-numbingly monotonous task. And futile.

He hadn't come across any Graysons or Gregs among the list of same-day travelers so far. And the more he thought about it, the more convinced he was that Grayson would want to head back to Boston.

By the mid-nineties, many of the Gardner's former employees, tired of being constantly questioned about the theft, had moved out of the area. Not Grayson. Grayson had stayed on. At first the agents on the case had suspected Grayson was more closely involved than he'd let on.

But before long it had become apparent that Grayson simply didn't have it in him to start a fresh life someplace else.

Blake rubbed his tired eyes and forced himself to concentrate. It was tedious work but it had to be done, he told himself.

"You can stop looking at those. You won't find Grayson there."

Ella's voice startled him out of the stupor into which he'd fallen. Intent upon his papers, he hadn't heard her step into his office.

He raised his head, his pen still poised over the manifests he'd been studying.

"Grayson hasn't left San Luis Obispo," Ella informed him, coming into the room. "And I don't think he plans to in some time to come."

"And you know this how?" Blake felt the pen slipping out of his fingers. Too tired to tighten his grip, he let it fall to his desk.

"Because of the prepaid card he purchased at the Pioneer Market & Newsstand before he left Paso Robles."

Ella pulled out the chair on the other side of Blake's desk and plonked herself into it.

"That was a stroke of genius, by the way," she went on, "asking me to check whether he'd bought prepaid cards and phones."

Blake blinked. "Grayson used his credit card to buy a prepaid card and phone?" Could the man truly be that dumb?

"No. No burner phone. Not yet. And he used cash."

"Then how—?"

Chapter Twenty-Five

Ella smiled, brushing imaginary wrinkles off her lap. "I circulated a composite," she said. "I remembered you'd said he'd left his toothbrush and shaving kit in his motel room. I figured he might have developed a stubble."

The smile widened.

"So I asked a Boston PD sketch artist to modify the photo we used to create the ID for his code name. And I focused on 24/7 businesses selling the items he'd be interested in."

"Boston PD?" Blake wasn't sure he wanted Boston PD knowing about his lost CI. Not when the CI in question was involved, however tangentially, in a murder case.

"I figured you wouldn't want word getting around the FBI office that you'd lost sight of your informant." She gazed at him, head tilted to one side.

Blake shook his head. No, he wouldn't. That would be even worse. But still—

"Don't worry," Ella reassured him. "As far as the sketch artist is concerned, we're looking for a Greg Peters, not a Grayson Pike."

"Okay." Blake gripped his temple.

Lack of sleep was making him lightheaded.

His fingers kneaded his forehead. "So Grayson has a prepaid card, but not a phone. And this tells us he's going to remain in San Luis Obispo County because . . ." He let his voice trail off and gazed expectantly at his assistant.

Ella leaned forward.

"Remember, we were wondering why Grayson had taken the Amtrak bus to the LOVR stop at Laguna Village?"

She paused—for dramatic effect, Blake supposed.

"Turns out it's an eleven-minute walk from the bus stop to Costco."

"He got himself a Costco membership?"

"Sounds like it. He bought clothes, shoes, toilette items."—All stuff he would need, Blake thought to himself—"And a ton of food. All with his prepaid card. Pretty clever strategy."

Blake had to agree. He wouldn't have considered checking any Costco warehouses to see if Grayson had made an appearance. Men on the lam didn't shop at Costco, which required all its shoppers to be members and insisted upon seeing some form of ID before issuing a membership card.

Moreover, what single man needed to buy items in bulk? Blake had let his own membership lapse years ago when a former girlfriend had left him. She'd been Indian—it was inevitable that she would.

Not that he was bitter about it. It was what it was. And there'd been plenty of other women since then.

He picked up his pen and tapped it against the sheaf of papers that littered his desk. "Good work, Ella."

She looked up at him, surprised. He pretended not to notice. He rapped the pen against his desk again.

"Keep monitoring that prepaid card. The places it's being used in should help us narrow down Grayson's location."

❧

"I had no idea academics were so unforgiving," Julia commented as she climbed into Celine's Honda Pilot. "What Frank van Mieris did wasn't illegal. Unconventional and in-your-face certainly, but not illegal."

Celine nodded, waving good-bye to Simon as she settled in behind the wheel and pulled away. "Frank was thumbing his nose at the experts; and academics, more than anyone else, don't take kindly to that kind of thing. But, yes, it was harsh, what happened to him."

The professor had seen an opportunity to prove his point when, shortly after their breakthrough, Boston University agreed to host an exhibition of Dutch painters, including several by Vermeer. *Girl With a Pearl Earring* was to be the main attraction of the show.

Frank, Simon said, had persuaded his students to replace Vermeer's original with their reproduction, created using the methods they'd uncovered.

If the reproduction could fool all eyes, the team's theory would be conclusively proven. It was a magnificent, dramatic stunt. But in successfully pulling it off, Frank had caused a furor in the Boston art world and at the University.

As a tenured professor, Frank couldn't be fired. But his career was all but over. He'd lost most of his research funding and the Dean of Faculties kept a close eye on his teaching. "Making sure he wasn't leading students astray by encouraging them to create forgeries," Simon had recounted with a wry smile.

Understandably, neither he nor his friends had ever spoken of their involvement with van Mieris.

"Are you still convinced Simon Underwood is Simon Duarte?" Celine wanted to know as she made a right onto South Street and cruised down to Main Street. She was more than ever certain now that Simon Duarte was dead.

And that Simon Underwood, one of Morro Bay's most prominent painters, was in danger.

Just as they'd left his house, she'd glimpsed the Lady. The vision had made her turn around to ask if he still kept in touch with friends in Boston. "Yes, my friend, Bella," Simon had said. "Annabelle."

Simon had been a close friend of Bella's younger brother. "Bella nearly came apart when he died; he was so young." She'd looked to Simon for support, needing him to take her brother's place.

As soon as Simon mentioned the name, Celine had recalled the wine baskets the Delft regularly sent on behalf of the painter to an Annabelle Curtis in Boston. Because Simon was an old friend, Dirck had never charged for the shipments. He'd been generous like that, Celine thought.

Was it Annabelle she'd seen in her dream, Celine wondered, smoothly steering left onto Main Street. Annabelle who would soon have to learn from Celine that Simon Underwood had been killed—just like her younger brother?

Because there was no way of averting that tragedy.

Tears pricked Celine's eyes; she blinked them back, swallowing hard. They'd warned Simon about the mob. It was all they could do. The white-haired painter had refused Celine's offer that he move into one of the guest cottages on the Mechelen. "I'll take my chances," he'd said.

"No," Julia said as they traveled down Main Street.

No, what? Celine's head pivoted sharply toward her; her foot tapped the brake. The car slowed.

"You asked whether I still think Simon Underwood is Simon Duarte," Julia explained as Celine continued to stare blankly; it had completely slipped her mind that she'd posed the question. "I don't."

"Good to know." Celine eased off the brake, allowing the car to resume speed just as the vehicle behind them honked impatiently.

"I still think there's some connection, though," Julia went on, looking out the car window. "I just can't put my finger on what it is."

The former federal agent sniffed hungrily at the delicious smells of fried seafood that wafted toward them from the cafés and restaurants that lined Main Street. "I could do with some of that. I'm famished." She turned toward Celine. "Want to stop for a bite?"

"Sure. How about here?" Celine pointed at a brick building on the right; a green awning projected over the glass door, overhanging an outdoor café teeming with diners. Potted geraniums were artfully lined against the wall on either side of the door.

Julia leaned her head out the window and peered at the name written in bold white letters on the face of the awning: *Oyster Bay Café*. "I think it's perfect!"

Chapter Twenty-Six

After a smiling young woman in a white shirt and black apron had taken their order—breaded Calamari strips served with garlic-seasoned fries and a can of coke for Julia; sole with lightly sautéed, crisp-tender broccoli and sparkling water for Celine—Julia gazed out at the traffic on Main Street.

"I didn't know John," she said a few minutes later, "but from the little I knew of Dirck, I would have pegged him as a Rembrandt fan, wouldn't you?"

Celine nodded, although the gesture was lost on Julia, still staring out the window.

They had opted for a table by one of the two large windows inside the Oyster Bay Café instead of sitting amidst the bustling lunch crowd on the sidewalk. It was quiet inside, with only one other table occupied by a burly man who'd walked in minutes after Celine and Julia.

Celine had been just as surprised as Julia to hear Simon say that John and Dirck had been fascinated by Vermeer—his subjects, his techniques. The portraits they'd painted of each other suggested instead an admiration for Rembrandt.

For one thing, Vermeer's known oeuvre, unlike Rembrandt's, hadn't included a single self-portrait. Rembrandt, on the other hand, not always able to afford a model, had painted himself close to ninety times.

But then again, was it such a stretch that someone who'd started out by liking Vermeer would go on to appreciate his older contemporary from Leiden? After all, both artists had concerned themselves with contemporary life. Vermeer had merely narrowed his focus to domestic life, while Rembrandt had turned his gaze out to the world.

She was about to share something of this when their server returned. She placed a bottle of sparkling water in front of Celine and handed Julia a chilled can of coke; the burly diner peered over his menu at their server. But just as

Celine started to direct the young woman's attention to him, he dropped his gaze.

The server smiled. "He's probably not ready to order, Miss. But thank you for letting me know. Enjoy your beverages. Your entrées will be ready in just a moment."

Julia opened her can as the server left their table and took a long gulp. "Strange, isn't it," she mused, "that two such avid fans of Vermeer should have names that have such significance for the artist himself?"

The comment startled Celine. "I'm not sure I understand what you mean." But tidbits from her art history courses were returning to her.

Julia took another long swig. "I suppose it's only fitting that the bar is called the Delft. That was Vermeer's hometown."

"Yes, it was." Celine fingered her bottle of sparkling water. Her throat felt parched, but somehow she couldn't bring herself to quench it.

"Isn't it strange that a man called Thins would be so intrigued by an artist who lived all his married life with his mother-in-law, also named Thins?"

"Yes, I know. Maria Thins. It's just a coincidence. What else could it be?"

"And what are the odds that a man named Thins would meet and befriend a man called Mechelen—the name of the inn that Vermeer's father owned?"

Celine felt her green eyes widen; she brushed the red-gold strands of her waist-length hair back. Where was the former federal agent going with this?

"Maybe it was the coincidence of their names that made them feel especially connected to Vermeer. Clearly, it wasn't a fascination that lasted. In all the years I've known them, I can't remember either Dirck or John ever mentioning Vermeer. And who can blame them, after what happened with van Mieris."

Her temper rose as Julia, instead of responding, continued to stare coolly at her.

"What exactly are you trying to say, Julia? That . . . that . . ." She found herself unable to voice the thought.

"I'm not sure what I'm trying to say, Celine," Julia said mildly. She reached over and enfolded Celine's cold fingers in her own warm, rough palm. "It just occurred to me how odd it was that two men with the names Mechelen and Thins should be such close friends and should both be so captivated by Vermeer. That's all."

Julia squeezed her hand. "I'm sorry if I upset you."

Celine looked away. "It's okay." But it wasn't so easy to forget the tenuous notions—insinuations, almost—that Julia had thrown out. They'd taken root in her consciousness, and her mind struggled to encompass them.

"Here you go!" Their server had returned with steaming platters and a wide smile. She slid the food onto the table, placed a stainless caddy stashed with packets of salad dressing, salt, and pepper between them, and, with another cheery smile, left.

"What happens to the wine bar and the winery now?" Julia asked, tearing into a packet of salt and dusting her fries with it.

"Nothing," Celine said as she speared a floret of broccoli. "I'm not planning to sell. Not just yet, at any rate." She raised her eyes. "It turns out I've inherited the business. But I'm sure you knew that already."

❧

Julia is only trying to help, Celine.

Sister Mary Catherine's voice was at her ear again. It had nagged her all through lunch as she toyed with her food.

Celine wiggled her key in the Pilot's door lock. They were in the parking lot of the Oyster Bay Café. Lunch had been a tense, silent affair—except for Sister Mary Catherine's voice.

Celine knew the nun wouldn't let go until she made things right.

You can't get to the truth without asking uncomfortable questions. You know that.

Celine raised her head and looked across at Julia, waiting on the other side of the vehicle. "Sorry, I got snippy back there," she said. "I . . ." But there was nothing she could think of to explain her reaction.

"Don't be." Julia's smile was warm. "You were upset. I get it. You've lost a close friend, and a woman you barely know is nosing around, asking questions."

Questions that should be asked, Sister Mary Catherine said. But Celine wasn't going to repeat that. It wasn't a sentiment she shared.

Celine pulled the car door open. "I'm just not ready yet to go where you're going with this, Julia. But I need to know what happened and . . ." She gazed out at the long line of cars proceeding slowly down Main Street. "And we need to keep Simon safe."

They needed to do it, she thought, even if the effort was going to be futile.

Julia climbed into the car. "Are you sensing that he might not be?"

When Celine nodded, she continued, "I don't think the damaged painting will be enough to convince Detective Mailand to provide Simon with police protection. But if you can give me something more concrete, I might be able to talk him into it."

"I'll try." Celine eased herself behind the wheel. As she buckled herself in, her leather tote bag, sitting on the seat beside her, slipped to the floor. A wallet, a vanity kit, a couple of pens and notepads tumbled out along with other odds and ends.

"Let me help with that," Julia offered as Celine swore under her breath. She wasn't usually such a klutz.

"Where did you get this?" The former federal agent picked up the last item on the floor—a bulky silver wristwatch—and held it out on her palm.

Celine's eyes widened as she stared at the watch. Damn, she'd forgotten all about that! "It needs to go in Lost and Found," she explained. "I found it"—*was it just this morning?*—"on the side of the building. One of our customers must have dropped it as he made his way back to the parking lot."

"Can you remember who it belongs to?" Julia's voice had a quiet urgency that startled Celine.

"No . . . why?" she faltered. She scanned her memory, but the only name that popped into her head was *B-aw-ston* Greg.

"I don't know why I keep thinking of Greg," she said. It was probably because they were headed to the Paso Robles Police Station to give a police sketch artist a description of his features. "I don't even remember if he was wearing a wristwatch."

"This isn't a watch, Celine." Julia's expression was grave. "This is a state-of-the-art tracker—made just for the FBI." She turned the watch over and Celine saw the rectangle with *LSS3i* inscribed into the back.

A surge of excitement powered through Celine—She was right, then; Dirck was innocent—as Julia continued.

"We wanted Light Security Solutions, the manufacturer, to come up with something light and innocuous that undercover agents and CIs could wear while on a sting. It was a way of keeping tabs on the operation without putting the person on the ground at risk."

"Dirck must have called the FBI with his information." Celine's eyes were glued to the watch. And this was proof, wasn't it? Dirck was just an innocent citizen doing his civic duty.

"And there must have an FBI operative—agent or civilian—at the bar last evening," Julia agreed. "What I don't understand is why this thing got left behind. If it was being used in an operation"—she clicked a button on the side—"there'll be phone numbers programmed into the memory."

"You can make calls with that thing?"

"Make and receive," Julia said, calling up and scrolling through what looked like a series of menus on the small black screen. "And it looks like someone's been trying to call it."

She tapped the screen. "Time to find out who."

⁂

If he'd been looking at his laptop when the phone rang, Blake might have had second thoughts about answering it.

But by the time he'd briskly uttered the words: "Special Agent Blake Markham, FBI," it was already too late.

His eyes drifted to his computer screen as he spoke, realization thudding into him like an unwelcome bonk from a baseball bat. The hit was just as unpleasant, and accompanied by the same stinging sensation of dismay.

The call had been made from Grayson's tracker.

Determined to go on the offensive, Blake sat up straighter.

"Ms. Celine Skye?" He didn't wait for her response. "Ms. Skye, you're in possession of an FBI tracking monitor. May I ask how you came by it?"

Chapter Twenty-Seven

"Special Agent Blake Markham. So you are aware that your man jettisoned his tracker."

The voice—sardonic, husky, deep enough to be almost masculine—was familiar. It took Blake a moment to place it—Julia Hood—and he was instantly on his guard.

Retired agent Julia Hood was a loose cannon. No doubt about it. In the Boston office's rogue days, she'd been tight with the likes of John Morris and John Connolly—Whitey Bulger's handlers and enablers.

Hood had survived the scandal that had ensued when the story came out in the 1990s—one of the few agents in the Organized Crime Unit to do so. Even Edward Quinn, the man responsible for taking down mob underboss, Gennaro Angiulo, had been tainted.

Not Julia. She'd emerged from the business unscathed.

But as far as Blake was concerned, Hood's credentials had always been shaky.

He played it cool, however.

"Julia Hood! Long time no hear."

Although, frankly, it hadn't been nearly long enough. She'd retired barely a month-and-a-half back in January.

"What's a retired federal agent doing with an FBI-issue tracker?"

And what was she doing in Paso Robles, Blake wondered. Checking out the same rumors Grayson had been? Was that the reason Dirck Thins was dead?

Julia's presence in Paso Robles at the time of the Delft owner's murder was a coincidence too strong for Blake to stomach.

"What's a current FBI agent doing losing his CI?" Julia countered. "Any ideas where he might be? I assume you know he's wanted for murder."

"Wanted for murder because he misplaced his tracker at a bar?" Blake allowed his feigned skepticism to ring out loud and clear.

"At a bar where a man was murdered, Blake?"

"And yet the tracker remains in your possession instead of in police custody. Why is that, Julia?"

She'd withheld it for some reason, Blake was certain. To threaten him? Into doing what? Revealing Grayson's location to her? Well, Blake wasn't about to do that. He wanted to find Grayson. But he wanted Grayson alive. Not dead.

"I had no idea of its existence until just a moment ago," Julia replied. "Celine, who picked it up"—she was on first name terms with the lady, Blake noted—"thought it was just a watch."

Her tone hardened. "Now what exactly is going on? Your man was sniffing around the Delft last evening, then hours later Dirck Thins, the owner, was killed."

"He was following up on a tip we received," Blake said. "About the Gardner heist."

"Called in from the Delft?"

"We believe so. At any event, the tipster asked to meet with our guy at the bar."

He drummed his fingers on his desk. Time to ask a few questions of his own. "I'm curious to know how you're involved in all of this, Julia. What took you to Paso Robles? How do you know Dirck Thins and Celine Skye?"

"I'm just a bystander caught up in this affair, Blake, nothing more than that. I came here for a much-needed vacation. It so happens that the guest cottage I'm renting is on the winery Thins owned."

It was mere chance that had brought her to the Mechelen? Blake wasn't buying that.

"And Ms. Skye just happened to ask for your help with the investigation?"

"A mutual friend asked me to look in on Celine when he realized I'd be here. Celine was aware of my background right from the start. And she knew she could call on me anytime she needed help. When she found Thins' body that's exactly what she did. There's no mystery here, Blake."

She paused, then went on: "The only mystery is the location of your man, Greg. That's his name, isn't it?"

"I'd leave the investigating to Detective Mailand, Julia," Blake replied, referring to the Sheriff's Office detective on the case.

He heard her sharp intake of breath. "You know him?"

"Well enough to know that he's more than capable of handling the case." Blake didn't know the man. But it was a reasonable assumption to make, and he would find out one way or another soon enough. He intended to call the detective the minute he got off the phone.

With the element of surprise on his side, Blake pressed on:

"Have you informed Detective Mailand that you've tracked down Simon Duarte?"

"Simon Duarte?" Julia still sounded stunned. "You've heard about—"

"It was the lead Greg was looking into." He deliberately used Grayson's code name. Once Julia got something into her head, she was like a dog with a bone. Feeding her bits of inconsequential information might help to head her off. "The last time we spoke, he reported seeing Duarte. At the Delft."

"So he's alive!"

"Isn't that why you drove all the way to Morro Bay to Simon Underwood's studio?"

"Yes, we met, but I don't think Simon Underwood is Simon Duarte. He —"

Blake wasn't willing to listen. He'd determine for himself whether or not Underwood was Duarte. "Does he have the Vermeer?"

He'd risked tipping her off with that bald question, but it had to be done.

There was a moment's silence. The penny had dropped, obviously. This was what the FBI was searching for in Paso Robles—Vermeer's *Concert*.

"No, Underwood doesn't have any Vermeers."

Another pause.

"But he does have a flawless method to produce one that could fool any expert."

❧

The police sketch artist wasn't an artist at all. He was a police officer trained in the use of SketchCop, a computer software program.

"Budget doesn't run to the expense of hiring forensic artists, unfortunately," he said with a rueful grin as he ushered Celine and Julia into a pair of narrow, hard chairs in the tiny interview room.

"Afraid you'll have to make to do with me." He lowered himself into a chair at an adjacent corner of the table.

"I'm sure you'll do just fine, Officer," Julia replied with a smile. "It's the interview that's the most important aspect of this process, isn't it?"

"That's right," the officer said. He'd introduced himself, but Celine had already forgotten his name.

He turned to Celine. "This isn't gonna be an exact rendering of the person. But if we can get enough details to jog someone's memory, we'll call it good."

Celine nodded. "Sounds good."

The officer set a notepad on the desk and grasped a freshly sharpened pencil. "Well, anytime you're ready, ma'am, just tell me what you remember of this guy."

It took no more than fifteen minutes to record her impressions, with the officer asking follow-up questions at intervals. He showed her a few reference photos as well, and then retreated to the computer lab to work on the initial sketch.

Celine sat back with a sigh. "That was pretty painless," she said.

"Um-hmm," Julia murmured. She shifted in her chair and crossed her left leg over her right. "We ought to get a hold of Mailand when we're done here. At least we know why Dirck's killers were so interested in the art hanging on the Delft's walls."

"They were hoping to find a Vermeer."

The FBI agent Julia had spoken with hadn't been very forthcoming. But it had been clear that the tip phoned in to the FBI had been about Vermeer's *Concert*.

The painting, about twenty-eight inches by twenty-five, showed a woman seated at a harpsichord next to a man with a lute. A female singer, portrayed in profile, stood next to the two musicians.

What Celine couldn't understand was how Dirck could've known anything about the painting's whereabouts. "Why didn't he tell anyone? He never said a word about it to any of us. Not his lawyer. Not Simon. And he certainly never mentioned it to me."

"If it was even Dirck who made the call," Julia said. "Just because the call was made from the Delft doesn't mean—"

"I know. But who else could it be?"

Julia didn't respond.

Celine turned sharply toward her. "You think Simon Duarte called in that tip? Even if he's alive—which I doubt—why would he, after all these years?"

"For the reward money, of course," Julia said. "That's why certain works of art are stolen. They're too well known to palm off in the black market. But you can arrange to have the work returned. The reward museums and collectors offer to recover stolen works is considerable. And for the thief, it's pure profit."

"Then why didn't Greg recover the painting?"

Julia shrugged. "Maybe he did. We won't know until we find him."

"But then . . ." Celine paused. Julia's theories weren't making much sense. "Let's say, Greg did make off with the Vermeer—that's what you're implying, isn't it? Well, in that case, he couldn't have been working with the mob. He couldn't have directed the mob to Dirck—"

"We don't know that either, Celine," Julia interrupted her. "We don't know anything at this point. All we know is that Greg, a CI for the FBI, is on the run."

"Maybe he saw something."

"Something he didn't bother reporting to his handler?" Julia's right eyebrow rose, giving her face a lopsided look. "Blake can spin this however he likes, but you have to admit, the whole situation smells fishy."

Celine subsided. She was certain Greg had intended to meet Dirck later that night and that Dirck had been expecting the CI. But if that were the case, the only person with a motive to kill them both was someone she was equally certain was dead: Simon Duarte.

So much for certainties, she thought.

Trust your instincts, my dear, Sister Mary Catherine whispered into her ear.

How can I, Celine thought, *when they make no sense?*

❧

"Here we go." The police officer returned to the room and handed Celine a printout of his computer-generated composite.

"Wow! It looks hand-drawn." Celine heard Julia's indrawn hiss of breath and her murmured, "Looks very familiar!" but she ignored it.

Instead, she glanced up at the officer. "I thought it would be more like a photograph."

The officer shook his head. "Too misleading. We want something that looks hand-drawn, that's open to interpretation. Folks understand that about a sketch. All of the features don't have to match for them to see and recognize a resemblance to someone they know."

He pointed to the sketch. "Anything you'd like to change?"

There were a few things. Celine pointed them out; then there was another wait.

When the officer returned with his second draft, Celine was sufficiently pleased with the likeness he'd captured to sign the back of the image.

She'd barely finished thanking the officer when Julia grabbed her arm and marched her out of the room. "We need to find Mailand. I recognize that face. Blake wasn't being straight with us."

Chapter Twenty-Eight

"Information?" Detective Mailand rose halfway out of his chair as he repeated Julia's words. "You have information for me, and you've graciously consented to share it. What can I say, I'm touched!"

They'd seen his office door ajar, and before Celine could think about knocking, Julia had thrust her head around the doorway and informed the detective that it was imperative they speak.

"Please come in." Mailand waved Julia and Celine in.

The room the Sheriff's detective had commandeered at the Paso Robles Police Station looked suspiciously like an interview room—sunless, windowless, and constricted. A desk, a file cabinet, and three chairs had been crammed into the tiny space.

After they'd all sat down, Mailand stretched his arm out across the desk, palm facing up.

"I understand you have evidence for me as well, Ms. Hood."

"I beg your pardon?"

"The tracker, please."

Celine pulled it out of her purse. "It was my fault this wasn't turned in sooner, Detective. I thought it was a watch misplaced by one of our patrons. If Julia hadn't recognized it . . ." Her voice trailed off as she saw the expression on his face.

Wordlessly she dropped the tracker into his open palm.

"It belongs to an FBI informant," Julia began to say.

"I'm aware of that, Ms. Hood."

Julia stared at the detective. "And his name, Detective Mailand? Were you aware of that as well? He's been going by Greg Peters. But his name is Grayson Pike. He used to be a guard at the Gardner Museum in Boston."

There was a bored expression on Mailand's craggy features, but Celine's eyes widened. "You mean he was a guard when—"

"He was on duty the night of the infamous heist," Julia replied tersely. "He's always been on our radar. As someone who knew more than he was letting on, even if he wasn't directly involved in anything."

Celine pondered this. *B-aw-ston* Greg had certainly acted as though he had some secret information. And he'd known about Simon Duarte and Earl Bramer, even though their involvement wasn't common knowledge outside of the FBI.

But what had *B-aw-ston* Greg wanted with Dirck? Why had Dirck been so eager to meet with him?

"The man's on the run, Ms. Hood," Mailand's voice addressing Julia penetrated Celine's musings. "His name and his former occupation aren't going to help me find him." He paused for a fraction of a second. "Fortunately, I have a more concrete lead."

"Already?" Julia's eyebrows rose. "And what is it, if I may ask?"

"You may ask, and I'll tell you—not that it's any of your business. We're tracking the purchases he's making on his prepaid credit card."

"And you know this how?" Julia was leaning forward now.

"A former colleague of yours gave me the courtesy of a call the moment he realized what his CI might've been involved in. Which is more than I can say for you."

"So Blake called. Trust him to get ahead of a story." Julia sat back in her chair, expelling a gust of frustration. "I've already explained why we didn't bring in the tracker sooner. We were on our way here when we realized what it was.

"As far as calling the tracker was concerned, it may not have been protocol, but at least it confirmed my suspicions that Dirck Thins' death is connected with the Gardner Museum heist."

Celine cleared her throat. "Dirck's killers were looking for the Vermeer stolen from the Gardner, Detective Mailand. That's why all the art was taken down. You were asking me earlier what Dirck had known. Well, maybe Dirck had seen the Vermeer or found out about its whereabouts—"

"I know about the tip called in to the FBI. We haven't determined who made that call. But"—Mailand's gaze shifted to Julia—"I understand the Vermeer the tipster was referring to could've been a forgery created by Simon Underwood. You've begun investigating him, I hear."

"We went to see Underwood to inform him of Dirck's murder and to let him know his work had been damaged in the commission of a crime." Julia's eyes met Celine's briefly before she continued. "Ms. Skye asked me to accompany her."

The lie made Celine uncomfortable, but she sat impassively as Mailand searched her features. His eyes lingered upon her face as he addressed his next remarks to Julia. "You thought he was Simon Duarte?"

"I don't anymore," Julia replied firmly. "Underwood didn't act like a guilty person when we went to see him, Detective Mailand."

Celine nodded. "Simon was genuinely shocked to hear what had happened. Besides, if he'd been responsible for Dirck's murder, he'd have been on the run, too, wouldn't he? Just like Greg Peters."

❧

"Well, that went well," Celine commented wryly as she backed the Pilot out of its parking spot onto Park Street. Their exchange with Mailand had been so contentious, she wondered if he'd be willing to even consider any further information they brought him.

Julia smiled. "It wasn't that bad. At least we've learned something."

"We have?" Celine gave Julia a quick look as she made a right onto 9thStreet.

Julia nodded. "We know they're close to finding Grayson. If he's using a prepaid credit card, there's no doubt about it, he's on the run. And"—she turned toward Celine—"we know to a fair degree of certainty that it was Dirck who called in that tip to the FBI."

They'd agreed that *B-aw-ston* Greg—Celine still couldn't think of him as Grayson—must have made his asinine reference to Rembrandt for Dirck's benefit. There'd been no other male within earshot that Celine could think of.

And Mailand had let fall that the anonymous tipster had specifically asked that any FBI contact use the artist's name as a code word to identify himself.

Of course, Dirck hadn't immediately responded. He'd been busy attending to departing customers. It was only when *B-aw-ston* Greg had mentioned his hometown that Dirck had come over. Still, the scenario fit.

"You still want me to look for his phone records?" she asked Julia.

"Absolutely. What we have now is just an assumption. A reasonable assumption. But we need evidence to back it up."

They were cruising down Niblick Road when Celine asked her next question.

"Was Greg—Grayson—a guard at the Gardner Museum at about the same time Simon Duarte and Earl Bramer were working there?"

"Yes. He probably knew them both."

"Well enough to recognize them nearly three decades later?"

Julia shrugged. "Hard to tell. People change as they age. Some more so than others."

She crossed her legs. "You know, I was in my forties when I went to my first—and last—high school reunion. An elderly, white-haired man came up to me. Wow, someone brought their dad to the reunion, I thought. Until he introduced himself."

"Someone you knew?"

"Someone I'd had a crush on and had fantasized about meeting. I just could not believe he'd turned into this gray-haired, doddering old geezer."

"Must've been a shock," Celine murmured, her mind elsewhere.

"I got over it," Julia said. "But what brought this about?"

After a moment's silence, she said again: "Celine?"

Celine gripped the steering wheel hard. She'd told Julia that *B-aw-ston* Greg had brought up Earl Bramer and Simon Duarte, but she hadn't mentioned what exactly had triggered that conversation.

And now she'd begun to wonder—

"Celine?" Julia said a little louder. "Is there something you've remembered?"

Celine sighed. She didn't want to talk about it, but this was something she had to get out of her system. Brooding quietly over it would just drive her insane.

"After John died, Dirck began falling to pieces. I could see it. We all did. I thought it was the stress of running the winery as well as the bar. But Julia"—Celine inhaled deeply—"what if Dirck made some kind of discovery about John—something that would've completely shattered his confidence, something so devastating . . ."

She shuddered. The steering wheel felt sweaty, the leather sticking to her palms.

She turned to Julia. "What if Dirck uncovered some evidence that John Mechelen was Earl Bramer."

"He couldn't have. They were together at Boston University—according to Simon Underwood, who says he knew them both."

Celine exhaled heavily, tension oozing out of her shoulders. That was right. Simon Underwood had known both Dirck and John.

"What put that into your head, in any case, Celine?"

"When *B-aw-ston* Greg saw John's portrait at the Delft, he seemed convinced—not that he said it in so many words—that John and Earl Bramer were the same person. I figured he'd just seen photos of Duarte and Bramer in the newspapers, but if he actually knew them—" She broke off.

No, if John was Earl Bramer, he'd have needed to take both Dirck and Simon Underwood into his confidence. What possible reason could either of them have had for helping to conceal Earl's identity?

"Of course, there is one other possibility," Julia said. "Maybe it wasn't the fact of Mechelen's true identity that bothered Dirck. Maybe Dirck Thins and Simon Underwood were both aware of it and were willing to cover for a friend they both thought was innocent."

"Until Dirck found out otherwise?" Celine asked quietly. Was that how Dirck had come across the Vermeer—as he went through John's possessions? If so, it must've destroyed Dirck to find out. It would've been such a betrayal of their friendship.

Had Dirck died trying to make amends for John's crimes?

If that was the case, Celine vowed his effort was not going to be in vain. She'd do everything in her power to recover the art looted from the Gardner.

Fifteen minutes later the Pilot scrunched to a halt in front of Julia's cottage at the Mechelen Winery. Celine turned off the ignition, waiting for the former federal agent to gather up her things. Waiting to broach what could be a sensitive topic.

Law enforcement agents tended to be leery of sharing information with civilians. But Celine was prepared to battle her way through Julia's objections on this one.

"I'd like to see whatever you have on the Gardner theft," she said when Julia, her hand on the door handle, finally turned toward her.

For what seemed like an eternity, Julia's shrewd blue eyes scanned her features. Then her gaze softened. "You want to help?" she asked.

"I want to understand what Dirck gave up his life for," Celine replied. Over Julia's shoulder, she could see a blurry reflection of her own green eyes, large and unflinching in her pale face, on the passenger-side window.

Her gaze shifted to Julia. "And, yes, I want to help. For Dirck's sake. This is what he would've wanted me to do."

Chapter Twenty-Nine

Julia smiled. "I've had something put together for you, Celine. And I've been wanting to show it to you for some time now. But I didn't want to impose on you. Not . . ." she spread her hands wide. "Well, especially not after what you've been through."

Celine acknowledged the remark with the briefest of nods but couldn't trust herself to say anything. The tears were already brimming over into her eyes. She'd given up art—any association with it—thinking it would keep her friends safe. Thinking she could prevent what had happened to her parents. But—

It isn't your love of art that's killed anybody, my dear, Sister Mary Catherine's voice, soft as the delicate breeze outside, rustled at her ear. *This was all meant to be. You are where you were meant to be.*

Inside her cottage, Julia busied herself at her coffeemaker. "Sure you don't want to join me in a cup?" She turned to Celine.

Celine grinned. "I wish I could guzzle caffeine the way you do. But it affects my ability to see."

"Psychically, you mean?" Julia looked to her for confirmation, then turned around and pulled open a drawer. From where she sat, Celine could see the colorful oven mitts and kitchen towels the winery provided its guests.

Julia slipped her hand underneath those items and withdrew a buff manila folder.

"Here you go," she said, handing the file to Celine and sinking into the chaise beside her.

Celine flipped through the pages. The robbery had taken place in the pre-dawn hours of March 18, 1990. Two men disguised as police officers had gained entry into the museum, overpowered the night guards, and in a matter of a little over an hour proceeded to loot the museum.

Thirteen works had been stolen, including two artifacts—a Chinese vase and a bronze eagle finial. Celine slid long, tapering fingers over the glossy photos, her eyes drawn for some reason to the finial. A gilded bronze affair about ten inches high, it wasn't particularly appealing, yet the image of it seemed to jump out at her.

"Is this valuable?" she asked. *General,* she thought inexplicably. *General.* Not understanding its significance, she thrust the thought aside.

"Not particularly, no. It's probably currently valued at about a hundred thousand dollars. It's a mystery why it was taken. They were actually after the flag, but they couldn't unscrew it from its frame. Guess someone was a fan of Napoleon."

Ah! That would account for her repeatedly seeing the word, *General.*

"Someone must've been a Degas fan as well," Celine remarked. Her eyes shifted to the four sketches and the single watercolor. "It's almost as though two different thieves robbed the museum at the same time," she murmured.

"What do you mean?"

"Well, the Rembrandts and the Vermeer and even the Flinck, I suppose, were genuinely valuable. I can see why a thief would want to steal those. But the sketches, the finial—those seem more like a made-to-order theft. For someone who absolutely had to have them." Celine shrugged. "I don't know. I'm just thinking aloud."

The coffeemaker beeped.

"No, it's an interesting theory," Julia said as she rose to pour herself a cup. "We've known there's a mob angle to these thefts. But it's hard to explain why a bunch of rough-and-ready men would've wanted those sketches."

"You're right, though. Only a genuine art lover—someone who appreciated the role of a sketch in the finished composition—would have wanted them. It's probably why Isabella Stewart Gardner bought them in the first place."

"Maybe the Rembrandts and the Vermeer were supposed to be payment —in kind—for committing the theft."

Julia smiled. "Now that's a theory." Taking a cautious sip from her cup, she returned to the chaise.

Celine returned to the file, poring over its contents. "I don't see anything about Simon Duarte or Earl Bramer." Puzzled, she looked up at Julia.

"It was just a rumor—brought to us, believe it or not, by Grayson aka Greg. Unverified. The person he named as his source denied it."

"I don't understand." Her lack of sleep was getting to her; her brain felt weary, befogged. "You're saying now they didn't exist?"

"No, they did. They worked, as I mentioned, in the museum garden. And shortly after the heist, they were burned to death in a fatal car crash. Those are undeniable facts, but whether we can connect Duarte and Bramer to the heist . . . We have no real evidence."

Julia shrugged. "On the other hand, I've never been one to believe in coincidences. And it's true, despite our best efforts, the art—all of it—has eluded us."

Celine flipped over the next few pages, skimming paragraphs of background about the museum and its inception. The Gardner Museum had been designed to showcase a rather eccentric woman's eclectic collection. She'd never had an opportunity to visit, but she'd heard the stories.

"It's nice to have some background, I find," Julia explained as Celine perused the file, "when you're investigating a case. You may not need it. But it's still helpful to know."

Celine turned to the last page. What she saw made her catch her breath.

"Who is this?" she demanded.

Julia leaned closer, peering down at a woman clad in black. "That's her—Mrs. Jack—Isabella Stewart Gardner. It was painted by John Singer Sargent." Julia smiled. "Hard to believe, but in its day that painting created quite a stir."

"I imagine it did!" Celine said, staring at the image of the Lady. The familiar black form-fitting gown, the strand of pearls around her waist, the daring neckline.

"What's the matter, Celine. You look like you've seen a ghost!"

"That's because I have." Celine looked up. "This is the woman who's been haunting me since I was two, Julia. I see her every time I sense an untimely death." Her gaze shifted downward. "This is Mrs. Jack?"

"Or Belle, as she was called in her younger days."

Belle needs you to restore her museum, Celine, Sister Mary Catherine's voice sounded in her ear. *She's always known you'd be the one to do it.*

❧

The Gardner Museum heist had taken place a few weeks before Celine had been born in April. And when Isabella Stewart Gardner—Belle, as she liked to be called—had realized that Celine would be the one to recover the art, she had decided to watch over her.

Her presence was a sign—the only sign you had as a child—of your intuitive abilities, Sister Mary Catherine said.

"Why did you never tell me?" Celine demanded. She pulled up in front of her cottage and turned off the engine.

She'd left Julia's cottage confused. If the Lady who'd haunted her since she was two was Belle—Isabella Stewart Gardner—then who was Bella, the woman in her dream? What did Bella want from her?

Belle didn't want me to. She felt you weren't ready, Sister Mary Catherine replied. *And I could see you weren't. Oh, Celine, you didn't even want any visions. Don't you remember?*

She did remember. Sensing murder and being involved in it—unable to do anything to prevent it—had taken a toll on Celine. She'd asked for a respite.

Belle protected you from all the things you might have seen—until your parents died. She showed you that.

"And I was devastated," Celine whispered.

She thought you'd be able to handle the visions as you grew older. But that didn't happen. And when you asked to make it stop . . .

"You agreed." The memories were returning. "But you also reminded me a time would come when I'd need my ability to see."

Celine sighed. "So this is it?" It wasn't really a question.

"And Bella, the woman I dreamed of? Who is she?"

Someone both Dirck and John were very fond of.

"And Simon Underwood still keeps in touch with her, doesn't he?" In her dream, she'd seen a relatively young woman, a woman in her thirties. But the only woman Simon had made reference to, Annabelle Curtis, must have been at least about his age—close to sixty.

"Is Bella a young woman?" Celine asked.

Not anymore, dear, Sister Mary Catherine said. *You see her the way Dirck remembered her.*

Remembered her, Celine repeated to herself. That meant Dirck hadn't kept in touch with her all these years. Why not?

But Sister Mary Catherine's presence had faded; a fog of weariness enveloped Celine instead. She sensed there were dots that could be connected, but her brain was going around in circles.

"I need sleep," she muttered, pushing the driver's-side door open and stumbling out of her car.

❧

Celine hadn't taken more than a few steps up the driveway when the visions assaulted her. Polished black shoes stomping determinedly down the path; rough, bear-like hands closing upon the door handle; picking up a stone and —

The vision abruptly left, jolting her awake. The window on the right side of the door was shattered. A sliver of light showed between the door and the jamb. Whoever had broken into the house had left the door ajar.

Were they still inside?

Pulling her phone out of her shoulder purse, Celine cautiously crept toward the door. The same raw energy she'd felt outside the Delft in the pre-dawn hours of that morning assailed her.

They're here, she thought. *Dirck's killers are here.*

With the phone out in front of her, aimed like a gun, she slowly opened the door, craning her neck to peer inside. The open kitchen-living room area was empty. But someone had rifled through her belongings.

She pushed her way in. Prints had been pulled down off the walls. Drawers were left open; kitchen towels, cutlery, and other odds and ends were strewn on the countertops.

"Who's in here?" she called. "You have no business here. Show yourself." She looked around. "Now!"

The pages of an open magazine rustled as a slight breeze wafted in through the door. Other than that, there was utter silence.

They'd either left or were waiting inside to ambush her. Hitting 911 on her phone, she made her way to the bedroom.

The same disarray jumped out at her. Her quilt and sheets had been swept off the bed. The closet door was open, her clothes swept to one side. A coral, carry-on suitcase and another larger suitcase had both been dragged out of the closet—both unzipped.

Celine ended the 911 call. Whoever had come in here had left. This was a matter for Detective Mailand and the PRPD crime scene technicians. The fingerprints they found here would match the ones they'd found at the Delft.

She sank down on the bed. What had Dirck's killers been looking for? The Vermeer? Or—

Dear God! An image of the cardboard box Dirck had entrusted to her erupted out of the depths of her consciousness.

Chapter Thirty

Bob Massie, Mechelen's handyman-slash-guard, was on his knees in a se-cluded area behind the barn, rinsing sprinkler heads. Six-foot-tall hedges enclosed a rectangular, concrete-paved area equipped with a hose, buckets, and outdoor shelves lined with tools—drills, coils of wire, air hoses, and other odds and ends.

He glanced over his shoulder as Celine sprinted into the area, panting.

"Did they find it?"

The question stopped Celine in her tracks. "Who?" she wanted to know, her mind going instantly to the box she'd hidden for Dirck. "Did who find what?"

"Your friends," Bob said. Celine came up closer and stood behind him. He had a blue shop towel in his hands, and he was diligently scrubbing between the ridges of a cylindrical tube attached to the head.

"What friends?" Celine frowned. She was beginning to feel like Echo, the Greek nymph reduced to repeating whatever everybody around her said. But it wasn't her fault. Bob and his cryptic replies weren't making a lot of sense.

Bob stopped scrubbing. "Your friends from back East, Celine." He twisted around to face her. "You know, Andrea was real pissed at the last-minute additions to the wine tour group. Next time you invite folks to join in a tour, think about letting him know, okay?"

If there'd been last-minute additions to the group, Celine could well be-lieve that their winemaker had been anything but happy. Andrea preferred conducting small groups. It was a more intimate setting; and it was easier to keep an eye on visitors, ensuring they didn't wander off to areas off-limits to outsiders. He'd learned that lesson in Italy.

The men who'd set fire to Andrea's vineyard had slipped in on one of the many wine tours his winery offered.

"What did they look like, these men who said they were friends of mine?" Celine asked.

She didn't think there was any point revealing to Bob that her cottage had been broken into. She didn't have time to answer his questions. She needed information. And she needed it now.

Bob held the sprinkler head up to the outdoor light and examined it.

"Hefty, burly guys. Mid-forties. Frankly, I was surprised to hear that you hung out with people like that. They looked like wiseguys straight out of the Sopranos."

"Is that all they wanted, to join a wine tour?"

"No, they said you'd asked them to pick up a box. Something you'd brought back from the Delft last night. Wanted to know where it was. But you hadn't mentioned anything to me."

Dirck's killers must have been watching the bar last night. They'd seen Dirck hauling those hefty bags into her car. It wouldn't have taken them long to realize that if whatever they were looking for wasn't in the bar, it had to have been smuggled out.

And what better place than the winery? She squelched the feeling of nausea that arose within her.

"So what did you tell them?"

Bob turned to face her. "Well, I figured it out, didn't I? You'd brought that box back from the bar yesterday. I told them you'd taken it to your cottage. Don't tell me it wasn't there?"

Celine closed her eyes. *Dear God*, they'd conned their way into the winery and they'd broken into her cottage. What next?

"*Jeez*, Celine!" Bob's voice startled her. "You need to start communicating better. Especially if you're going to be running the show from now on. You can't expect people to read your mind."

She opened her eyes, willing herself to be patient. "You're right, I suppose I do. Listen, Bob, I need the front windowpane on my cottage replaced." She glanced at his hands, held over his red bucket, clutching the canister the sprinkler head fit in. "Pronto. It's completely shattered."

Bob put the canister down, a frown forming on his broad forehead. "What d'you mean shattered? How did that happen?"

Celine hesitated for just a second. "I think it was those men who lied about being my friends, Bob—and got you to tell them where I live."

She saw his jaw drop open.

"Next time, could you please give me a call before taking every Tom, Dick, and Harry who passes by at their word?"

❧

Inside the barn, Celine took stock of her surroundings. The place was undisturbed—everything just as she'd left it last evening. Hard to believe it was only last night. It felt like an eternity had passed since then.

"Everything okay?" Bob was behind her.

His voice had startled Celine, but by the time she looked around she'd recovered her composure. And her anger. How had Bob allowed himself to get rolled like that?

"I know Dirck and John must've mentioned this to you, Bob," she began, "but in light of recent events, I feel I need to reiterate the Mechelen's rules. No visitors are to be allowed anywhere near the guest or staff cottages or the barn."

Seeing Bob's mouth open, about to argue the point, she went on, her voice sharper.

"Is that understood? Not unaccompanied, not without my permission. It doesn't matter who they say they are." Her tone brooked no argument.

Bob stared at her; Celine stared back. Then, he slowly nodded.

"I can go look at that window of yours, now."

"Good." She tossed him her cottage keys. He was leaving when another thought occurred to her.

"Bob, wait!" She fished her car keys out of her shoulder purse and extended them toward him. "When you're done, bring my car here, will you? Ms. Hood asked for some gardening supplies. It'll be easier driving them to her."

Bob frowned, a question fermenting in his brain; she headed him off.

"After you help me unload the supplies at her cottage, you can take the Pilot to get that pane of glass you'll need to fix my window." It was a smoother ride by far than the old jalopy Bob drove.

He smiled. "Done deal."

Celine waited until he was out of sight, then, latching the door behind her, she went over to the wheelbarrow.

It seemed heavier than she remembered it; the wheels emitting a rusty squeak as she braced herself against the floor and heaved. It moved at last. With a quick flick of her palms, she brushed the soil and dirt aside, and then lifted the floorboards up.

The black hefty bag with its cardboard box hadn't been touched. For a brief second, Celine wondered if it would be safer where it was. But she dismissed the thought just as quickly. Dirck's killers had broken into her cottage. They'd have no compunctions about raiding the barn.

Putting the item in Julia's custody seemed like the best strategy. They'd have to find a way of getting it back into Annabelle's hands. If she was right that was whom it belonged to.

⸎

By the time Bob returned with her Pilot, Celine was waiting outside the barn. She'd found an old bottle of linseed oil and rubbed down the entire barrow with it. There'd been a grease gun on one of the shelves; she'd squirted as much as she could squeeze out of it onto the axles.

Then, she'd loaded the barrow with bags of potting soil and every gardening tool in sight.

Bob eyed the barrow, glanced back at the Pilot with its tailgate lifted all the way up, and then turned toward the barrow again.

"It would be easier to load that thing into your car without all that crap, you know."

"That's not such a good plan, Bob." He was right, but she had no intention of giving in on this point. "We'd just have to put all that stuff back in."

"But—"

Celine held up her hand. Fortunately, she'd already anticipated his objections.

"I have a better idea." She tipped her head back at the barn.

"There's a large piece of plywood in there. We can use it as a makeshift ramp and wheel this baby in. No point trying to lift it. Even without all the potting soil and tools, it'd be much too heavy for the both of us."

Bob just shook his head. "Whatever you say, Boss Lady."

⸎

"You're back." Julia stood at the door.

Her eyes roved past Celine's slender figure to Bob Massie's portly person and then down to the wheelbarrow.

"With gardening tools." The inflection of surprise in her voice so slight, it had surely eluded the handyman.

At least Celine hoped it had. She stole a glance at Bob. He stood behind her, his features impassive.

She turned back to Julia. "These belonged to Dirck and John." The explanation was meant to serve as a hint, but Celine wasn't sure the former fed had caught on. "Brought here all the way from Boston."

"Ah!" Julia's eyes widened. "Let me help you wheel it around to the side."

"You still need me around?" Bob Massie's gruff voice interjected. "I need to get that glass for your window."

"No, that's quite all right," Celine said. "And, yes, you'd better get going. Before J&P Glass closes."

"What's in there?" Julia asked once Bob had left.

Celine shook her head. "I don't know. I just know it's important. It was hidden in the bar. Dirck asked me to bring it back last evening and find a secure place for it."

"And you've brought it to me because—"

Celine sank against the doorjamb. "Because they were here, Julia. Dirck's killers were here."

"What? When?" Julia drew her into the cottage. "Come inside."

"You need to bring it in. They broke into my cottage, Julia." Celine twisted back toward the door. But she was too tired to resist Julia's efforts and allowed herself to be taken in and helped onto a couch. "They broke in while we were gone."

She recounted the details.

"Did you call Mailand?" Julia wanted to know.

"Not yet. I just wanted . . ." Celine gestured at the door, exhaustion taking over. "Dirck said it belonged to someone he and John were very fond of. It needed to be returned, he said." She looked up at Julia. "I think he was referring to Annabelle."

"Annabelle?"

"Bella, the woman I dreamt of. The woman Simon Underwood was telling us about. Bella is Annabelle Curtis."

"Annabelle *Curtis*? Did you say *Curtis*?"

But Celine's eyes had closed. "We need to get in touch with her . . . we need . . ."

"Celine?" She felt Julia's hand on her shoulder, heard her voice as if from a distance, but her eyelids remained closed, pressed shut. Her last conscious thought was of a blanket being thrown over her as she sank deeper into the couch.

Chapter Thirty-One

Blake absently regarded the note Ella had left on his desk while he'd been speaking with Julia Hood. It was a message from Penny Hoskins. Annabelle Curtis was Simon Duarte's sister.

Penny had provided Curtis's current address and phone number as well.

The information was redundant. Blake had already discovered these details for himself. But after his conversation with Julia, he'd found himself agreeing with the Director of the Gardner.

The Duarte-Bramer angle needed to be re-opened.

Blake fingered the note and pondered what he'd learned. He'd been able to confirm Simon Underwood's identity. The man checked out. He was also capable of forging a Vermeer.

The source of this information had offered Blake yet another tidbit.

One so compelling, it had convinced Blake that Duarte's sister was worth a visit. But even without that, a consideration of the facts had led Blake to dismiss the notion of a forgery being at play.

If Underwood had wanted to con the Gardner with a forged Vermeer, he would have done it years ago. To do so now, at the height of his career, made little sense.

Involving Dirck Thins in the affair made even less sense. It was a pointless complication. And, financially, neither man would've benefited from the paltry reward being offered.

That aside, why would the mob waste its time worrying about an attempt to return a forgery?

Well, all right, maybe it would. If the loot from the Gardner was being used as collateral for unsavory deals in the underworld, the return of even a potentially forged item could cause quite a stir.

The current possessor of the Gardner art would be in the unenviable position of trying to establish that the art was genuine—and, worse, might never even be given an opportunity to do so. In the criminal world, the mere suspicion of betrayal could cause heads to roll.

It was a dog-eat-dog world; you murdered first, repented later.

But then again, if either Dirck Thins or Underwood had been planning on returning a forged item, why bother hiding the work?

Blake set Penny's note down. He'd left a message with her personal assistant, informing her that the tip they'd been following had fizzled out; that the Vermeer the tipster had promised to return had turned out to be a forgery. But Blake didn't believe that to be the case.

Whatever Thins had been planning to return had yet to be found. Blake knew that because Mailand had called back with some unexpected news.

The detective had received a report of a forced entry into Celine Skye's cottage. The fingerprints on that scene matched the ones lifted from the Delft.

It was clear Dirck's killers had been looking for something—something quite specific. They hadn't found it at the Delft, so they'd turned their attention elsewhere. From a mobster's perspective, killing a man to prevent him from returning a forgery made sense; looking for said forgery did not.

No, most likely, the story Grayson had brought to the FBI all those years ago was true. Duarte and Bramer had made off with the Gardner art.

Had the mob found itself with nothing? That would explain why no trace of the art had been found.

Or had Duarte and Bramer left the mob with a bunch of forged items? An offense as brazen as that would merit instant death.

But it was Dirck who'd been murdered.

Why?

Because he knew where Duarte and Bramer were and had refused to divulge their location? Or because Thins had taken charge of the art?

Either scenario seemed likely. Especially if Grayson was right, that Duarte had survived the car crash all those years ago and sought refuge in Central California.

If that was the case, how had the mob come to learn that Duarte was still alive? And where was Duarte?

Blake tapped his fingers on his desk. He had his suspicions about the former. As to the latter, maybe Annabelle would know.

A man Celine couldn't see sat on the faded red couch—wrapped in an oblique beam of sunlight that obscured Celine's vision. Bella wiped her tears with a fierce swipe of her palm.

You need to tell her I'm gone, Celine. Dirck's low voice was tinged with regret. *Tell Annabelle I'm gone at last.*

"It wasn't an accident, Simon." Annabelle's voice trembled. She pressed the crumpled sheaf of papers in her hands to her stomach.

"Bella—" The man began. The light changed and Celine caught a glimpse of his face and the thatch of white hair.

Simon Underwood!

"That's what the police say. But it wasn't. They were killed." Strands of dark hair fell over Bella's young face. "And Simon, poor boy, knew they were after them."

Why did Bella look so young, Celine wondered. Why did Simon Underwood look so old? Weren't they the same age?

Tell her I'm sorry, Dirck whispered into her ear.

Sorry for what? Celine wondered . . .

❧

Annabelle Curtis lived in a red brick house on Beach Street in Revere. It was a ten-minute drive from the FBI office. Blake pulled up to the house, parking behind a brown UPS delivery truck.

In the fading light of dusk, he could make out the white Nissan parked along the side of the house. Annabelle was at home. A flight of four steps led up to a white door with a black handle. The windows were white, the sash on both sides thrown open.

The woman who answered Blake's knock was slender, the loose gray-black curls framing her face the only sign of age.

She peered at him. "Yes?"

"I'm from the FBI's Art Team, ma'am." Blake showed her his badge. "We're following some new leads in the Gardner Museum case."

She stared at him, face expressionless. Her hand remained on the door, though, and she stood motionless.

"Your brother was an employee at the Gardner Museum, wasn't he?"

"That was nearly thirty years ago, Special Agent . . ." She looked questioningly at him, his name already forgotten.

"Blake Markham," he prompted her.

"Well, Special Agent Markham, my brother's long dead. He can't help your case from the grave."

"No, but perhaps you can. May I come in, Ms. Curtis?"

"Mrs. Curtis," she corrected him, stepping aside.

Blake followed her into a small living room. Out of force of habit, he scanned his surroundings. The prints on the wall; the bottle of wine on the coffee table; the family photos on the mantelpiece above the faux fireplace.

Annabelle was either an excellent actress or she really was unaware that her brother had survived the car crash that had supposedly killed him all those years ago. They'd been close, according to Penny Hoskins. If Duarte had survived and deliberately chosen not to stay in touch with his sister, how would she take it?

For the first time since the beginning of this investigation, Blake felt a twinge of—not guilt exactly or even shame. But he was certainly not going to be proud of himself for the can of worms he was about to open.

"What leads are you following?"

The sound of her voice startled him. She pointed to the couch.

"You told me you were following some fresh leads. I imagine you had some reason for wanting to share them with me." Her smile was gentle, not warm, but certainly not unfriendly.

Blake sat down. They were days when he really hated his work. His instincts told him she knew nothing, but he needed something more concrete than that.

"We received a tip that the Vermeer stolen from the Gardner and the bronze finial have both turned up in Paso Robles. While the items haven't been recovered yet, our investigator"— Grayson didn't deserve to be exalted with that title, but there was no way Blake was going to admit to a civilian that the FBI had sent in a CI to investigate a lead—"did report something unusual."

He paused, trying to read the expression on her face. But Annabelle merely looked mildly curious. She raised her eyebrows.

"Yes?" she prompted him.

"Our investigator reported making contact with your brother—Simon Duarte."

"Is this some kind of joke, Special Agent Markham?" Annabelle didn't have an especially expressive face, but the fury written in her features was unmistakable.

Blake waited for her anger to subside. "We were as startled to hear of this development as you are—"

"Did it occur to any of you that your investigator might have been mistaken? That the man he spoke with may have been lying? Simon and Earl were brutally killed years ago—so badly burned their remains couldn't be identified. No one bothered to investigate."

"It was an accident, ma'am. An unfortunate incident. Their car ran off a cliff."

"And how do you think it ran off, Special Agent Markham?"

"You're saying there was a second car?" It was the first he'd heard of it. He didn't recall seeing any mention of it in the reports of the accident.

"Whoever robbed the museum killed my brother and his friend, Special Agent Markham. I tried telling the police that. No one was willing to listen."

Blake sat back. "Tell me what you know," he said. "I'm here. I'm willing to listen."

"Dirck and Earl loved that museum." Annabelle looked down at her folded hands and swallowed. "Like everyone who worked at that place, they were concerned about security."

"Or the lack thereof," Blake said.

She nodded. "Someone—I don't know who—came up with a plan to force the trustees to take notice. Dirck and Earl had a small part to play. But it went horribly wrong. It was all very wrong. That's what they kept saying over and over."

"That it was all wrong," Blake repeated softly.

Annabelle nodded again. "They wanted out, but they were threatened. They had to go along with the plan." She looked up at him, her eyes haunted. "And they knew they were going to die. Those poor boys knew."

She clenched her lips. Blake waited.

"A few days after they were killed, a friend of theirs came to see me."

"Simon Underwood?" Blake said, voicing it as a question, although he already knew the answer. Underwood had worked with Duarte and Bramer on those Vermeer forgeries that had taken the BU art world by storm and resulted in their professor losing his reputation and most of his grant money.

Underwood had kept in touch with his undergraduate friends even after the affair.

"He brought a letter with him," Annabelle said. "My Simon had set his affairs in order. There was a little bit of money he'd saved. He wanted me to have it—a college fund for Bryan, my son."

She raised her eyes. "All those years ago, the police wanted to know what evidence I had that Simon and Earl were killed. Well, that envelope and that money *were* the evidence."

"Where had he kept the money?" Blake wanted to know. That part of the story could be easily verified.

"At the First Street Credit Union. They've never had very many branches, but they have good rates for students."

"I'll check it out," he promised. His gaze circled the living room. "You've kept in touch with Simon, I see."

A couple of the prints showed the Mechelen Winery vineyards. The wine on the coffee table was a Mechelen product as well.

Blake's eyes returned to Annabelle's face. He wanted to see her reaction.

"My brother was twelve years younger than I, Special Agent Markham. When he died, it was like losing a son. I think Simon understood that. Those gifts of wine remind me of what my Simon could've done with his life. Earl and Simon and I grew up in a farming community, you see. Our families owned apple orchards.

"The boys were fascinated with art, but they soon realized they'd never be able to make a career of it. The job at the Gardner sparked a passion in them. They talked about owning farmland, growing peaches and plums or maybe even grapes."

Annabelle sighed. "John Mechelen and Dirck Thins nurtured their vineyard and built their winery from scratch. It's nice to hear of two Boston boys fulfilling a dream like that."

"I see," Blake said. John Mechelen had accomplished what Duarte might have had he remained alive.

Chapter Thirty-Two

The evening gloom had deepened by the time Blake emerged from Annabelle Curtis's house. The sound of an engine starting caused him to glance up. The UPS van parked up the street was pulling out of its parking spot.

It was rounding the corner when Blake pulled away from the curb. He followed the van around the corner, up a driveway, and into a garage. The white garage door slid down into position behind Blake seconds after he pulled in.

A lanky, uniformed individual with a handlebar mustache and a nerdy expression jumped down from the van.

"All set, Trevor?" Blake poked his head out of his car.

Trevor gave him a thumbs-up sign and grinned. "She took the bait, and it's working like a charm, bro."

Following a rushed court order to wiretap Annabelle's cell phone, Trevor had spoofed a call to Annabelle. Pretending to be a representative from her phone company, he'd persuaded her to make a few *security updates* on her phone.

The updates had resulted in Annabelle downloading LSS spyware capable of listening in on both her phone calls as well as any conversation she had within earshot of the device. Blake's call to Annabelle requesting an interview had served to activate the spyware.

"Stayed behind to test it," Trevor explained. "Heard you guys in there loud and clear."

"Great!"

"You think it's gonna work?" Trevor asked as Blake stretched his legs out of his car.

"It better," Blake replied. It had taken all his persuasive powers to show probable cause. If Duarte was still alive and Annabelle was aware of it, Blake's visit would prompt an immediate phone call to Duarte.

Even if Annabelle wasn't aware of Duarte's immediate location, Blake felt sure she'd call Underwood. And who knew what calls that might trigger?

Yes, they were finally getting somewhere. And with Mailand's upcoming raid on the San Luis Obispo address where Grayson had holed up—keeping tabs on his prepaid credit card had yielded rich dividend—Blake Markham hoped all the pieces of his case would fall into place.

A minor crackling from the van put both men on high alert. Their target was making a call. They rushed into the van, putting on their headphones in time to hear a phone stop ringing.

"Simon?" Annabelle said.

"Bella, what a pleasant surprise."

"Simon, someone from the FBI was here."

❧

Concealed in a Revere, Massachusetts residential garage, Blake and Trevor heard Simon Underwood sigh.

"This have something to do with the Gardner Museum heist?"

"Yes, how did you guess?" Annabelle said.

Blake couldn't hear Simon's response. Annabelle was talking over him.

"They've traced the art to Paso Robles. The Vermeer and the finial, at any rate. That's what they say."

"An FBI agent was here as well. Same story. They think—" Simon cut himself short. "I have some terrible news, Bella."

A short pause. Underwood must have been waiting for Annabelle to respond, but she said nothing.

"Dirck Thins—"

"Is he okay?"

"I'm afraid not, Bella. Dirck's dead."

"Oh no! I'm so sorry to hear that, Simon. I had no idea he was ill? What was it? A heart attack?"

"No." Simon's voice was so soft Blake had to strain his ears to hear him. "He was killed."

"Good God!" Annabelle gasped. "I'm so sorry. What you must be going through! And here I am calling, imposing on you."

"There's nothing you or I could've done about it, Bella. Besides, it's nice to hear your voice. Takes my mind off things. Tell me, what can I do for you?"

"Simon, the special agent who came here, Blake Markham, said his investigator reported seeing—" Annabelle hesitated. "It seems so crazy. But the investigator reported seeing my brother. In Paso Robles!"

"Oh, Bella!" Underwood sighed. "I'm so sorry—Simon never meant . . ."

"I told Special Agent Markham his investigator had been lied to. But who would do such a thing? It was such a cruel joke to play!"

"Bella, I need to—"

An unidentified noise interrupted the conversation.

"There's someone at the door, Bella," Simon said. "Can I call you back?"

Tell her I'm sorry.

Dirck's words played repeatedly in Celine's mind. But what was he sorry for?

Killing Simon Duarte and Earl Bramer!

The thought flashed behind Celine's closed eyes. She was awake, the dream still fresh in her mind. Dirck's words still rang in her ears. He'd known Duarte and Bramer.

Had he killed them?

Dear God, no! Celine's eyes flew open. Sunlight streamed in through the cottage window. A faint breeze carried with it the distant chirping and chattering of birds.

This wasn't her cottage! Where was she?

A jumbled assortment of memories flooded Celine's mind.

"Coffee?" Julia's voice intruded upon her consciousness just as Celine recalled the events that had brought her to the former federal agent's cottage.

She turned her head, feeling the soft pillow Julia had put under her head and the colorful quilt she'd thrown over Celine's sleeping form.

"I hope you're feeling well rested," Julia continued. "We need to talk. Simon Underwood—"

"I know." Celine sat up. "He was lying. He knew Duarte and Bramer. He visited Bella Curtis, Duarte's sister, after the car crash."

She recounted the dream she'd had. "Bella was certain it was no accident. Someone was after her brother and Earl Bramer."

The Boston mob, clearly. But had Dirck been part of the mob? Or somehow been involved in the two men's death? Was that the reason for the wine baskets he'd given Underwood to send to Bella? Prompted not by generosity, but by a sense of guilt?

These were thoughts Celine couldn't bring herself to mention to Julia. If Dirck had killed Simon Duarte and Earl Bramer, why hadn't he turned himself over to the police?

It sickened Celine to even think of the possibility. The Dirck she knew wouldn't have been capable of such a crime . . . *would he*?

"The question, of course, is why?" Julia's voice startled Celine.

"What!"

"Why was Underwood lying?" Julia brought Celine a steaming cup of coffee. "He pretended not to have heard of either man." She sat down and took a sip of her own brew.

Celine wrapped her chilly hands around the hot cup. Its heat and the aromatic steam that arose from the mug were somehow comforting. She took a sip, swirling the liquid in her mouth like a connoisseur swishing wine.

"How did you figure all this out, though?" Celine was genuinely puzzled. There'd been nothing to suggest Simon Underwood had been lying to them, had there?

Julia sat back, a smile illuminating her broad features. "While you were out, Sleeping Beauty, this former fed was at work. I made a few calls. By the way, Mailand says the fingerprints at your place match those at the Delft, meaning—"

"Meaning we were right. Dirck's killers were looking for something specific—the Vermeer, I suppose."

Julia nodded. "Then I called Francis van Mieris. He remembered Underwood and the two students who'd come up with the breakthrough idea of making tracings on oil paper. Want to take a guess who they were?"

"Simon Duarte and Earl Bramer?"

"Yes. I called Boston University. No one by the name of John Mechelen graduated from their art program—"

"Maybe he didn't finish the program," Celine said. "Didn't Simon tell us that Dirck and John began to think they'd never make it in the art world? Their background in farming was perfect for the venture they did have in mind."

But Julia was shaking her head. "No, Celine. No one by that name was ever enrolled in that program. It's not hard to see why. You see the real John Mechelen died as an infant."

"Then who was—?"

"I don't know."

"But Simon Duarte and Earl Bramer are dead. My dreams confirm that."

"And yet our friend Blake's CI reported seeing Duarte just the other evening. Speaking of Blake, he called van Mieris minutes before I did. So Blake now knows as much as we do about Underwood's relationship with Duarte and Bramer."

"If Underwood knew them both, then"—Celine frowned, trying to gather her thoughts—"then, do you think he knows where the Gardner art is?"

"I'm betting he does. And that's the other reason I wanted to talk to you. About that item you brought here last evening, any idea where Dirck might have got it?"

Chapter Thirty-Three

Blake swiveled around in his chair, winced as the morning sunlight hit his eyes, and quickly swung the chair back around to his desk. He'd returned to the office—exhausted, head pounding—after an all-night stakeout in the chilly, damp Revere garage Trevor had found for them.

They'd waited the entire night for Underwood to call Annabelle back. But he never had.

It had been frustrating. Blake was certain—and Trevor had agreed—that Underwood had been on the verge of making a significant revelation. Had he thought better of it?

Or had Underwood been prevented from revealing what he knew?

Blake tugged his tie loose and passed a handkerchief around his neck. But the cold, clammy sensation that had washed over him remained.

Who'd been at the door when Underwood ended his call with Annabelle? Simon Duarte?

That Duarte was still alive was apparent. Underwood's apologetic tone and the explanation he'd been about to provide had been evidence enough —to convince an investigator, at least, even if it wouldn't hold up in a court of law.

Had Duarte faked his death to escape the Boston mob? Or had he simply wanted to make off with the Gardner loot?

Blake was veering toward the latter explanation. Duarte may not have killed Dirck Thins—he doubted Duarte would have garroted his victim— but it did look like he hadn't wanted to be found.

Not if he'd intentionally cut off all ties with his sister, allowing her to believe for nearly three decades that he'd been brutally murdered. They'd been very close, Penny Hoskins had said.

For a brief moment, Blake thought about calling the Gardner Museum Director. If it hadn't been for Hoskins, he might never have considered getting in touch with Duarte's sister.

But what could he tell her—that Duarte might still be alive? And, no, he still had no idea where the Gardner's former employee was. And no way of tracing the man, either.

Nope, there was no point getting Penny's hopes up at this stage.

Blake reclined back in his chair and massaged his forehead. His head was still pounding. His mind returned to Duarte's sister.

Blake hadn't expected to, but he'd found himself liking her. She'd reminded him, oddly enough, of his own older siblings. And although it made his work more difficult, a part of him was glad Underwood hadn't gotten around to returning her call.

He didn't want to think about how she'd react to the news.

But Underwood's failure to return the call he'd promised to make was worrying. From the little Blake had heard, it seemed very out of character. And he didn't think Underwood would flake out on Annabelle quite so easily either.

No, there was probably a very good reason for Underwood's failure to call. A reason Blake didn't really want to consider. But he knew it would have to be checked out.

The suspicion gnawing at his mind that something was wrong refused to go away.

Eyes closed, Blake drummed his fingers on the desk. Was it worth collaborating with Julia Hood on this? She was in the area, familiar with the case, and she'd already made contact with Underwood.

His fingers tapped out a swing rhythm. Tempting as the idea was to involve a former colleague, he had to remind himself that Julia was a loose cannon. Moreover, her presence in Paso Robles had coincided with a murder connected to the Gardner case.

Blake didn't believe in coincidences any more than any other law enforcement agent.

"Coincidences are unicorns, ladies and gentlemen," one of his instructors at Quantico had declared.

Blake tended to agree.

He was wondering what to do when his cell phone rang. He opened one eye, forefinger stretched out, about to hit cancel, when he realized the caller presented the perfect solution to his problem.

"Do you know what's in here?" Julia pulled out a cardboard box from the cabinet under the kitchen sink. Gray duct tape dangled from the partially opened flaps.

Judging from its size—a fourteen-inch square—it was the container Celine had concealed between the floor joists of the barn for Dirck.

"Some type of bronze figure, I gather," she replied. "Nothing special, but not exactly a piece of junk either."

"I take it you didn't look inside." Julia pushed the flaps apart, put both hands in, and carefully lifted the object out of the box and set it on the floor. "Recognize it?"

Celine didn't—not at first.

It was a ten-inch-high eagle with its wings outspread. The head and large beak were turned to the viewer's right; the single eye that faced the viewer was elongated, wide, and angry; and the creature's talons grasped a ridged object with ends that tapered on either side.

"It used to be displayed in the room where we found Dirck's body," Celine said. She raised her eyes. "But that was quite some years back. The last time I remember seeing it was in an old photograph of Dirk and John taken in that room."

She'd used the photo some months back on a Facebook ad promoting both the Delft and the Mechelen. The eagle had so dominated the picture, she'd tried—unsuccessfully—to photoshop it out. Eventually, she'd just let it remain.

"Dirck didn't really like my using photographs of either him or John in the Facebook ads I created."

"But you did it anyway?" Julia was looking closely at her.

Celine shrugged. "Ads with faces and people get a better response. What was I supposed to do?"

"Who would have seen those ads?"

"Anyone in the country with an interest in wine or alcohol as well as art. Why do you ask?"

Julia let out a sigh. "Because I think we've just discovered what led the Boston mob to your employer and your bar?"

Chapter Thirty-Four

"You can't be referring"—Celine pointed, incredulous—"to *that*?" Her eyes roved over the bronze eagle.

There was something else vaguely familiar about it. Hadn't she seen it somewhere else? A photograph of it, perhaps—?

But the thought fled—chased away by Julia's sudden bray of amusement —before Celine could pursue it.

"Yes, *that*! Because that, my dear, is the Napoleonic finial, which—"

"I remember now."

She'd seen a photograph of it just yesterday in Julia's folder on the Gardner Museum heist. How could she have forgotten?

"But if I recall, there was more than one model created. How do we know this is the one from the Gardner? Or that it's not just a replica?"

There had to be a better explanation than the one Julia was foisting upon her.

"Because of the numbers on the base, Celine. The accession number, T17SI.a, identifies the finial as the property of the Gardner. But after it is a separate series of four numbers, the existence of which was never publicized.

"Deliberately, as you can imagine. So, no forger would ever be able to discover those numbers even existed, let alone what they were."

The former fed's words were like hailstones pelting Celine's brains. She looked up to find Julia's shrewd blue orbs on her.

"I don't understand," she said. "That thing has been here a long while. How . . . ?"

She shook her head, struggling to frame the questions in her mind. There were so many.

How had the finial come into Dirck and John's hands? How had they not known what it was? And if they had . . .

The sour aftertaste of the coffee she'd been sipping assaulted her senses.

Dear God! Why hadn't they returned it?

Julia ran her hand gently up and down the eagle's body. "It's interesting. I can feel no dents. No signs of fire damage or exposure to extremely high temperatures. You know what that means, don't you?"

"No," Celine's voice was soft. The images from the dream she still hadn't shared with Julia were beating incessantly against her mind. She'd tried to ignore them, but their implications in light of this discovery couldn't be denied any longer.

She wrapped her arms around herself, rocking back and forth to quell the nausea that threatened to overwhelm her.

Oh God! Oh, dear God! What had Dirck done?

Julia's voice penetrated her consciousness.

"Isn't it obvious? Duarte and Bramer faked their deaths. They didn't die. Therefore, neither did the art."

"Simon Duarte *is* dead, Julia." Celine glanced up, still clutching her stomach. "I told you . . . my dream—"

"We have to look at the facts, Celine. This finial, Grayson Pike's report of seeing Duarte, it all adds up."

"There's something I need to tell you, Julia. Something I heard in my dream that I haven't mentioned to you."

❧

Blake grabbed his phone.

"Detective Mailand? I hope you have good news for me."

A vague hemming accompanied by a crestfallen sigh told Blake that the news would be anything but good.

"We raided the address, Special Agent Markham, but . . ."

"But what?" Had Grayson already fled San Luis Obispo?

Mailand sighed again. "We were met by a frail, elderly lady. Fran Schumann."

Fran Schumann, however, had been very cooperative. She'd readily admitted to using the prepaid credit card. In fact, she still had a small amount remaining on it.

Blake was puzzled. "But this is the card our guy bought at a Paso Robles newsstand. How did it end up in this woman's hands? Where did she find it?" Not on Grayson's dead body, he hoped.

"It was given to her—"

"By?" Blake inquired, interrupting the detective. It was either a man by the name of Grayson Pike or someone named Greg Peters.

"By a man she met outside the local Costco."

That figured, Blake thought. Greg had been traced to Costco.

After a small hesitation, Mailand continued: "He claimed to have been heading for the airport, but apparently his wife, who was supposed to take him there, screwed him over. Fran says she saw the woman hurtling past them in the parking lot. She was driving like a maniac."

The story about the wife didn't make a lot of sense, but Grayson had evidently conned some woman into giving him a ride to the airport. *Clever.*

But Mailand's next words contradicted that expectation.

"She got his name—and most of his purchases—but it doesn't match either of the names you gave us. Fran Schumann claims to have gotten the card from a Geoff Brandt."

"*Geoff Brandt*?" The name sounded familiar. He'd seen it or read it somewhere quite recently. Where?

His wandering gaze settled on the untidy pile of passenger manifests on his desk.

Oh!

The penny dropped instantly. Grayson had made a deliberate detour to the Costco, made some purchases there to throw them off the scent. He'd succeeded, but just barely.

Blake pulled the pile of manifests closer, dug through it until he found what he was looking for.

Geoff Brandt had been a passenger on the Alaska Airlines Flight at 11:10 a.m. Its destination was Seattle, but most of the passengers booked on the flight had taken a second connecting flight to Boston.

So Grayson was back in his neck of the woods.

"Detective Mailand, could you follow up at the local Costco. I want to know—"

"Already on it, Special Agent. Anything else you want me to do?"

"Actually, there is." He explained about Underwood and Simon Duarte.

When he hung up, he pressed his finger down hard on the buzzer.

His finger was still on it when Ella poked her head in, wearing an annoyed frown.

"You can stop that. I'm not deaf, you know."

"Get on the horn with San Luis Obispo County Regional and find out what type of ID a passenger by the name of Geoff Brandt used to get on his flight. I'm betting it was a recently issued Costco membership card."

"Since when is that a crime?"

"I didn't say it was, Ella. But I have reason to believe Grayson is using that alias. That's why he went to Costco. *That* was his fake ID."

"Good grief!" Ella looked suitably stricken. "I'll fax over the composite I had made, shall I? I wish I'd done it first thing. We'd have been saved the runaround."

❧

"Why would Dirck say he was sorry, Julia?" Celine pressed the point, willing her friend to see the significance of her dream. "Why would he apologize right after he and I both heard Annabelle say her brother and Earl were killed? Simon Duarte told his sister someone was after him."

"Then that might explain why he and Bramer were on the run," Julia said. "You don't rip off the mob and expect to get away with it. That doesn't happen."

Celine expelled a frustrated sigh. Julia refused to accept that Duarte and Bramer were dead. Worse still, the former fed seemed unable to grasp Celine's suspicions about Dirck either.

Celine simply could not bring herself to express them any more openly than she already had: that Dirck was in some way responsible for what had happened to Duarte and Bramer.

"I know what you saw in your dream, Celine," Julia continued. "But when you first had it, you thought you'd find yourself telling Annabelle that Simon Underwood was dead. We know now that's not the case."

"I still think Simon Underwood is in danger." It was a feeling that refused to go away.

"Yes, but based on your current dream, he's still alive."

"Dreams are symbolic, Julia."

"My point, exactly. And learning to interpret them is a fine art that you, my dear, by your own admission have yet to master."

Celine sighed again. "Look, I don't know why the facts of the case contradict what I'm seeing in my dream or my feeling that Simon Duarte is dead. I just don't know."

Oh, Celine, Sister Mary Catherine's voice whispered in her ear, *you have everything you need to figure out what the truth is. Just put on your thinking cap.*

She ignored the voice. She couldn't stop feeling Duarte was dead, and yet she also sensed that *B-aw-ston* Greg had genuinely felt he'd made contact with Duarte two nights back.

Or thought he had. There was always the possibility that he'd been mistaken.

People change in thirty years. And *B-aw-ston* Greg had been more than a little inebriated.

"Why was Dirck apologizing?" she demanded. "What did he have to apologize for?"

Julia shrugged. "Maybe for the same reason that Underwood should be apologizing. They both knew Annabelle's beloved brother was still alive, and they kept that knowledge from her. They allowed her to needlessly grieve."

She heaved herself up from the couch. "Look, we can argue about this until the cows come home, but our best bet would be to go see Underwood again. Let's see what he has to say for himself once we confront him with the truth."

"And the finial?" Celine asked.

"It's going to be in a dryer full of clothes for now," Julia said. "And I've put a decoy container in the wheelbarrow just in case your friends decide to return or Bob Massie unwittingly blabs to someone."

She stretched her back, wincing as she did so. "It'll need to be returned to the Gardner. The sooner the better." Her gaze returned to Celine. "Are you up for a trip to Boston?"

"I guess." Celine wasn't at all sure she wanted to go. But there was little to keep her in Paso Robles. "The bar's going to be closed for a while. And I suppose Andrea can manage the winery by himself."

Who knew, maybe the change in scene would be good for her after all. It had been years since she'd traveled anywhere.

Chapter Thirty-Five

The First Street Credit Union was at the corner of Longwood Avenue and Binney Street. A little over a half-mile northwest of the Isabella Stewart Gardner Museum, Blake noted. And about a mile away from Boston University. Conveniently located for students—and anyone employed at the Gardner.

Blake wasn't surprised Simon Duarte and Earl Bramer had opted to bank here. Although the credit union had grown since the nineties—it boasted four branches now—its fees were still student-friendly, far lower than at the average bank.

He parked his car on the narrow road—the bike lane was as wide as each of the two lanes running down the two-way street—and prayed he wouldn't bump into the Museum's Director, Penny Hoskins.

It was the last thing he needed, he said to himself, eyeing traffic on both sides before jaywalking across.

He pushed through the glass doors into a brightly lit, pleasant space. Comfortable couches upholstered in muted shades of carmine, thick rugs patterned in white, gray, and crimson, and wall art painted in cheerful reds and oranges gave the place an inviting air.

A slim woman in a dove-gray business suit was at his side the moment he walked in.

"Special Agent Blake Markham?"

Blake nodded.

"Mr. Kevorkian is waiting for you," she informed him with a smile as she led him across the marble-tiled floor, through a door in the back, into a small office.

A graying, middle-aged man rose from his chair and reached across to take Blake's hand. "Special Agent Markham? Michael Kevorkian."

"Armenian?" Blake asked when the woman had left, and they'd settled down at the manager's desk.

Kevorkian smiled. "Yes! How did you guess?"

"It's the i-a-n," Blake explained. "It's a dead giveaway." He'd grown up next to an Armenian family, and his buddy Arman had provided that particular clue to Armenian identity.

"So it is," Kevorkian agreed. "But I imagine that's not what you're here to discuss." He pressed his palms together, interlacing his fingers. "What may I do for you, Special Agent?"

When he'd requested an appointment, Blake had explained that he needed records for an old account. But he hadn't mentioned any particulars. He did so now.

"The holders of both accounts are dead, Special Agent, and the accounts have long been closed. May I ask what this is about?"

It was a question Blake was prepared for. "Their names have come up in connection with a more recent case, and we've reason to believe that their deaths may not have been the accident we thought it was."

"Ah!" Kevorkian's bushy eyebrows shot up. "In that case, I have some interesting information for you." He pushed a slim manila folder across the desk to Blake. "A few days before the accounts were permanently closed, both young men came into the bank. They not only provided instructions on the disposal of the funds in their accounts in the event of their death—"

"Bramer declared a beneficiary as well?" Blake interrupted. "Whom did he name?"

"The same person as his friend Simon Duarte: Annabelle Curtis. Bramer apparently had no living relatives to leave his assets to."

"I see." Blake nodded. "I'm sorry I interrupted you. You were saying . . ."

Kevorkian leaned back in his leather chair. "They had a considerable amount of money in their accounts. They withdrew the bulk of it. Annabelle Curtis received a sizeable inheritance, but both men took out about eighty percent of what was in their accounts."

This was interesting. "How much was that?"

"Between the two accounts, close to a million."

Blake whistled. "As much as that!"

How had two presumably impoverished art students managed to get their hands on that much money? By selling the treasures stolen from the Gardner Museum?

At the time of the theft, the stolen art had been valued at about two hundred million dollars. Then as now, the Vermeer alone would have accounted for half that amount. At black market rates, a savvy thief might have expected to net close to twenty million for his efforts. About half that for just the Vermeer.

But for two young men such as Duarte and Bramer, a million dollars would have been a king's ransom. Moreover, a rube in the art theft field would need to rely on a fence. And in that case, a million would be a fairly generous amount.

"Special Agent Markham!" Michael Kevorkian's voice penetrated his wandering mind. He looked up. "Could the money have been the cause of their death?"

"It's a possibility," Blake replied. It had more likely furnished a means for their disappearance, but that was not a thought he could share with the bank manager.

He leaned forward. "All that money, suddenly withdrawn, didn't it strike you as being extremely odd? Suspicious even?"

Kevorkian smiled. "I was just a humble clerk back then. Manning the counter out there." He tipped his head outside the door at the four tellers attending to the credit union's few customers.

"Either the manager at the time saw no reason to ask any questions. Or, if he did, he was satisfied with the replies he received."

"I see," Blake said. "Any chance, the manager's still around."

Kevorkian's expression became grave. "I'm afraid not. Rawlins died very shortly after. Murdered. It was an unfortunate affair. His house was broken into; the intruders killed him. A senseless crime." He sighed.

"Murdered?" This was getting even more interesting. "By whom?"

"The case was never solved. There'd been a spate of bank robberies in the neighborhood. The police theorized that the killers may have wanted access to our vaults and that Jerry Rawlins refused to comply. Although whether they would've let Rawlins live after he'd provided the information is doubtful."

Blake agreed, although he didn't think Rawlins' killers were after bank codes or vaults. They were most likely enforcers for an enraged mob that had just discovered it had been swindled by a couple of rookie criminals.

Rawlins likely had no information about the whereabouts of Simon Duarte and Earl Bramer. But even if he had—and been willing to share it—he would have been no less dead.

The crime scene tape and the police cars around Simon Underwood's residence were visible as soon as Celine turned onto South Street.

The sight was jarring to her. Gripping the steering wheel hard, she eased her foot off the pedal. She turned to Julia.

"What do you think is going on there?"

"This must be Blake's doing." Julia leaned forward and peered through the windshield. "He probably uncovered some information that ties Underwood to the stolen art. I'd love to know what, though."

"I thought the statute of limitations had run out on the theft." The Pilot lurched forward as Celine pushed the gas pedal down.

"It has," Julia replied, her eyes still on the scene up ahead. "But you could still be charged for possession of stolen property. And if I'm not mistaken that's exactly what's happening here. Cruise forward, will you, so we can find out what's going on."

They'd barely approached the corner of South Street and Morro Avenue when a Morro Bay police offer stepped forward with his badge held out.

"I'll have to ask you to turn around, ma'am," he said when Celine rolled down her window. He jerked his thumb back at Simon's house. "Crime scene."

Julia leaned across. "I'm retired FBI, Officer." She showed him her badge. "May I ask what happened here?"

The officer hesitated, looked over his shoulder, then turned back around. "I'm not at liberty to say, ma'am. But if you'll wait here a minute, I can ask Detective Mailand if he'll talk with you."

"Just as I suspected," Julia said when the officer had left them. "This is connected with what happened at the Delft. And the Gardner."

"I have a bad feeling about this." Celine's eyes were riveted on the house. Simon was nowhere to be seen. *He's dead.* The thought flashed across her mind. Her fingers, wrapped tightly around the steering wheel, felt cold and clammy.

It seemed like an eternity before Detective Mailand walked out to them. The craggy lines on his face had deepened, settling into a forbidding, dour expression that intensified the moment he saw Julia.

He bent down and peered in through the open window. "What brings you here, Ms. Hood?"

"We were here to see Simon Underwood," Celine replied for her. "We had some questions for him."

"Some things that, upon reflection, don't add up," Julia added. "May we have a moment with him?"

"I wish I could say, yes." Mailand's gaze drifted toward Celine. "I'm afraid I have bad news for you, Ms. Skye."

Celine had to bite her lip to keep it from trembling, but her voice quavered nonetheless when she asked: "How did you know? How did you know to come here?"

Mailand's eyes were on Julia when he replied. "Your colleague at the FBI asked us to check up on him. He feared Underwood might be in danger." He paused. "Unfortunately, he was right."

"Same perps?" Julia asked.

"Looks like it." Mailand stood up. "Same MO."

⌘

Back in his car, Blake wondered why no one had questioned the timing of the deposits into and out of Duarte's and Bramer's accounts. They had occurred so shortly after the Gardner Museum heist, it was hard to believe no one at First Street Credit Union had thought to report the transactions.

He leafed through the file Kervokian had given him. The money had been deposited in four separate checks—two going into Duarte's account and two into Bramer's. Even so, the deposits were larger than any the two had made in their entire history with First Street Credit Union.

Either an overworked teller had slipped up, failing to report the amounts to Jerry Rawlins, the manager, or someone in the credit union—a teller or Rawlins himself—had been bribed to keep the amount under their hats.

Certainly, there'd been no additional scrutiny other than an automatic three-day hold on each check. A hundred dollars of the amount had been made immediately available, five thousand after the first business day, with the rest being made available by the third day.

The checks had clearly passed scrutiny, although nothing in the file told Blake who had signed them.

He set the file down on the passenger seat, started the car, flicked on his left turn indicator, and waited. A steady stream of cars drove past.

The deposits were suspicious. Clearly, Duarte and Bramer had been involved in something illegal. But the withdrawals were even more telling.

They were the clearest indication so far that Duarte and Bramer had intended to go on the run.

Why? Because they were genuinely in fear for their lives? Or because they'd double-crossed the mob? Blake didn't know.

He peered into his side-view mirror, waiting for traffic to sufficiently clear to let him merge in. The steady tick-tick of his indicator accompanied his thoughts.

No one had told poor Annabelle Curtis about the large withdrawals her brother and his friend had made shortly before their "accident."

"She never asked," Michael Kevorkian had told Blake. "I still remember her coming into the credit union to close the accounts. She was so distraught. All she wanted to do was get on with the business at hand. She barely paid attention to the information we did give her."

The withdrawals and everything Blake had learned thus far provided the first faint glimmer of corroboration for the cockamamie tale Grayson Pike had brought to the FBI years ago.

Duarte and Bramer had made off with the Gardner Art. And Blake was beginning to suspect they'd staged the car crash and faked their deaths. What better way to escape the mob than to die before they could dispose of you?

A lagging car afforded Blake the opportunity he needed. He was about to take it when his phone rang. He glanced at it.

Penny Hoskins.

He could swear the woman had a sixth sense for his whereabouts—and for the exact wrong time to call.

Sorry, Penny, you're going to have to deal with voicemail for now.

He pushed the gas pedal down and steered smoothly into the gap in traffic.

He'd call her just as soon as he possibly could.

Chapter Thirty-Six

Simon Underwood had been garroted with a thin wire and left for dead some time during the previous evening. Mailand had been able to ascertain that Underwood had received and responded to a phone call around about 6 p.m. Someone—his killer, or killers in all likelihood—had knocked on the door shortly after.

"There were no signs of a break-in, so he must have let his killers in."

How the Sheriff's detective had ascertained these details or even why Blake Markham had suspected Simon Underwood might be in danger, Celine didn't know. She sat with Julia in Mailand's makeshift office at the Paso Robles Police Station, her mind grappling with the news.

It felt oddly surreal to be here again. To be dealing with murder for a second time.

But at least Mailand wasn't treating them like suspects this time. If anything, he was being surprisingly forthcoming.

"Was anything found in Underwood's residence?" Julia's voice interrupted her thoughts. "Any paintings not by him?"

Mailand shook his head. "The place was in disarray. Whoever killed him had searched the place pretty thoroughly. The paintings that were there were pretty roughed up. There's nothing missing from what we can tell.

"And nothing that doesn't belong to Underwood either—other than a few fingerprints that matched the crime scene at the Delft and the break-in at your cottage, Ms. Skye."

"Then it couldn't have been Greg—Grayson, whatever his name is."

It was the one thought that stood out clearly in Celine's mind. She'd initially thought he'd had something to do with these events, but her cottage had been broken into and Simon killed after the man had already left Paso Robles.

"Unless, of course, he drove down from San Luis Obispo," she added.

"His fingerprints weren't a match for the ones we found. It wasn't him," Mailand said. "Although we still think he's a person of interest in that he might know or have seen something that could help explain who's behind this."

"Any luck finding Grayson?" Julia asked.

Mailand shook his head. "I'm afraid he led us on a wild goose chase. He conned a cashier at Costco into giving him a Costco Membership card without verifying his identification. He used that to fly into Boston. The prepaid credit card we were tracking down . . . he gave that to an elderly lady. It was a deliberate strategy to get us off the scent."

"Sounds suspicious," Julia remarked.

"No, he was probably just afraid," Celine said. She didn't know how she knew that. The thought had just popped into her head.

It was followed by another. "He's probably hiding in a church somewhere."

"I beg your pardon?" Mailand looked puzzled.

"She means," Julia said with a hard glare at Celine, "that churches often provide sanctuary to people—even those running from the law or the federal government. We were talking just the other day about illegal immigrants who take refuge within Catholic churches."

Mailand shrugged. "I guess that's as good a possibility as any. Of course, the other important bit of business is to find Simon Duarte. It seems he may have known both Dirck Thins and Simon Underwood. Now both men are dead. Can't be a coincidence, if you ask me."

"Anything useful on Dirck's cell phone?" Julia wanted to know. They'd stopped by his cottage before setting off for Morro Bay. But Dirck's phone bill had only shown phone calls to and from an unknown number. Simon Duarte's number, they'd both thought.

"And I was so sure Dirck was the one who'd called in that tip to the FBI." Celine had let the bill slip from her fingers, disappointed. Could she really have been so wrong about her employer?

The number had a Paso Robles area code, but the phone company, when Julia had called, had been unable to provide any information on it.

Mailand nodded when Julia shared that snippet with him. "Must have been the burner number Thins was using to call the feds," he said. "There was a burner app on his phone." He turned to Celine. "Any idea why he may have wanted to conceal his identity?"

Celine shook her head. Dirck hadn't told her he was calling the FBI. He hadn't told her how or why he'd come into possession of the Gardner's bronze finial. But at least he'd been attempting to return it. That was something.

"He must have thought he was in danger." What had Simon Underwood said—something about the FBI being in bed with the Boston mob? Could that have been the reason for Dirck's caution?

Julia had pooh-poohed the idea so strenuously when Simon suggested it that Celine hesitated to broach it again now.

She glanced at her companion. Why was Julia really here, she wondered. Two men had been killed since her arrival in town. And last night, Celine had conked out—so deeply unconscious, Julia could've come and gone, and she'd not have a clue.

Now Julia had the finial. Was she going to mention it to Mailand?

❧

Ella looked up from her computer, her round glasses gleaming, the moment Blake opened the door to the outer office. He felt a guilty start as their eyes collided. Why his personal assistant had that effect on him he had no idea. But she did.

She'd been waiting for him; he could tell from the way she leaned back in her chair and folded her arms across her chest.

"There you are," she said in the mildly disapproving tone of an elementary-school principal chastising a tardy first-grader.

She pushed her chair back and came around to him, a folder in her hands. "I've been fielding calls for you all morning."

Calls, Blake thought. There'd been more than one? He opened the door to his office and gestured Ella in.

"Penny Hoskins?" he asked as she strode past him. He didn't see who else it could be.

Mailand had already called in from the Sheriff's Office in San Luis Obispo County to report Underwood's murder.

"First Street Credit Union," Ella replied. "I thought that's where you went."

"I did. That's where I'm coming from. Traffic was—" He stopped himself. She was his assistant, goddammit, not his boss. She didn't need an explanation.

"Well, the manager called. More than once."

"What about?" He pulled a chair out for her and then went around behind his desk to his own comfortable black leather swivel chair.

"About the accounts you were interested in." She opened the folder and passed a paper across the table to him. "Simon Duarte and Earl Bramer each received a check for two hundred and fifty grand on March 11 and then a second check for the same amount on March 18, 1990."

Blake glanced at the paper. The checks had been from a Boston-based art dealership, Lawrence & Young. The first deposited a week before the Gardner Heist, and the second on the day of. It may not have looked suspicious then. But it sure as hell did now.

"First Street," Ella continued, "conducted the usual safeguards, checking with Lawrence & Young's bank to make sure the dealer's account had sufficient funds for the checks to clear, but it was just a formality."

Lawrence & Young had banked with Citizens Bank, Blake noted. It was a fairly prominent financial institution in the New England region. Respectable, well regarded, with never a sniff of anything remotely shady.

He looked up. "Go on."

"As a noted art dealership, Lawrence & Young habitually dealt with large amounts of money—cash and check. On a few occasions, they had made sizeable payments—although nothing to the tune of what Duarte and Bramer received—to clients of First Street, many of whom were up-and-coming art students at Boston University."

In other words, there'd been nothing untoward about the transactions.

Blake nodded to indicate he was following her. The additional transactions on the document Ella had handed him showed Duarte and Bramer receiving five hundred dollars each from Lawrence & Young just six months prior to the amounts they'd received in March 1990.

"So, when Duarte and Bramer showed up with these checks, First Street simply assumed their clients had struck gold?"

"That's right," Ella said. "Naturally, they saw no need to file a criminal referral form."

Because Lawrence & Young had been seemingly above suspicion, Blake realized. A known commodity. At least within the banking community. If only they'd heeded Ronald Reagan's advice to "trust, but verify."

"And when the teller casually asked the two men about their sudden fortune, they said their work was finally getting the interest it deserved. A couple of art collectors from Ohio thought they were destined to be the next big thing in the art world."

"A couple of art collectors?" Somehow Blake didn't buy that story. Art collectors, no matter how naïve, simply do not drop a quarter of a million dollars on works by unknown artists.

"It sounded fishy to me, too," Ella said, noting his skepticism with something akin to approval.

"You looked into it?"

"And missed my lunch doing so."

Ah! That's why she'd been so grumpy. Ordinarily, Blake would have been the one making phone calls.

"I haven't eaten either," he confessed. "Want me to have something brought in"—he pulled the phone toward himself, his fingers ready to lift the receiver—"and we can continue this conversation over lunch?"

Ella regarded him, head tilted, lips pursed, then smiled. "Okay. But make sure it's from Floramo's."

❧

Floramo's—about a two-minute walk from the FBI office—ordinarily didn't offer takeout. But an exception was usually made for the clientele at 201 Maple Street.

Blake placed an order for the veal cutlet sub, extra mushrooms for himself, and the chicken cutlet sub with extra cheese for Ella along with an order of fries and onion rings.

When it came, he allowed Ella to tuck in before pursuing details of her investigation.

He bit into an onion ring, chewed, and swallowed. "So you called Lawrence & Young, I assume," he began.

She shook her head, mouth full. "I tried to," she said after she'd swallowed. "But they went out of business five years ago when Lawrence passed away. Young had already died some years back. After Lawrence passed on, there was no one—except Lawrence's son who wasn't interested—to carry on the business. The son just liquidated the dealership's assets."

"So you called Citizens Bank," Blake ventured a guess.

"Who wouldn't tell me anything. They point-blank refused to send over any records pertaining to Lawrence & Young."

"Not surprising, all things considered," Blake remarked. He couldn't believe Ella had even gone that route. They had no probable cause for demanding the art dealership's financial statements.

"That they couldn't get a hold of you to confirm my requests didn't help either," Ella informed him.

Yet another reason for her initial irate greeting, Blake realized. "So what did you do?"

"I told them we were looking into a potential money laundering case that went all the way back to the nineties, and that Lawrence & Young may have been unwittingly involved. I mentioned the two checks issued in March 1990. Had they, I asked, looked into the individual who had paid Lawrence & Young just before they issued those checks?"

She took the last bite of her sub, washing it down with a quick gulp of Sprite.

"That got their attention. The manager still wasn't willing to reveal very much, but he did look into Lawrence & Young's deposits for that month. Turns out the dealer received four checks—signed by four different individuals—but all drawn upon an account owned by a company called Gold Star, Inc."

"A shell company," Blake guessed.

"Yup. It took me some digging to find out, of course. Care to take a guess who the director of the board of said shell was?"

Blake frowned. The name of the company had sounded familiar, but he couldn't place it.

"One William Longfellow Worth," Ella said.

W.L. Worth? Blake straightened up in his chair. W.L. Worth was the shady fence who—according to Grayson—had indicated that Duarte and Bramer had made off with all the Gardner Art.

When questioned, Worth had denied making that statement. But now here was a connection between Worth and the museum's two assistant gardeners. That was surely not a coincidence.

"Well done, Ella!" Blake said. He meant it.

"There's more."

He waited expectantly.

"Shortly after the FBI brought W.L. Worth in for questioning, Gold Star was dissolved. Its assets went into a bank account in the Cayman Islands."

"So something shady was going on—whether Lawrence & Young was aware of it or not?"

"Absolutely," Ella replied. "Citizens Bank suspected nothing. They went so far as to mention that Gold Star had made prior large payments to Lawrence & Young."

"All shady, I'm guessing." Blake scratched his chin. "If only we could get a look at those transactions."

But the connection to the Gardner Museum heist was too tenuous to convince a judge to give them the go-ahead.

Ella dabbed at her mouth with a paper napkin.

"Well, if my plan works out, we just might."

He gaped at her, visibly startled.

She pushed back her chair, amused by the expression on his face.

"Don't worry, Blake, it's all on the up-and-up."

Chapter Thirty-Seven

"You didn't tell Detective Mailand about the finial," Celine remarked as she put the gear into reverse and backed out of their parking spot. The Pilot made a smooth, wide arc onto the street.

"Why not?" Celine depressed the brake pedal, her hand on the gear, ready to move it into drive. She turned to face Julia.

You can trust her, Celine, Sister Mary Catherine had softly murmured into her ear. Based on that, Celine had decided against mentioning the finial to the Sheriff's detective. But now she wanted to know Julia's reasons.

If they were going to work together, they would have to trust each other. And for that, Celine needed more than her guardian angel's voice.

"There's a car behind us," Julia said, tipping her chin at the rearview mirror. "We'd better get moving."

Celine shifted the gear and took her foot off the brake, letting the Pilot roll forward. Her gaze slid to the right and then shifted back to the road. Julia looked as though she was collecting her thoughts, so Celine waited.

Julia sighed. "It was a spur-of-the-moment decision," she said eventually. "Not something you really think about. But"—she expelled another breath—"there were several fairly good reasons behind that decision. First, on the surface of it, the finial has nothing to do with either murder. We're assuming it does."

"We are?" Celine asked.

"Think about it. If you were on its trail, would you rip a painting out of its frame to find it?"

"I guess not," Celine agreed. It was the reason she hadn't initially considered it worth mentioning that Dirck had given her a container to hide hours before his murder.

"Second, if Grayson came to Paso Robles, drawn by the photo of the finial you inadvertently advertised on Facebook, then his presence in town coincides with one murder and has been followed by a second. Best that we keep our discovery on a need-to-know basis."

Celine stole another look at Julia. "I thought you said that my ad might have attracted the mob's attention."

Julia seemed to hesitate a fraction of a second. "I'm not so sure anymore. Given your targeting criteria, I think it's more likely that Grayson saw the ad. He's a lush—always has been. More into beer than wine, but you said you targeted anyone partial to alcohol. And he is heavily into art, I'll give him that."

"Then how did the mob come to know? Their enforcers obviously followed him here."

"That's what I'd like to know," Julia replied quietly. "If Grayson thought he'd discovered the whereabouts of the Gardner loot, he'd go straight to the FBI. It seems like he did just that. They bit, so there was no need to blab to the mob."

She paused, then said: "On the other hand, maybe he did blab. Perhaps it slipped out of him while he was drunk. But somehow I don't think that's what happened. He was after the reward money; why would he jeopardize his chances of getting his hands on it? No most likely Grayson kept this little tidbit to himself."

"And they found out . . . how?"

"I wish I knew. That he took off his tracker is telling."

"You think the FBI . . .?"

"I don't know." Julia cut Celine off. "What I'm more interested in is why Dirck offered up the Vermeer when he called in his tip to the FBI, but not the finial. Was he unaware of what it was?"

Celine thought back to the last time she'd seen her employer alive. Dirck had emphasized the value of the object he was giving her. It needed to be kept in a safe place, he'd said. *Away from prying eyes.*

"Dirck said he'd been keeping it for someone he and John cared for very deeply. He didn't think he could keep it any longer. It needed to be returned."

"You think he was referring to Simon Duarte? Or Earl Bramer?"

"He was talking about a woman. I can't help but think it was Annabelle Curtis."

"Duarte's sister." A playful gust from Niblick Road whipped Julia's ponytail to the front. She rolled up her window. "I wonder if that bronze eagle was stolen for her. It's not particularly valuable. Never has been. Its appeal is more historic than aesthetic.

"We ought to pay her a visit when we get to Boston," Julia said.

"And I'm going to have to tell her Simon Underwood is dead, after all."

It was clear to Blake that Simon Duarte and Earl Bramer had been involved in an underhanded scheme to sell some—or all—of the stolen Gardner art to disreputable collectors.

A premeditated scheme, given the dates on the checks. Duarte and Bramer must have approached William Worth and Gold Star well before the heist with a fairly clear idea of the works they'd dispose of.

And a fairly good idea that they'd soon be on the run.

Funneling the art through Lawrence & Young, a seemingly legitimate art dealer, would have been Worth's idea. Had Worth arranged for false papers and new identification for the two as well?

Blake rubbed his chin as he pondered the various threads of the case.

If Worth had helped Duarte and Bramer acquire false ID, it would make sense for him to surmise that the stolen art had been destroyed along with the two men—burnt to ashes in the fatal car crash that had supposedly taken their lives.

"And if I were Worth—and the FBI brought me in for questioning," Blake said to himself, "I'd deny making that surmise, too." To admit it would have forced Worth to confess to having knowingly dealt with some of the stolen Gardner art.

But for Worth to have drawn that conclusion, the checks issued to Duarte and Bramer could certainly not have been for the entire body of stolen art.

No. Blake shook his head. *Definitely not.*

Besides, if Dirck Thins' tip was to be believed, the Vermeer, at any event, had ended up in Paso Robles.

Had the four separate checks, then, been payment for four separate works of art? Or just the one?

Blake pressed his fingers into his temple. His cogitations were making his head hurt.

He opened his drawer, about to reach for his bottle of Tylenol, when his phone rang.

Penny Hoskins, according to the caller ID.

Jesus Christ! The woman was relentless.

❧

"You're a hard man to get a hold of, Special Agent Markham." Penny Hoskins' breathy, high-pitched tones made Blake's ears tingle.

He put a fraction of an inch between his head and the earpiece on the receiver. "I was out in the field," he said.

"Indeed." The rising tone of Penny's voice as she uttered the word made it clear she was expecting a report.

Blake wasn't about to give it to her. But he did owe her an account of his visit to Annabelle Curtis the other evening.

"Was Simon Duarte attached to his sister?" he asked.

"Very much so," Penny replied. "She was like a mother to him. I take it you've discovered he's in touch with her. I told you—"

"Actually, Penny, what I've discovered is that Annabelle Curtis mourns her brother today as much as she did when she first learned he and Bramer had been killed."

"She could've been . . . you know . . ." Penny hesitated.

"Lying?" Blake voiced her unspoken thought. "If you've met her, you'll know she isn't capable of dissimulation. Annabelle isn't just grieving for her brother. She's furious that what should have been investigated as a murder was allowed to go down as an unfortunate accident."

"Murder?" Penny sounded incredulous. "I just don't believe that, Blake."

"They were in fear for their lives," he told her. "They'd unwittingly agreed to be part of a heist that was meant to get the museum to be more proactive about security. When they realized that wasn't the case, they wanted out. But they knew too much."

Blake had bought that theory when Annabelle had first broached it. But after his recent investigation into Duarte's financial affairs, he'd begun to have his doubts. Had Duarte fed his unsuspecting sister a bunch of bull?

He wasn't ready to admit his suspicions to Penny Hoskins, however. Not just yet. And he certainly wasn't ready to admit to her his strong suspicion that Duarte might still be alive.

He thought he'd made a powerful case to the contrary. And there was one fact that made it even more compelling.

"You can't really believe that Duarte would have allowed his sister to believe he was dead all these years." That cinched it—or so he thought.

He wasn't prepared for her reaction.

"I think the evidence suggests that he might just have," she replied quietly.

What evidence? Blake wanted to ask, but didn't.

"The finial has turned up. In Paso Robles—exactly where your tipster hinted the Vermeer was."

"And you know about this—?" Blake let the question dangle.

"From your retired colleague, Julia Hood. She's flying it here. There's no question it's the real thing."

He heard a rush of air as Penny exhaled.

"Special Agent Markham"—they were back to last names, he noted, and this time she wasn't being playful—"The FBI has consistently given us the runaround. For three decades, we've had to press for the few updates we've been given.

"I really thought things would be different with you. That you'd accord us some respect, treat us like partners. But clearly, I was wrong. I'm just grateful that Julia Hood hasn't given up on us. And I'm grateful, that unlike you, she thought to inform us of this important new development in the case."

Blake lowered his eyes—a tacit apology—not that she was there to see the gesture. He hadn't known about the "new development," he wanted to explain. But she wouldn't have believed him.

"I apologize," he said. "I didn't want to offer any false hope. And over the years, despite our best efforts, we seem to have done just that, Ms. Hoskins. But with all due respect, how does the re-appearance of the finial prove that Duarte is alive?"

It was the only item stolen that could've escaped complete destruction from the fire that had consumed Duarte's vehicle. If indeed, that was what had happened.

"Because there are no signs of fire damage on the finial, Special Agent. None. It was never in a fire. I'm guessing Duarte and Bramer weren't either. The bodies found at the site of the car crash were too blackened and charred to be properly identified. Clearly—"

"I understand," he interrupted gently.

He really did. The pieces were beginning to fall into place.

Grayson had mentioned the finial. It was in Paso Robles, Grayson had said. If he hadn't lied about that, there was no reason to believe he'd lied about seeing Duarte either. The only question was: where was Duarte?

Chapter Thirty-Eight

Celine unlocked and pushed open the front door of the Delft. A stale, musty odor greeted her when she stepped inside. The bar was no longer a crime scene—all the evidence Detective Mailand and his team might need had been bagged and tagged.

But the cleaning crew the Coroner's Unit had recommended to Celine wasn't going to be available until the following week. By then Celine would be in Boston. That was yet another task their winemaker would have to supervise.

Andrea hadn't been too happy about her decision to leave at a time like this, but he'd fortunately offered no argument against it.

"Are you still up for this?" Julia asked, following her in.

They'd returned to the bar to search for any trace Dirck might have left of his doings prior to his death. Anything at all that could tell them what and how much Dirck knew of the Gardner heist. If he'd promised to return a Vermeer, surely some clue to its whereabouts could still be found here.

"Sure," Celine said. Her throat felt hoarse—as though she was being choked. A sensation possibly due to the residue of negative energy that remained from the murder. She cleared it as she surveyed her surroundings.

Someone—possibly one of the crime scene technicians—had set the bar stools and chairs upright. But the walls were mostly bare—bereft of the paintings that gave the Delft much of its character. And a thin layer of dust had settled on everything.

All of that could be cleaned. But the stain of death would mark the bar forever. There was no getting rid of that.

"Shall we?" Julia's voice interrupted her brooding. The former fed gestured toward the room where Dirck's body had been found. The wall panel separating it from the bar was still retracted. It was a secret space that no one but she and Dirck and John had known about.

Now, thanks to the news of Dirck's murder, all of Paso Robles—possibly the entire county of San Luis Obispo—was privy to its existence.

"This is where—" Celine averted her eyes, flailing from the images that accosted her the moment she set foot inside the concealed room. She gripped the door jamb, suppressing the nausea that threatened to overwhelm her. "There's a closet in here where Dirck and John kept their most significant belongings, their most important possessions. Anything of a sensitive nature, really."

Celine sighed as she recalled what Dirck had told her the last time she'd seen him alive. "Most of it pertains to the business. Wine recipes, business plans." She tapped out the code on the thermostat and waited for the closet door to slide open. "But it's possible Dirck thought to keep other important items here."

The finial had been stored in the closet until Dirck had entrusted it to her that night. Could the Vermeer be here as well?

The closet door was now fully open revealing rows of shelves stacked with overstuffed files and folders; sheaves of paper with crinkled corners protruded untidily from each. A four-foot-high safe stood in the center.

"I don't think Mailand's team had a chance to search in here" she informed Julia. "This is a cleverly constructed space, and you'd have to know it existed to even begin to wonder how to access it."

"Pretty fortuitous that Dirck happened to tell you about it just before he died."

"He must have had some forewarning of what would happen," Celine said. Dirck's odd behavior that night was finally beginning to make sense. "That entire evening he was bidding me farewell. And he must've wanted me out of there before his attackers arrived. That's why he was rushing me out."

A wave of nausea overcame her again. "Oh, God! I can't believe he's gone. And Simon, too."

She doubled over, clutching her midriff.

Julia's strong hands gripped her shoulders. The former fed remained silent, but the heavy pressure of her hands was comforting.

"We can do this another time if you'd prefer," Julia said softly.

Celine shook her head, bracing herself. "No, we're here now."

Besides, they were leaving in a couple of days. There would be no other time to return.

They sifted through the papers, finding nothing more interesting than business plans, tax returns, and documents pertaining to the living trust the estate had been put in.

"The safe," Julia said. "You wouldn't happen to know the combination, would you?"

Celine shook her head. Dirck hadn't gotten around to revealing the numbers that opened it. But she had an idea. "Dirck liked to keep things simple," she said as she twisted the dial clockwise three times.

Then, she proceeded to twist the dial, first clockwise, to the first digit of the code that opened the concealed closet; then counterclockwise to the second digit; clockwise again to the third digit; and counterclockwise to the last digit.

A welcome click sounded in their ears, indicating she'd cracked the code. "I'm guessing that's why he changed the code to the closet every week. He probably reset the combination to the safe at the same time."

But when they opened the door to the safe it was apparent that *The Concert*, a painting about 28.5 by 25.5 inches, wouldn't have fit within it. The metal shelves were welded in, each at a height of about eight inches from the one below. The safe itself had an overall depth of a little over two feet.

An envelope with color photos spilling out of it lay on the topmost shelf. On the next was a bundle of correspondence. Celine pulled out the bundle and examined the postmark on each envelope.

They'd all been mailed from Boston. And they were all addressed to Simon Underwood.

"What was Dirck doing with these?" She pulled out a few handwritten sheets from one of the envelopes and turned to the last page. "From Annabelle Curtis."

"Are they all from her?" Julia wanted to know.

"Looks like it." Celine sifted through the other letters. They all ended with Annabelle's name, inscribed in a large, rounded hand across the page. Many were accompanied by photographs of herself, her son, and her husband.

"What could Dirck have wanted with these?" Celine asked again. "And why would Simon have let him keep them?"

"I'm guessing it was so that the other Simon—Simon Duarte—could stay in touch with his sister."

"Then Dirck must have known where he was." At least, he hadn't been responsible for the man's death.

"It would seem so." Julia's tone was oddly non-committal. She reached for the packet of photographs. Most were pictures of a fruit farm.

"Appleway Farm," Celine read the sign. "Isn't that where Simon Underwood said Dirck grew up?" According to Underwood, the Thins had sold the farm shortly after Dirck had left for Boston.

"Umm … hmmm," Julia murmured. She continued to shuffle through the photos. In one, a middle-aged couple stood smiling in front of a sprawling farmhouse. The man bore a faint resemblance to Dirck. A few showed a slender young woman with a baby in her arms.

"That's Annabelle," Celine exclaimed. "I had no idea she knew Dirck that well. They must have grown up together."

"Looks that way," Julia said. Her voice remained neutral. Celine glanced at her. They were far closer to finding Duarte—and the truth—than they had been. But Julia seemed strangely unenthused.

Celine wondered why.

Don't close your mind, Celine. She heard Sister Mary Catherine's voice in her ear. *Don't close your mind to the truth.*

And what truth might that be, Celine wondered, but her guardian angel hadn't stayed behind to answer that question.

❧

Blake had just begun to draw a few tentative conclusions about Duarte's whereabouts—he'd combed through the notes on his interviews with Annabelle Curtis and Michael Kevorkian three times before an insight surfaced, bolstered by a playback of his last conversation with Grayson Pike when Ella poked her head in.

"SAC wants an update on the Gardner case."

He looked up, mildly irritated.

"Couldn't you do it?"

Some key details needed to be ironed out before he could confirm he was on the right track. The time wasted gabbing with Special Agent-in-Charge James Patrick Walsh could be better spent working the case.

Ella shook her head. "Sorry. He wants you. In person, he says."

But when Blake walked into the anteroom, he was met by a smiling intern who informed him that SAC Walsh and his personal assistant had both just gone into a meeting. An unscheduled meeting.

The news—delivered with an apologetic smile—did little to appease Blake's irritation. It was typical Walsh. But he swallowed his ire, giving the young lady a brief message for her boss—and his.

"Developments in the Gardner Case," she repeated, jotting Blake's words on a notepad. "Anything specific you'd like to report, sir?" She glanced up at him expectantly.

Blake hesitated. But the intern—Mary, according to the nametag pinned to her breast—was the person who'd received Dirck Thins' tip. It was her initiative that had resulted in the call being traced to Paso Robles and her diligence that had resulted in the detailed report that had landed on Blake's desk.

She'd been rewarded with a transfer from the hotline to the SAC's office. But a few more details about the case would not go amiss, Blake figured. She'd make a good agent. And people like her needed to be encouraged.

"We have some reason to believe our missing CI is back in Boston. And —this is big news—the finial has been recovered."

"Wow!" Her eyes widened.

"Absolutely," he agreed. "Give Ella a call when the SAC is available to meet, will you?"

It was just a few minutes after he returned to his office when Ella showed Mary in.

"SAC wants a written report, sir," the intern said.

"I'll email it to him within the hour," Blake promised.

Mary hesitated. "He'd prefer it handed in to his office, sir. Reasons of security."

"Fine," he said. He didn't understand Walsh's reasons, but he wasn't about to argue. Not with an intern at any rate.

Chapter Thirty-Nine

Celine leaned forward to peer out of the cabin window. She and Julia were in the first class cabin of Flight AA 518, which was now approaching Boston Logan International. The seat belt sign had come on several minutes ago when the plane began its descent.

Slender wisps of cloud floated in a crisp, azure sky that overlooked a splendid expanse of cyan blue water. It was a breathtaking view, but the knot in Celine's stomach tightened as she gazed down at it.

"Cold?" Julia asked, her warm hand closing over Celine's icy palm.

"I'll be fine." Celine forced herself to smile.

Paso Robles was enjoying a spell of warm weather. It had been in the high seventies when they'd left. Boston was going to be at least ten degrees cooler. But although Celine could sense the change, it wasn't the temperature that was making her shudder.

From the time they'd made the decision to come to Boston, the Lady—Celine still found it hard to think of her as Isabella Stewart Gardner—had made her presence felt.

There's danger where you're going, Celine, Sister Mary Catherine had whispered to her. *Belle's watching over you.*

Recalling the warning, Celine forced her eyes away from the view of Boston harbor below and turned toward Julia.

"We'll need to be careful." She fingered the pendant Julia had given her—a silver cross with a tiny heart-shaped amethyst in the center. It was, Julia had said, a gift from Keith Elliot, the psychic detective she'd come to know in New Hampshire.

"It should help hone your psychic energies," Julia had told her when she'd given it to her.

There are choices to be made, Celine, Sister Mary Catherine now whispered as Celine's eyes fell on the red duffel bag sitting between her and Julia.

The bronze finial, carefully wrapped, was in it, tucked between two layers of Julia's clothing. *You'll need to make the right one.*

"You're sensing danger," Julia said. It wasn't a question. "You think Dirck's killers are on our tracks?" The former fed's expression was grim as she followed Celine's gaze to the duffel bag.

"I'm not sure how they know." Celine closed her eyes. The attempt would be made as soon as they landed. She was sure of it. Within her stomach, it felt as though her intestines were twisting themselves into tight knots. The pain was excruciating.

"I can't imagine how they could have found out," she said again.

The only person Julia had called had been Penny Hoskins, the director of the Gardner Museum. And that call had been made on a secure line.

"I wonder if the Gardner Museum phone was tapped," Julia mused out loud. "Or could Penny have mentioned the fact to someone else? I did tell her to keep it quiet. But this is an exciting development, and . . ." Her voice trailed off.

She patted her hip. "We'll face whatever comes our way. I'm armed."

"But"—Celine felt Julia's eyes on her—"I am worried about you. Protecting myself is one thing. Taking care of an unarmed civilian . . ." Julia inhaled deeply. "Well, it is what it is."

Celine nodded, opening her eyes. The plane had descended even lower. A building caught her attention—a square structure constructed of glass and metal with a staircase unfurling, ribbon-like, onto a deck that projected out onto the harbor.

She pointed. "What is that?"

Julia leaned across. "The tall glass building is Pier 4. The shorter structure next to it is the Institute of Contemporary Art. Remarkable, isn't it?"

But Celine didn't reply. The view below had faded, replaced by a deserted wasteland. Rickety piers extended out onto the water. Dilapidated warehouses loomed up toward a dark sky. A truck lumbered into an empty parking lot.

"This is it, man," she heard a long-familiar voice say.

It belonged to Dirck.

In the arrivals lounge at Boston Airport, as she and Julia waited for the carousel to deliver their luggage, Celine braced herself for trouble. The Lady stood directly across from them, staring so intently, Celine found it impossible to look away.

There's danger, Celine, Sister Mary Catherine warned again. *It's not a question of "if," but "when." Think carefully about the choices you make.*

Julia glanced at Celine. "Everything okay?" she asked.

Celine nodded. Her face, reflected in the shiny metal column rising above the carousel, looked pale and wan. Her hands felt cold and clammy. It didn't help to know that a single decision of hers could either put them in harm's way or keep them safe.

But then it didn't help to know a lot of things, Celine reminded herself bitterly

She wasn't sure what was making her more nauseous—the prospect of running into Dirck's killers or the implications of the vision she'd had as the plane landed.

The truck she'd seen had been transporting the stolen Gardner art to the Seaport district. In the early morning hours of March 18, 1990—hours after the theft. And there'd been no mistaking the voice she'd heard.

Her murdered employer was clearly more closely—and more directly—involved in the Gardner Museum heist than she'd realized. To what extent had he profited from it, she wondered. And the business he and John had built up—had that been financed by the Gardner's stolen treasure?

God! No wonder, Dirck had attracted the attention of the mob.

Focus on the present, Celine, Sister Mary Catherine's low voice cut in through the thoughts swirling in her brain.

How can I? Celine was beginning to respond when Julia's voice penetrated her consciousness.

"Well, what do you think?" Julia hauled her baggage off the carousel.

"About what?" Celine forced herself to concentrate.

"You haven't heard a word I've said, have you?" Julia's lips twitched, forming an amused half-smile. "Oh good! There's yours," she exclaimed as Celine's light-blue bag came into view. She lifted it down effortlessly and turned to Celine.

"Rent a car or take a cab?" she asked. "There are pros and cons with either choice. It would be good to have our own ride in case we're tailed. On the other hand, I don't like the idea of being liable for damages to a car we don't own."

"It's still the better choice," Celine said quietly. "If we took a cab, we'd be drawing an unsuspecting individual into our situation—a life-and-death situation."

"Rent it is, then." Julia turned decisively around.

Celine followed the former fed, fingers crossed, hoping she'd made the right decision.

"I'll be glad to get the finial out of our hands and safely back at the Gardner," Julia said over her shoulder as she briskly walked toward the Enterprise-Rent-a-Car counter at the airport.

A long line of people waited ahead of them.

"Great!" the former fed huffed. "This could take forever!"

"Or not." Celine smiled as she caught sight of a uniformed man holding up a placard with their names. "Looks like Penny Hoskins sent someone for us." Relief set in for the first time since they'd landed.

She caught his eye and held up her hand—two fingers and a thumb extending upward.

"Exce—" Julia began to say as she turned around, but the word was instantly replaced with an imprecation.

"You were right," she hissed. "Trouble's here!"

Celine frowned. "I don't understand." Sister Mary Catherine was uttering her warning about choices again. The Lady was obscuring her vision—a semi-transparent screen through which little was visible. "What is it?"

"Blake Markham." Julia's voice was tight.

❧

A tall, well-built man in a suit was striding purposefully toward them.

"Julia! Ms. Skye?"—he held out his hand—"Blake Markham, FBI."

There are choices to be made, Celine. Judge wisely.

She took his outstretched hand as he turned to Julia and said: "I'll be escorting you to the Gardner Museum."

"There's no need for that, Blake," Julia replied coldly. "I'm quite capable of handling the situation."

Celine's head swiveled from Julia to Blake. The hostility between the two agents was palpable. Her gaze shifted to the sea of people beyond.

The Gardner's uniformed chauffeur was pushing his way through the crowd. She'd need to make another quick decision.

She turned to Blake.

"How did you even know—?"

"About the item you've recovered?" Blake's eyes—narrowed to suspicious slits—never left Julia's face. "I'd say common courtesy dictated we should have been told. This is still our case. I'm even more surprised that you didn't think to mention it to Detective Mailand.

"What could your motive have been, Julia?"

Julia cocked her head to one side. "I'm guessing Grayson Pike came to you with a story about having discovered the location of the item."

Blake didn't respond, but the sudden widening of his eyes gave him away.

The uniformed chauffeur was approaching. Celine held up her forefinger —silently asking him to stay put. He nodded to indicate he understood and kept his distance.

"Grayson wanted the reward money, didn't he?" Julia continued softly. "He wouldn't have jeopardized his chances of getting it. And the reward for bringing back the Vermeer would be even greater.

"So why would he have brought the mob to Dirck Thins' bar? The answer is, he wouldn't? The leak must have come from somewhere else."

Julia's insinuation that the source of the leak stood right in front of them was so thinly veiled, it took Celine by surprise when the special agent agreed with her friend's assessment.

"That's why I'm here," he responded with a smile. "To ensure the item does actually find its way back to where it belongs." The smile grew wider. "We wouldn't want to hear that you were unfortunately waylaid, now, would we?"

His innuendo was even more plainly voiced than Julia's had been. But his words had unexpectedly illuminated the path for Celine. There was just one thing she needed to clear up.

"Special Agent Markham, you haven't answered my question: How did you know the *item*"—she was using their euphemism for the finial—"was in our possession?"

He turned to her—his gray eyes cold. "From Penny Hoskins, the Director of the Gardner Museum. I understand"—his gaze returned to Julia—"that you did at least inform her of its discovery."

"Fine, we'll go with you." Celine turned to Julia. "I have no objection to that."

"Why?" Julia looked both outraged and betrayed. "The Gardner's sent a car and—"

"And we'll dismiss it," Celine said firmly. She turned to Blake. "I do fear we might be attacked. If it does happen, I'd prefer that a federal agent be a witness to the crime. Someone who's armed and able to protect us.

"We don't accept the Gardner's car," she explained to Julia, "for the same reason that we weren't going to take a cab. The strong potential for drawing an innocent bystander into the fray.

"I assume," she went on, gaze shifting back to Blake, "that you're armed and that the car is armored."

He gave her a curt nod. "Yes, ma'am, it is."

Chapter Forty

The chauffeur from the Gardner had at first been startled when Celine dismissed him. But when she'd cut through his objections, a flicker of displeasure had crossed his features.

"As you wish, ma'am," he'd said coldly.

His reaction had taken Celine by surprise and annoyed her no end. But Julia had intervened before Celine could say anything. "Please thank Ms. Hoskins on our behalf," the former fed gracefully interjected. "We'll be with her very shortly—"

"They'll be accompanying me." Blake held out his badge. "Special Agent Blake Markham. Ms. Hoskins knows who I am."

He ushered them out of the airport. "The sooner we get out of here the better."

Celine found herself agreeing as she hurried after him. The image of the Lady had faded, but she could sense they weren't completely out of danger. Not while they still lingered at the airport.

"I hope you know what you're doing," Julia hissed into her ear. "If the finial doesn't reach its destination—"

"It will," Celine said, more confident in her decision now that they'd emerged from the arrivals lounge. A black Chevrolet Suburban slid up to the curb alongside them and purred to a stop. Blake held open the door.

The interior was more spacious than a Tahoe, but Celine was still partly miffed—and partly amused—to find herself sitting between Julia and Blake.

She pulled the seatbelt over her shoulder, struggling to find the slot for the buckle. "Feels like an outing with Mom and Dad," she muttered.

Blake glanced down at her. "Sorry about that. But you'll be safer between us."

He turned to Julia. "You should probably call Penny and tell her we're on our way. Knowing her, she's not going to be too pleased about your dismissing the car she sent."

"Already on it," Julia responded curtly. She clutched her phone to her ear.

"Hello, Penny!" She launched into her apology. "What!" Her blue eyes had widened. "Oh, I see . . . No, no. Nothing to worry about, we're on our way." She hung up.

Her palm—fingers still gripping her phone—dropped to her lap.

"What is it?" Celine ventured after several minutes' of silence had elapsed and the shell-shocked expression on Julia's face had yet to subside.

Julia's head swiveled slowly to face her. "The Gardner didn't send a car for us."

"You mean—"

Julia nodded. "Yes. That was the attempt you feared. I ought to have realized something was fishy. I never requested a car. And Penny had no way of knowing when exactly we were arriving. I didn't share our arrival time with her."

The former fed hadn't shared those details with the FBI either. But it was one thing, Celine realized, for the FBI with all its resources to discover those details. Quite another for Penny Hoskins or anyone else to have come by them.

Julia's eyes shifted to Blake, her expression grim. "You know what this means, don't you?"

Blake stared back at her. "I just don't believe it," he snapped, but Celine could sense he was worried.

"Did you mention our arrival to anyone?" she asked.

"SAC wanted a report," he muttered.

"Special Agent-in-Charge," Julia explained for Celine's benefit. "He heads the Boston bureau."

"Then that's where the leak came from." Celine couldn't have explained how she knew that, but as soon as the words fell out of her mouth, she was certain she was right.

"Don't be ridiculous!" Julia and Blake snapped simultaneously.

"An intern," Celine uttered the words as they flashed across her mind. "Is there an intern?"

"No . . ." Blake began to say, then his face turned pale. "Oh God! Mary. She's the intern who took Dirck's initial tip about the Vermeer, took the initiative to trace the call, and—"

"Immediately informed her boss on the dark side," Julia commented drily. "When was she moved up to the SAC's office?"

"Shortly after her work on that tip. I can't believe—" Blake stopped himself, grabbed his phone, and barked out a few instructions. He waited a few minutes, his expression earnest. Then his face fell.

"Oh great!" he said—and hung up.

"She didn't show up to work today," he informed them. "Nothing about her checks out. The name so generic, she could be anyone. The address is fake. She's gone—like a fart in the wind," he concluded bitterly.

"Doesn't matter. We still have the finial." Celine was determined to look on the bright side. Then as another thought occurred to her, she turned toward Blake. "I'm curious—why didn't you let the SAC know you were planning to meet us at the airport?"

"It was . . . uhmm. . ." he hesitated, a faint trace of red suffusing his cheeks.

"A spur-of-the-moment decision," Julia guessed. "To ensure the FBI had a presence at the Gardner when one of its lost pieces was returned. Even though you had nothing to do with its recovery."

"Something like that," Blake mumbled.

Celine found herself reaching out and squeezing his hand—now, why had she done that? It was inexplicable. Special Agent Markham was a grown man not a youngling in need of reassurance.

"We're both glad you did," she informed him. "You were instrumental in saving us—and the finial. Julia and I were on the verge of taking that car. I thought it was a Godsend when I saw that guy holding up a placard with our names on it."

The memory made her shudder. She'd made the right decision. But what if she'd been swayed by Julia's hostility toward a former colleague? What if . . . ?

"Way to give a man credit, Celine." Julia rolled her eyes. "And for something he had no idea he was even doing."

The Suburban sped through Williams Tunnel under Boston Harbor—"We're ninety feet underwater," Julia informed Celine, her voice sounding hollow —and then emerged onto the 90 West.

"Seaport's to our right." Julia seemed determined to make what was essentially a business trip seem like a tourist visit.

Celine started to say she knew where Seaport was but stopped herself just in time. She wasn't ready to explain how she'd come by that knowledge just yet. But Julia's remark had dislodged a memory or two and these in turn had raised questions—issues that only one person could clear up.

"We'll need to see Annabelle Curtis." She'd kept her voice low, but Blake had overheard and turned sharply toward her.

"Why?" The single word uttered so forcefully, it sounded like the explosive report of a gun.

She wasn't prepared for the question either, and it took several seconds before she was able to frame a response.

"She was close to Simon"—Celine's voice choked as she uttered the name —"Simon Underwood."

"I understand." Blake dropped the matter as abruptly as he'd brought it up.

"And I want to know if she recognizes the finial," Celine softly added.

"I beg your pardon!" Blake's torso twisted around to face her.

Celine felt herself squirming under his piercing gaze. *He likes Annabelle,* she thought. *Respects her even.*

"Celine has psychic abilities," Julia intervened before the silence could grow any more uncomfortable. "Her visions suggest the finial was intended for Annabelle."

"What visions?" Blake demanded. His gray eyes—darkening in anger— bore through Celine.

He couldn't have been more outraged, Celine thought, if she'd put forward the bizarre notion that it was his sister who was the intended recipient of the finial. She provided her explanation, attempting to gently guide him to her conclusions.

"There's also the fact," Julia added once she'd finished, "that Dirck never mentioned the existence of the finial when he called in his tip."

The former fed inhaled deeply as though forced to confront a difficult truth. "He may, I suppose, have been concerned that the FBI had a mole within its ranks—someone who'd instantly deduce that the existence of the finial meant that his friend Duarte, at least, was still alive. I think it's safe to conclude that John Mechelen was, in fact, Earl Bramer—and he died some months back."

"Or Dirck had no idea what he had," Blake said. Celine couldn't understand why the special agent was giving Dirck the benefit of the doubt. But she could contain herself no longer.

"I'm pretty sure Dirck knew exactly what he had," she burst out.

"Celine!" Julia gently touched her arm.

Celine shrugged her hand off as the Suburban slowed smoothly to a halt in front of a large, square steel-and-grass structure.

"Let me get out. It's stifling in here."

So this was the Gardner, she thought as she stood on the sidewalk. She'd barely had time to take in the new wing and the art installation on the façade —a rough, almost crude, line drawing in blue of a fish—when she found herself gazing at the yellow exterior of the museum as it had appeared on a dark night decades ago.

There'd been a hatchback parked on Palace Road—directly behind Evans where they were now—on the night of March 17, 1990.

"The truck was on Tetlow in the rear of the museum," she said as the images receded.

"What truck?" The question erupted from the mouths of her law enforcement companions at the same time.

Celine closed her eyes, the bile rising within her yet again.

"The truck that transported most of the art to Seaport," she said.

She opened her eyes and met Julia's gaze straight on and elaborated:

"The truck Dirck was driving."

❧

Celine Skye's revelation hadn't been as much of a bombshell to Blake as it had for Julia. He followed them into the lobby, gazing out at the tall lacebark elms and witch hazels of the Lynch Garden as his companions approached the admissions desk.

He'd initially been skeptical of the woman's abilities, barely able to refrain from an involuntary eye-roll when Julia mentioned them to him. But he was compelled to admit: she was pretty good.

But Blake could tell that even Celine Skye hadn't put it all together. Yes, Dirck Thins had been involved in the Gardner heist. Blake had come to that conclusion shortly after his last conversation with Penny Hoskins.

But the special agent had uncovered far worse. He'd hesitated to reveal every last detail, however. Despite Julia needling him when he'd agreed with Celine.

"You're trying to say Dirck Thins returned from Canada, making his first stop in Boston to join forces with the mob on an art heist?" Julia's ponytail had flicked from side to side as she shook her head. "And there was no record of his presence here?"

"Returned from Canada?" Celine's head had pivoted from Julia's to Blake's, but neither agent had cared to elaborate any further.

It had taken Blake a good measure of self-control not to blurt out the key detail he held. But one glance at Celine's face had convinced him the young woman was neither psychologically nor emotionally ready to face the truth about her employer.

He didn't know much about the occult, but he wondered if Celine's emotional state was blocking her intuition—providing tantalizing half-truths.

He could tell Julia felt the same way he did. It didn't take a psychic to sense that his former colleague had shared none of the details she'd dug up about Dirck Thins with her young friend.

"She'll have to face the truth someday," he said to himself, his gaze lingering upon Celine's slender, erect back. She looked so fragile, so young.

Annabelle would have to face the truth as well, but Blake was convinced she could handle it.

"She's waiting for us." Celine looked over her shoulder and gave him a smile. "Fourth floor."

He smiled back. "Up we go, then."

Chapter Forty-One

Penny Hoskins, Director of the Gardner Museum, was waiting for them in a spacious office in the new wing designed by Renzo Piano. The tastefully displayed floral arrangements and lush potted plants on their way up had helped Celine relax.

She took in the Director's beautifully appointed office, noticing that it afforded an expansive view of Evans Way Park just across the street.

"Oh, there you are!" Hoskins rose—a slim woman in her fifties with gray shoulder-length hair framing her classically beautiful features in a bob. "I hope you enjoyed our art installation—*Blue on Blue.* Put together by our artist-in-residence. Fabulous, isn't it?"

Her green-blue eyes homed in like a pigeon on Celine's face.

"Absolutely," Celine tactfully agreed, although the rough line drawing, left uncolored on a plain white background, hadn't much appealed to her.

Hoskins' eyes traveled toward Julia, and her face took on a rueful expression. "I'm sorry about all that confusion with the car. I didn't realize you were expecting to be met . . ." her fluty voice tapered breathlessly off.

"We weren't," Julia assured her quickly, providing a brief account of their encounter at the airport.

"I have to ask," Julia went on, "did you happen to mention our recovery of the finial to anyone—anyone at all?"

Hoskins' eyes, Celine noticed, flickered toward Blake. She didn't appear particularly happy to see him, and if Celine had to take a guess, she'd wager Special Agent Blake Markham had lost all credibility in the Director's eyes.

Blake, for his part, seemed to bristle under Hoskins' gaze. "Other than me, Julia meant—obviously." The addition of the final adverb didn't seem to endear him to the Director.

"Of course." Hoskins' eyes snapped back toward Julia. "Other than the Head of Security and myself, no one's been informed about this happy turn of events. We've kept this quiet—as you requested. But"—her pupils suddenly expanded, a slender, well-shaped hand fluttering to her mouth—"Oh my God, this must mean someone's after the finial. Again!"

"It does." Some ideas were beginning to crystallize in Celine's mind. "I don't think whoever was behind the heist received the entire consignment of stolen art."

"And, naturally," Blake added, supporting Celine to her surprise, "they've been on the lookout for the works for about as long as you have."

"I—" Penny broke off abruptly, a frown marring her smooth brow. "Oh dear, where are my manners?" she exclaimed. "Come in, sit down. Let's look over the finial, and then you can tell me all about this theory of yours."

❧

Several minutes later, Penny Hoskins was gazing enraptured at the bronze eagle finial.

"My God, it's the real thing!"

Her voice was low and breathy as she passed her hands gently over the finial, her head lovingly following its contours.

"I can't believe it."

Penny smiled at Celine. "All these years later, one of our treasures back where it belongs. I can't thank you enough—for doing the right thing."

Celine shrugged. "I was aware it needed to be returned. I just didn't know to whom. If it weren't for Julia recognizing the piece . . ." She lifted her shoulders in another delicate shrug.

It felt awkward to be thanked so effusively for simply doing what was right.

"But how," Penny began, her eyes still on Celine, "did you come up with your theory—that the person behind the theft was robbed as well? You're not a detective, are you?"

"No, she has psychic abilities," Julia explained.

"*Oh!*" Penny's eyebrows arched up ever so slightly, as though she'd been presented with an obvious forgery. "And so you contacted—"

"No, I contacted Celine," Julia interrupted the Director. "And roped her in."

"Not that it would take a psychic to come up with the theory Ms. Skye's put forward. It's the only explanation that fits," Blake came out in support of Celine as well. *For the second time in fifteen minutes.* She must have made quite the impression on the man.

"This is the mob we're talking about, Penny," Blake went on, oblivious to Celine's glance of surprise. "They don't take too kindly to being ripped off."

"Ripped off?" Julia leaned across Celine, staring hard enough to bore a hole through her former colleague's brain. "What exactly have you found out, Blake?"

Blake hesitated—his pupils sliding toward Penny—and cleared his throat. "I owe you an apology," he addressed his remarks to the Director. "When I met Annabelle Curtis, she was adamant her brother and his friend were both dead. Murdered, she said."

"Just as I suspected," Celine murmured. She'd sensed right from the start, hadn't she, that Simon Duarte was no more alive than Dirck?

"Annabelle insisted the two men were in fear for their lives. To corroborate her story, she offered up details about the steps they'd taken to name her as a beneficiary if anything happened to them—apparently not long before they actually died."

Blake paused, loosening his tie. "I checked out the credit union—mainly to verify her story." He paused again. "And what I discovered about their accounts and their final transactions convinced me that Duarte and Bramer had faked their deaths."

He summarized the financial details for them.

"The only thing I'm not sure of," he said, wrapping up his report, "is whether the money they received was for only a part—or all—of the stolen works."

"So I was right?" Penny asked. "They're still alive?"

"Was Grayson Pike employed here about the same time as Duarte and Bramer?" The question was out of Celine's mouth before she could rephrase it to sound less like a complete non-sequitur.

Penny looked bewildered by this sudden change of subject, but responded readily, nevertheless. "Yes, they were all hired around the same time."

"Then, I guess he'd have been able to identify them if he saw them decades later. When he came to the Delft, he saw a portrait of John Mechelen and instantly pointed out his startling resemblance to Earl Bramer. In fact, at first he tried to insist that it was Bramer pictured in the frame."

"The real John Mechelen," Julia added, "died as an infant in Boston. So it's safe to say, under the circumstances, that the man masquerading as him in Paso Robles was Earl. The faux Mechelen died of natural causes a few months back, so there's no hard evidence to back us up. But I think we're on the right track."

"And Simon Duarte?" Penny was watching them intently.

"Probably still in Paso Robles," Julia replied at the same time that Celine and Blake blurted out, "Dead as well, most likely."

Celine looked at Blake. That was the third time, he'd agreed with her. But another question had surfaced.

"If Duarte wasn't killed in a car crash, then how did he die?"

Blake's eyes drifted toward Julia's. A look passed between them that Celine didn't quite understand.

"I'm afraid the reasons for my conclusions are somewhat tentative. I . . ."

Penny nodded. "Can't share them, until you're absolutely certain?" she asked, still nodding. "We understand."

She looked at them all in turn.

"Now, is there any chance some of the art might have remained here in Boston?"

Chapter Forty-Two

The hopeful, eager expression on Penny Hoskins' face caused Blake a surge of anxiety.

He leaned forward. "Why, what have you heard, Penny?" It wouldn't be the first time the museum had received a bogus tip and chosen to act on it.

She glanced down at her slender fingers drumming a nervous beat on her desk.

"I thought we'd agreed," he said after another minute had elapsed, "that you would allow the FBI to conduct an initial assessment before responding to any tip."

Penny's features hardened into an expression of stubbornness.

"It's been thirty years, Blake. We owe it to ourselves—and the public—to act upon any viable tips that come in."

Blake sat back, trying to digest this information. The Gardner had received a tip and not considered divulging it to the FBI. He wanted to ask if it was even viable, but Julia beat him to the punch.

"And you think this one is plausible?" Julia asked. She sounded encouraging not adversarial, and Penny nodded, opening up instantly.

"Well, after what you've just said," Penny replied, "I think it is very credible."

It irritated him that his former colleague had gotten that much out of Penny, whereas had he asked the question, she would have instantly jumped down his throat.

He saw Julia give Penny a reassuring, "do go on" nod. *Jesus, why encourage the woman*, he thought. But he realized, too, it was the only way they could coax any details out of Penny.

Penny smoothed her skirt. "You said didn't you that you think not all of the stolen art remains in the hands of the original thieves? Wouldn't that suggest that some of it does? And Blake's already confirmed the Vermeer isn't in Paso Robles—"

Blake felt heat suffusing his cheeks as all three women turned toward him. He hadn't voiced it in quite such categorical terms, had he?

"I meant the tip we received hadn't panned out," he backpedaled.

"But there've been two murders in Paso Robles," Julia countered.

"I'm aware of that." Blake was having a hard time containing his anger. He glanced at Celine. What did she think of this nonsense? She hadn't said a word since Penny had brought up the tip, but her forehead was wrinkled.

"Two things seem very clear," Julia was saying to Penny. "Dirck Thins was murdered by the mob; and his killers were looking for something. I doubt it was the finial. It would be impossible to conceal a bronze figure behind a canvas."

"No, no." Penny frowned, considering the implications of what Julia had revealed. "So you think the Vermeer is in Paso Robles?"

Blake had had enough.

"We don't know that," he said, his words colliding with Julia's: "It's not something we can rule out."

Penny turned to him.

"What *do* you know then, Blake?" she snapped. A blaze of anger he'd never before seen flashed in her eyes.

Regaining her composure, she turned to Julia.

"I'm sorry, Julia. But nothing you've said assures me that it would be a good idea to reject this offer out of hand. In fact, I don't think we can afford to reject it."

"You've received an *offer*?" Celine's frown had deepened. She wasn't liking the sound of this any more than he was, Blake thought. "Not information. But an *offer*?"

Blake had wondered at the choice of word, too. Out of the corner of his eye, he saw Penny nod.

"The person who called," she elaborated, "has offered to return the Vermeer."

"In exchange for—?" Blake probed.

"A monetary consideration," Penny replied stiffly.

He waited for her to provide the figure, but she remained silent.

"And where and how will this exchange take place?"

Penny shook her head. "I'm sorry I can't provide those details to you, Blake. Any suggestion that the authorities are involved, and the deal's off.

We'll never see our Vermeer again. The last time we allowed that to happen —" She broke off abruptly, shaking her head.

"April 1994," Julia said softly. "I remember that. The anonymous letter offering to return the entire stolen collection in return for 2.6 million dollars wired to an offshore bank."

"Ten percent of the value of the stolen art at the time," Penny said. "And" —she turned to Blake—"if we hadn't shared the information with the FBI, we might've gotten our art back."

The tipster had divined, somehow or the other, that the FBI was monitoring the situation and had immediately backed off. Blake had been about ten at the time and nowhere near the FBI. But, of course, that didn't prevent Penny from personally holding him responsible for what had happened.

He had read the report, though, and he wasn't so sure the Gardner had any chance of regaining its art at the time.

"Or stood to lose a pile of money for a portfolio of rubbish," he muttered in response to Penny's remark.

The letter had seemed authentic enough, but the money was to be paid regardless of whether the art checked out or not. In fact, he didn't recall the letter-writer giving the museum a chance to even examine the works before shelling out the ransom.

Penny glanced sharply up at him. "We're willing to pay ten million dollars just for information, Blake. I don't think a few million dollars for the return of a painting—the most expensive one of the lot—is too much to ask."

"Not if it's genuine," Celine said quietly. "The question is: is it?"

Chapter Forty-Three

The armored FBI vehicle turned right, skirting the beautiful eleven-hundred-acre chain of parks known as the Emerald Necklace. Celine suppressed a sigh. The nine-minute drive to the Revere Garden Inn would have been enjoyable were it not for the endless bickering between her companions.

Celine pushed herself back against the leather backrest as Blake leaned over her to address Julia—they were seated in the same configuration as on their earlier ride with Celine between the two agents.

"I don't understand why you're supporting Penny in this foolhardy scheme."

Celine didn't understand it either, and when Julia shared her reasoning it made even less sense.

"This is a good way of flushing out Grayson Pike," Julia explained calmly. She spoke slowly, drawing out each syllable as though conversing with an idiot. "Who else do you think could have come up with this offer?"

Celine wasn't sure Grayson was involved at all. In fact, she wasn't sure he had the Vermeer—or any other work of art, for that matter. But it was also clear that Penny Hoskins wasn't going to be deterred from her plan. And who knew, something might develop from allowing Penny to follow through on it.

Celine's gaze flickered toward Blake. The special agent was exhaling slowly as though willing himself to be patient.

"When Grayson fled Paso Robles, Julia," Blake reminded his former colleague, "he was in a hurry. He had nothing on his person. Neither did Geoff Brandt, his alias, as he boarded a plane out of San Luis Obispo Airport. Nothing resembling a painting, at any rate."

"What other leads do we have? This is still worth a try. If nothing else, it'll lead us to Grayson."

"How?" Blake demanded. He sounded frustrated. "We don't even know where the exchange is taking place."

The Director of the Gardner had also made it clear she wasn't going to divulge any details of where and when the ransom would be paid in return for Vermeer's *Concert*.

"Round house." Celine spoke for the first time. She'd seen the words over and over again in her mind as Penny spoke of the offer she'd received. Celine had no idea what the words meant. They hadn't been accompanied by any images that made sense.

"Round house!" Blake repeated.

"Do you mean a house or structure that looks round?" Julia probed.

Blake looked away and snorted. "God, this could be anywhere. In Boston, out of Boston. Who knows!"

"I don't know," Celine said. "I just saw the words when she was speaking. It must mean something."

"What else did you see?" Julia was gazing intently at her now. "The psychics I've worked with frequently receive words and images in disjointed fashion. They have no idea how they connect up, but those disparate pieces of information can make sense to the intended recipient."

Celine shrugged. She gazed out the window. The car was turning left onto a street called Riverway. They were surrounded by greenery. It was exquisite. The trees jogged her memory.

"I saw green—trees. A park, I guess. At dawn." But Julia had ceased to listen.

"A round house," the former fed murmured to herself. "Trees. Park." She repeated the same words in the same sequence a couple of times before throwing her head back and loudly exclaiming: "*Oh!* Round House!"

"What!" The expression on Blake's face suggested he thought his former colleague had lost her mind.

Julia jabbed a finger at the window. "Riverway. The historic Round House at Riverway, Blake. That's where the exchange is taking place. Well done, Celine!"

"Riverway?" Celine wasn't getting it.

"It's a thirty-four-acre park," Julia explained. "We're driving alongside it. There are paths that follow the course of the Muddy River. And there's a round, brick structure. It's called the Round House. That's why you kept seeing those words."

A veil seemed to have lifted from Blake's face. "I can work with that," he said. "You don't happen to have guessed the day and time as well?" He turned expectantly toward Celine.

"Early morning is my best guess. Sometime this week. Probably in the next day or two." Logic was taking over. "I doubt she'd have mentioned it if the arrangements hadn't been finalized."

"No, you're right, she wouldn't." Blake clutched his phone, fingers tapping feverishly upon the screen.

He wasn't going to make any phone calls, Celine guessed, until after he'd dropped them off at the inn.

❧

The Revere Garden Inn was a three-story, powder-blue Victorian clapboard structure at the corner of Littell Road and Stearns in Brookline. The FBI armored vehicle eased to a stop by a narrow sidewalk and let Celine and Julia out.

Blake rolled his window down and thrust his head out. "I'll call you as soon as Annabelle lets me know when she's available to meet," he promised as the Suburban began pulling away from the curb.

Julia acknowledged the words with a nod and a brief palm-up gesture of farewell. Then she turned around and gazed up at the front porch, extending out before the inn in a wide semi-circle.

"I'll be glad to put my feet up for a while," she confided as they climbed the short flight of steps to the porch. She pressed the tip of a stubby forefinger to the doorbell. "I'm beat."

"Me too," Celine said as the door opened.

"Ah, there you are!" An attractive woman in her mid-thirties greeted them with a smile. "It's Celine and Julia, isn't it?"

She barely waited for their nod before going on: "I thought your flight must've been delayed. Stuart and I have been expecting you for hours." She stepped back from the doorway. "I'm Ann, by the way. Ann Revere."

Celine gave her a friendly smile, then allowed her gaze to wander. The lobby was cozy, its floor carpeted in red and its walls covered in a pink, floral-patterned wallpaper.

"They're here," Ann called over her shoulder.

A corridor ran past a red-carpeted staircase on the left and a partially open door on the right that led to what looked like a parlor.

A stoop-shouldered, bespectacled man emerged from the parlor just as Celine spotted it. "I hope you've had a pleasant flight." He held out his hand. "Stuart Revere." The smile widened. "No relation to the more famous Paul. Welcome to the Revere Garden Inn."

"Built by Rupert Revere, landscape designer." Julia's words earned a smile from their hosts. She'd taken the trouble to read up on the inn's history when she'd booked their rooms.

"The house was built by Rupert," Stuart said. "My grandfather—Rupert's son—decided to turn it into a bed-and-breakfast. It was too big for the family. So he figured he'd let the rest of the world enjoy our house and grounds."

The Reveres seemed like a pleasant, chatty couple. But God help anyone who tried to get a word in edgewise, Celine thought. Not that she was complaining. She was quite content to just listen.

Ann signed them into the inn ledger and produced a couple of keys. "You're in the Rose Room," she informed Celine. "You, Julia, get the Lilac Room."

She handed Julia a key and gestured toward the corridor. "Both rooms are down that way. The only other room there is the Garden Room. That's occupied as well, so you'll have some company."

Celine murmured her thanks and was about to pick up her bag when Stuart stopped her with a smile. "Allow me," he said. He grabbed her bag and Julia's. "I'm afraid we're short-staffed this week. No bellhop. Just Ann, me, the cook, a new cleaning woman, Rosa, and the other cleaning staff. But we'll do our best to make you comfortable."

"There's a fresh pot of coffee and refreshments in the dining room when you're ready," Ann added. "Do help yourselves."

Chapter Forty-Four

In the Revere Garden Inn's dining room, Celine had just selected a pot of apricot preserves to go with her blueberry bread when Julia entered the room.

The former fed picked up a plate and surveyed the spread. "What do you make of it all?"

The question clearly wasn't about the food. It was about the bombshell Penny Hoskins had lobbied at them. Celine pulled a chair out for herself and waited until Julia had helped herself to a muffin and joined her at the oval dinner table.

"Dirck must have known he was risking his life calling in that tip. Why else would he have gone to such trouble to conceal his identity and his location?" Mailand had told them Dirck had been using a burner app on his phone to contact the FBI.

Julia buttered her muffin, but her eyes, as she took her first bite, remained on Celine.

"I'm convinced Dirck knew exactly where *The Concert* is. He wasn't lying to the FBI. And he must have realized that calling in that tip would be like drawing blood in shark-infested waters."

"Meaning . . . ?" Julia frowned.

"Meaning that whoever Duarte and Bramer double-crossed has been on the lookout for the art. This individual doesn't have the Vermeer. Dirck does —or did. And he didn't reveal its location"—*what in the name of heaven had her employer meant that it was hiding in plain sight?*—"Whoever called Penny is just trying to palm off a forgery."

"That's a possibility." Julia took another bite of her muffin and chewed thoughtfully. "Or maybe it was Grayson trying to capitalize on what he has."

"You think he'd risk his life to do that? He's running scared." Celine had no proof of this other than her own strong feeling that this was the case.

"And I doubt he has the Vermeer." Nothing anybody said would make her doubt that.

Celine wasn't sure if the Vermeer was in Paso Robles. She strongly suspected that it was. But she wasn't sure. She was absolutely certain, though, that Grayson didn't have it.

"I still think Penny's tip is worth pursuing," Julia said. "It could lead somewhere."

"It might," Celine agreed. She ate the last bite of her blueberry bread and helped herself to another slice. The bread was delicious, and she was unusually ravenous this afternoon. Her hand hovered over the pot of apricot preserves, then moved on to the jar of strawberry preserves.

"But I don't think it'll lead to Grayson." She spread the strawberry jam on her slice of bread and licked the spoon.

Julia's only response was a sigh of resignation.

"We do need to find him, though," she said a few minutes later. "Find Grayson, and we'll be one step closer to finding Dirck's killers. And, if you're right, nabbing his killers will bring us one step closer to identifying the mastermind behind the Gardner Museum heist."

The word "General" fluttered across Celine's mind. It was accompanied by an image of the finial. The name "Napoleon" followed it. Napoleon had risen to the rank of general, she thought—only to realize her mind was wandering.

These words and images obviously meant nothing. Celine pushed them to the back of her mind and forced herself to concentrate on Grayson.

"He's in Boston, that much is clear." Special Agent Markham had confirmed that. "Holed up in a church, I'm pretty sure." A word surfaced in her consciousness.

Celine repeated it. "Sanctuary."

Julia set her mug down. "You mean the sort of church that provides sanctuary to illegal aliens? There are at least two that I know of. The Old South Church on Boylston Street and Bethel AME Church."

She helped herself to a hard-boiled egg. "But there's got to be others."

Not that kind of church, Celine thought. Not that kind of sanctuary. But before she could unravel the ideas her intuition was throwing up, a bright voice interrupted them.

✄

"Churches? Did I hear you mention churches?"

A slim woman about Celine's age stood at the doorway, an inquisitive expression on her face.

Celine took in the woman's sensual figure leaning against the doorway, lips parted in a slight smile, head thrown back. How long had she been standing there?

Celine turned to see Julia's startled eyes on her. The same question must have crossed her friend's mind.

"A passenger on our flight was telling us about a church." Julia glanced over her shoulder at the woman. "A must-see place, according to her. But we can't for the life of us remember the name."

"There are plenty of churches here that are rich in history and worth visiting."

The newcomer sashayed in, walked past a display of tourist brochures, and pulled out a map.

She handed it to Julia.

"There's the Old South Church that your friend was mentioning." She pulled out a chair next to Celine's. "I'm Lillian, by the way." She smiled; her eyes, strangely wide, unblinking, roving over Celine's features as though taking their measure. "In the Garden Room."

"That makes us neighbors, then." Celine forced herself to smile. There was nothing overtly suspicious about Lillian. She seemed friendly enough. But something was putting Celine on edge.

It was probably just social awkwardness and her usual inability to warm up to strangers, she told herself. Celine had never been as vivacious as her mother. But what little social ability she'd possessed had vanished when her parents had died. Celine had withdrawn into herself, and never quite recovered.

"What other churches would you recommend, Lillian?" She forced the words out of her mouth.

"Depends on what you're looking for." Lillian's gaze shifted toward Julia. But the former fed was too busy buttering up another muffin to respond.

In the silence that followed, Celine perused her mind. What kind of church were they looking for?

The kind that Grayson would be comfortable in. A church ready to extend a hand to anyone genuinely in need. Not to make a political statement, but because it was the Christian thing to do.

Where kindness ruled and traditional values mattered.

She had no intention of revealing any of this to Lillian.

So the silence dragged on, heavy with the weight of Lillian's disregarded remark—a casual, barely voiced question that nevertheless demanded an answer.

"Trinity Church has architecture worth seeing," Lillian finally offered. "Old North Church and Leonard have gardens, if that's more your style."

An old church, Celine thought.

She must have spoken aloud, for Lillian immediately said, "Well, First Church on Marlborough Street is ancient. It was founded in 1630."

"Old North Church would be worth a visit, too." Ann Revere had poked her head in. "It was founded in 1722. Paul Revere was a bell-ringer there."

She smiled at her guests. "I'm glad to see you're getting to know each other. Lillian's been here a few days, so she might be able to help you plan your stay." She glanced across at Lillian. "You know, they might like King's Chapel on Tremont Street."

Ann turned back to Julia. "Then there's Park Street Church."

Julia smiled, nodded, then looked at Celine. "Do any of these sound familiar?"

Her question reminded Celine of the fiction they'd concocted for Lillian's benefit. But Julia was also asking whether any of the churches named had struck a psychic chord within her.

Unfortunately, they had not. But potentially, they all fit the bill.

"They all sound interesting," she said.

Close to Belle, Sister Mary Catherine's voice rustled in her ear.

Celine's eyes widened. Now that was a clue. "I think the church Whatsername mentioned might be close to the Gardner Museum."

Lillian smiled widely. "That narrows it down quite a bit." Her eyes met Ann's. "An old church near the Gardner Museum. We should be able to help with that."

Chapter Forty-Five

"You must be Celine." Annabelle Curtis's fingers lightly touched Celine's cheek. "Special Agent Markham"—Annabelle's gaze flickered toward the federal agent—"said you needed to talk with me. It's about Simon Underwood, isn't it?"

Celine nodded. In the face of Annabelle's manner—warm, compassionate, maternal—the hard rock of grief Celine had been holding onto dissolved. Her lips trembled; she felt her eyes moisten.

Annabelle enfolded Celine in her arms. "You poor child! You're too young to be dealing with death."

In the living room, while Celine clung to Annabelle, unable to restrain her tears, Julia quietly introduced herself. "How did you know?" the former fed wanted to know. As far as they knew, Blake Markham hadn't yet broken the news of Underwood's death to their host.

"I've been worried about him," Annabelle said. "I haven't heard from him in some time." She exhaled heavily. "Then when Special Agent Markham called to let me know Celine was in town, I knew something was wrong. Simon would have let me know she was here."

"He spoke of her?" Julia asked.

Celine felt Annabelle nod. The older woman held her even closer. "My younger brother—also a Simon—always wanted a daughter. Had he lived to have one, she'd have been about Celine's age.

"Celine was such a quick study at the winery, interested in art, Simon Underwood was truly impressed. 'Duarte would've liked her,' he told me. 'He'd have enjoyed taking her to the Gardner.' Belle's museum, my brother used to call it. Or sometimes just *the old girl*."

"*The old girl?*" Celine wiped her tears.

Annabelle smiled. "The boys liked to think the museum was their girlfriend. It was just a joke. The Gardner Museum was the woman they lived for.

"That's how I know"—her face hardened—"that Simon and Earl Bramer and all of those boys who worked there would never have stolen any of the museum's treasures."

Tell her I'm sorry. The voice in her ear belonged to Dirck.

Sorry for what? Celine wondered. Luring Simon Duarte into a crime he'd otherwise never have committed?

Another thought surfaced. The finial couldn't have been stolen for Annabelle. Blake Markham had already filled her in on Annabelle's theory—that any involvement Simon Duarte and Earl Bramer might have had in the heist would have been to protect the art, not to steal it.

Had the pair taken the finial to prevent its theft?

Was the woman the finial needed to go back to the Gardner Museum? Not Annabelle, but Belle's museum—the museum both men had loved.

Celine cleared her throat, her eyes sought Julia's. *Don't show her the photograph of the finial,* she wanted to say. But before the words could come out, Julia had pulled the photograph out from her purse and was handing it to Annabelle.

"Did your brother ever show you this bronze eagle? Did he ever bring it by to your house?"

Annabelle looked at the photograph, then up at Julia.

"No he did not," she replied evenly. "It's an insult to Simon's memory to even suggest such a thing."

Tell her I'm sorry. Dirck's voice was insistent.

"The finial was found among Dirck's things, Annabelle," Celine said. "And we know that Simon Underwood and Dirck and your brother all knew each from taking Frank van Mieris's course at BU."

Annabelle drew back. "My Simon never knew a Dirck Thins, my dear."

"Your brother *never* mentioned Dirck Thins?" Celine was having a hard time believing this.

"If he had, I'm sure he would've mentioned it. I first heard of Dirck when Simon Underwood went west. And by that time"—a shadow of pain passed across her features—"Simon and Earl were already gone."

Celine's gaze flew toward Julia's. Her friend looked as stunned as she felt. Was Annabelle so furious with Dirck she refused to acknowledge his existence?

Somehow that didn't make sense. And Celine hated to believe the older woman was lying.

The only person who didn't seem at all surprised was Special Agent Blake Markham.

"What makes you so sure Duarte and Bramer knew your employer, Celine?" Blake leaned forward to ask. "Is that what Simon Underwood told you?"

Tell her I'm sorry. The voice was driving her crazy.

Celine forced herself to calm down. What had Simon Underwood said?

"Underwood claimed never to have known or heard of Simon Duarte and Earl Bramer," Julia explained dryly. "He was so convincing I believed him—until I did some digging."

"That's when you found out about Frank van Mieris, I presume," Blake said.

Celine shook her head.

"No, Simon told us about him. He talked about having met Dirck and John through Frank van Mieris. They were trying to discover how Vermeer created his paintings."

Annabelle nodded. "Simon and Earl were fascinated by what they learned in that course. They could never stop talking about it."

"It was Dirck and John," Celine continued, "who, apparently, discovered that a tracing on oil paper impressed upon canvas could produce a tonal image of a composition—an image without lines."

"That wasn't Dirck!" Annabelle's objection sounded like an explosion in Celine's ears. "Simon and Earl had that insight. The revelation made them heady! They couldn't believe they'd finally cracked Vermeer's secret." She smiled sadly. "I can still remember them talking about it."

Tell her I'm sorry, Celine.

"If Simon Underwood was lying about the one thing," Blake interjected. "Not knowing Duarte and Bramer, that's to say, couldn't he have been lying about the other? What's to say he didn't concoct some fiction about how Dirck Thins and Mechelen and he met?"

Celine shook her head. Simon Underwood hadn't been lying.

Not about everything. There'd been a kernel of truth somewhere.

"He sounded pretty convincing," Julia insisted. "They all knew each other from their Boston days."

Dirck's voice buzzed in Celine's ear again. And again.

Tell her I'm sorry. Tell her, Celine. Tell her.

Celine clapped her palms to her ears, willing Dirck to stop. *Make him stop, Sister Mary Catherine*, she pleaded with her guardian angel.

Convey his message, Celine, the nun advised her.

"Annabelle." Celine gazed into the older woman's eyes. "Are you sure your brother never mentioned Dirck Thins?"

She waited. But Annabelle continued to look blank—and mildly puzzled, as the silence grew.

"Because Dirck keeps saying he's sorry."

"Sorry for what?" Annabelle stared.

Celine subsided. She didn't know. Somewhere deep in the recesses of her mind, it occurred to Celine that it was fortunate Annabelle hadn't asked her how she knew.

Talk to me, Dirck. Why are you sorry?

But the voice in her head had faded. And Sister Mary Catherine's explanation was too vague to mean anything. She repeated it, nonetheless.

"He feels responsible." If only she could be more specific than that. "Dirck feels responsible for what happened to your brother."

"How could he be?" Unless she was an excellent actress, Annabelle's astonishment was authentic. "He didn't know my Simon."

❧

"Are you sure?" Julia's voice broke the silence.

They were beginning to sound like a couple of broken records, Celine thought. But Julia wasn't just questioning the veracity of Annabelle's memory, she was handing her proof—the bundle of photographs they'd discovered in Dirck's safe at the Delft.

"They were taken on the farm Dirck grew up on in the Boston area." Julia tapped the bundle. "And there's a photograph of you."

"So there is." Annabelle stared at the image of her younger self. "Wonder where he got these from?"

"From your brother, perhaps." Julia's voice was soft.

She sat—still as a statue—as Annabelle looked up, blue eyes blazing.

"We believe your brother might still be alive."

"That's nonsense."

Annabelle turned toward Blake, but he ignored the question in her eyes.

"Does anything else about those photographs seem familiar?" he asked instead.

Annabelle sifted through the photographs. "Mom and Dad." Her voice caught. Her eyes remained glued to the picture. "This went missing from my album about the time Simon died. I remember looking through its pages after Underwood broke the news to me."

She held up another photograph. "Appleway Farm."

"That's where Dirck grew up," Julia informed her. "According to Simon Underwood."

Annabelle's head jerked up. "Why would he tell you that? Appleway Farm was my parents' farm. Simon and I grew up there. Earl's parents owned a farm not too far from ours. That's how we knew each other."

She frowned. "You're saying . . ." Annabelle paused. She lowered her gaze to the photographs in her hand. "You can't be saying . . ."

Julia sat back. "Frankly, at this point, I'm not sure what we're saying. Dirck's identity checks out. He was born in the United States, his family left for Canada when he was a young boy—"

"But Dirck never spoke about living in Canada," Celine burst out. "He did mention growing up on a farm. Even I knew that. Not the name of the farm, of course—not until Simon Underwood gave us the whole story—but—"

"And he returned to the United States as a young man," Julia finished. Her head swiveled toward Blake. "You can corroborate this."

"No." Blake looked down at his hands. "Look, after I spoke with Annabelle, I began to suspect . . ." He drew in a prolonged breath. "I couldn't get over the similarities in background. Duarte and Bramer had been art students, too. But they wanted to return to their roots—to farming."

Just like Dirck—and John, Celine thought. *Interested in art, but not good enough, or so they thought, to make a living at it.* She was beginning to feel sick.

"Annabelle said hearing about Dirck and John Mechelen reminded her of her brothers. Two Boston boys making it in the West. Just like her brother and Earl had wanted to."

"But Dirck's identity," Julia protested.

"Doesn't check out," Blake interjected. "I did a little digging, too. Dirck Thins did not return to the United States. He never left Canada. The man who was Dirck Thins died a few years ago in Canada. Of natural causes," he hastened to explain as a collective gasp greeted the news he provided.

"So, then. . ." Julia began.

"Simon survived." Annabelle's face was white. "But he let me believe . . . he was gone all these years?"

"That's what he's sorry for." Celine finally understood. "He didn't mean to hurt you."

Chapter Forty-Six

"A church connected to the Gardner?" Penny Hoskins' voice crackled over the speakerphone as she repeated Celine's question. "The museum isn't associated with any church. Never has been. Why do you ask?"

Celine exchanged a glance with Julia. They were seated on the queen-sized bed in the Lilac room where they'd spent a sleepless night mulling over what they'd learned from Annabelle and Blake.

Celine was still struggling to come to terms with the fact that Dirck Thins—the father-like figure she'd come to know seven years ago—was actually Simon Duarte, the man who'd absconded with the Gardner's eagle finial and its Vermeer.

Dirck—Celine couldn't bring herself to think of him as Simon Duarte—had, by his own admission, been in possession of *The Concert*. The finial as well—which he'd told her, the day he was murdered, had to be returned. But Celine was reluctant to believe he'd taken anything else.

"Then what do you think he and Bramer sold to fund their getaway?" Blake had demanded.

Not a question Celine had been able to answer, and she'd put it aside for the moment. But she was beginning to come around to Julia's view that Grayson Pike—the last person aside from Dirck's killers to have seen her employer—might have some inkling of the *Concert's* whereabouts.

Might even, she had to concede, *be the person calling the Gardner with his offer to return it.*

"Celine? Julia?" Celine's iPhone crackled to life. "Are you still there?"

"Yes, we are, Penny." It was Julia who responded. "We've been able to confirm that the tip about the Vermeer came from Dirck Thins, Celine's employer in Paso Robles. He was murdered last week before he could divulge any more information to the FBI—"

"Oh, my God, that's awful! I had no idea. I am so sorry."

"Penny, the last person to see him alive," Julia went on, "was Grayson Pike
—"

"And you think he might have the Vermeer now?" Penny sounded breath-
less and uncertain.

"It's a possibility," Julia said. "We believe he's back in Boston."

"Well, then, that would dovetail with the tip we received. I'm glad I trusted
my instincts on that."

That elicited an amused smile from Julia.

"We have information Grayson might be hiding in a church somewhere."

"Oh I see! But what makes you think it would have to be a church associated with the museum?"

Julia hesitated. "When you said yesterday that Grayson and Duarte had
been employed at about the same time, we surmised the two might have
been close. So Celine and I paid Duarte's sister a visit." She paused.

Anyone else would have assumed the Gardner connection had come from
Annabelle. But not Penny.

"And . . . ?" Penny's voice rose a little in anticipation.

"We wanted to find out more about Grayson," Celine spoke up. "Churches
that he frequented, that kind of thing. But Annabelle said that neither Simon
nor his friends were particularly religious. She did mention that they were
fascinated by an old church somehow connected with the Gardner."

Other than the last five words, nothing Celine had said was an outright
lie. Duarte and his friends had been fascinated by an old church.

"She couldn't recall the name," Julia added. "We figured you might know."

A rush of air sounded through the iPhone's speaker. "I wish I could help
you, but I have absolutely no idea what church that could be. Of course,
there are several in the vicinity. That doesn't narrow it down very much,
does it?"

"No," Julia agreed with a rueful smile, "but it's a place to start."

"I could have one of our staff look through the archives. There might
be something in Mrs. Gardner's letters and documents . . ." Penny's voice
trailed off.

"Whatever you can do," Julia said. "Meanwhile, we'll do some legwork of
our own and see what we can come up with."

"Well, it's got to be a church close by. In fact, that would make perfect
sense, given—" Penny interrupted herself. "I'm sorry I shouldn't be revealing
any more details. It could jeopardize, you know. . ."

"Understood," Celine said. "And thanks for your help."

But Penny didn't seem ready to end the call.

"No, thank you. If it weren't for you, we wouldn't have our finial back. And it looks like our luck is finally changing." Penny paused. "Would you two like to be here tomorrow when . . . ?" Another pause.

Celine looked at Julia—was Penny trying to tell them something? Julia nodded and mouthed, *yes*.

"Absolutely," Celine spoke into the mouthpiece. "At what time?"

"Early morning," Penny said. "If you can make it."

Julia was out of the bed and on her feet by the time Celine disconnected.

"I don't want to jeopardize anything, but I think you'd better call Blake."

❧

Blake scanned the Excel sheet on his laptop as Ella rattled off the information she'd dug up in the last half-hour.

"There are only three churches that fit in the Fens area." She tapped the laptop screen. "But if we extended our search to the Back Bay area, we'd have five more to look into."

Blake's gaze scrolled down, obediently following her finger. Ella had typed in tidbits of information next to the relevant churches. Saint Cecilia Roman Catholic Church had been built for Irish maids and coachmen. The Holy Trinity Orthodox Church had been founded in 1910 by immigrants from Russia and the Austro-Hungarian Empire.

The phone rang just as they reached the end of the Excel worksheet. Blake was about to pick up the receiver when he heard the muted scuff of Ella's chair scraping against the carpet.

"It's Celine," he told his assistant, indicating with two raised fingers that he wanted her to remain in the room. "Blake Markham," he announced himself into the receiver as Ella subsided into her chair.

"It's going down tomorrow," Celine informed him. "We thought you'd want to know."

Blake knew instantly what she was referring to, and to say he was thrilled by the news would be putting it mildly.

"Absolutely!" he agreed fervently. His men were getting tired of staking out the Round House, and in a few days, if nothing went down, he'd have to call off the surveillance. "Are you sure, though?"

It almost seemed too good to be true.

"You've interpreted your psychic feel . . ." he stopped himself. He wasn't quite sure what the terminology was, but even he realized referring to Celine's intuitions as "feelings" wouldn't be kosher.

Celine laughed. "I have it from the horse's mouth."

"You mean, Penny?" Blake was incredulous. Even his assistant, resourceful as she was, wouldn't have been able to pull that off. His eyes met Ella's. *Tomorrow*, he mouthed to her.

Ella frowned. "You sure about this?" She kept her voice low. Her plan to access Lawrence & Young's transactions with Gold Star had been put on hold since Celine's arrival, and Blake knew she was eager to get back to it.

Yup, he mouthed back, pressing the receiver closer to his ear.

"She wants us there," Celine was saying. "And from what she revealed, we're right about the hand-off being where it is—not far from the museum. In fact, that's why she's certain Grayson must be hiding in a church nearby."

"You talked about that?" What he really wanted to know was whether Penny had divulged anything useful about Grayson's whereabouts. He put Celine on speakerphone. He wanted Ella to hear the conversation verbatim.

"Yes, but she couldn't be very much more specific than that." Celine sounded disconsolate. Blake was about to tell her about Ella's research when Celine went on: "Penny couldn't think of any church associated with the Gardner."

"Wait, you're looking for a church connected to the Gardner?" Blake pulled his laptop closer and peered down the rows of the Excel worksheet. "You didn't mention that yesterday."

"I didn't realize that's what my guardian angel was trying to convey to me. I thought we were looking for a church near the museum. But I think now it must be connected to Belle Gardner—or more likely her museum—in some way."

"A church connected to the Gardner?" Ella was smiling. "That's a no-brainer."

Blake's head jerked up. "What do you mean?" He leaned into the mouthpiece. "Celine, Ella might be able to help. Go on, Ella." He directed the mouthpiece at his assistant.

"The church you're looking for is Old South Church. The "new" building —if you can call it that—was designed by Willard Sears, the architect Isabella Gardner hired to design the Gardner Museum."

"That sounds like it, Celine. Old South Church is in the Back Bay area, less than two miles from the Gardner. And if they were designed by the same man, there's the Gardner connection you were looking for."

"But . . ." Celine didn't seem convinced.

"It fits on all counts, Celine." Blake glanced at his watch. "Look I've gotta run. Does Julia have her laptop? Yes? Great, I'll email you the list of churches Ella narrowed down for us"—he pulled up Outlook and attached the workbook—"in Fenway and the Back Bay area. But I think you'll find Old South Church is the one. If your information is correct, that's probably where Grayson is."

By the time the call was over, Blake had sent Julia and Celine the information. He glanced at his watch again. There was work to be done if they wanted to get the bastards trying to cash in on the Gardner's desperation.

At a hundred million dollars, it was the most outrageous con Blake would have the satisfaction of putting the kibosh on. And there was absolutely no doubt in Blake's mind that it was a con.

Chapter Forty-Seven

The bus dropped them off at Copley Square. Celine and Julia would have to trace their steps back on Boylston Street to get to Old South Church. But directly in front of them, rose the ancient spires of Trinity Church.

It was apparently designed in the shape of a Greek cross, but to Celine's untrained eyes, the structure bore a greater resemblance to a small European-style castle or fortress. The façade was a brown square topped with a tower in the center and two smaller ones at the sides. A couple of slender turrets hugged the center tower.

She glanced down at the Revere Inn notepaper clutched in her right fist. Trinity was on the list of churches Blake Markham's assistant had gathered for them.

"We're here," Julia said. "Want to drop in and see what we can find out?"

"Yes, thanks." As they headed down a path toward the three arches of the façade, Celine tried to identify the presence she was sensing. It didn't seem to belong to Grayson. Yet it had directed her attention to the church.

Had Grayson come here, and been turned away? Had he sought shelter here for a brief time, and then moved on?

More importantly, would anyone respond to their questions? The knot in her stomach intensified.

A figure sweeping the section of yard up front glanced up as they approached. "Visiting?" He greeted them with a pleasant smile. "You'll want to go around to the Clarendon Street entrance."

The friendly, informal greeting eased Celine's tension. She returned his smile as she and Julia followed the path his arm indicated.

"Let me handle this," Julia whispered as they sprinted up the steps, walked past a series of columns that evoked classical Grecian architecture, and approached a smiling greeter with straw-colored hair and rounded shoulders.

"Welcome to Trinity? Are you here for a tour?"

"Actually, we're looking for a friend," Julia began. "A recent member of the parish, I believe. Grayson Pike? We were supposed to join him here, but . . ." She looked around helplessly. "You wouldn't happen to know if he's already arrived, would you?"

The man shook his head, apologetically. "I'm sorry, the name's not familiar." He hesitated, glancing over his shoulder. "Our Verger might be able to help you. Would you like me to take you to his office?"

Julia's eyes brightened. She was quite the actress, Celine thought, amused.

"Yes, if it wouldn't be too much trouble."

Outside the Verger's office, the greeter knocked on the door, poked his head in and called out a muffled message. He waited a moment, then returned to them.

"Patrick will be with you in a few minutes," he informed them, seeming relieved to be able to wash his hands off them.

A portly Hispanic man, about three inches shorter than Celine, emerged from the office.

"Are you the visitors Bill was telling me about." He stretched out a plump hand. "Patrick Reyes, Verger."

"We're hoping you can help us find a friend of ours," Julia responded. "We were supposed to meet him here"—she glanced at Celine—"we think."

Reyes raised an eyebrow. "You think?"

Julia slumped her shoulders. "Trouble is we don't remember the name of the church he was so excited to show us. And we can't get through on his cell phone."

Reyes looked amused. "Well, let's see if we can't help you. What is your friend's name?"

"Grayson Pike."

Reyes frowned. "Name sounds familiar."

"He's about medium height, late fifties." Celine paused. "Looks a bit like Liam Neeson. Not quite as good looking, though."

Reyes burst out laughing. "A man like that, I would remember for sure. But, no, we don't have any members or staff by that name. But—" He glanced over his shoulder. "Give me a minute. That name does sound familiar."

He headed back into his office.

"Good instincts, Celine," Julia murmured. "Looks like we're getting somewhere."

Reyes emerged from his office again, carrying a sheet of paper.

"Is this the man you're looking for?" He held the sheet out to them.

"Yes!" Celine gasped. "But where did you get that?" It wasn't a photograph Reyes had in his hands, but a sketch. The kind used by law enforcement. Not a perfect likeness, but showing enough of a resemblance to trigger recognition.

The sketch she'd been instrumental in providing, and which Detective Mailand had shared with Blake.

Reyes shrugged. "Seems your friend is very popular. There was someone else around just this morning, asking for him."

"Tall guy in a suit, dark hair, walks like he's God's gift to womankind?" Julia was describing Blake. Although it seemed odd he'd leave a composite behind.

"Nope. Short, dumpy, beefy hands." Reyes shook his head in disbelief. "I'll never forget those hands. Raw and red and huge."

Celine swallowed. She'd never forget them either. Those were the hands that had taken Dirck's life.

"Were you given a number to call in case he came by?" Julia asked.

If Reyes noticed the change in her manner from flustered tourist to interrogating FBI agent, he didn't comment on it.

"On the other side of the sketch." Reyes turned the paper over.

❧

Outside Trinity Church, Celine and Julia found a secluded bench on Copley Square. A solitary pigeon fluttered between the bronze Tortoise and Hare dedicated to the Boston Marathon runners. Diagonally across from them, a couple sat on the steps of the Copley Square Fountain.

While Julia called Blake's phone and hers to organize a three-way call, Celine glanced down at the phone number scrawled on the back of the composite Dirck's killer had left behind at the church. The Trinity's Verger had expressed no hesitation in handing the paper over to them.

"We're always glad to help. But we don't have the resources to keep track of all our visitors and reunite them with their loved ones."

That the composite she'd been instrumental in providing had found its way to Dirck's killers didn't surprise Celine. The FBI intern responsible for leaking the details of their flight must also have been responsible for this particular leak.

But it had been especially chilling to see the phone number they'd left behind. Did it mean anything? Or had it been left behind as a veiled threat?

We know where you are. We know what you're doing.

Celine shivered.

Why had Dirck's killer left behind the phone number of the Revere Garden Inn? The few guests at the Inn didn't include anyone with hands of the sort Verger Reyes had described.

A muffled "Hello!" called her attention back. Blake Markham had joined the conference call.

"We have some disturbing news," Julia began without preamble. She kept her voice low, her eyes constantly scanning their surroundings. "It looks like Grayson Pike's gotten himself on a kill list."

"This isn't good," Blake said when he'd heard Julia out. In the background, the faint sound of a pen repeatedly tapping a hard surface came through. "This is definitely not good."

"What I don't understand," Julia said, exchanging a glance with Celine, "is how they're following so closely our logic on this issue. They know we think Grayson's holed up at a church. They've honed in on the same churches, it looks like. We'll need to confirm that."

"And they know where you're staying," Blake said. "That's especially troubling."

"That would suggest there's a plant at the Revere Garden Inn," Julia said. "But how could anyone have even known—?" She glanced at Celine again, puzzled.

"The FBI intern." The answer had come to Celine instantly. "She knew when we were arriving, right? Could she also have known where we were staying?"

"Damn!" Blake cursed. "I should've booked you somewhere else the minute we realized she was the leak."

"It's not too late to do it now," Julia said. "Is it?" She eyed Celine.

"No!" Celine's denial was sharper than she'd intended it to be. She wasn't going to be scared away by Dirck's killers. She didn't care how powerful they were—or thought they were; she'd confront them. "Let's stay and flush out the leak. I'm willing to bet it's Lillian."

"She overheard you . . . talking . . . ?" Blake sounded perplexed.

"No, Blake. The Reveres, their staff, and the few guests they have are all aware Celine and I are interested in churches—churches close to the Gardner Museum."

"Which would include all the ones you're looking into," Blake agreed. In her mind's eye, Celine could see him slowly nodding his head. "Any particular reason to find this Lillian especially suspicious?"

"Just a hunch," Celine said. Or maybe it was that Lillian reminded Celine of every bitchy, underhanded girl she'd encountered growing up. There was something about Lillian—something insidious—that was the quintessence of *mean girl*.

But Blake accepted her rationale easily enough. "Let me go to the Revere Garden Inn and put out some feelers," he said.

"Go easy, Blake," Julia warned. "If it is Lillian, we don't want to tip her off. Not too soon, anyway."

He laughed. "Not to worry, Julia. This isn't my first rodeo." But he didn't seem particularly offended.

Celine was relieved. She liked them both—Blake and Julia—and she was glad they were getting along just fine.

Chapter Forty-Eight

It was lunchtime at the Revere Garden Inn when Blake arrived there. And most of the guests with the exception of Lillian were in the inn's Victorian dining room.

"Would you care to join our guests?" Ann Revere peered anxiously up at him—the FBI badge and his own appearance causing their predictable nervous reaction. "I don't think anyone's looking for a missing friend . . . Well, Celine and Julia might be . . ."

"They did mention a friend," her husband agreed. "But I don't think she's missing." He turned to Blake. "Of course, they're not here either."

"That's okay." Blake gave them what he hoped was a friendly, reassuring smile. He indicated the parlor. "I think I'll wait there, if that's alright, and meet your guests one at a time."

None of the mostly elderly guests who joined him in the quaint, old-fashioned parlor had reported a missing person. And no one expressed anything more than polite interest when Blake casually mentioned that the FBI might have a line on the missing individual and were looking to provide the information to whoever was scouring the city in search of them.

That didn't surprise Blake. Celine had said she suspected Lillian, and he trusted her instincts. That Lillian wasn't at the inn was mildly suspicious as well. But then again she was a young woman, probably disinclined to be indoors when she could be out and about.

He stood up to go; he'd leave a message with the Reveres for Lillian. With any luck, she'd take the bait.

"Special Agent Markham." The sultry voice caught him off-guard.

He glanced up, felt his eyes widen and his Adam's apple bob as he swallowed once, twice, a third time while he stared at the curvy brunette draped against the doorjamb.

She smiled. "I'm Lillian."

Blake nodded stiffly, watching her sashay in and—without waiting for an invitation—drop gracefully into the couch in front of the window. She leaned back against the pile of cushions. Her lips stretched wider into an inviting smile.

Off-duty, in a bar someplace, he'd have had no hesitation responding to that smile. On duty, knowing who she was, Blake tamped down the response she elicited in him.

"What can I do to help you?" Lillian looked up at him.

"I'm not sure you can." Blake sat down and, on a whim, plucked the composite of Grayson from his folder. He hadn't shown it to any of the guests.

"Is this someone you're looking for?"

Her eyes swiveled slowly—too slowly, Blake thought—toward the photo. The nostrils flared. She looked at the composite far longer than was necessary, her body unnecessarily still.

"What makes you think anyone here is looking for him?" Her head pivoted back toward him as she spoke.

It was an interesting question. Blake countered with one of his own.

"I take it you're not?"

"No." The shake of the head and the curt denial came a fraction of a second later than he'd have expected.

Lillian looked at the photo again, then back at him.

"Why do you ask?"

Blake put the composite away.

"Whoever was looking for him left the number of the Revere Garden Inn." He began to stand up.

"And . . . ?" Lillian's voice stopped him.

Blake looked at her. "And now that we know where he is, his friend might want to be reunited with him."

He made for the door.

"Special Agent Markham"—he turned instantly—"I don't know if Ann mentioned it to you, but there are a couple of our guests you haven't spoken with." Lillian was leaning forward now. "I'd be happy to pass on a message."

Blake smiled down at her, feeling more in control now than he had when she'd first walked in.

"No need. I can leave my card with the Reveres in case the other guests want to get in touch with me."

✒

At the corner of Dartmouth and Boylston, Old South Church was larger and even more imposing than its neighbor three-quarters of a block away. The black doors at the foot of the campanile were thrown open.

As she and Julia waited for the short line of people before them to go in, Celine craned her neck back to get a good look at the campanile. But following its soaring lines skyward was a dizzying experience, and she quickly lowered her head.

"I think we go official this time," Julia whispered as they stepped through the doorway.

"Probably the best way," Celine agreed. Something about the church's atmosphere suggested its staff would be less accommodating and far less forthcoming than that of Trinity Church.

At the reception, a black woman with short hair glanced up as she and Julia approached her desk.

"What's this about?" she asked, eyes widening as Julia held up her badge.

"Has anyone been here this morning asking about this man?" Julia held out the composite of Grayson that they'd retrieved from Trinity's Verger.

The receptionist—Tamara Williams, according to the brass nametag pinned to her jacket—stared at the composite, then at Julia's badge, and then shifted her gaze back to the composite.

She pushed her chair back, rising quickly. "Let me get someone to help you," she said, and disappeared behind a door.

"Notice, how we didn't get invited in this time." Julia put her badge away.

"I doubt posing as hapless tourists would've got us back there, either." Celine looked at her. "Does it matter, though?"

"No, it just means we won't get very far here," Julia replied as the receptionist returned with an overweight, long-haired, white woman.

"Kayleigh Byrne." The newcomer stretched her hand out. But her hazel eyes held no warmth. "I'm the Interim Associate Minister here. How may I help you?"

Julia repeated her question.

Kayleigh regarded her, a watchful, wary expression on her face.

"May I ask what this is about?"

Julia's nostrils flared ever so slightly. Celine didn't blame her. Kayleigh Byrne was treating them as though *they* were the enemy. When all they were trying to do was their job.

"It's about a very dangerous man on the track of another man who's about to be very dead if we don't find him in time, Ms. Byrne."

"We did have someone inquire after him," Kayleigh conceded. "But we didn't tell him anything."

"Because you didn't have anything to say?" Julia asked. "Or because you weren't willing to?"

The Associate Minister rolled her eyes and expelled an exasperated sigh. "Look, it's not like we hide fugitives or anything like that."

"I'm not suggesting you do," Julia countered. "But this man"—she tapped the composite—"could be in a great deal of danger. Is he here? Has he ever been?"

Kayleigh Byrne ignored the question. "Why do you think he'd come here?"

"Because"—it was Celine who answered the question—"we have reason to believe he's at a church with a connection to the Gardner Museum. Your church is the only one that fits the bill."

Kayleigh Byrne seemed to see Celine for the first time.

"If that's the case, we're not the only church you should be looking at."

❧

Celine was about to call Blake—they needed to find a second church with a connection to the Gardner Museum—when her phone rang.

"It is Lillian," Blake said the moment she answered.

She cupped her hand over her phone. "Blake," she mouthed to Julia. "Seems we were right about Lillian."

"No doubt about it, she's the plant," Blake was saying.

"Did you arrest her?"

A low, amused rumble of laughter greeted her question.

"I wish I could have."

She put the phone on speaker, listening closely as he explained.

"So what now?" Julia lowered her head to the mouthpiece.

"I've asked the Reveres to make sure the Beech Room is empty—the number you gave me connects to that room. The phone's going to be disconnected. And they'll let me know if any of the guests ask to be moved up there.

"But Lillian knows the cat's out of the bag, and she may not try anything. Anything that'll tip us off any further, that's to say. But I'd advise the usual precautions. Be aware of your surroundings. Don't cue anyone in to your plans or whereabouts. Watch for anyone following you. And be careful not to take any calls on the Revere Inn lines."

"Got it," Celine said. She asked the question she'd originally intended to ask.

There was a pause.

"I have absolutely no idea," Blake said. "I can ask Ella to check again, but . . . I'll just ask her, okay? If there actually is another church in the city with a Gardner connection, she'll find out which one it is."

Chapter Forty-Nine

Lunch was over at the Revere Garden Inn by the time Celine and Julia returned, but the table fortunately hadn't yet been cleared. They'd decided to head back to the inn for a quick bite to eat before researching churches again.

Old South Church's Kayleigh Byrne had been tantalizingly unhelpful—throwing out an intriguing possibility but refusing to elaborate on it any further. "You're the FBI. I think you can figure it out yourselves," she'd said primly before turning on her heels and walking away.

"Too bad you can't get a warrant to force people to talk," Julia had grumbled again as they settled down in their cab. The conversation with Blake hadn't put her in a much better mood. "And now I guess using the Revere's Wi-Fi is out of the question as well."

They'd stopped at a Verizon store on the way back to the Inn for a portable Internet device that Julia could plug into her laptop. And now all they needed was lunch.

"You must be famished," Ann Revere greeted them with a smile.

"We are," Celine told her. "It's been a long day."

"You're in luck, then. The table hasn't been cleared yet, so help yourselves." Ann leaned conspiratorially closer. "There was an FBI agent here," she informed them.

Julia looked up, her expression impassive. "No trouble, I hope."

"Oh, no." Ann shook her head. "Apparently someone reported a friend missing and left our number as their contact information." She cocked her head and regarded them. "It wouldn't by any chance have been . . . ?" Her voice trailed off as she searched the desk. "He left his card here, if you need to call."

"We haven't lost anyone." Julia smiled. "Not yet, anyway."

They were about to head into the dining room, when the phone rang. Ann answered it, gesturing to them to stay as she listened intently. "It's for you," she said, handing the receiver to Celine.

"Celine? It's me, Penny."

Remembering Blake's advice, Celine quickly spoke up. "Penny, can I call you—"

But Penny didn't seem to have heard.

"I have some news. As luck would have it—"

"Penny, please," Celine tried again. "I'll need to call you back."

"Call me back?" Penny sounded puzzled and . . . hurt? Celine felt terrible, but she had no choice.

"Yes. I'll call you back in just a second, okay?"

Celine took a notepad and pen off the desk and went out to the porch, dialing the number on her cell phone.

"Sorry about that," she apologized when she reached Penny.

"What was that all about?" Penny wanted to know. "I thought you guys needed this urgently and . . ."

"Prying ears," Celine spoke softly into the phone. She glanced back into the inn, hoping Ann hadn't overheard.

"Oh, I see." Penny, at least, seemed to understand. "Well, I was looking into Mrs. Gardner's papers. I assume you know she lived at 152 Beacon."

"Yes." Celine hadn't been aware of that tidbit. But she didn't want to have a long conversation about Belle Gardner's houses.

"It was a wedding gift from her father. Then later, Jack Gardner bought 150 Beacon. It was to house their growing collection of art. The Gardners decided to remodel and connect both houses."

"I see." Celine pressed the phone closer to her ear.

"Well, the architect they used was one John Hubbard Sturgis."

And Sturgis had built a church—a church in Boston. A church Isabella Gardner herself had been quite fond of.

Celine rested the Revere Garden Inn's notepad against the wooden railing surrounding the porch, and hastily scrawled the name of the church on the topmost sheet.

A surge of excitement rushed through her as she hung up and swept down the hall into the dining room.

"I think lunch will have to wait, Julia." She handed Julia the notepad.

Julia glanced at the pad, her mouth full of roast beef.

"I guess it will," she agreed, tearing off the sheet and stuffing it into her purse.

"But what about lunch?" Ann protested as they dropped the notepad and pen off at the front desk.

"Sorry, gotta go."

Julia and Celine hurried out onto the porch and down the stairs to the curb.

❧

"I don't understand it," Ann stared after her guests.

Out of the corner of her eye, she saw Lillian emerge from the parlor. "Where are they going?"

"I don't know." Ann was still staring out the open front door, bewildered. "They just got back, and they're off again. Without lunch."

When she turned around, Lillian was standing in front of the desk, her fingers on the notepad.

Ann was about to ask if she needed a sheet of paper, but Lillian just smiled. "I guess I'll go in for a nap," she said.

Chapter Fifty

"I'm not Greg." The man Celine had privately dubbed *B-aw-ston Greg* stretched out his hand. "The name's Grayson." His pale blue eyes flickered toward Julia. "But I guess you'd figured that already."

Celine nodded. It had taken a moment to recognize the man who'd walked into the Delft a week—it seemed more like an eternity—ago. His frame had shrunk, like a slowly leaking balloon. The faded blue eyes had a haunted look. And a scraggly growth of gray-studded hair covered his chin.

Out on the street, she wouldn't have recognized him as the same man.

He gestured toward the spindle-back Windsor armchairs set against the wall of his tiny hiding place.

"How'd you find me?" Grayson asked when they'd sat down.

They were at the Church of the Advent, an Episcopal church on the corner of Brimmer and Mount Vernon Street in Beacon Hill. Learning that Grayson had been a witness in a crime and could prove helpful in bringing the perpetrators to justice, the Rector had reluctantly admitted to Grayson's presence at the church.

"I'll see if he wants to meet you," he'd said. "But it's going to be his decision."

Grayson had fortunately agreed to see them.

He glanced at the door now. Reverend Patrick Donegal had left it ajar. But the room on the other side was the Rector's office. No one was likely to disturb them.

Not without the Reverend's permission. And he'd seemed like a shrewd individual, unlikely to be taken in by . . .

A name crossed Celine's mind.

The General.

Nothing more specific than that. But now at last she was able to put a name to their adversary.

The General.

She thrust the name aside, bringing her attention back to the present.

"Good detective work," Julia was responding to Grayson's question. She glanced at Celine. "And a little bit of intuition."

"We met Annabelle Curtis," Celine added. "Simon Duarte's sister."

Grayson nodded. "She tell you about Belle's church?"

"She couldn't remember the name," Celine said. "But how many churches are there in Boston with a connection to Isabella Stewart Gardner?"

Grayson smiled. "Most people would've thought of Old South Church. The connection there is overt. But it was the Church of the Advent that Belle Gardner was especially fond of.

"Its"—his smile widened—"The word 'progressive' has such negative connotations these days, but the church did have a progressive outlook for its time. Not wanting to rent pews so that rich and poor could sit together. That must have appealed to Belle's sense of justice.

"And John Hubbard Sturgis was a parishioner in addition to being the man who designed its house of worship."

"What brought you here?" Julia wanted to know.

Grayson sank back against his armchair. "Only safe place I knew. We used to know the Rector here. Not Donegal. Another man. He was the one who urged us to go to the FBI when we realized the heist hadn't been planned as a wake-up call. It was designed to take advantage of the security breaches at Belle's museum."

He sighed. "Obviously no one knew going to the FBI would be such a bad decision."

"He's dead now, isn't he?" Celine said. "The man you went to?"

She wondered why Julia hadn't asked for a name. She glanced at her friend. Julia sat tight-lipped, hands crossed primly on her lap. Celine sensed that the former federal agent had a pretty good idea who Grayson was referring to.

"Oh, yes, he's dead all right." Grayson nodded. "Guess that's why Duarte thought it would be safe to call in his tip. But the General must still have his tentacles in the department?"

"The General—he was behind the heist?" Celine asked softly.

Grayson nodded again.

"I kept hearing the word when we were going through Dirck's wheelbarrow," Celine addressed Julia, deliberately keeping her explanation vague. "I didn't know what it meant at the time. I do now. It's what he calls himself?"

"The General?" Julia repeated in disbelief. She turned to Grayson.

"That's the moniker he goes by," Grayson said. "And before you ask, I don't know who he is. No one does. Someone with a lot of influence, I imagine."

"You recognized Dirck—Simon Duarte—the minute you saw him, didn't you?" Celine asked.

"And he knew me. Knew who I was. Knew it was okay to trust me."

He and Dirck had met later that night, Grayson told her.

"Very briefly. He wanted me out of the way so he could clean up and get the Vermeer down for me. Guess he didn't entirely trust me. I was supposed to come back for it and then he'd take me to the vineyard to grab the finial."

"Okay. Where is the painting now?" Julia leaned forward. "Where did you stash it?"

Grayson looked at her. "I didn't. Duarte never had a chance to give it to me. It's back wherever he had it."

"At the Delft?" Julia looked at Celine. They had scoured the place. There'd been no sign of a Vermeer. "Are you sure?"

"Unless the General's men got hold of it," Grayson said.

"I don't think that happened," Celine said softly. She was remembering the images that had flooded her mind when she'd entered the bar hours before dawn. Dirck had been taunting his attackers.

Hiding in plain sight.

What had he meant by that?

An unrelated thought flashed through her brain. She turned to Grayson.

"Why didn't you call 9-1-1? When you saw what was happening, why didn't you call for help? Why did you let him die?"

Silence greeted her question. Grayson averted his eyes.

"I was scared," he said flatly.

"You let your friend die," Celine accused him. Anger pulsed through her. "How could you do that?"

"Hey, now!" Grayson's head jerked up. "Duarte and I were never close. I was simply—"

"Looking out for yourself," Celine finished for him. "I know."

Disgust filled her. *You're such a piece of shit*, she thought unable to look at him anymore. Julia squeezed her hand, the older woman's touch soothing her ragged nerves. Gradually, her breathing slowed.

She heard Julia pressing on with her questions. Grayson had seen the men who'd attacked Dirck.

"You don't double-cross the General, you piece of shit!" one of them had growled.

The name had caught Grayson's ears, and he'd run.

"Don't ask me to testify against them. I'm not doing it."

"They haven't been caught yet," Julia replied, her grip tightening around Celine's wrist. Her friend seemed to be willing her to stay calm. But Celine was calm.

"There's just one piece of information we need from you." Celine forced herself to look at the coward who'd let Dirck die. "You don't know who the General is. But you recognize the name, right?"

Grayson dipped his head.

"Do you know whom he'd use as a fence? To offload high-end goods?"

His eyes widened. She knew he'd read her mind.

His voice was quiet when he replied.

"I wouldn't play games with the General if I were you. It could get dangerous."

❧

Blake shifted, stretching his legs in the cramped space beneath the archway of the Chapel Street Bridge.

"You sure this thing's gonna go down today?" Tony, his partner, asked in a low voice.

"Yup." Blake shifted again, his gut wrenching despite the certainty in his voice. It was not that he didn't trust Celine's intuition. It was just that . . .

Just that her word was all the confirmation he had.

The dampness of the ground seeped in through his jeans. They'd been hunched under the bridge, their eyes trained for hours on the stone gazebo known as the Round House Shelter.

A team of agents he'd handpicked for the job were posted at key points along the Muddy River all the way from Shattuck Visitor Center at Fenway and Forsyth to Longwood and Riverway, just past where he and Tony were posted.

Penny, Blake was pretty sure, would bring the money. He could only hope that her caller kept his side of the bargain. He adjusted his earbuds and the mouthpiece that wrapped around his mouth, preventing his words from carrying into the night air.

"Just another hour to go," Blake spoke into the mouthpiece, his eyes on the lightening sky. They'd agreed to share the watch during the night at each post. In reality, no one had gotten much shuteye. But it was time now for every agent to be awake and alert.

Through the noise-canceling earbuds, he listened for the sound of his men reporting in.

The wait was interminable and his gut tensed again as dawn broke, casting a pale, gray light over the part of Emerald Necklace known as Riverway. In the silence, the quiet crunching of grass and leaves came to his ear.

He glanced at Tony. Someone was approaching.

He leaned cautiously forward, peering out from under the arch. Penny's slender figure emerged from the trees, a leather case in her hand. She looked uncertainly, first to the left, then to the right, and then entered the gazebo.

A short time later, she re-appeared at the gazebo doorway, this time without the leather case.

Blake took in a breath and let it out slowly. The first part of the mission had gone off successfully. Penny hadn't been aware of their presence. And Celine had been right about the timing of the drop-off.

Blake spoke into his mouthpiece. "The bread's here. Repeat. The bread is here. Any sign of the ducks?"

The ducks had not arrived.

Several minutes passed.

He was about to inquire after the whereabouts of the ducks again when a heavier footfall caught his ear. He exchanged a glance with Tony.

"Looks like they're here," Tony whispered into his mouthpiece.

"White yacht docking at the harbor," Blake heard Nick, the agent posted at the Shattuck Visitor Center, report at the same time. They'd code-named the visitor center the harbor and the white yacht referred to a white van. "We have eyes on it."

Blake acknowledged the report, craning his neck out in time to see their target. He yanked his gun out, pulse racing. It was almost time for action.

The short, heavyset man gave his surroundings a cursory glance, then made his way into the Round House. He was back out a minute later, Penny's leather case in his hand.

"When?" Tony moved restlessly beside Blake.

"Let's give it a minute." Blake crouched by the arch, watching as their target uttered a few words into his radio. He wanted Nick to confirm the connection between their guy and the yacht at the harbor.

"Duck Two just hopped off the yacht," Nick said. "He's got a package."

"Now!" Blake erupted into his mouthpiece. In one fluid movement, he swooped out and up from under the archway, his gun pointed squarely at the heavyset target.

"Drop the case." He didn't bother identifying himself as FBI. "Drop it now!"

Chapter Fifty-One

"It should be any minute now." Penny stood at the window, scanning the view outside her office. "The call should come at any minute."

She tugged at the gold band of her watch, then swung decisively around to give her visitors a tight-lipped smile.

"Were you given any indication of when to expect the call?" Celine asked.

She exchanged a glance with Julia as the Director of the Gardner Museum began pacing the length of her spacious office again—covering the distance from window to bookcase in short, elegant steps.

It had been over two hours since Penny had dropped off the money—bundles of cash stuffed into a discreet brown leather case. Nearly two hours since Celine and Julia had joined Penny in her office, waiting to hear where and when the Vermeer they were receiving in exchange could be picked up.

Penny shook her head in response to the question Celine had asked.

"No," she said, tucking her shoulder-length gray hair behind her ear. "I wish I'd thought to ask."

Celine chewed uncertainly at her lip. The painting, if Penny even received it, was unlikely to be the real thing. But Blake and Julia had insisted they keep that bit of information from Penny.

If they were to have any chance of nabbing the guys behind the ransom demand, the operation needed to go down as planned.

"Any idea where they'll leave the painting?" Julia asked. She'd stayed more or less silent, quietly sipping her café latte, the entire time.

Penny turned to face her, her blue-green eyes shrouded with anxiety. "I can't imagine they'll come to our doorstep, do you?"

"Highly unlikely," Julia agreed, lowering her head to draw another swig of her latte.

Penny was back by her desk. She propped herself against the chair, clutching the backrest for support.

"The thing is, this was such a lot of money. And if it doesn't pan out . . . " She closed her eyes. "*Oh dear God*, what have I done?"

Celine exchanged another glance with Julia. "It'll be all right," she wanted to reassure Penny. If all had gone according to plan, Blake had recovered the money—and the art.

Out of the corner of her eye, she saw Penny move to the window again, searching the street below. Julia's gaze followed her, then turned to Celine.

"Paperwork," the former fed said quietly. "Protocol. He'll call as soon as he can."

BRR . . . RRR . . . RING.

The sudden ringing of the phone was like a jolt of lightning lancing through their bodies.

Penny spun around, her hand on the receiver.

"Yes," she breathed the word into the mouthpiece.

A flurry of emotions swirled over her features, flitting by too quickly for Celine to detect what they were. Alarm, anger, relief, and then a strange calmness.

"Come on up," she said, and replaced the receiver in its cradle.

☙

Blake was still in his jeans and the dark turtleneck he'd worn all night when he walked into Penny Hoskins' office. He'd managed to run a comb through his hair and brush his teeth, but he hadn't been able to dispel the discomfiting sense of scruffiness that followed an all-nighter.

"Got your money." He dumped the leather case unceremoniously onto Penny's desk—she was sitting behind it—and nodded a greeting at Celine and Julia. "We've documented it, photographed it. You can have it back."

"And the art?" Penny jerked her head at the rectangular, brown-paper-wrapped package under his arm.

He looked at her, his eyes feeling sandy and gritty. "I brought it here for you to take a look at. But it'll need to go into evidence." He used his leg to yank a chair toward him and sank into it. "If it's any consolation, I doubt you'll want it."

"Meaning?" Penny leaned forward.

He couldn't prevent his gaze drifting toward where Celine and Julia sat. Penny caught the movement.

"They were in on it?" Her normally fluty voice sounded brittle and edgy.

"Penny . . ." Blake heard Celine begin and found himself interrupting immediately.

"Celine just sensed that your caller likely didn't have a genuine Vermeer. No hard evidence, just a psychic sense." He emphasized the last words.

Penny already didn't trust him. He didn't want her incipient trust in Celine and Julia broken as well. He'd been forced to admit to himself that the two women were their only hope of recovering the Gardner's lost art.

"Okay." Penny dipped her head, considering his words. "But how did . . . ?"

"We've been discreetly staking out the surroundings ever since you told me you'd received a tip. Celine and Julia had no idea."

He caught Celine's eyes widening and gave her and Julia a hard stare, imperceptibly shaking his head.

"Okay," Penny said again. "But what makes you think the Vermeer isn't genuine?"

"We found Grayson," Blake replied. "I can't tell you very much more other than that his testimony suggests the painting, if it exists, is still in Paso Robles. He never got to set eyes on it."

"I'd still like to take a look at it." Penny indicated the painting.

"Sure." He lifted the work up. "That's why it's here."

❧

It may not have been painted by Vermeer, but it was still breathtaking. The artist had captured the vibrant glow of Vermeer's paintings, the subtle gradation of light and shade.

"It's beautiful," Celine breathed, leaning over the work.

"So vibrant," Penny agreed. "So striking."

"Too much so, perhaps," Celine suggested. The delicate technique Vermeer had used on this painting would have been susceptible to abrasion. Yet there was no sign of it on the work Blake had recovered.

She gently touched the edge of the wooden frame and closed her eyes.

An image of Simon Underwood swirled into her mind. She saw him as a young man sitting before an easel.

"This is an Underwood," she proclaimed with certainty. "Not a Vermeer." Her eyes opened. "He was able to figure out how Vermeer captured his compositions—a tonal image making no use of lines."

"But where's the hard evidence of that?" Penny stared at the work, enraptured.

"You're not just going to take it on faith that this is a genuine Vermeer, are you?" Julia sounded horrified.

"I'm not going to dismiss it out of hand," Penny shot back. She glanced up. "Look, it's been thirty years, Julia. And now, finally, we have this—the most valuable of the works stolen. I'd like to believe . . ."

She took a deep breath. "I just don't want to be too skeptical is all. Not based on . . . on . . ." Penny's hand swept through the air, a gesture of frustration.

"On psychic hocus-pocus?" Celine voiced the words Penny had suppressed.

"That's not what I said," Penny replied tersely. She turned to face Celine. "Look, did Simon Underwood ever confess to making a copy of the *Concert*?"

"No." Celine felt her spirits sinking as she made the admission. Penny's features remained obdurate. There'd be no persuading the Museum Director of the truth she saw. "No, I can't say that he did."

"But that doesn't mean he didn't paint this." Julia's voice was firm.

She rested her hand on Celine's shoulder. "Let's just take it slowly, and see what we can find, okay?"

Penny nodded, reluctantly.

"Whatever it is, it'll be something obvious." Celine scanned the paintings, her confidence resurrected by Julia's open show of support. "Underwood always included some detail that would enable the careful observer to distinguish a genuine Vermeer from one of his copies."

"What about these fine brown hairs?" Blake was studying the work through a magnifying lens. "Would a forger allow brush hairs to remain on his work?"

"Someone like Underwood, who knew what he was doing, would have," Celine pointed out. "After all, bristles have been found on *The Music Lesson*. That dates back to the same period as *The Concert*."

"Vermeer used hog's bristles for his paintings," Julia said. "Should be easy enough to find out what those hairs are."

"I'll have our conservators test for that." Penny scribbled a note on a pad. "But it'll take a while." She looked questioningly at Blake.

"I'm sure we can find a way to let you keep it for as long as that," he said. "But let's see if there's anything more easily detectable that gives this away as an Underwood copy." He bent low over the painting, inching the magnifying lens along the canvas.

He'd moved the lens along the singer's dress to the black frame around an older Dutch painter's work that Vermeer had represented on his canvas, when he abruptly stopped, and peered closer.

The movement made Celine catch her breath. She wondered what the special agent had seen.

"Dirck van Baburen's *Procuress*," Penny murmured. "I don't see anything wrong with it."

"There's a signature here," Blake said. He lifted his head and handed the magnifying glass to Celine. "Take a look."

Celine held the lens over the canvas. Had Underwood really signed his name? Now that would be a dead giveaway.

But what she saw on the canvas made her heart sink as though it were weighted by an anchor.

On the black frame of the *Procuress*, painted in a medium blue-gray were the letters "Meer" with an uppercase "I" nestled within the plunging valley of the "M." It was the most characteristic of Vermeer's signatures—he'd signed his works in a couple of different ways.

But what Celine was seeing was the signature he'd most frequently used.

The Music Lesson had been signed in a similar fashion. On the black frame of a painting included within the work, if memory served.

Dear God, had she really been so wrong about this work?

She lightly touched the canvas and closed her eyes. An image of Underwood swam into view again, confirming her initial impressions.

No, this wasn't a Vermeer. It was an Underwood. She couldn't be mistaken about that.

But what about the signature?

A possibility—a very remote possibility—occurred to Celine.

"I guess Underwood could've copied that signature." She stretched up. "Only a handwriting analyst would be able to confirm that, though."

"Wait, there's a Vermeer signature on that painting?" Penny frowned. She turned the painting around to face her and picked up the lens. "But . . ."

"But the only problem," Julia said quietly, looking up from her phone, "is that *The Concert* was one of the few paintings Vermeer left unsigned. Whoever painted this work, it was definitely not Vermeer."

Chapter Fifty-Two

"The question is: why now?" Celine considered the painting.

"What do you mean?" Penny asked. The revelation that the work Blake had recovered was not a genuine Vermeer had clearly come as a shock. The realization that she'd nearly squandered a hundred million dollars on it couldn't have helped her state of mind, either.

Celine looked up. "Underwood's copy has been floating around since the time of the theft. Why hasn't anyone tried to capitalize on its presence until now? Why do it now?"

"Because something's changed," Blake said softly. He fingered the frame.

Penny crossed her arms and looked at their faces. "I still don't understand. What's changed? We're no closer to finding the stolen treasures now than we were before."

"You're forgetting Dirck's tip," Blake reminded her. "We were on the verge of recovering *The Concert.*"

"Only Dirck was killed," Julia added, "before he could give it to Grayson, Blake's CI. The men who killed him were looking for the painting—meaning that they didn't have the original."

Celine was struggling to follow their logic. "Therefore they returned Underwood's copy?"

Blake nodded. "Yes, because once the Gardner recovered the original—an eventuality that must look like a strong probability—it would be all over the news. And being in possession of a fake would've been bad for business."

"Art thieves and their associates don't have recourse to art appraisers and authenticators," Julia explained. "All they do have are newspaper accounts that detail the thefts of big-ticket items and their values. With that information, they can use stolen works as collateral or even as payment for drugs, arms, you name it."

"*Oh, I see.*" Understanding hit Celine. "But they've been doing it all this while with a forged work."

A shadow of a smile appeared on Penny's face. "There'll be hell to pay when their business associates discover that fact."

Julia nodded. "Whoever's behind this must be very desperate to find the original. They've killed two people—to no avail. Desperate times call for desperate measures."

Penny's face twisted. "And they almost got a hundred million out of the deal. I can't believe I was that dumb."

"Not your fault," Blake said. "But I have a feeling your tipster will be calling before long. We'll need to figure out how to play this thing."

Celine's eyes drifted toward Underwood's copy—the woman seated at the harpsichord, the man seated near her with his theorbo-lute, and the singer who stood by them. Had Vermeer realized that this serene gathering of music-makers would be the cause of so much death?

"We need to draw him out into the open," she said. "And I know just how to do that."

⁂

Penny wrapped the tight coils of the telephone cord around her fingers. The call had come just as Special Agent Blake Markham had predicted it would.

"The Gardner has its Vermeer, Ms. Hoskins." The caller's voice was deep, menacing. "But I don't have my money."

"I left it where you asked me to." Penny clutched the receiver to her ear. The phone was on speaker so that Celine, Julia Hood, and Blake could listen in on the conversation. The FBI had made arrangements to track it, although Blake had warned her the caller was probably using a burner phone.

"The individuals acting on my behalf were arrested for theft, Ms. Hoskins. You were told not to involve law enforcement."

Penny licked her lips, searching her visitors' features. Blake passed her a note; she glanced down at it, dipping her head to acknowledge that she understood.

"That seems to have been a misunderstanding, Mr. . . ." She allowed her voice to trail off, but her caller didn't rise to the bait.

"My name is of no consequence to you, Ms. Hoskins. You may keep the painting. But I want my money. I also want my men out of jail."

Penny looked down at the note. "I actually don't have the painting. I've been informed it's a forgery."

"Don't try my patience, Ms. Hoskins. You know as well as I do, there's been no time for any comprehensive tests."

That got Penny's goat. She sat up. "It didn't require comprehensive testing for us to know it was a fake. There were key details the forger got wrong. Besides—" She paused, glancing at Celine. The girl was too young to be used as bait.

It had been her own idea, of course. But that didn't make Penny like it any better.

"Just do it, Penny," Celine said, her voice barely detectable.

Penny looked at Julia and Blake, but their eyes slid uncomfortably away from her gaze.

She took a deep breath and spoke into the mouthpiece. "You may not, of course, have realized you were in possession of a forgery. But even without the details we uncovered, I'd have to proceed with caution."

"And just why is that, Ms. Hoskins?"

Penny hesitated. The thumbs-up sign Celine gave her did nothing to increase her confidence. She drummed her fingers on her desk, hesitating some more.

"I've just received a visit from a young woman"—she took another deep breath and slowly let it out—"She says she's discovered the whereabouts of Vermeer's *Concert*. I have every reason to believe this is genuine. Her employer called in a tip to the FBI shortly before he died."

"Tips are a dime a dozen." Her caller sounded amused. Then his tone turned menacing again. "We had a deal, Ms. Hoskins. I want my painting back."

"That's something you'll have to discuss with law enforcement," she snapped. "As I've already mentioned, I don't *have* your painting."

Chapter Fifty-Three

Celine studied the mug shots Blake had taken out of a manila folder. John —*Shorty*—Bruno had well-fleshed features, dark hair slicked back from a prominent widow's peak, and finely drawn eyebrows. His eyes glittered like black pebbles from slightly upturned eyes.

They were back at FBI quarters, returning with Blake to see if they could help identify the men arrested at Riverway earlier that morning. Bruno had been tasked with bringing Underwood's forgery to the Shattuck Visitor Center.

His partner Frankie—*the Tub*—Agnello had been the man Blake had arrested outside the Round House with Penny's leather case. Celine turned her attention to his mug shot.

Agnello looked older than Bruno—in his forties, Celine guessed. His gray-streaked hair receded from a wide forehead. The fleshy folds of skin under his chin and his flushed, bulging cheeks had clearly provided the genesis for his nickname.

Julia and Blake eyed Celine in silence as she examined the mug shots. They'd wanted to know whether Shorty Bruno and Tub Agnello had been responsible for Dirck's murder as well. It was a likely hypothesis, but they needed something to confirm it.

"Any of them ring a bell?" Julia broke the silence eventually.

Celine shook her head.

"No psychic feelings or hunches?" Blake asked hopefully.

"Afraid not." She looked up. "I didn't see any faces, remember? Just hands. But those I remember distinctly."

"So if you saw their hands . . ." Julia turned to Blake. "It's a stretch, but it's worth a shot, don't you think?"

"A hand identification?" Blake's eyebrows rose. Then he shrugged. "I guess there's always a first time for everything." He reached for his phone.

"What about their fingerprints?" Celine wanted to know. "Couldn't you match them to the ones found at the Delft and in Simon Underwood's home?"

"Already on it," Blake said as he sifted through a stack of business cards on a chrome Rolodex. "Or Mailand is, to be more precise." He flipped another card back. "Ah, here we go. They're being held at the District D-4 Station on Harrison Avenue," he explained as he dialed the number.

"Didn't want to tip off whoever Bruno and Agnelli are working for that this is anything more than theft at this time. Or that the FBI is involved. But if we can confirm those two killed Duarte and Underwood, we'll have some leverage to get them to talk. Give up who's behind this whole thing."

"I wouldn't bet on it," Julia commented wryly. "Enforcers get paid to take a hit for the family. That's what those two are doing."

"Doing time for theft is one thing," Blake responded. "Going down for murder is quite another. It's worth a try."

"Didn't say it wasn't," Julia said. "Just don't hold your breath expecting too much."

Celine had a feeling Julia was right. Neither Agnelli nor Bruno would reveal who the General was. But sitting back and doing nothing was not an option. "If we can nail them for murder, that'll be something. And . . ."

She paused as a thought struck her.

"Wait! I wonder if Grayson saw their faces."

Boston Police District D-4 was a brick building at the corner of Harrison Avenue and Plympton Street. Blake eased his car into the only available parking spot just outside the police station.

They hadn't bothered with an armored vehicle this time, taking Blake's sedan instead. Julia had decided to ride shotgun, leaving Celine with the rear seat. It was a definite improvement to being sandwiched between them, but sitting in the back only reinforced Celine's sense of being a little girl on an outing with her parents.

"So here's the plan." Blake cut the engine and looked over his shoulder at Celine. "We go inside, take our time. If you think Agnelli and Bruno are the guys we're looking at for the murders in Paso Robles, we'll risk bringing Grayson out of hiding to provide a confirmatory identification."

Celine nodded. A hand identification wouldn't hold up in court. But Grayson's eyewitness testimony would bolster a fingerprint analysis—assuming Detective Mailand was able to match their fingerprints to those found at the Delft and in Simon Underwood's home.

"And if we do need him, Grayson can go into witness protection?"

Blake had already mentioned the possibility of witness protection. But Celine needed to be absolutely sure the arrangements would be made.

Her nails dug into her palms. There'd already been two violent deaths she'd been unable to prevent. God forbid, that in her quest for justice, she should cause a third.

"Of course." Blake held her gaze, but he made no further attempt to persuade her.

Satisfied, Celine nodded.

"Ready?" Julia asked softly.

"Yup." Celine swung open the car door.

Inside the station, a Detective Hornby strode out to meet them.

"We have everything set up." He ushered them through a narrow hallway into a small room equipped with a television. He motioned toward the chairs, but his visitors ignored the invitation.

Hornby shrugged in a "suit yourself" gesture.

"Agnelli and Bruno are in the next room." He picked up the remote and switched on the television.

A grainy, black-and-white image flickered to life showing two sets of masculine forearms stretched out on the wide surface of a wooden table pitted with scratches.

"Cameras have been adjusted to focus on their hands, just like you requested."

Celine concentrated on the screen. Agnelli and Bruno were sitting across from each other, the camera cutting off their heads.

"Never done one of these before," Hornby broke the dead quiet that had filled the room. "Unusual, isn't it?"

"Yep," Blake replied tersely.

Hornby subsided into silence.

Celine moved closer to the television. Her gaze swept the screen from left to right. The guy on the left with the muscular, well-toned arms was Shorty Bruno, she figured.

"Could you focus on his fingers, please?"

"Sure." There was a phone attached to the wall. Hornby lifted the receiver and rapped out a few staccato instructions.

The image adjusted until a set of short, stubby fingers came into view. Celine gasped as another image swam into her mind. Stubby fingers stabbing a glowing cigarette into Dirck's worn cheeks.

She swallowed the nausea that threatened to overwhelm her.

"Focus on the other man's arms, please."

Intent upon the screen, she was barely aware of Hornby conveying the instructions. The camera shifted up and to the right.

Tubs Agnelli had huge arms. Not flabby, but the muscles weren't as well defined as Shorty's.

"And his fists."

Celine's eyes followed the moving camera. A second swell of nausea surged up as Agnelli's large, raw, beefy fists and his misshapen knobby knuckles came into view. His were the hands that had tightened the piano wire around Dirck's throat.

Clutching her throat, Celine turned away.

"Everything okay?" Julia put a comforting arm around her shoulder.

Celine managed a nod.

"*Oh God*, it's them," she said, speaking through tightly clenched lips. "It's definitely them."

❧

"Touring churches again?" Ann Revere's eyebrows arched up as she took their room keys.

Julia muttered something inaudible as she browsed through a stack of tourist leaflets propped up on the front desk. Ann turned to Celine, who responded by shrugging her shoulders and flashing Ann a quick smile before discreetly scanning the hallway.

They had returned to the Revere Garden Inn for a quick bite before tackling Grayson.

"Where is Lillian?" Celine's gaze shifted back toward Ann. The proprietor now had her nose buried in a ledger in which she was making entries. "We didn't see her at lunch."

All the other guests had gathered together in the Victorian dining room. Lillian, oddly enough, had failed to make an appearance.

"Oh, didn't you hear?" Ann's head remained bent over her ledger. "She checked out this morning." Ann raised her eyes. "Quite a surprise, that was.

We were expecting her to stay at least a couple more weeks. But apparently something came up."

"I'll bet," Celine said softly.

Somehow the news wasn't quite as welcome as she would have expected it to be. Not understanding why, she brushed the thought aside and lightly touched Julia's arm. "Let's go."

Julia replaced the brochures she'd been leafing through and joined Celine at the door. It was only after they were in their cab that she commented on Lillian's departure.

"I'd like to know what took her away, but I can't say I'm not glad she's gone." Julia settled back in her seat. "Now we won't have to worry about her getting too nosy."

"I'm not so sure." Celine's sense of unease was growing.

"What do you mean?" Julia's head spun sharply around.

Celine met Julia's narrowed gaze.

"It occurred to me," she said, carefully searching her way around her impressions, "that Lillian may have checked out because she has the information she needs."

Julia stared at her.

"About Grayson and where he is?" Her voice was quiet, but Celine sensed the undercurrent of anxiety that lay—barely hidden—beneath her words.

"What else?" Hadn't that been the information Lillian was after?

"But how?" Julia protested. "We've been nothing but careful."

"I don't know." Her own lack of clarity frustrated Celine. "I just know that she knows. Which means whoever she's working for knows as well."

Her throat tightened; her chest constricted.

"Grayson is in danger."

"All the more reason to get him out of that church, then," Julia said grimly.

Chapter Fifty-Four

"I'm not doing it." Grayson stared at them, his eyes cold and determined. "I'm not testifying against them." He pointed to the photos in Celine's hand.

Celine and Julia had been in Grayson's tiny room at the Church of the Advent for nearly twenty minutes now, arguing with him. But Grayson hadn't budged.

He had cast a reluctant eye over both mug shots. He'd even admitted that Agnelli and Bruno just might have been the men he'd seen torturing Dirck. But he'd steadfastly refused to handle the photos.

"You can't hide here forever," Julia pointed out. "Don't you want to go back home?"

Grayson looked at the former fed as though she'd lost her mind. "You seriously think helping to put the General's men away is a good strategy to get him off my back?"

He waited for them to respond. Neither of them did. In all honesty, there was no effective argument to counter what he'd said.

"Do you know they've already sent people here?" he demanded. "Ask Father Donegal."

"I know," Celine whispered. She'd seen the Lady hovering by the door to Grayson's room the moment they'd come in. Heard the nun's voice warning her of danger.

The Lady lingered by his chair now. If Grayson chose to stay in this room, he would die.

He's in danger, Celine, Sister Mary Catherine warned her again.

Celine clenched her fists. *I know, I know. But he won't listen. They never do.*

"All right." Celine met Grayson's eyes. "What do you suggest? How do we get the General off your back?"

He looked at her, an amused smile tugging at the corners of his mouth. "You really want to know?"

"Yes, Grayson." Celine forced herself to be patient. "We want to help you."

"Okay." He leaned back. "Give him what he wants, then. Return the art Duarte and Bramer stole from him."

"There's just one problem with that, Grayson," Julia said. "The art doesn't belong to the General. It belongs to the Gardner Museum. If you know where it is . . ."

"I don't. I've already told you that." Grayson turned to Celine. "He'll never stop looking for me until he gets what he wants. And what he wants is in your possession. Just return the art to him. All of it."

Celine shook her head.

"If Dirck knew where the rest of the art was, he would've mentioned it when he called in his tip. But he only mentioned the Vermeer. I'm inclined to believe that's all he had."

"Oh yeah?" A sardonic smile spread over Grayson's sunken cheeks. "How did Duarte and Bramer get the money to start their wine business? Land was cheap in the nineties. It wasn't dirt cheap."

"No, they . . ." Celine paused.

She exchanged a glance with Julia. They'd surmised that Dirck and John had sold the Vermeer in exchange for the money and the papers they needed to make their escape. But in that case, how had had they ended up with the genuine Vermeer?

Unless . . .

"They conned someone into buying Underwood's copy." Julia straightened up in her chair. "They kept the original—for whatever reason. As proof of their story, perhaps. And they got someone to buy Underwood's work."

"And that someone took it to the General," Celine said. "That's why Simon Underwood is dead."

"Glad you figured that all out," Grayson interrupted their conversation. "Now, how are we going to get the General's men off my back?"

Celine looked at him. "Grayson, they know you're here. You're not safe here. You know, you're not. Father Donegal won't betray you."

"No, he won't." Grayson's lips were set in an obdurate line. He set his head back defiantly.

"But you know these men," Celine continued. "They'll kill him—the Rector of a church—to get to you. That's how desperate they are."

She knew she'd gotten to him. Grayson's lips trembled and his eyes widened as her words sank in.

"You don't want to be the cause of Father Donegal's death, do you, Grayson?" Julia pressed the point. "A man who's gone out of his way to help you?"

"No. No, I don't. But . . ." Alarm flickered in his pale blue eyes. He looked old and uncertain.

"There's an armored vehicle waiting outside for us, Grayson." Julia took out her phone. "Blake Markham's in it. All I have to do is tell him you're ready to come with us, and the car will be at the church steps."

He's in danger, Celine, Sister Mary Catherine repeated her warning. *He's in danger.*

It's okay. He's coming with us, Celine assured the nun.

She could see the hesitation in Grayson's eyes crystallize into a decision.

"It's okay," she whispered to him and to Sister Mary Catherine.

"Okay." Grayson stood up. "I'll come with you. Let's do this."

Blake wasn't happy to be on Pinckney Street. It was farther than he would have preferred from the church Grayson was holed up in on 30 Brimmer Street.

But the entire length of Brimmer—from Mount Vernon Street to Pinckney—had been lined on both sides with parked cars.

Mount Vernon had been equally devoid of available parking spots.

Worse still Pinckney was a one-way street.

Blake clutched his phone. Julia and Celine and their charge were on their way out of the church. His phone would start buzzing as soon as they were at the church door.

"When the call comes, back up to make the turn onto Brimmer," he instructed his driver.

"No problem, boss." The driver, a recent FBI recruit, gave him a quick thumbs-up in the rear-view mirror.

The driver looked idly out the window.

"Looks quiet today. But I'm sure glad we have the other unit closer to the church."

"What other unit?"

The driver swiveled around, taken aback by the sharpness of Blake's tone.

"The FBI vehicle—"

Blake was out of the car before his driver could complete the sentence. There was no other vehicle. He hadn't thought to deploy another unit. Hadn't thought they'd need it.

He sprinted back up the street to Brimmer. He'd just turned the corner when he felt his phone buzzing.

He hesitated, undecided whether to return to the car or to continue on foot to investigate?

Probably quicker in the vehicle.

He'd just made the decision when a loud ttha-TTTHHUUUD jolted his senses, forcing him down.

As the sound ricocheted away from him, he eased himself up.

Goddammit!

Chapter Fifty-Five

Celine was out the church door, sprinting down the steps, when she heard Sister Mary Catherine's voice.

Stay back, Celine. Back.

She whirled around, not understanding the reason for the warning. But the nun's tone was too urgent to ignore.

Before she could wave Julia and Grayson back, a single explosive bang —like a car backfiring—reverberated through the narrow, car-filled street. Instinctively, she began to duck down, wincing as a flash of scalding heat streaked past her ear.

Too stunned to call out a warning, she saw Grayson lurch back as though struck by a powerful force, his midriff crumpling. His chest opened up in a spray of red just as her knees finally hit the ground.

"Oh my God, no!" She tried to rise.

"Stay down, Celine. Stay down." Julia tugged Grayson's lifeless, bleeding form back through the church doors.

Still crouching, Celine turned to face the street. Where the hell was Blake?

"Ms. Skye." A pair of arms helped her to her feet. She took in the blue trousers of the men before her, the blue windbreakers with *FBI* inscribed on them in yellow letters.

"He's hurt." She gestured back toward the church. "You've got to help him. Grayson's hurt."

"Get into the car, ma'am." The man holding her propelled her toward the black SUV parked on the curb. Hands pulled her into the vehicle; the door slammed shut behind her. Then the car powered forward.

"Celine."

Who was that calling her? Julia?

Celine looked through the tinted rear window.

The last thing she remembered was the stinging sensation in the back of her neck, and the chaos on Brimmer Street that swam in and out of view and then faded out.

❧

"Go, go, go," Blake yelled as he climbed back into the vehicle, his gun already in his hand, cocked and ready to fire. "Shots fired. Go."

His startled driver slammed the Suburban into reverse, peeled back and then squealed forward into Brimmer.

A black Chevy was pulling away from the curb up ahead.

"That's the car I was telling you about, sir."

"Follow it."

But a parked sedan a few cars ahead of them swerved out into the street, then went back and forward in a valiant attempt to execute a three-point turn on the narrow, car-packed street. A curly-haired, flustered woman peered out the driver's side window and mouthed an apology.

Jesus F'in' Christ!

Blake maneuvered himself halfway out of the car and roared, "Get the hell outta the way, lady!" Unaware that he had a gun in his hand, he lunged his arm repeatedly in the direction of Mount Vernon Street.

The woman's jaw dropped; she stared petrified at the gun.

"Please don't kill me."

"Police business, ma'am." The driver took over, speaking in a calm, firm tone. "Head that way."

The woman nodded, eyeing them warily as she re-started her engine. Swiftly, she turned her car's nose toward Brimmer. But it was too late.

❧

"She's gone, Blake." Julia rushed toward him. She gestured helplessly at the empty spot by the curb where his driver had seen the black Suburban that had taken Celine.

His car had turned right onto Vernon, but there'd been no sign of the SUV they'd been following. And as usual in a big city, no one seemed to have heard or seen anything.

At first he thought they'd taken Grayson. But Grayson was . . .

Blake's eyes veered past Julia to the blood pooling on the church floor.

"Grayson's gone," Julia informed him. "Sorry . . ."

"Don't be. Mailand called back. The fingerprints are a match. Agnelli and Bruno aren't going anywhere." But it was a hollow victory.

Grayson was dead. And Celine was . . .

Kidnapped.

Why? Because she could lead them—whoever they were—to the Vermeer?

"What about Celine?" Julia looked up at him anxiously. "We need to get her back."

"I have agents pinging her phone."

Julia nodded. "Good thought. Although . . ." She hesitated, looking up at him again.

His phone rang before he could wonder what had given her pause.

"Yes."

"Bad news, sir."

"You lost her phone?"

"No sir. Her kidnappers did. We traced the cell to the Charles River. They must've tossed the phone out."

The Charles River. Jesus Christ. He turned away, unable to face Julia.

"I should've had backup. We were using her as bait. I should've . . ." He fisted his right hand and crashed it into his left palm.

Why hadn't he, an experienced agent, considered the possibility that Celine might—no, make that *would*—be a target? He'd lost control. Once again, he'd lost control. Because he hadn't been thinking.

Just like he hadn't been thinking when he'd let those kids he'd been in charge of at boy-scout camp play hide-and-seek in the woods. He'd been fourteen, then. Too young, his therapist had said, for such a heavy responsibility.

But he was thirty-five now. That excuse wouldn't fly any longer.

"I don't know how we'll find her," he said softly.

He'd gotten lucky at fourteen. Charlie had been found—not uninjured and not immediately, but at least not dead. Hard to believe he'd get lucky again.

He felt the pressure of Julia's hand on his upper arm.

"We'll find her, Blake."

He nodded. Of course, they'd find her. They had to find her. He wasn't going to let the mission go south like this.

"If her phone's in the Charles River, they must have taken her to the other side. That's where we concentrate our efforts."

"Good thinking," Julia said. "But there might be a better way."

He looked at her, startled. She was speaking to herself now, but he caught the words.

"As long as her kidnappers don't realize what she has on her."

Chapter Fifty-Six

Celine, wake up. A voice tugged at her consciousness.

Sister Mary Catherine?

Uneasily, Celine stirred, aware of the woozy feeling in her head, the heaviness of her neck.

Questions drifted in and out through the fog in her brain.

What day was it? How long had she been asleep? The Delft? Was there something that needed to be done there? The clean-up?

She sank back into the comforting depths of fog, unable to remember. *Whatever it was, it could wait.*

Celine, wake up.

Why, Sister?

Celine moaned, reluctantly willing her head to move.

The pain of the effort jabbed at her sagging senses. Memory returned. Her eyelids, scratchy and heavy, opened to . . .

Blackness . . .

It took a moment for her brain to put it together. She was under a rough-textured blanket. It covered her face as though she . . . *was a corpse?*

The shock of realization propelled her upright. Her body was aching and sore. She ignored the sensations, forcing her mind to take stock of her surroundings.

She was in the cargo area of what seemed to be a van.

She frowned. So they'd changed vehicles? Why? And Julia, Grayson? Had someone gone to their aid?

Grayson is beyond help, Celine. Sister Mary Catherine's voice seemed to come from a great distance. *Look outside. Observe your surroundings.*

Look outside?

It was only when Celine tried to turn that she realized that under the blanket her wrists were bound together.

She jerked her body, desperate to get the blanket off her. Then she looked down.

She'd been . . . No, that wasn't possible.

She stared at the shiny gray duct tape wound tightly around her wrists. She tried to prise her arms apart, but the duct tape refused to yield.

She'd been restrained. Why?

She remembered being herded into a vehicle by . . . She closed her eyes, recalling the baggy blue windbreakers, the yellow lettering.

If they'd been federal agents, why had they taken her prisoner? Had she been kidnapped?

Yes, Celine. By the General's men. Now for God's sake, look out.

The nun's urgent tone got her attention.

Obediently, she twisted her body around, moving her head closer to the sliver of window near the top of the van.

The vehicle curved around providing a panoramic view. A pier-like structure projecting out over a body of water. Chain link fences. Rough, pockmarked road. Blue dumpsters.

It had all the charm of an industrial area wasteland.

Owww!

Her head slammed against the side of the van as it thudded up and down. A few more bone-shattering jolts later, they scrunched to a halt in front of an enormous shed. Celine committed the rusting corrugated iron and the dull green-brown patches of disrepair to memory.

Jesus Christ, where was she? She didn't recognize this place.

Stay calm, Celine. Julia will find you.

"I don't believe in micromanaging my agents, Blake, but . . ." Special Agent-in-Charge James Patrick Walsh paused and leaned back in his chair.

The softly worded objection lingered in the air like a threat.

But a CI had been killed—in the open, in Blake's presence, and he'd been able to do nothing to prevent it. Worse still, a civilian had been kidnapped. Walsh's criticism didn't have to be voiced. It was self-evident.

Blake gripped the armrests of his chair, feeling the rising onset of a panic attack. He idly wondered if the large glass window behind the SAC's chair let in any air at all. Had the SAC's office ever been ventilated?

He took a deep breath of what was probably stale, regurgitated air.

"We're doing everything we can, sir." *And they were, dammit!*

Walsh regarded him quietly, his fingers steepled upon his midriff. He was a lean, gray-haired man with a deeply wrinkled face that now wore an expression of extreme concern.

"What have we got so far?"

It's in the report, Blake wanted to yell, but he forced himself to take another breath instead. The act did nothing to calm him. The room seemed hermetically sealed, its oxygen supply rapidly depleting.

Breathe. Easy, breathe.

"Both the killing and the kidnapping were well planned, sir." He clenched his teeth, willing himself not to start shaking like an addict in desperate need of a hit. "Extremely well planned."

Goddammit, they must have been lying in wait for Grayson to emerge from hiding. Figuring he eventually would. Although how they'd traced Grayson there was another question altogether.

Walsh said nothing, waiting for Blake to continue.

"The shot came from an upper unit at 27 Brimmer Street. Hunting rifle. Reported stolen a week back."

"The condo belonged to the woman who blocked your car?"

He'd been expecting criticism. Walsh's statement—or was it a question?—eased Blake's mind. The SAC was either confirming what he knew or seeking more information. Either way, Blake was okay with it.

"Amy Hudson. She was an unwilling accomplice in all of this," he explained, somewhat calmer now. "She's a single mother. The killer threatened to kill her and her baby if she didn't cooperate."

Hudson had been visibly distraught when he'd gotten the details out of her. The agents he'd sent in had seen the hunting rifle on the living room floor and heard the baby's mewling the moment they entered the condo.

It had taken a while to locate Hudson herself. She'd been instructed to wait an hour before returning to her condo.

"Any leads on the guy?"

The question caught Blake off-guard. If the SAC had read the reports filed so far, he already knew the answer to that question. But then the purpose of the meeting hit him.

Blake was here re-treading ground that had already been covered to give Walsh an opportunity to sniff out every wrong move he'd made.

The vise around Blake's chest tightened. Walsh was regarding him with the cold curiosity of a predator waiting for a weakness to surface.

But it wasn't the prospect of potentially losing his job that was stimulating Blake's urgent need for a Xanax. It was his own stupidity.

He had almost laid eyes on the killer. *Almost.* Had he looked a second longer, he would've seen the guy.

He'd noticed the plumbing van pulling into the one spot left on Brimmer as his own vehicle circled the block looking for a place to park. Seen it and not thought anything of it.

Observed the van pulling in, but in his haste to get to the church doorstep, failed to see it leave.

"Blake?"

Walsh's voice reined in his runaway mind. Blake marshaled his facts. He wasn't going to twist himself into a pretzel attempting to defend himself. *Just give him the facts, Blake.*

"Security cameras in the building didn't capture a good image of the guy."

The bastard had avoided turning his face to the cameras.

"All we have is Hudson's description of the guy who threatened her and her baby. The plumbing van was stolen from a twenty-four-hour plumbing service. The plumber who usually drives the van went missing at the same time."

SAC Walsh fiddled with a pen on his desk. "I take it the missing plumber doesn't match Hudson's description of the killer."

"He doesn't." It was in the report. The missing plumber was a short, thick-set man in his late forties. But the image the security cameras at 27 Brimmer had captured showed a younger, well-built man of medium height.

A man who'd disappeared from right under Blake's eyes.

By the time agents and Boston police had begun securing the street, the plumbing van and the killer—dressed in a business suit now instead of the plumbing overalls he'd been wearing when he went up to Hudson's apartment—had long gone.

"So a lot of information." Walsh made a show of thumbing through the pages in front of him. "But none of it relevant," he summed up the situation dryly.

Blake's hackles rose. Nervousness had turned to anger. Walsh couldn't find fault with anything he'd done.

The details his team had garnered might not seem useful. But eventually, those details along with the composite they'd been able to develop from Hudson's description would yield results.

The SAC knew this as well as Blake.

Rather than point out the obvious, Blake allowed himself one little jab.

"The recent leak in the department hasn't helped, sir."

Walsh turned a particularly virulent shade of beet.

"Mary came highly recommended."

From a golfing partner Walsh barely knew. And who likely knew little enough of Mary the intern. Other than that she'd expressed an interest in going to Quantico but wanted some on-the-job experience before committing to the training.

The anxiety was subsiding when Walsh managed to arouse it yet again.

"Where are we on the kidnapping?"

Chapter Fifty-Seven

Where is she?

Celine strained forward to hear the voice. The movement caused the sharp edges along the sides of the chairback to press harder into her arms. Her ankles, tightly secured, scraped painfully against the raw, exposed wood of the chair legs.

She fought to keep her attention away from the discomfort that throbbed through her arms and stung the skin on her ankles.

That voice outside—it sounded familiar. Who was it?

She'd been in the dingy, musty shed for what seemed like hours, alone, chair-bound but not gagged. Her captors hadn't even bothered to warn her against screaming for help.

That was troubling.

It meant they'd chosen a place so isolated, her screams would go unheard.

"They'll find me," she'd spoken up as they turned to leave the shed. "My friends will find me."

The taller of her two captors looked over his shoulder.

"Don't count on it." He smiled, following her gaze to the phone in his palm. "Your phone's not here to betray your location."

She felt a momentary pang of alarm. What if someone at the Mechelen needed to get a hold of her?

The thought was absurd and laughably irrelevant. She was worrying about the implications her lost phone had for the business she'd inherited? Instead of freaking out about what it meant for her chances of being rescued. *Way to go, Celine!*

"Where is it?"

The shorter man grinned. "With the fishes. Where your friends're gonna think you are—if they ever find it."

An image flashed into Celine's mind. She heard Sister Mary Catherine's voice in her head.

"We're on the other side of the Charles River."

Shock mingled with anger shot through the shorter guy's features. His head jerked toward his companion. "How the hell does she know that?"

"Beats me." The taller man shrugged. "Maybe you should've used a stronger dose of tranquilizer—like I told you to."

"It was plenty strong," the other man reiterated.

Their squabbling was oddly reassuring. If she could find a way to widen the breach between them . . . The thought helped to settle her unease.

"I know because I'm psychic," she said.

She caught a fleeting expression of panic on the shorter guy. But the taller man looked at her, his cold gaze shrewdly assessing.

"Too bad, your friends ain't," he said.

A cold chill ran down Celine's spine. No, they weren't.

Julia will find you, Celine. Sister Mary Catherine's voice was firm.

But how?

The question penetrated her consciousness again as she tried to focus on the muffled voices outside the shed. The newcomer was . . . *female?*

That was unexpected.

Her voice sounded so familiar. Where had Celine heard that voice before?

She'd barely figured it out, when the door opened?

SAC James Patrick Walsh drummed his lean, tapering fingers on his desk. "You're telling me you didn't see an SUV containing men masquerading as FBI agents?"

His eyebrows rose, marking his skepticism.

Blake felt the same knot of frustration that had twisted his intestines when he'd lost little Charlie in the woods all those years ago. He'd been a fourteen-year-old eagle scout. The youngest to achieve the rank—just like his father.

An irresponsible, immature eagle scout not deserving of the rank, Markham.

He could still hear the scoutmaster bawling him out—his harsh voice strident with anger.

Aware of Walsh watching him, Blake marshaled his thoughts.

"They weren't wearing their windbreakers at the time, sir." *They couldn't have been.*

He'd been focused on finding a parking spot, true, but he hadn't been so fixated on the issue that it had obliterated his sense of situational awareness.

Still, it was a feeble attempt to explain his lapse—in both judgment and awareness. Walsh's face as he digested Blake's words was devoid of expression. But Blake knew what the SAC was thinking.

He'd been irresponsible. He tried to repair the impression.

"We've found the vehicle, sir. It had stolen plates. We're processing it for fingerprints and any other evidence."

The SUV had been abandoned a short distance away from the Church of the Advent. Pity the kidnappers hadn't also abandoned their faux FBI field jackets. There might have been a chance—a small chance—of tracking down purchase records.

"Any chance of finding any?"

Walsh's voice caught Blake by surprise. He must have looked as dumbfounded as he felt because Walsh immediately clarified: "Any chance of finding fingerprints?"

Blake didn't respond. If he was being honest, he'd have to say no.

"Thought not." A sour expression settled on Walsh's face. "And you managed to lose the victim's phone as well."

It wasn't a question.

"It seems likely they're on the other side of the Charles River," he pointed out hopefully. If Celine's kidnappers had ditched the phone in the river, it must have been because they were crossing it.

"That doesn't exactly narrow things down, Special Agent."

"Julia—Julia Hood—seems to think she can. Narrow down the area, that's to say."

Walsh's eyebrows shot up yet again. "She's back on the job? After retiring not more than a month back?"

"She knows the victim." It felt odd to refer to Celine that way. She was quiet, seemingly fragile, but Blake had sensed an inner strength in her and a rare fortitude that made her an unlikely victim.

Walsh leaned back in his chair; his weight thrust the backrest out of its ninety-degree angle. The chair squeaked out an indistinct protest that Walsh ignored.

"I'm stunned neither one of you anticipated that something along these lines might take place. You used the woman as bait. What did you expect?"

It was a fair question. One that Blake had struggled to answer to his own satisfaction.

"We underestimated his desperation," he said. "We thought he'd make contact with Celine, try to persuade her to give up the painting to him."

Walsh didn't ask who he was referring to. It was clear that the mastermind behind the Gardner Museum heist had—all these years later—come out into the open. Triggered by a tip called in to the FBI hotline.

But Blake had misjudged the man. Could that fatal error prove to be his undoing?

"If we find her," he said, trying to ignore the fact that it was still a very big *if*, "we might have a chance of finally solving the Gardner case."

"You think she knows where the Vermeer is?"

Blake hesitated. If Duarte had been telling the truth, the Vermeer was somewhere in Paso Robles. Either in the Delft Bar or at the Mechelen winery.

Celine may not have worked it out yet. But she was the only person who had a prayer of figuring out where Duarte had concealed the painting.

He wondered whether to mention any of this to Walsh. The leaks from the SAC's office had undermined his confidence in his superior.

"It seems likely." Blake chose his words with care, unwilling to commit himself one way or another.

"Then, we'd better find her, Markham. ASAP."

Chapter Fifty-Eight

"We meet again." Lillian took a few steps in and paused, one slim hip jutting out in what was no doubt meant to be a sexy pose. She gave Celine a bright smile.

Celine was in no mood to return the greeting. "What do you want, Lillian?"

She ignored her kidnappers, who'd followed Lillian into the shed and stood on either side of the door, arms folded.

"Eager to get down to brass tacks, aren't you?" Lillian said.

She pulled a chair over to the middle of the shed and straddled it, facing Celine.

"Well, I guess the sooner we get done with this the better." She regarded Celine, the fake smile still pasted on her face, but she made no move to make her demands known.

"You want me to tell you where the Vermeer is, don't you?"

The smile on Lillian's face widened into a grin, as though Celine had just cracked a hilarious joke. "Hey boys, you were right," she called over her shoulder. "She really is psychic."

The taller guy allowed himself a laugh, but a momentary expression of panic flickered across the shorter guy's features.

"Pity your psychic skills weren't good enough to warn you of the predicament you were going to get yourself in."

Lillian's statement was like a slap in Celine's face. But what she said next was like a dagger driving deep into Celine's consciousness.

"And getting that scab Grayson killed, you must find it hard to forgive yourself."

Celine's eyes widened. Wrapped up in her own situation, she'd failed to reflect upon what had happened. But Lillian was right. She'd seen Grayson's death. Sensed it as surely as she'd sensed every other death since the age of twelve.

Unlike her parents, Grayson had heeded her advice. But it was Celine's counsel that had gotten him killed. He should've stayed in the church.

No, Celine. Sister Mary Catherine's voice boomed in her ear. *They would've found Grayson and killed more people in an effort to get to him. You did the right thing.*

She shivered, teeth biting down hard on her lip to fight back the tears that trembled at her eyes.

Don't let her get to you, Celine. Don't let her win.

Was that Sister Mary Catherine or her own ego?

She gazed squarely at Lillian.

"You're right, my skills do leave much to be desired. But they're good enough to know that we're by the Mystic River."

Lillian's face hardened, but she said nothing.

"They're good enough to know," Celine continued, "that the General has been making do with forgeries; that he'll be the laughing stock of the criminal world if word gets out."

"How does she know that?" She was finally getting to the taller guy.

"And my psychic skills are keen enough to know," Celine said with a faint smile, "that the General will soon tire of you and get rid of you. Just as he has all his other women."

"That's nonsense!" Lillian snapped. "You have no idea what you're talking about. Now, where is the Vermeer?"

"Where it always has been," Celine said, trying to pull off a shrug, but not quite managing it. Her arms were too tightly bound for that. "If Shorty and the Tub had looked for it"—she deliberately used their nicknames—"they'd have found it."

Lillian strode over to her deliberately and struck her across the face. "Where is the painting, bitch?"

"Where it always has been." Celine repeated the words Sister Mary Catherine was whispering into her ears. The nun was conveying Dirck's words to her. But Celine didn't understand what they meant. Her mind traveled back to the Delft. In her imagination, she stood in the middle of the bar, surveying her surroundings.

The painting is where it always has been. Safe, waiting for you when you return.

"Where?" Lillian shrieked. Celine flinched, anticipating the slap. But it didn't come. Instead, Lillian stood over her, glaring down at her.

"Tell the General," Celine said, "that I have no intention of speaking with his minions. If he wants the location of the Vermeer, he'll need to speak directly with me."

"That's not gonna happen."

The taller guy whipped out a gun and trained it at her.

Celine looked at him. "I don't think the General would appreciate your killing the only person in the world who knows where that painting is. But try it and see what happens. Maybe you'll live to see your firstborn. Then again, maybe you won't."

He shrank back. "What kind of witch are you?"

The painting is where it always has been. Look, Celine. Hiding in plain sight.

In her mind's eye, she was back in the Delft. Dirck stood behind her, his hands lightly gripping her shoulders as he swiveled her around, encouraging her to see.

"Do you see it now, Celine?"

Chapter Fifty-Nine

Blake stormed out of his office into the anteroom.

"Where is she?"

Ella glanced up, unperturbed. "Who? Julia?"

She adjusted her glasses and peered over them at him.

The action and her words irritated Blake. "Who else would I be looking for at this time?"

He'd assumed Julia was at his desk, working on tracking Celine down. But neither she nor her voluminous beige leather tote were anywhere to be seen.

Ella pushed her desktop screen out of the way. "There's no need to get snippy, Blake. Julia's at the airport."

"At the airport?" Blake was dumbfounded. "We have a missing person, and she's at the airport? Why?"

Ella shrugged. "Beats me."

"Is she going to be back?"

"Don't be absurd, Blake. Of course she is. She hasn't gone on vacation."

"Send her in when she gets here." He charged back into his office and slammed the door.

Jesus F'in' Christ, this was a disaster! What was Julia playing at?

He tried her phone for the third time only to get voicemail—yet again. *Damn!*

Calm down, Blake. You can figure this out yourself. Look at a map.

He powered his laptop and pulled up a map of Boston. Celine's captors had crossed the Charles River. That meant they were in Cambridge. But where in Cambridge could you stash an abductee?

Had they remained in Cambridge or gone farther afield into Somerville?

"Blake?" Julia's voice startled him. He looked up.

She was standing by the door. Strange, he hadn't heard it open.

"Blake," Julia said again, coming into the room, "this is Lieutenant Keith Elliot."

A tall, gray-haired, burly man followed Julia into his office. He wore jeans and a baggy green-and-blue plaid flannel jacket over a white tee shirt that stretched over the wide expanse of his gut.

He stretched out his hand. "Retired. I used to work homicide at the Durham PD in New Hampshire."

Blake took the older man's hand, struggling to make sense of this development.

"Julia asked you to come out here? You can help us find Celine?"

Elliot smiled. "Sure can." He looked at Julia. "But, no, Julia didn't have to call me. I figured she might need my help."

"Elliot's a psychic cop," Julia explained. She pulled out a chair for Elliot, inviting him to sit down.

"Okay." This was beginning to make sense. "You're going to make use of your skills to find Celine."

"Nope. Not good enough for that." Elliot sat down and reached for the laptop case Julia was carrying. "I'm gonna use technology."

"What technology?" Blake was still standing.

"Ever heard of GPS tracking?" Elliot squinted at his laptop.

Blake found himself getting irritated. "Her phone's lost. Or didn't Julia mention that little detail to you?"

Elliot looked up. "Don't need her phone." His eyes returned to the laptop. "Takes a bit of time to load, but once the software's up and running, it's pretty fast."

"I don't understand. What does Celine have on her person that's enabled with GPS tracking?"

But neither Julia nor Elliot responded. They were staring at the laptop. Blake resisted the urge to walk around his desk to take a peek.

A little ping sounded.

"Is that her?" Julia pointed her forefinger at the screen.

"Yup." Elliot dragged his finger over the mouse. "So let's see, this is . . ."

"Charlestown." Julia's eyes were gleaming with excitement.

She bent forward, peering at the screen.

"She's in Charlestown, Blake." Julia straightened up. "In a warehousing facility near the Mystic River." She grabbed her tote and crossed the room toward the door.

Blake couldn't believe it. They'd found her—actually found her?

"Are you sure?"

"Absolutely." Elliot closed his laptop. "This thing is very accurate."

He strode over to Julia. "Are you coming?"

Blake remained behind his desk.

"For the last time, what is this damn thing?"

"Just a little gift I gave Celine. It's supposed to enhance her psychic visions. Don't know how well it works as far as that's concerned. But the tracking app is pretty useful."

"Come on, Blake." Julia was sounding impatient. "Let's go."

❧

"Ms. Skye, I believe you have information for me." The voice Celine heard over the phone was smooth, urbane, polished. She turned away from her captors and Lillian, focusing her attention on it.

After several minutes of bitter wrangling, her kidnappers had forced Lillian to make a call. The General had agreed to call back.

"It's the best you can hope for," Lillian had coldly informed her.

He's using an untraceable phone, Celine now thought. Her senses sagged. She'd hoped an examination of Lillian's phone—once Blake had arrested the woman—would yield useful clues. But, clearly, the General trusted no one.

"I asked to speak with the General," she spoke into the phone. "I don't believe you're him."

There was a lengthy pause, then what sounded like a chuckle.

"You seem like an intelligent woman, Ms. Skye. I won't insult you by lying to you. You're right, I'm not the man you asked to speak with. I'm his executive assistant. I'm in his presence as we speak. This is about as close as you're going to get to him."

She decided not to argue the point.

"You were the one who made contact with Penny Hoskins, am I right?"

"We're wasting time, Ms. Skye. You don't have to be involved in this situation. Give us what we want, and you can go free."

"Here's the thing." Celine looked down at her ankles. They were still bound to the chair. The shorter of her captors had untied her hands; she'd insisted upon it. "If I tell you where the Vermeer is stashed, what guarantee is there that you'll let me go? Your boss has had three men murdered."

"I can tell you one thing"—the voice had hardened—"if you refuse to cooperate, your friends will never find you."

"You'll kill me and dispose of my body so well it'll be like I never existed." Celine allowed herself a smile. "I have a feeling you'll do that even if I do cooperate."

Good work, Celine. Keep stalling. Julia will get here.

Thank God for Sister Mary Catherine, Celine thought. She had no intention of divulging the Vermeer's location. But finally understanding where it was had boosted her confidence.

You have the upper hand, Celine. They need you.

"You're wasting time, Ms. Skye."

"No, I'm negotiating," she replied. "This must be worth a lot of money to you."

"You expect us to pay you for the information?"

Julia is coming, Celine.

"Why not? The Gardner Museum was willing to pay. Not as much as I'd hoped to get, of course."

The amethyst in the pendant Julia had given her was getting uncomfortably warm. Almost as hot as the cell phone Celine held to her ear. She moved the phone to her other ear, but just as she was reaching up to adjust her necklace, Sister Mary Catherine's voice arrested her.

Don't finger the chain, Celine. Don't call attention to it.

"You do realize that there's more than money at stake here, don't you, Ms. Skye? At this point, my employer is more than inclined to cut his losses and move on."

Julia was getting closer. Celine knew that. But she didn't know how much longer she could hold out.

"If you do that, there's one thing you should know." She struggled to keep her voice from trembling. "I haven't told Julia where the Vermeer is. But she has all the clues she needs to figure it out."

She could only hope he believed her. *Where was Julia?*

"My death won't prevent her finding—and returning—the Gardner's Vermeer."

She paused. A faint sound caught her attention. The shadow of a movement flickered in the gap between the shed door and floor.

Keep talking, Celine. Keep him on the phone.

"If you release me, I can show you where it is."

With a loud thud, the shed door slammed open.

"What's going on?" Alarm thrummed in the voice over the phone.

"Goddammit!" one of her captors swore as agents stormed in, guns in hand.

"I think the General lost his chance," Celine said softly. Dead silence filled the air as the phone disconnected.

*

"Am I glad to see you!" Celine threw her arms around Julia, hugging her tightly. They were out of the dingy shed in the bright sunlight. "I didn't think you'd find me." She stepped back from the embrace. "*How* did you find me?"

"It was Keith." Julia drew her toward the portly, gray-haired man standing a few feet away near an FBI vehicle. "You remember him, don't you?"

Celine looked at him. Keith Elliot, the detective who'd been instrumental in bringing Sonia and Nicole's killer to justice in Durham. Who'd been there for her when she'd been working at the Montague Museum.

He was older, grayer, and considerably heftier than he'd been when she'd been living in New Hampshire. But she recognized him.

"You look the same," Keith said, drawing her into his arms. "All these years later, you still look the same."

"As do you, Keith." Celine returned the hug gratefully. "Thank you for finding me. And thank God for psychics!" She turned to Julia. "If we'd been relying on my GPS tracker, we'd have been straight out of luck."

"We *were* relying on your GPS tracker," Julia informed her. "That silver cross you're wearing has a chip embedded in it. Keith thought you might need something like it."

Keith laughed. "That's as far as my psychic skills went, I'm afraid.

Celine squeezed his arm. "Don't sell yourself short, Keith. If it weren't for your intuition and this pendant of yours, you guys never would've found me. I'd be dead." She touched the silver cross. It was still warm. "It was burning up my skin in there. I couldn't understand why."

"The battery activates only when someone's using the wireless app to call up the data on the tracker," Keith explained. "It was designed that way to save battery life."

Celine nodded. Her captors and Lillian were being handcuffed and led away by Blake's team.

"They may not talk," Julia said softly. "You know that, don't you, Celine? We may never know who they were working for."

Celine's gaze shifted toward Julia. "I know, and it doesn't matter. We'll get him—sooner or later. I'm certain we will. But for now, we need to get back to Paso Robles."

"Of course. You've had a traumatic experience, and you need to return to familiar surroundings."

"No, it's not that, Julia. We need to get back because I know where the Vermeer is. Dirck showed it to me. We have to return the Gardner's painting. That's what Dirck wanted to do. It's what John wanted him to do when he realized his heart was getting weaker and he didn't have long to live."

Chapter Sixty

Celine faced the front door of the Delft, the heavy weight of expectation emanating from behind her as palpable a force as the waves that crashed against Morro Rock.

"Are you sure this is where it's at?" Julia surveyed the green-awning-fronted cafés and restaurants that neighbored the bar. A few cars were parked alongside the curb on either side, but 13thStreet was relatively quiet on this warm spring morning.

Few of the passersby paid attention to the small group crowded in front of the Delft's door. Penny Hoskins and Blake Markham had accompanied Celine and Julia back to Paso Robles.

"I want to see it for myself, Celine," Penny had said. "I simply can't wait."

"Mailand's men scoured the bar as did you and I," Julia went on, turning back toward the door. "We didn't find any sign of that painting."

"It's in here," Celine assured her. Her fingers trembled as she inserted the key into the lock. It felt strange to be opening up the bar—her bar now. The key turned. She pushed open the door, wincing as the sterile odor of bleach and a mixture of other cleaning products assailed her nostrils.

The cleaning crew had obviously been here. The leather chairs had been pushed back against the wall. A stack of brown-paper-wrapped canvases stood at the foot of the horseshoe-shaped bar counter—the artworks Mailand's men had taken as evidence.

She opened the door wider, stepping into the shaft of warm sunlight that slanted in a wide swathe across the wood floor. She was about to turn around and invite the others in when something caught her eye.

A flutter of movement on the other side of the bar. It solidified into a familiar figure.

Dirck? It couldn't be!

He turned to face her, so vividly present, she could hardly believe her eyes.

He's still alive! Exultation pulsed through Celine's being. She hurried forward.

The vision shimmered and faded from view.

"Celine, are you okay?" Penny's voice seemed to come from a distance; her fingers squeezed Celine's arms. "You look like you've seen a ghost."

Dirck's still here, Celine, Sister Mary Catherine said softly. *His spirit is here. He needs to see this thing through.*

"I'm fine." Celine forced herself to smile, trying to ignore the heavy disappointment that weighed her spirits down.

"So where is it?" Blake swiveled around, scanning the walls of the Delft. They were bare but for the few paintings Dirck and John had worked on.

Celine hesitated, wondering how to explain what she knew. She'd found it hard enough to believe when Dirck had revealed the facts to her. The truth was far simpler than they'd surmised.

"Do you remember when Dirck called in that tip?" she began.

"He refused to give his name," Blake said. "Insisted that whoever we send meet him here at the Delft and ask for Rembrandt."

"Right. Dirck and John may have been fascinated by Vermeer, but Rembrandt was the key."

"Rembrandt was the key?" Julia and Penny exchanged glances.

"Yes," Celine nodded. "I think Grayson understood that. See that portrait there?" She gestured at the large canvas—a little over two feet in breadth and quite a few inches more than that in length—that hung in a prominent position behind the bar counter.

"That's the portrait of Earl—John Mechelen—that Dirck painted, isn't it?" Julia asked. "The one Grayson recognized rightly as portraying Earl Bramer."

"Yes, but initially, he suggested it was a Rembrandt," Celine said. "That's what called Dirck's attention to him. Not the fact that he was from Boston."

Penny crossed the room toward the bar and peered curiously at the portrait. "It is in the style of Rembrandt," she said over her shoulder. "A three-quarter view of the sitter wearing dark clothes and a brown turban."

She turned to face them.

"It resembles a Rembrandt self-portrait in the Royal Collection Trust in England. It's an oil on panel that some experts think was painted by one of his students, Isack Jouderville. But the monogram looks right, and many people have no doubt it's a Rembrandt."

"Dirck and John and Grayson would've been familiar with the work," Celine said.

"I still don't understand what any of this has to do with the Vermeer," Blake spoke up. "Are you saying that portrait of Earl—John—conceals a valuable Vermeer?"

Penny swiveled around to face the portrait. "It is the right size," she said thoughtfully.

Julia frowned. "But there are two portraits in that style at the Delft, aren't there? Dirck painted that one and Earl created a similar portrait of Dirck. Why create two? Unless one of them was . . . a decoy?"

Her frown deepened. She looked at Celine, seeking confirmation.

Celine smiled. "You're right, one of them is. If you had a valuable painting—even if it had been painted over to conceal what lay underneath—you wouldn't keep it out in the open, would you?"

"No, of course not," Julia said. "I'm guessing they painted over the Vermeer and hung it in the room where we found Dirck's body. No one had access to that room except for Dirck and his partner, and you, of course."

"So, this is the decoy?" Penny pointed a slender finger at the portrait of John Mechelen in a turban.

"No." Celine shook her head, still smiling. "Dirck said it was hiding in plain sight, remember? This is it."

Penny looked confused.

"That can't be it," Julia protested. Celine nodded.

"I don't believe it!" Blake looked astounded. "You mean all these years that we've been looking for it, *The Concert* has been right here under a portrait of Earl—John, whatever you want to call him?"

"Yes." Celine's smile widened.

She was enjoying the astonishment on her friends' faces. It had taken her some time to understand Dirck's clues.

"Few people would've guessed a tongue-in-cheek portrait concealed a priceless work of art. And anyone who entertained the notion would immediately assume this one—hanging in plain view—wasn't it."

She turned to Blake. "Dirck didn't know whether he could trust Grayson. He'd used the code word, but then it seemed unlikely he'd come as a representative of the FBI. He was going to call you after he sent Grayson away—"

"I didn't receive a call."

"I know. His attackers stormed in before he could make it."

Celine sighed and stepped closer to the painting.

"Can you help me take it down?" she asked Blake. "It's heavy."

Despite Blake's help, Celine's arms were straining as they lifted the canvas in its heavy wooden frame off the wall and lowered it onto the counter.

"We'll need to get the frame off," she said.

"Please be careful with it," Penny urged, her slender palm covering Celine's. "It's an old canvas. I'm not even sure we can get the top layer off without damaging what's underneath."

"We don't have to destroy Earl's portrait to get to the Vermeer, Penny."

But the uncertain expression remained etched on the Gardner Museum Director's features. Even Julia looked skeptical. "Are you sure?" she asked.

"You'll see"—Celine smiled reassuringly—"You'll both see, once we've taken the frame apart." Her gaze shifted toward Blake. "Got that pair of pliers?"

"Of course." Blake withdrew a pair of blue-handled pliers from his jacket. "Let's turn this thing over so I can pull out the staples."

It took a few minutes of concentrated effort to remove the staples. Then Blake took out a screwdriver from his pocket, wedged it under the black spline all around the frame, and carefully peeled that out as well. Under the spline, a few more staples attached the canvas to the frame. Blake removed those as well.

"I'm going to stand this up now," he told Celine. "Hold it up for me, while I push the stretcher out." He gently tugged back on the frame, while pushing the stretcher forward with one hand.

When the stretcher finally popped out of the frame, Penny caught it. "Now what?" she asked.

"We snip the canvas off at the back." With Blake's help, Celine turned the stretcher over. Dirck had left the canvas untrimmed, allowing it to cover the entire back of the stretcher.

Celine pointed to the stitches gathering the edges of the canvas into a little pouch at the center of the stretcher. "We need to get those off."

She took a small pair of sewing scissors out of her tote and carefully cut through the stitches.

The canvas fell away, revealing the stretcher with an older gray-yellow canvas fastened to it.

"*Oh my!*" Penny gasped softly. Her palm covered her mouth.

"Let's turn it over. Everybody ready?" Julia's hands closing around one edge of the stretcher. "Grab a corner." She waited for the others to follow suit. "All together now, on the count of three."

One. Two. Three.

An exquisitely rendered Dutch interior met their eyes. Apart from the lemon yellow hue of the seated woman's jacket, the painting wasn't as bright as Underwood's copy had been. The theorbo-lute player's garments were a dull brown. And the standing singer was clad in a gray gown.

"This is it," Penny whispered. "It's our Vermeer." She pointed to the singer's gray gown. "These are the signs of abrasion Underwood's copy didn't capture. Vermeer used a thin glaze of ultramarine blue over a gray ground for the dress. But you can see how the blue has degraded over time."

There were tears in her eyes when she turned to Celine.

"I don't know how to thank you, my dear. I don't know what to say. I can't believe we've got back not one but two of our treasures. And it's all thanks to you."

"Thank Dirck," Celine said, blinking back her own tears. "He and John kept your treasures safe all these years. And Dirck lost his life trying to return them."

A flicker of movement caught her attention. She lifted her eyes. Dirck stood at the rear of the bar, his figure shimmering in a radiant glow of light. The Lady—Isabella Stewart Gardner—stood beside him.

He's ready to say goodbye, Sister Mary Catherine whispered. *He's ready to go.*

Goodbye, Celine said. A haze of tears obscured her vision. She wasn't ready to let him go. But she didn't have a choice.

Goodbye, she whispered again.

Don't worry, Celine. Belle will lead Dirck into the light.

The End

Author's Note

On March 18, 1990, the Gardner Museum in Boston was robbed. Thirteen items were taken. and these have yet to be recovered. While the heist remains unsolved, Stephen Kurkjian's *Master Thieves* provides the most comprehensive account of the theft and the most plausible theory of what might have happened.

I have naturally concocted my own theory.

We know very little about either Johannes Vermeer or his technique. But reasonable speculations can be made based on what we see in Vermeer's art.

Philip Steadman's *Vermeer's Camera* provides a thought-provoking argument about the artist's use of the camera obscura. But even Steadman has been unable to explain a curious quality of Vermeer's underdrawings. There are no lines.

How can that be?

Artist Jane Jelley answers that question with a highly unusual but extremely compelling theory in *Traces of Vermeer*. I've attributed her ideas to my fictitious professor, Frank van Mieris.

Jeffrey Wands' *The Psychic in You* and Noreen Renier's *A Mind for Murder* were my primary sources for Celine's psychic abilities.

A former journalist, Nupur Tustin misuses a Ph.D. in Communication and an M.A. in English to paint intrigue. She also orchestrates mayhem in composer Joseph Haydn's Europe.

In addition to writing, she enjoys composing music and painting. She lives in Southern California with her husband and three rambunctious children.

For more details on the Joseph Haydn Mysteries and the Celine Skye Psychic Mysteries, visit: NTUSTIN.COM.

Get Three FREE Stories at NTUSTIN.COM

Subscribe to the Mystery Blog at ntustin.com/blog

www.ingramcontent.com/pod-product-compliance
Lightning Source LLC
Chambersburg PA
CBHW021645110726
47902CB00007B/1828